BLOOD SHACKLES

ROSEMARY A JOHNS

I slowly stood to face the bastard, who'd started all this: Head of the Retrieval Team in Bangkok, who'd hunted me on his monstrous black motorbike and trashed my Triton. He'd kidnapped me - not like a person - but like a wild bird, which'd been trapped and sold into captivity. A pet to be tamed and trained, presented in a gilded cage on some rich man's wall. From the moment Mohawk had shot me full of tranquillizers, I'd been a slave. My blood roared louder than those motorbikes. It wasn't terror I trembled with any longer: it was rage.

I0628789

FANTASY REBEL

FANTASY REBEL
First Edition 2016

All characters, places and events in this publication, other than those clearly in the public domain, are fictitious and any resemblance to real persons, living or dead, is purely coincidental.

Cover design by JD Smith

ISBN-13: 978-0995557925

ISBN-10: 0995557926

Fantasy Rebel Limited
rosemaryajohns.com

For A.

'There's nothing but snowflake patterns.'

The Slave Journal of Light

MAY 3

Look, it's all about the pain, right? Pretty playthings. Forever young. And no guilt.

The Lost reduced to nothing but a possession. Property. Slaves to you sodding humans.

See at the heart is the Blood Club: the new, most exclusive club for Russian oligarchs, sons of Arab princes and the brats of Silicon Valley.

Here we are - two species in this world of ours - and I should have my nut examined for reckoning it was big enough to share.

Ruby, my Author, once showed me a macabre museum: La Specola. She warned that you First Lifers would stuff and mount us Blood Lifers (like all the other animals you've screwed over), if you ever discovered we existed.

Ruby swore we had no place but the shadows.

I, however, didn't listen.

It doesn't look so bloody clever now, does it?

I'm sprawled on the bed of my cell; I'm still starkers except for the silver ring on my left hand – S.L.A.V.E standing out in stark relief. And yeah, it's a cell: Egyptian cotton sheets don't cancel out the lock.

Didn't they teach you that in *How to Be a Mistress* school?

Earlier I'd heard footsteps outside my door. I'd also caught the whiff of gorse and sunlight. You'd smelled just like that, the first time I saw you, when I was just one of many slaves - tiger-striped and bruised - waiting for your inspection at Abona House. But then the scent had faded.

To be owned by Finlo Cain's daughter – Grayse - now *that* takes the piss. I'd forgotten you were *Master's* spawn, until you told me your name was Manx.

And even your name is torture: it strips me back, layer by painful layer. To my first love and betrayer. To the woman, who destroyed my heart and then got me killed. To the bitch, who became my first ever prey. *Grace.* That was her name. Still, your name's spelled differently. So best we don't take it as a bad omen, yeah?

I can't hear anything in the dark of the night anymore; you must be kipping by now.

I take another quick shufti around: there's nothing but four off-white walls, this strange bedside table (a stiff cube of crochet), and an eerie blue glow from the window blind, as if it's infested with magical ivy. You'd explained you'd had it fitted with electroluminescent fabric, which becomes brighter at night and dims as the sun rises: an early warning system for the dawn.

It looks like you're a dead thoughtful slaver.

Still, there'd also been this journal on my pillow.

A5 textured Italian calf leather, framed by smooth burgundy; it's so deep red I could suck the blood from it. The pages are buttery between my fingers.

I guess you're not big on irony, springing for such luxury on a slave. I imagine you only buy the best: this journal and now me.

The journal even came in a cracking navy presentation box; the bang was bloody satisfying when it hit the wall. It doesn't have any lines, so your thoughts can flow free. There's no lock. But then I don't know why I expected one: privacy's for the free. There was, however, this blinding pink gold fountain pen, so...swings and roundabouts.

And its name – 'The Slave Journal of...'

See, that's where I got stuck.

You lot call me slave *shadow* to mock. Because my true name?

It's *Light*.

I feel like I'll be struck down or...beaten down at least, simply for writing that. But it's the truth. And truth can't be erased as easily as words.

You must be a mug if you reckon you can keep me here – tamed - as a willing slave. But then, I'm not exactly *willing*, am I?

Do you get off on it? The power?

If folks were honest, everyone bloody would (given half a chance). The thing is, most First Lifers never do. It takes being reborn as a Blood Lifer to taste that splendour.

I haven't forgotten the majesty of the night, even if the black's consumed me. I've more than a century on you. I'm a predator - not to mention a Rocker. You can take the clobber from a bloke but you can't take that.

Freedom means so little, until you lose it. But I will find it again, I promise you.

So, dear Reader (because I know you're reading this, there's no use pretending otherwise), did you reckon giving me this poncey journal - all softness and stink of leather - would make me spill my Soul? You already have my body, bought and paid for. You *think* you have my mind.

My thoughts, however..? They're my own.

Write in it every day, you'd ordered, with that little smile.

What do you think this is: *Bridget Jones's Diary*?

I'm not a performing monkey. I'll write, when I write. You want more?

Good luck with that.

You want to know how I was captured? Enslaved? Defanged?

I won't guarantee you'll like what you read. No one does when it's the truth: raw and flayed. Bloody.

But not tonight.

The glowing ivy is dimming in the blind. The sun is on its way. And I'm knackered. I need a kip and a wank. That's what comes of you not giving me any clobber: black jeans and t-shirt please. Nothing fancy.

Maybe you won't even read this. Why would you? I'm only a slave now. What difference could my thoughts make?

MAY 5

So, I guess you did read my journal then?

The look on your mug this evening when...

I noticed the journal had been straightened on the crochet table. It's not like *I* leave anything straight, is it? Because rebel here, yeah?

I knew you'd read my pissed off ramblings, when you tossed the black jeans and t-shirt at me, before slamming down a cup of blood and banging out. Not a single glance at me. Not one word.

OK, wanker here, and you're a... I don't know yet. That's what brings me out in a cold sweat - the uncertainty, which haunts all slaves - because nothing is under their control, least of all what their new *owner* will be like.

Still, if you don't want honesty from a Blood Lifer, don't demand it.

In the 1950s, I knew this Blood Lifer from Darwin, who was so blindingly honest he'd tell you to your face you were a *crook* or a *fiddler* (and sometimes both).

I asked him once if he didn't get tired of all the barnies.

The bloke had stared at me evenly out of his purpled peepers, before shrugging. 'The truth is free.'

Turns out, however, that the git wasn't right: he copped it when some *crook* or *fiddler* took exception, shanking him through the heart.

Shame that - because wouldn't it be nice and comforting if life could be tied up pretty in a bow?

Anyway, now you've left me alone for the night. I don't know if it's punishment, or if that's simply the way it's going to be. If it is, I'll start scratching lines on the wall to record the dawn, as the ivy brightens and dims, transforming this into a proper gaol.

I've paced up and down to burn off the buzz and roar of the blood, as my muscles bunch and tense, dancing on the balls of my feet and gagging for a go with my fists and my non-existent fangs.

Or a shag – I'm not fussy.

You've been feeding me cows' blood, which is richer than my normal pigs'. It trickles into the system slow and sensuous, manna to a starving man, after all these months.

Christ in heaven, can it really be so long..?

The blood's not human. But after existing on so little, it firework sparks technicolour, until overloaded I could lick the walls and kiss the stars dancing in front of my peepers.

There's nothing to do in my cell. I've lain for hours counting, losing myself in the exquisite coloured song of numbers: whorls of plaster on the high ceiling, strands of entangled crochet cotton, moulded into servitude and leaf tendrils on the alien ivy.

Then I've played with the numbers, drawing out the game to fill the void: ordering them into sequences and memorising the never-ending tumble of morphing shapes.

I should be used to my bondage. When I was first captured, I drowned in it. And now..? Sometimes I think it'll turn me touched after...

No, you haven't earnt that memory. Not when you've locked me in here. Alone.

I tried the door earlier, just before I started writing this entry.

It's a heavy, original affair, or it'd splinter with one good boot. I've broken through enough doors in my time (you don't want to know why). There was no budging it.

Then I lost my blasted temper.

All of a sudden, I was hammering on the door and hollering.

You sodding well let me out... I'm not your bleeding pet... Open this...

Until reality crashed in: Abona House's severe grey façade, the dark stables, *Sir*, the slaves, who I'd left behind and the parades of punishments for just such rebellion.

I freaked out. Trembles shook every nancy boy inch of me, as I fell back, scrambling to the illusory safety of the corner. I hugged my arms tight over my nut.

Good boy. Got to be a good boy. I promise to be...

I huddled there - I don't know for how long - but you never came. The blind showed it was still twilight. You must be out.

Lucky break for me.

That's why I reckoned I should write this entry...you know, honesty and that. To show you I can be a *good boy* too.

You can't imagine how much I hate myself for that slave thinking. But you're free. You have options.

I don't.

Still, writing this has given me something to do in the vast expanses of boredom, seeing as you've abandoned me in this cell. It keeps the nightmares out: the ones of my past and future. Spectres of what's been done to me and shadowed fears of what will be.

It doesn't half bring home a fellah's helplessness, however, to have the long length of an empty journal spread in front of him, with all these blank pages to fill, like these walls and my slavery.

How about I write what it was like when you came to buy me?

Maybe then you won't leave me in isolation. A bloke's got to hope or else he's truly dead - and I've already tried that. I didn't fancy it much.

It was the rebirth, which was glorious.

'Whoa, this one's wicked frickin' busted. What did he do, Mr Yates?'

A line of us had been herded into a wing of Abona House, which I hadn't seen before: a humungous entrance hall, with a baroque chandelier, all smoky flourishes and brass scrolls amongst the sharp glint of Austrian crystal. I'd only caught a shufti of the room, before we'd been ordered to *kneel*. Then all I'd been able to see, as I'd bowed my nut, has been the cold black-and-white chequered marble floor.

When I heard the woman's unexpected voice, I risked a quick glance up from underneath my eyelashes.

It was some bird, tall and willowy in a lace Victorian knit sheath dress, who'd come to inspect us, as if we were expensive antiques for sale.

The bint was a First Lifer; I could smell the blood pumping through her.

Christ in heaven did I crave to violate that dainty throat and gorge my starved fill.

I told you this would be the truth flayed bare, didn't I?

The woman's grey, piercing peepers caught mine, before I had the sense to lower mine.

'The pretty leech makes trouble he does,' *Sir* - I could feel him hovering behind me. I tensed. I could imagine *Sir* pushing his black framed glasses up his neb, in a habitual gesture of disappointment. 'You don't get nowhere without discipline, see. It was all on your dad's orders, Miss Cain.' I flinched. This bint was the *owner's* daughter? *Master's* daughter? *Bollocks.* Shrinking down, I tried to look as uninteresting as possible, as you strolled closer. I sensed your hand reaching out towards my cheek. Just for a moment, I allowed myself to imagine you intended to caress it, rather than clout it. 'You carry on now,' *Sir's* voice contained a hint of impatience in its Cardiff lilt: that never boded well.

I struggled to stop myself fidgeting; the stripes across my back and arse ached deep into the muscle.

Stuff *Sir*, I was going to risk another look.

This time when I raised my peepers, you were staring right at me. Neither one of us looked away.

'I'll take this one.'

'What? I mean...' For once *Sir* seemed lost for words at your announcement, and wasn't that just harmonious, orchestral backed choirs in Heaven music to my lobes? 'Look you, the boy's not ready. His training's only... Your dad's been thinking on this leech for the Estate.' *The Estate.* Two words, which hung over us Blood Lifers, as the ever present threat, which made Abona look like a sodding kiddie's nursery. I only realised I'd begun to gasp in panicked breaths, when *Sir's* manicured talons landed on my shoulder and squeezed painfully. 'See? Not right at all. But isn't this little one a lovely job?'

When he released my shoulder, *Sir* tried to drag you on to the next Blood Lifer - this blue-eyed teenage crush of a Dutchman - who was staring vacantly ahead.

My breathing slowed at last: that was me forgotten then.

'Na-ah,' you shrugged *Sir* off, 'I've already told you - I'm taking *that* one.'

'But I need a few more months to break him. If I was given a couple of weeks, maybe I could--'

'Naw,' I was surprised by your sharpness, 'I want him like he is. Right now. Intact.'

I nearly laughed.

Intact?

I sodding wish I was, sweetheart.

'Up. Inspect,' *Sir* barked. I jumped up, standing to attention, with my legs spread apart, as I balanced on tiptoe. I clasped my hands behind my nut and arched my back - my whole bloody wares on display. When you circled me, I felt your hand close to my skin, skimming it but never quite touching: it was torture. Your fingers hovered over the lash marks. *Sir's* voice was low. 'It's a mistake.'

'You want me to call my daddy?'

'No, no, look here... But the leech'll have to be sent to you.' Panic. There was definite panic in *Sir's* tone.

I sensed you directly in front of me; you were studying me. 'I want to talk to him alone. We could walk in the gardens. He'll be on his best behaviour, right?'

I ventured a small nod.

'How about some pants and a t-shirt for him? It's wicked raw out tonight.'

I tensed.

Sir had never yet shown his *other* side to a human, but – and I had to give it to you – you had the skill to right royally piss him off.

There was a significant pause, before *Sir* replied, with what I knew was a supreme effort of restraint, 'These creatures don't feel the cold.'

'That's why they're like, shivering their asses off?'

This time I couldn't help it. I spluttered with laughter. Then I yelped, as *Sir* grabbed me by the scruff of the neck.

'What slaves *feel,*' *Sir* spat, 'doesn't matter.'

A moment later and it was your soft fingers on my neck instead of *Sir's*, as you prised him away, before steering me out of the room.

We strolled in silence through the kitchen gardens at the back of Abona House, the herbs – basil, mint and chime – melding in sunbursts of scents and hollowing my starved belly with the memories of long ago dinners. We wove past the ice house and down to the large walled gardens and horse pond; I could see the fat koi sleeping under the black mirror of the water. The gravel of the drive was sharp under my bare feet, nicking my soles bloody, but I bit back my pain because I was outside and that was...like breath.

I was desperate to tip my nut back, stare up at the stars and howl at the crescent nibbled moon, like I was off my bloody trolley.

Yet I didn't dare.

You just kept on walking, tense as I felt.

When we reached the long, low stable block, I couldn't repress the tremble, which ran through me. I wished I could forget my last trip there but I was still welted in rainbow stripes.

You glanced at me. 'Cold?'

'Yeah, it is rather parky, darlin'.'

You gaped at me, as if you'd been expecting me to speak some strange Blood Lifer tongue and not the Queen's English. Like you hadn't assumed I'd sound...human. Then you gathered yourself together. 'Here,' you led the way to a sheltered trio of arches, which made up the poncey fakery of a loggia. 'Better?'

'Almost like I wasn't starkers.'

You gave a tight smile.

I leant against a column, as I had a gander back at the silhouette of the great house, its steep terrace, the wood encircling it beyond and the drive sweeping down to it, between the dark sentinels of oaks.

In some screwed up world, this was the worst Jane Austen scene ever.

Well, maybe not *ever*...

You were giving me these quick, surreptitious looks. 'This is, like, fried.'

I shrugged. After the year I'd had, this new twist to my existence had some dead stiff competition in the *fried* department.

You edged closer. 'You don't have to look so scared; I'm not gonna scoop ya.'

I raised my eyebrow. 'Good to know.'

That flummoxed you.

You ran your fingers nervously through your ash blonde hair, which I now noticed hung in a bob to your shoulders. I had the sudden thought of how soft it'd feel on my lips...and then wanted to scrub my brains out.

I haven't long been alone - utterly, truly alone - since my first death. Since I lost the only person, who mattered to me in this brutish world, I feel too easily.

Us Blood Lifers do that; every emotion is amplified.

I looked down, but you forced my chin up.

Reluctantly, I met your sharp gaze.

'I meant it. I didn't want...one of those broken *things*. Though you've gotta be soft making trouble for daddy. He's the one, who's insisting I buy one of you. He's eager for me to learn about the business now I'm back. It's not like *I* want...' Embarrassed, you looked away.

'Don't worry, I wouldn't want me either.'

'Naw, it's just...I've never even looked after a dog before.'

'Lucky I'm not a mutt then.'

The wind whipped through the gaps in the arches, goose bumping my skin. The air was fresh and sharp. For the first time, I could smell more than my own blood and sweat.

'Look, it's late. I'd better get you back.' *Bugger it - me and my big gob*. I hopped from sore foot to sore foot after you down the drive, leaving a crimson snail-trail in my wake. 'Just tell me what luggage you'll need sending with you?'

I built up the bottle to reply, 'I had a coat. A leather motorcycle jacket – studded - with a gold ace of spades on the back. I don't know where it is; the buggers took it. It's vintage, from the '60s. It's a bit faded now but...' You were staring at me in surprise. I dropped my gaze. 'It's a blinding coat,' I muttered. When I looked up again, I almost caught a smile.

You may be a Cain, but it doesn't have to mark you. We're more than what our families, ancestors or species make us.

At least I used to reckon so.

There isn't bleeding anyone, who won't try and control you. The system's set up like that, cradle to the grave.

But that doesn't mean you have to play their game.

For the first time in months, as the Stuart shadow of Abona swallowed us again, I let my mind wander to escape – and it smelled just like you: of gorse and sunlight.

Then again, you've shut me up in solitary now, so I got that wrong, didn't I?

Maybe you *are* marked by Cain.

MAY 6

Your little pinkie stroked mine, when you passed me my blood just now, so that's progress..?

No, you're right, I'm barmy: too much blood and boredom.

I noticed something though, when you handed the blood to me, inked on the inside of your wrists, before the delicate pulse points (and trust me, you don't want to know why my gaze was drawn there).

Tribal black outlines of a Manx cat, with long hind legs and shortened, stumpy tail.

There's one other place I've seen the same design. It signifies white, searing agony. Snaking fire. Schumann playing wild carnival.

Do you have the tracker?

That thought makes me shudder. I remind myself just who you are – a daughter of Cain.

The Manx is marked out by its genetic mutation: the shortening or nonexistence of its tail. That makes it no different to us Blood Lifers.

It's all in the evolution – venom and fangs – which are from Komodo dragons, if you're interested (although I reckon your sort isn't).

We're simply numbers on a page. Cash in the wallet. You prefer to commodify us. Pretty up the image.

Trap us in a tattoo.

MAY 9

I'm writing this in your kitchen: humungous, blinding white and stainless steel affair, with silver brocade wallpaper, Smeg fridge and a Rangemaster gas stove, which has more dials than I know what to do with (and looks like it's never been touched).

I'm writing this entry because you stuffed the journal in front of me, before ordering me to do something *quiet*, since you had *like so much work*. You'd reckon I was a snotty nosed brat with a colouring book - not a century and a half old Blood Lifer.

It's not as if the last week has been a picnic, shut up in my cell.

This evening started the same. Except that the call of the blood – the night, in all its electrifying glory – beat in my veins. Until my nut felt like exploding bloody firework. Until I struggled not to scream from the pulsating migraine agony.

All I wanted was to drive the pain away...*bang, bang, bang*...to the *beat, beat, beat* of the blood. My nut against the wall, painting it crimson.

The new pain grounded me. There was no thought or sensation, except the...*bang, bang, bang*...

I didn't even hear the door open.

The next thing I knew, you were dragging me away from the wall and hollering at me.

My blood was dripping sticky into my peepers. Shadowing you into a spectre.

Then you quietened. To my surprise, there was the light touch of your fingers down my cheek, followed by the firm grip of your hand in mine, as you led me out of the cell for the first time.

You parked me here in the kitchen, before swabbing me with balled cotton wool, pinking a bowl of tepid water, as you cleaned my cut.

Ruby would've licked the blood from me like a proper feast. Then buzzed, we'd have shagged right there on top of the gleaming counter, shoving the avocado knives, nut milk bags and kombucha jars smashing to the marble white tiles.

You, however, just threw the used cotton wool into the rubbish. 'Well, that was frickin' stupid.'

I shrugged.

'Ya huh! You're not getting off so easy. You're telling me what that was about on account of I don't want you decorating my tasteful apartment a vivid shade of red.'

All right then, veiled truth time.

'I don't like to be caged. Alone. I'm sorry.'

And there was that piercing look of yours.

Then you sighed, settling down on the stool next to me, before piling out an iPhone (that was miraculously charging inside your monochrome tote bag), workbooks and a handful of rollerballs onto the counter. So definitely no shagging then...

Your hair was hanging in damp strands, as if you'd recently been caught in a downpour.

I flipped open one of the workbooks. '*Masters in Management*?'

You snatched the workbook back, as if I'd sully it. *Right, I've got the memo, sweetheart.* 'It's why I've been...distracted this week. Daddy wants me trained. But it's so intense. I mean, wicked exciting, with global experts and networking, you know? But this week there've been evening summits and--'

'So you reckoned... What? You could stuff me in a spare room like a...hoover?'

'A hoover?'

I couldn't help grinning. 'Alright, not my best analogy.'

You shivered, running your fingers through your wet hair. Tiny rivers streamed down the vast bay window out in the dark. I craved to feel them coursing down my skin too. 'It's wick raw out. Does it do nothing but rain in this city?'

'Drizzle. It drizzles mostly. And making small talk about the weather? That marks you as an honorary Londoner right there.'

'Yah, I'm from Boston; it's not like I don't get it.'

'So, that's it then? I mean...' I ducked my nut.

'I grew up with my aunt in Beacon Hill. After that it was Harvard, of course. Do you wanna see my resume too?'

'Right little bluestocking.'

'Right little killer.' Your peepers were hard now.

Bugger. My chest was tight. *Breathe, bloody breathe*. 'You don't know the half of it, sweetheart.'

The look on your mug was worth it. When you slipped off your stool, however, stalking down the hallway towards my cell, I tensed for flight.

Fight or flight – they're our two most basic, ancient responses. I used to imagine I'd always fight. That's been tested, however, these last few months.

We none of us have one identity alone and immutable.

To the Blood Club I'm *shadow*. But my true name is *Light*.

Yet what does that even mean?

In First Life I was *Thomas*. In Blood Life we must all transform, when we're rechristened into our new world: I chose *Light*. I was, however, to change again, when I met... Let's just say she was a First Lifer - like you - and I never saw anything the same way. *I* was never the same. I shed the Blood Lifer I'd been, like snake skin.

Now she's gone. And who am I without her? In the blackness of this new life and grief?

It was *Sir* who rechristened me once more as *slave shadow*.

So who am I now? The type of bloke who scarpers in terror from a First lifer?

When you returned to the kitchen, however, just as I was poised to leg it, I saw you were only holding this journal. When I caught a glimpse of its blood-red cover, it was strangely comforting.

You thrust the journal down in front of me, with that order to do something *quiet*.

Since then you've been tapping away at your laptop.

I don't know what's wrong with pen and paper.

You know, it's not as comfortable as you'd reckon travelling by crate. No, you're right: no one reckons it's comfy.

That first night, when they delivered me to you like the product I've become, I'd been travelling for so long in the stink of brittle straw and the dark, that the bright light of your chandelier blinded me.

I lay there, wedged in and tied down by red nylon ropes, which had bruised my wrists and ankles (even purpling my throat), gasping for air and slowly opened my peepers.

I squinted up at the light refracted by the vast chandelier, which my muddled mind realised was hundreds of pieces of plastic rubbish, the type that could be washed up on a beach: bottles, bags, balloons and fishing lines.

Then I could feel rough hands dragging the tight ropes off me. Finally, I was hauled upright, like a sodding statue.

You were simply standing there – watching - your hands clutched together. I didn't know which of us was paler.

Your apartment was Georgian, panelled in polished mahogany, with a classical, fluted fireplace at one end and two high bay windows with heavy blinds and silver velvet curtains. It felt Bohemian, however, rough around the edges. The furniture was a mix of antiques, modern pieces (more like art than anything else), and junk shop finds. There was a tree trunk bench along the back wall: a huge log, with traditional chair backs stuck into it. I wondered whether the plan was to similarly domesticate me.

The apartment reminded me of how a Blood Lifer would decorate, picking out what they liked from across the ages. It felt like...home.

You muttered something to the workers and they left, taking that bleeding torture device of a pine crate with them. You didn't tip. My kind of bird.

Then we had a silent staring contest. It was more awkward for me, considering I was starkers, except for the silver S.L.A.V.E ring. Somehow the ring only made me feel more exposed.

I hugged my arms close around me. 'Where might this be then?'

'My apartment.' Not a flicker. You should play poker, you'd be bloody blinding at it.

'And that's where? Exactly?'

'Exactly where it's meant to be.'

I wandered over to the far bay window and peered out.

A city.

Towers, small blocks of flats and the low black ghosts of estates. The occasional sharp church spire, like needles.

Yet only in the distance because the apartment was overlooking a park, with an avenue of tall sweet chestnuts guarding the street and the black hump of a hill to the north.

It was so familiar, my skin itched - of course, that could've been the nicotine withdrawal. Still, I couldn't help the smile, as I spun to you. 'London?'

Suddenly a memory flashed back with such vividness, I could taste the blood warm.

AUGUST 1866 PRIMROSE HILL, LONDON

Ruby and I had stalked this reprobate through the steaming heat of Regent's Park. He was a right ruffian in a dirty crimson choker and a crooked tile, which he kept pressing to his nut, as if expecting it to be swept off.

He stank of onions and sex.

The wanker was a kidsman; all evening thc little ones had flocked around him with their petty thievings - a billy or a jenny - as he knocked them around, whilst fondling their arses.

Ruby had let me pick our mark for tonight; the kidsman might as well have offered me his neck himself.

I reckoned he must be up to some caper or other, when he skulked into the park shifty-like; it suited us just fine because so were we.

Ruby grasped my hand, as we prowled under the London planes and oaks.

Authored in Elizabethan times, for a century Ruby was my red-haired devil, Author, muse and love. Together we were alone against the world - or so I'd thought.

I've since learnt never to trust such simple appearance.

We tracked the bloke past avenues of sweet chestnuts and limes, darting underneath the spreading arms of ancient oaks. The air was fresh, in a way it wasn't on the streets. You don't know what pollution is, until you've been in a pea-souper.

I sparked with the freedom, twirling Ruby round and unbuttoning my shirt.

We passed the darkened tea-rooms of Chalk Farms and their pleasure grounds. The bull *croak* and *bark* of the frogs from the preserve called out in the black. The rogue was still slinking onwards, up Primrose Hill.

I hadn't been back here since my election to Blood Life. I remembered, however, my papa bringing me and my sisters, Nora and Polly. We'd munched on Barcelona nuts from sellers and cocktail sticks of treacle and peppermint. We'd climbed to the top, out of the smoke of the city. I'd stared in awe over the vast lake of Barrow Hill Reservoir, the crowded cottages and public houses, the zoological gardens and Wren's domed St. Paul's, which was like a decoration on the horizon.

London.

It hadn't seemed large enough to me, laid out like that; I never could find a world, which was big enough. I reckoned I had, when a second life opened up, like a puzzle unfolding, in Blood Life.

But I'd been bloody wrong.

That day with my sisters when we'd reached the summit, my papa had picked two creamy primroses - sun yellow in their centres - and laced them into their long locks. Papa had gently kissed each of them on their foreheads.

A year later papa had been dead, and I never saw my sisters again.

I guess my little sisters are dead too. I hope they were allowed some happiness in their short First Lives.

At last, when the kidsman reached the junction at the top, we saw a whole gang of coves gathered in the darkness. I wondered what they were plotting. Their dark seeds, however, wouldn't make it past tonight.

When Ruby stepped into the dim glow of their gas lanterns in all the beauty of her crimson silk, the kidsman smirked.

I knew then he was going to have his baubles trampled.

The ruffian leered at her. 'You looking for a tup, pretty pinchcock? You show us your cunney, I'll show you my weapon. Here's something for your troubles.'

A copper tuppeny bit landed on the grass at Ruby's feet. There were sniggers.

I remained in the shadows, waiting for my cue.

'Faith, you are foolish slaves. Nothing but base beasts. By this hand, you will cry mercy before this night is over.'

The laughter died.

'What, you bitch..?' The kidsman tried to backhand Ruby, dropping his lantern. In one practised movement, a steel shiv had flicked into his paw.

Ruby twirled the ruffian round, however, as if he was a ragdoll. Then she sank her fangs into his neck.

I heard the bloke's shocked scream, before he began to shake, as he fought the paralysis that was setting in. Soon the second ingredient in the venom would stop his heart, just as it'd already sealed the holes in his throat.

And that's why we're the ultimate camouflaged predator: we leave nothing but natural death behind. We were always meant to be the *Lost* species. Being dragged from the shadows was Ruby's greatest fear. She was my Cassandra.

Ruby tossed the kidsman's frozen body back to me, as I too now joined in the game. I swung the bleeder round, before rolling him down Primrose Hill: a nice little snack for later. His slack limbs bounced over the holes and hillocks, before coming to rest.

Then there was uproar: shivs, coshes and cudgels appeared, as if by dark magic.

When the First Lifers rushed us, we took those crooks apart one by one, chucking them between us, before hurling them down the hill to join the mound of paralysed treats.

I copped a mouse - a right shiner - before I could drag the giant off me by his Newgate knockers. The ramper bellowed, as I tore tufts out of his greasy whiskers.

I dived for his throat, my fangs extended and sank through his skin, piercing two tiny holes and delivering the toxin. He struggled, trying to thrash away, even in his pain. When I booted him, however, he too tumbled down the hill.

At last, Ruby and I were alone: two Blood Lifers on top of a hill in the black, a pile of First

Lifers at the bottom and the velvet sky above pricked by stars.

We were conquerors of our world.

I noticed the primroses then, which had been crushed in the struggle. It reminded me of that day with my papa and sisters, who I hadn't seen for so many years. Who I knew I wouldn't see again.

I knelt down and plucked a primrose. Its face was tightly closed against the moon. I knew I'd never see it open. Still, I slipped it into Ruby's scarlet hair. It suited her.

'My dearest prince,' Ruby snogged me, biting my lower lip and sucking at the droplets of beaded blood, 'how did you like my game?'

'You were...breath-taking,' I couldn't help grinning. 'But I was taught by my mama not to play with my food.'

Then Ruby's long-nailed fingers were tight around my throat. Squeezing. She always liked to play rough, this one. I licked my lips. Just as suddenly, however, Ruby's grip loosened. 'Prithee,' she smiled, 'let's feast.'

Ruby clutched my hand, dragging me after her down the hill in skipping leaps. I noticed, however, that first she'd stooped to pick up something from the grass.

The boss was still twitching where he lay buried under the rest of his gang at the bottom of Primrose Hill. Ruby grabbed him by the leg, hauling him out. I heard the wet, messy *crunch* as his neb smashed.

When Ruby crouched over the kidsman, I could see she had something small pinched between her thumb and finger. Then she held it up high in front of the kidsman's terrified lamps: it was the copper tuppeny bit, which he'd tossed at her feet.

I could see his sauce-box working, like he was fighting to form words. Ruby lowered her mush to his, as if intent on hearing them, but his stiff tongue couldn't force out more than a garbled, 'Please...'

Ruby gently placed her soft fingers on the First Lifer's blue lips. 'Peace be quiet.'

Faster almost than even I could follow, Ruby was straddling the poor bastard and forcing the tuppeny bit between his gnashers...and then deep down his throat.

I tilted my nut, listening to the coughed, wet rasps, as the kidsman choked to death.

I hadn't heard someone cop it that way before. I'm a human camera: life is a series of shots, branded into my brain. A day or night is always richer for a new experience.

Then we feasted. Bloody hell, how we feasted.

And that's how I knew I was home. The memory. The *taste.*

'Primrose Hill?' I gazed at you hopefully.

'What's it matter? It's not like you're going out. Ever.'

I turned my nut away, trying to hide the sick dread. Yet you must've seen it, plain as day.

I hated the whole bloody lot of you First Lifers then. I imagined you in a pile of twitching corpses mounded at the bottom of Primrose Hill – you, *Sir*, *Maste*r – and felt better.

Bollocks to it all.

I straightened my shoulders. 'Well, figured. Not with no clobber on.'

You seemed taken aback. 'I'll order something. But that doesn't mean you'll... Follow me.' That's when you led me into this white and silver kitchen for the first time, setting me on a shovel-like, red-

and-black stool, as if you didn't know what to do with me. 'So, shadow, you hungry?' I couldn't hold back the flinch. You noticed. 'That isn't your real name, huh?'

I looked away. 'It's what I'm called now.'

'Na-ah, I wanna know. I'll tell you mine. I'm Grayse. It's a Manx name.'

I remembered the agony of the belt... *My name is Light...* Cane... *My name is Light...* Riding crop... *Light, Light, Light... Sir's* boot, fist and the *snap* of shattered bones.

'Light,' I whispered, 'my name is Light.'

'OK then, Light, you hungry?'

I nodded. Every molecule roared for blood.

You swung open the fridge, pulling out a baby's bottle - thick with crimson - which you held towards me with an expectant expression.

Starved though I was, a bloke's still got to draw the line somewhere.

I raised my eyebrow. And didn't reach for the bottle.

After a moment, you lowered your arm. 'I don't get it. She said this is what you needed on account of your fangs having been removed.'

Suddenly I found myself off the stool and right in your face. To give you your due, you didn't back away, although your fingers clutched at the marble kitchen top. I didn't miss that. 'What's next? Pretty little bowl with *Light* printed on the side for my din dins? Or a leash?'

'At least it'd go with the collar I've got you.' I drew back to study you. Your grey peepers were coolly amused. 'Joke.'

'Right. Ha-bloody-ha.'

'So, what..?' You waved the bottle of blood at me.

Hypnotised by the scent, I weaved after it, like you were a sodding snake charmer. 'A cup'll do me. Warmed.'

Before you turned away, you glanced back at me. 'You're not what I expected.'

'And how did you expect an unwilling Blood Lifer sex slave exactly?'

That amused expression in your peepers, which didn't quite make your serious mouth again. 'Not like you.'

'No one's like me.'

You busied yourself pouring the thick blood out of the bottle and into a bright red-and-black teacup; I liked that I matched your décor. 'I'm just figuring that out,' you murmured.

You look like you're finishing up now with your work. Your iPhone, however, is still beeping every few minutes, and your fingers are all *swipe*, *swipe*, *swipe*.

Buggering hell, you look knackered.

MAY 14

I guess yesterday you bothered to read my journal because this morning you bit my head off.

I forget you'll see what I write.

It's like there's *you* and then there's *Reader you*.

It's so much easier to spill my guts to *Reader you* because with her there's no consequences. We have an understanding: what happens in this journal, stays in this journal.

I guess *you* don't have the same understanding..?

If I wasn't such a daft berk, I'd be more circumspect and keep both my own counsel and skin.

When you're scrabbling through a list of chores, however, which have been set by your Mistress, scrubbing at the kitchen floor on all fours in pink Marigolds, it pays to at least still *talk* the part of the rebel.

But here's the thing: I'm not playing any part. You can't flay a rebel's Soul.

I reckon you learnt that today.

The first night you allowed me out alone in the apartment (because you didn't want me painting the walls of my cell red again), whilst you were at one of your seminars, I did nothing but sit exactly where you'd placed me on the tamed log bench.

'I've gotta go down the City,' you said, 'let's see if you can't get into no trouble tonight? Don't move.'

So I didn't.

You'd left the chandelier of beachcombed detritus off and candles burning instead - needle pricks of light in the vast dark. Waves of fragrance caught me in their currents: Fig Trees, Tahitian Gardenia and Mango. I was carried on their seas. Transported to faraway lands.

To freedom.

A bloke can dream, can't he?

Yet in the apartment there was only the blackness and the olfactory illusion as comfort.

It forced me to remember the others - frame by bloody frame - who were still shut up at Abona's pleasure.

My new family.

How could I have forgotten them? Even for a moment?

When I heard the key in the lock, I tensed but didn't move. I wasn't sure what you defined as *trouble*, but I was desperate not to be shut away again.

You bustled into the sitting room but stopped stark still, when you caught a gander of me. Again the silent staring contest. I was getting the better of it, now I had on some clobber.

'Have you been..?'

'All evening. Not budged a muscle. I've been good as gold, God's honest truth.'

You simply stared at me again, before dropping your tote to the wooden floor with a *clatter* – you should watch that, I bet it cost a bomb. 'Go to bed.'

Bollocks. Screwed that up, didn't I?

'Get up.'

Christ in heaven, make up your mind.

'What..?' Groggy, I squinted out of the covers. You were standing with your hands on your hips, glaring down at me. I groaned and burrowed back into my nest. The magic blue ivy was dimmed to nothing on the blind: sun up. 'It's morning. Sleep time.' The duvet was unceremoniously hauled back. 'Oi, undressed bloke here.'

'I said, get up.'

Grumpily, I sat straddling the stool in the kitchen, resting my nut in my hands.

You'd already shown me the computerised blinds, which you'd had fitted throughout the apartment to keep the sun out, with a kid's glee. I'd just had time to drag on my jeans and a t-shirt, as well as to run my fingers through my hair.

Take note: if you want your toy to look smart? Brylcreem.

So, I was sitting there, bleary-eyed, whilst you were all chirpy, blitzing yourself – *bzzzzzz* – a blueberry and banana smoothie.

You poured the thick swill into a tall glass and took deep gulps. Your neck looked so long and ivory. Bloody inviting...

Look, *Blood Lifer* here.

'Coffee – black. Two sugars please, darlin'.'

You slowly lifted the glass from your lips, licking a smoothie moustache away. 'You can drink coffee?'

'Well, yeah. How else do you expect me to stay awake at this time of the bloody day?'

'It's not like, early. It's nearly--'

'Nocturnal here.'

'Not anymore.'

'Come again?'

You shrugged your slim shoulder. 'It's not working out. I need my sleep.'

'Me too. And I need it when that thing, which can boil me down to melted goo (called the sun), is in the sky.'

Your peepers were as hard as I've ever seen in a First Lifer. 'Not happening. You'll just have to...adapt. Can't you do that?'

'More than you know, sweetheart.' I gritted my teeth together not to say more.

Your smile was one of cool triumph. 'Mint. Now I just need to think of things to keep you busy whilst I'm out, so you don't...you know. I've got a gym; you can work out in there for two hours each morning,' your mush lit with sudden enthusiasm, 'I'll set you a fitness programme from Instagram.'

'Then I'll need that coffee.'

You banged through cupboards in search of what must be sodding poison by your sour expression. As a last ditch attempt, you swung open the fridge, which was stuffed with long-stemmed globe artichokes, strawberry punnets, asparagus spears, waxy lemons, aubergines and loquats. You shook your nut.

Seeing all that grub, however, I wasn't able to keep the glazed-eyed salivation off my mug.

You snatched up one of my bottles. 'You want some blood?'

'That'll only take off the edge.'

'You mean,' I could see the cogs turning (*thank Christ*), 'you need *real* food too? Like a...' You'd been about to say *human*, but I reckon that would've been a step too far. 'She told me slaves...I mean...Blood Lifers....didn't need...'

'That right?' Again I wondered who this *she* was. The same *she*, who'd advised you that we drank from bottles, like baby animals on a farm.

Uncomfortable, you slammed the fridge shut. 'Why?'

'There aren't enough calories in blood. Without other food, we're in a permanent state of starvation. Plus, I like the taste, the same as you.'

'But I haven't fed you since...'

You hurled the bottle at the far wall with a holler of sheer frustration. The teat bounced off and cold, glutinous blood splattered across the silver brocade.

I jumped up. Shuddering, I forced myself not to dive on the blood and lick up every delicious, dripping globule of red life.

You Cains have spirit. It makes you prime candidates for election to Blood Life.

I inched towards you, before tentatively patting your stiff shoulder. 'It's alright.'

'Naw, it's not. I told you, I've never even looked after a dog before.'

I smiled. 'I guess you've got the collar though?'

For a moment, you were smiling the first genuine smile I'd yet seen. Then you were shoving the remnants of your smoothie into my hands. 'Drink that. I'll get you some more blood. You can have anything you want when I'm out today; there are sweet potato brownies at the back of the cupboard.'

'I'll be sure to look out for them.' I watched you over the rim of the glass, as I tried to take measured sips, rather than down it in one go.

You were busying around, pouring fresh blood into a cup, before transferring it to the microwave. Then you eyed the coagulating mess on the far wall. 'I had to fire the cleaner because of you. Do you know how hard it is to find a good cleaner in London?'

I shrugged.

Somehow both the tantrum hurling of the blood and the firing of the cleaner had become my fault. But with a slave's instincts, I knew better than to argue the point.

'That's gonna frickin' stain unless...you sort it. After all, you're the one with all the free time. Anyway, I don't want you getting bored. I'll leave you a list of chores.'

'There an apron to go with that?'

'You want one? Or how about a pretty French Maid's outfit?

Humiliated, I shifted uneasily.

I finished the smoothie, banging down the glass. It wasn't the strongest rebuttal, but it was all I had.

You tossed pink Marigolds at me and didn't take *no* for an answer, until I was wearing them like a right pillock. I knelt on the kitchen floor by a soapy bucket, washing up the gooey blood from the marble tiles and scrubbing it from the silver wallpaper.

It still left the ghost of a stain.

When you bustled out of the apartment, I shook myself awake like a mutt. Then I got down to some serious press ups in the sitting room so I wouldn't have to explore your poncey gym.

It got out my energy: if it'd been night-time and I hadn't been about ready to curl back to sleep on the cold, mahogany floor.

When I padded into the kitchen, I discovered that - true to your word - you'd left a chores list for me on a pink Post-it note.

It was neatly numbered too.

I started with the dishwasher.

DISHWASHER: DINNER PLATES, FRONT LEFT. SIDE PLATES, FRONT RIGHT. BREAKFAST BOWLS, BACK LEFT.

I stared at that pink Post-it note, which was a pink bloody rag to bull. My fingers itched. You'll be living on the wild side from now on with your dishwasher arrangements. I slipped a dinner plate to the back.

Next up: laundry. I nosed into the utility. There were already these smart little hampers, which were marked *light* and *dark*, as if even our dirty threads needed dividing.

LAUNDRY: WHITE WASH (WHITE ITEMS ONLY). DARK WASH (DARK ITEMS ONLY).

You know sometimes I wonder how you reckon I've lived for the last 150 years. And it's not by merrily mixing colours. But your machine of torture in snazzy scarlet with matching drier? Flashing lights and twenty plus bloody settings?

Sod that.

It's cotton, delicates or quick wash - that'll do me.

Chuffed with how well I was getting through the list, I decided to have a snoop around. I pushed into your bedroom. The first thing that hit me was a montage of photos, which covered an entire wall. In each one, you were laughing or smiling.

It was as if you were a different bird.

Some of the snaps were faded. They showed an older woman, elegant but with the same grey peepers as you. She was in Florence. I never forget a place I've been.

Most often, however, it was you in the photos with this dark-haired fellah. He was a stud (in an alpha geek way), with his checked shirt buttoned up to the neck.

I had the sudden urge to rip off the wanker's bleeding arms because they were draped over you.

I don't know why.

You were posed in front of an imposing, white colonial mansion, with an American flag caught just in frame, sprawled on the grass under shady elms or leant on large oaks, in front of redbrick and ivy-hugged buildings. You pulled goofy faces and cuddled, or dived into cool blue pools.

It was confusing and overwhelming. A slice of life lost, except on these walls.

I forced myself to turn away from your private memories. Yet as I did, I only just had time to notice the vast white bed, when instinct booted me in the goolies.

Blood.

A dark pool. At the foot of the bed.

I threw myself to my knees. My phantom fangs ached with their attempt to descend (the shameful reminder of my impotence), whilst I lapped at the blood.

Wrong – taste and smell – chemical wrongness.

Spluttering, I pulled back, wiping my arm across my mouth in disgust. I prodded the solid pool with my nail.

A fake.

A mock massacre, masquerading as a rug. Nothing but a ghoulish decoration.

I ran my hands carefully over the rug's outline: one body fully drained, if you guzzled it all.

I pushed myself away, sickened and ashamed by my reaction.

You reckon you know me? Who I am. What I am. A *killer*?

But for many years now I've lived as something different. Even when I was new to Blood Life, I killed to live. It was survival. At least that's what I reckoned. A quirk of evolution had elevated me above the moral quagmire.

But then I met someone, who changed me.

Still, it's you First Lifers, who are obsessed with death. We need blood to live but First Lifers create fake baubles, which obsess on death for the sake of art, narrative or because it matches the décor. Death fascinates you. You spend your short lives dancing towards it - sod it, *inviting* it.

You shouldn't be surprised there exist in the shadows those who are ready to welcome you.

That evening when I'd finished the chores, I settled in the sitting room in a brown Fjord relax chair, which was lopsided like a baseball glove, with my arms linked behind my nut, for a little kip.

I was just resting my eyes, when I felt someone watching me. I slowly opened my peepers.

You were standing over me, your ash blonde hair plastered to your nut. It was raining again then.

'Comfortable?'

I wriggled my arse further down into the seat. 'Yeah, not bad. It's better than the rest of your tat.'

Your eyebrows rose. After a day running around after the Nazi of the Post-it world, which was now (and with exultant joy), torn into tiny pieces and tossed into the rubbish, it was a treat to see. '*Tat*?'

'You can't tell me you've ever actually sat on that tree trunk thingy?' You chucked your tote against the fireplace – *bang* – something definitely broke that time. 'And what's with that... On the floor in your bedroom?'

'Why were you in my bedroom?'

'Why do you have a grisly murder as a rug?'

You frowned. 'It's art – *Heartbreak.*'

'Right. Real romantic.'

'It means--'

'It means you First Lifers are nothing but blood bags. You'll get no arguments from me. Who knows, maybe these bigwig artists of yours are Blood Lifers themselves? We're everywhere you know: in business, the music scene, nightclubs, entertainment... The world's 24/7 now. And that suits us just fine. If you reckon we're only slaves, you've got it dead confused.'

You paled and turned away. 'Where's the chores list?'

I sprang up. I don't know why I was so buggering close to having a strop. 'Why? Checking up, are we?'

'I just figure I can't have set you enough to do on account of you having time to lounge around - on my *tat...*'

I blinked. 'Now hold on a minute; you do realise daytime is upstairs to Bedfordshire time for Blood Lifers? Bit of credit here.'

You, however, only tiredly shook your nut.

All right, I'm a daft pillock.

There were longer and more detailed pink bloody Post-it notes after that. Also an increase in prescribed exercise to three hours a day.

I always make sure I look the *good slave* when you come back through the door now.

Wearing Marigolds, whilst on my knees and scrubbing is a look, which mollifies you.

This evening I'd been ordered to dust the dining room.

You were out. As always.

The dining room's high-ceilinged, with a fireplace at one end, with low relief carving and inlaid coloured marble. Every wall - floor to ceiling - is frescoed, with a pastoral scene of gentle rivers, oak trees and rolling hills.

When I'd first scrutinized the fresco, which is original to the house, I'd discovered the black outline of stumpy tailed Manx hidden behind tufts of grass and snaking streams. I'd wondered whether you'd had them added. I'd traced each one, counting the technicolour bursts. A splendid parade of numbers. They'd risen to a crescendo, when I'd spied the last one behind a holly bush.

Every time I touch the orange sun, I'm astounded it doesn't melt my skin. The joy is pure.

The last time I experienced such happiness in the sun I was a kid, under the weeping willow behind our Watford house.

I'd been teaching my sisters a trick of the light with silver halfcrowns. That was before mama had stumbled down the steps to tell us... Before everything had been lost for good. Childhood. The sun. My freedom.

And now it's lost for well and good yet again.

In the dining room, however, surrounded by that fresco, I'm outside - even though I'm trapped inside.

When every day I sit cross-legged and stare at it, it's as if I can feel the breeze. It flutters the leaves. I can smell the tangy grass. Hear the cold *splash* of the gently churning river, as the perch shift in shadowed patterns beneath the clear surface. I stare up at the indigo sky and the face of the sun - and I taste the freedom. In those moments, I fool myself at least.

It's beautiful.

Then the front door *bangs*, and I startle, jumping back to my body again.

You're home. And all I can taste is the ash of my captivity.

Tonight, when I traced the sun with the tips of my fingers, I couldn't help my foolish grin. I tapped the first Manx I saw, which was sheltered underneath the arms of an oak. I avoided glancing out of the windows over Regent's Park and the sea of the city, which I could no longer touch.

Instead, I dusted the sideboard in wide arcs. The sideboard was a patchwork of scrap timbre and salvaged planks polished to a brilliant shine.

You can appreciate the precious in the worthless when it comes to objects. Yet not the worth in a sentient being, when we fall short of your black and white morality.

Bloody hell, then *we're* objectified. Just something else worthless to be transformed by the omnipotent Cain family (and their *training* process) into the newly precious.

You know, maybe I got it wrong. We *are* just like this poor sideboard.

I gave it a more rigorous rub with my fibre cloth.

The silence was getting to me more than usual.

Didn't folks in the twenty-first century have entertainment blaring every minute of the day? You had the technology, but it sat there, like it was ornamental. I'd have found a way to use the internet to free myself - if I'd had anyone to contact on the outside. That's the problem with not playing well with others: when you go missing, there's no one to give a sod.

Backwards, forwards, backwards, forwards...

I could see the dust, like midges, rising before settling again.

There was a pile of well-thumbed books perched on the edge of the sideboard. I trailed my finger down their spines: *Mistress and Slave Relations: The Beginner's Handbook, Mistress and Slave: The Advanced Course, Protocol Handbook for Slaves...*

I pulled my hand back, as if from the flames.

I guess you'd decided to do some swotting up. Life lived through academia, not raw in tooth and claw - bloody, thrilling and *delicious*.

Life's not sanitised: the infantilised drip-feed of the Instagram generation, blended to the bland.

It's dirty. Painful. And intoxicating.

The sensation of being trapped ballooned. The dining room warped.

I was a predator. I should be on the hunt.

Not defanged and playing house, whilst you bought me books on slave protocol.

I struggled to keep my hands from balling into fists, as I reluctantly worked further along the sideboard. To the item, which I feared most in the whole bloody apartment.

It hunkered at the end of the sideboard. A fruit bowl. Except there was no fruit in it, apart for one lone apple for artistic effect.

Nothing but display. The same as me.

Like a lump of shrapnel, the bowl was a deformed nightmare of limbs and weapons melded together from hundreds of toy soldiers: innocence and horror in a handy fruit bowl.

I shuddered as I fingered the contours of one melted soldier. Only his head and right arm pushed up, as if from the fires of hell.

Boom, boom, boom... Trapped in a hole with Ruby during the Great War, under the rotting corpses. The bright lights searing my peepers. The guns so loud my eardrums bled...

My chest was suddenly tight. I was breathing too rapidly; I couldn't get in the air. The disabled soldiers wept out of the bowl's wounds, hopping one-leggedly from its sides and then determinedly across the sideboard's shining surface towards me in a grotesque parade.

'Go away! Go away! Go away!' I howled, as I slid down into the shadow of the sideboard. I huddled close to the wall, with my knees to my chest. I screwed my peepers shut. But I could still hear them... *Clack, clack, clack...* 'You're not real,' I whimpered. 'Not real...not real...not...' I didn't dare take a shufti. I clutched onto the wall behind me.

With a roar, I threw myself up, swiping everything off the sideboard. Blinded in my panic, I couldn't see the damage. But I heard the *smashes, bangs* and *clangs*.

Facing my fear, I jumped up and down – *stomp, stomp, stomp* – I could feel the crunch of plastic under my feet.

At last, my breathing calmer, I wiped my arm over my mush. The sweet gangrene aroma had died away. I couldn't hear the *boom* of the guns.

I could see, however, the fruit bowl smashed into tiny sodding pieces; hero that I am, I'd killed the little bastards. The apple was ground into pulp; the Mistress and slave books were sticky in the juices.

Bugger it, I was going to cop it.

That's when the true panic set in. I don't remember everything. All I know is, my body was set for escape.

I made it to the front door, wrenching at it. But you must've had it reinforced because there was no movement. Not a sodding thing.

I booted the door, until my leg ached.

My blood was up now. I was no longer weak from the starvation, which had dogged me since my capture. Predator energy sizzled in fury at becoming the prey.

I snatched an ugly monochrome vase from the sitting room's fireplace and hurled it against a bay window. The vase smashed, but the window behind the blind didn't even tremble.

Reinforced glass too then.

In 1964 I got this blinding Triton. On times like this, I'd take her out and tonne it down the motorway - a crimson ghost in the dark. That'd settle me.

But locked inside this silent apartment..?

I lobbed the Fjord chair over on its side, which was heavy, so...satisfying. Next went the soft blue Sponge chair, which was wrinkled, like an elephant's hide, before I overturned the glass coffee table with a dull *crash*.

When I stood there in the middle of the destruction, which I'd wrought, I was shot through with sudden terror. But then as I spun on the spot and had a better gander at the devastation, I was filled with squirming pride too.

The place was trashed. *I was back*.

Unfortunately, that's when I heard the key in the lock, because so were you.

You took one look at me standing frozen in the remains of your sitting room – and thank Christ you'd yet to discover your dining room – turned once on the spot, as if somehow you could've come into the wrong apartment and then trudged into the kitchen. 'Just...go to bed,' you muttered, without glancing round at me.

I didn't need to be told twice.

So now I'm sitting here, writing this and hoping you'll understand why...

Look, I haven't caught a wink tonight, and the eerie glow from the ivy is already dimming. I guess I could've simply said sorry. But that's not my style.

Are you sorry for enslaving me?

All right, I want to...

Yeah, sorry.

MAY 15

Stupid git, aren't I? Because I guess 'sorry' doesn't cut the mustard.

I stumbled out of my cell this morning, after only a few hours' shut eye, at your call. You were standing in the centre of the sitting room, like an owner poised to shove a puppy's nose in its naughty *accident*.

Anxiously, I twisted at my slave ring. 'Look, can I just say--'

'Naw, don't think so. What the frig were you thinking?'

I shrugged.

You pointed at me. 'You're clearing this up.'

'I didn't doubt it.'

You clutched my arm with surprising strength and marched me into the dining room. I'd forgotten you hadn't discovered this nice little surprise last night.

We both stared down at the shattered remains of the soldiers. At the books with their split spines.

I wondered which of us would break first.

'You do get that was, like, an original?' *That'd be you then...* 'It was wicked valuable.'

I remembered the mutilated soldiers crawling along the sideboard. Then as they'd swarmed down my neck, before covering my entire body, until I was nothing but a plastic soldier too. 'What's money?'

This time - to my surprise - you tried unsuccessfully to smother a grin.

I reckon the bird trapped in those snaps on your bedroom wall isn't totally dead.

I glanced around, with a shrug. 'Anything else you want me to..?'

'*Naw*,' you snatched my arm again, dragging me until my back was pressed against the fresco, as if out of harm's way. 'So you witnessed the wars against that guy...Philip II, huh?'

'What? I'm not that old.'

'But I thought..?'

'The Great War. 1914, yeah?'

'Why were you even..? What did *our* war have to do with you on account of you being a Blood Lifer?' For the first time, your shoulders had relaxed, as you leant next to me. Intrigued, you watched me, as if we were simply two mates having a chinwag.

It was...nice.

'Too bloody right. All that First Lifer mechanized slaughter? You reckon we gave two figs which side could massacre more of the other? But me and my Author, we got trapped for weeks, caught between both lines. We were going barmy. The *boom* of the guns...screams...lights...stink...' I shook my nut, battling to clutch onto the present. 'War's not a toy...or a sodding fruit bowl.' It was times like these I missed my ciggies: I needed something to do with my hands. I bit at my thumbnail. 'Bloody stupid First Lifers.'

And just like that, our moment was over.

You booted at the banks of paper leafs. 'These books? A whole notha matter to the bowl. My sis loaned them. And she's gonna...'

Sister?

I'd heard whispers of an older Cain daughter, whilst I'd languished at Abona. With blinding clarity, I realised who the *she* was, who'd been giving you instructions on slave management.

I was buggered.

False bravado, however, seemed my best bet.

I slouched further against the wall. 'What..? Box my ears?'

'For starters.'

I straightened up. 'Tell her the worm has turned.'

When you straightened too, you slipped your manicured fingers into the pocket of your flared shirtdress. 'Thing is...all this...it's only...things. But what I wanna know is why you tried to get out?'

When had you started caring about my motives? Or admitting you read this journal? Usually you pretended like I came with an instruction manual, rather than emotions.

'Wouldn't you?'

'I get that. I do. But you tried to escape, like, for real.'

Frustrated, I pushed closer. 'Look, you daft bint, if I hadn't been so bloody starved, I'd have tried it long before now. The first chance I got.'

That's when you pulled something out of your pocket, holding it up in front of me: a small touchscreen device, with a black Manx logo.

Shooting, spearing, white-hot agony. Lava snaking down my spine and then in sparking rivers down every nerve in my body. Paralysing. No escape, only suffering and enduring, as Schumann played in wild, hallucinogenic carnival.

The memory of all that was held within the one innocuous looking device, which you were now pointing right at me.

Why had I been stupid enough to reckon *sorry* would be enough?

I fell to my face at your feet in submission. 'Please...'

Horrified, you reached out your hand, as if to pet me but then curled your fingers closed. 'I don't..? It's only your tracker. Light..? I just wanted to remind you that we always know where you are. That's all. What's..? You'd be soft to risk anything with how my daddy feels about his property. Plus I reckon you should know there are hidden cameras in each room.' Even in my fear, I understood now how you'd known about my unsuccessful escape attempt. Once more, my world narrowed. 'Our Retrieval Crew'll come get you in less than an hour, if I touch this button...'

I flinched, waiting for the pain.

As if shocked at my response, you stuffed the tracker back into your pocket. 'What the frig?'

You didn't know. *You didn't sodding know.*

I could feel the manic laughter bubbling inside again but I held myself still. A fury was building. The owner's daughter - rich on blood money - training to join the Management...

Yet you didn't have a bloody clue.

Had you ever dirtied your lily-white hands?

You lowered yourself to your knees, before grasping my chin. 'Tell me.' When I simply stared at you, your mug hardened. 'I don't care about the... But you've gotta be honest with me. That's non-negotiable – honesty.'

Alright, sweetheart, so that's what you want? Because there's a cost. To know what I am, underneath the labels. To see the Blood Lifer beneath the skin. You're not ready yet to hear who your family are beneath *their* skin. Not without me being the one who pays for it.

I'll tell you about the blood then, before my fifty years of abstention. That'll give you an intensive course in *honesty*.

I won't tell you about the woman, who blazed through me, until her death because you don't deserve to know.

I'll write about the other one - the Blood Lifer. The wonderful whirlwind of Elizabethan blood and death.

Ruby.

She's snuffed it now, so you lot can't get your mitts on her. But her and me?

Together we were a force of nature.

AUGUST 1866 LONDON

Ruby and I were dossing in the rookeries, in the slums circling Westminster Abbey, before we set off for our Grand Tour.

We'd masqueraded as lodgers, who desired to share a dustman's dark room in the crowded apartments for 2d a day. He'd stuffed his room with the broken treasures of the wealthy, which he'd sifted from the ashes and refuse. We'd ended the dustman's miserable existence, moving in as eagles, rather than rooks.

We didn't share the world.

From the tiny window, we could see out over the squalid roofs of the quarter and *First Lifer watch*.

Ruby would laugh at that: *prithee, why do you hold to First Life so?*

I, however, loved the chaos and the clamour - the death, clinging to the back of life.

Tails haunted doorways, raising their skirts at passers-by with a wink, even as they coughed bloody into handkerchiefs. A shivering Jemmy, his naked chest purpled with bruises, sprawled in the muck of a side street; he was tormented by a pack of destitute kids, who were like tiny skeletons.

A ditch snaked down the middle of the street, which ran with sewage the colour of green tea; doorless privies for both blokes and birds were built directly over it. When you were outside, you could hear the *splash* of buckets into the ditch, which was also conveniently the water supply for the quarter.

Life and death, see what I'm getting at?

Ruby and me stuck to the blood.

I was leant against the grimy wall, staring out over Westminster (or the Westminster of the poor), when Ruby slipped her arms around my waist.

We'd spent the last few hours making the beast of two backs, Ruby educating me in my own body, as much as in hers. We fitted - virgin that I'd been in First Life - in ways I'd never dreamed a man and a woman could. Now, however, our hunger was up for something else.

'My turn to play the game,' Ruby rested her chin on my shoulder.

Down below, the early evening street bustled with First Lifers. A full moon had just pushed itself into the smoke-laced sky.

Shrieking. Bawling. Pleading.

A punisher (a swarthy bruiser with bushy beard and whiskers), was stamping on the legs of a young down and out, who'd earned himself a hiding. Next the cosh was out, and scarlet was streaming to join the green tea sewage.

I raised my eyebrow. Ruby, however, shook her nut.

Ah, ah, ah...dirty...little...blasted...whore...

Right beneath our window a toff, who was as ran-tan as they come, with his loosely knotted necktie eschew and his top hat fallen into the mire, was brutally buggering a Mary-Ann. The Mary-Ann was so young, he was lifted up onto his toes on each thrust.

Ruby started to nod but then she hesitated and instead, pointed further up the street.

This bloke and bird, who were bundled under tatty coats and shawls despite the oppressive London heat, were cautiously creeping through the shadows.

When the light of the moon struck the couple's smug, excited mugs, I knew what Ruby's instinct already had, even though they'd tried to veil themselves in rags: *they didn't belong here.*

They were masquerading as much as us Blood Lifers - the rich *slumming* it, as if the poor's lives were a tourist attraction for their amusement.

Come and see the zoo...

Ruby smiled. 'I'faith, I believe I have made my choice.'

We stalked our quarry through Westminster's narrow streets and back-to-back tenements. We passed match girls, starving street urchins on street corners, who were hoping to be sent on the wealthy's errands and rat-catchers wearing their ferrets like fashion accessories on their shoulders, as terriers trotted at their heels with their latest kill hanging limply from yellow-toothed jaws.

The undercover couple nudged each other, as the woman suppressed her giggles. When they reached the grander sweep of Victoria Street, they dived into a waiting brougham.

When Ruby hailed a hansom cab, the dour cabbie didn't even blink at our request to set off in pursuit of the private carriage, simply flicking the reins at his stamping nag.

We'd not long ridden through the gas lit streets, before we were pulling up.

I should've bloody guessed: Belgravia, where the fashionable ladies and gentlemen rented elegant stucco townhouses in this aristocratic but *dull* district.

We watched as the couple – husband and wife, back from their ghoulish jaunt – descended and were admitted to just such a three-storied mansion.

I dived from the hansom cab - my dander up - ready to swoop after our prey.

Yet Ruby dragged me back. 'Have patience, my darling Light, our tatty pheasants will change their plumage and fly again.'

At first I didn't get it. Then I realised the First Lifers' brougham was still waiting outside.

So it was playing dress ups, was it?

I booted at the cobbles. Belgravia was like being becalmed. I was used to the rattle and the roar. The confusion of the crowd. The bustle and the bother. Growlers, cabs, broughams and the whiny of steaming horses. The sharp, brutal, never-ending merry-go-round of London. But this tranquillity?

A butler eyed me disapprovingly, as he took his evening constitutional. There was a volley of double knocks on a door several houses up, whilst a powdered footman next-door lounged lizard-like on the doorstep of a mansion, as if he owned it. I watched a high-cheekboned swell trot his gelding past us, with the type of expression, which implied all life was a bore; I itched to ease him of that burden.

The rich man in his castle/The poor man at his gate...

You First Lifers have always ordered each to his *Estate*. Only the god now is named *Capitalism*. Look around London and see if the rich and poor don't still live cheek by jowl.

To your reckoning, Ruby was right when she insisted it was God, who'd lifted us up to Blood Life.

If First Lifers didn't question the natural order, why was I? And if we Blood Lifers were the apex predator, then you *were* the prey.

Between Darwin and God, they had it stitched up.

When the couple's door swung open once again, I nearly didn't recognise them. 'Christ in heaven.'

Cinderella fairy tale, they'd been transformed ready for the dance. She was dolled up in a short-sleeved light pink number, which was trimmed with tulle and embroidered in gold, which glinted when the rays of the moon caught it, as if she was caught halfway in the process of metamorphosis. He was in a black dress coat and trousers, with white linen shirt and cravat. His waistcoat was gold-studded, as if to match the preciousness of his wife's outfit. His overcoat was trimmed with black velvet.

It was a cracking coat.

'Do they not look splendid?' Ruby snatched up my hand, spinning me in a wild circle, in a parody of the waltz. When I stumbled to keep up, she *tsked*. 'We will hire you a tutor, dearest prince. Every man should know how to dance.'

Impatient, I eyed the couple, who were dithering in their doorway, collecting up the lady's ornate fan, gold and diamond bouquetier and white lace gloves. 'Must we wait all night for these lovers to go to the ball, whilst I--'

Ruby stopped me with a kiss. All too soon, she drew back. I followed her with my lips but found only air. 'Now, my lover. We hunt bloody, *now*.'

We rested our foreheads against each other, and I nodded. Then we swooped.

We took out the liveried footman first. One quick bite. Ruby tossed him into the opulent entrance hall, under the glare of the bright gas light, as we barrelled into the shocked pair of toffs. We slammed the door shut behind us.

Ruby caught the husband, and I caught the wife close in my arms. The wife was frozen still in shock and then a moment later with paralysis. Her fan clattered to the Oriental rug.

She was warm and sylph-like; I could feel the flutter of her terrified heart.

The husband? He struggled and thrashed like a hooked perch, as Ruby twisted both his arms behind his back. He stomped at Ruby with his patented leather boots, gasping out a litany of *Cynthia, Cynthia, Cynthia*, whilst he stared at his wife.

He jerked like he'd been shot, when Ruby slowly licked up his neck, tasting - the fear and rush of blood - beneath the surface.

Then Ruby bit and let in the toxin.

Ruby nodded at me, before glancing upstairs. I smiled because I knew she had something planned.

I was more the fangs and fists type of bloke.

I dropped the wife to the rug, before creeping up the stairs to the top of the house and the attic rooms – servant quarters.

The cook and the housemaid had retired for the night.

So, *honesty*...

The housemaid was a regular stunner, even in her plain cotton nightdress; if she'd been a debutante she'd have had her card filled for every dance, instead of being on her knees each morning lighting fires.

Cinderella is nothing but claptrap spun to kids, as an opiate against the pain of their inevitable future disappointments. Blood Lifers look beneath the surface. They taste the Soul, electing true beauties, thinkers, warriors and leaders. The mistress of this house might've ruled in First Life, but it was her maid, who would've been chosen for election.

But not tonight. Tonight was for feasting, not authoring.

The maid screamed because a man in her rooms could only mean ruin. And it did, although not the sort, which she'd fantasised about in the lonely hours before dawn.

The bird's squawking was getting on my wick, so I snapped her neck – *crack* – pushing her long black braid aside, before sinking in my fangs.

Blood.

I barely stopped to savour. The roar blasted through me. The world was undone and remade again in the moment.

I was so lost in the sensation, I almost didn't register the *clang* and sharp pain across the back of my nut.

Reluctantly, I withdrew my fangs, before dropping the maid. I turned to face my attacker - a portly matron in a nightgown and cap, wielding a ceramic bedpan like a cudgel. The cook, I'd wager. Plucky old girl that she was, she still staggered back at the sight of my dripping fangs.

How much honesty can you handle? Put it this way: mutton didn't taste as fine as lamb.

Afterwards, high on the blood and its intoxicating thrill, I took a shufti through the house, stumbling from their bathroom, which even had its own flushing khazi (no sewage in the drinking water for them), to their bedroom and discovered what had been keeping Ruby amused.

The bedroom was a grand room, as if it was a set in a play; it was rich and dark with heavy navy curtains, floral pink and blue wallpaper and over-stuffed furniture.

I caught a butchers of the bleeder's velvet trimmed overcoat, which had been discarded, like a seal's skin, on the rug.

It would really suit me when I half inched it.

Ruby, however, never did like that coat. It wasn't until the Great War that I acquired another blinder. The next was... Well, you know the one. Leather motorcycle jacket, with gold ace of spades on the back..? That was Brighton, May Bank Holiday 1964. I got it off some Rocker, who'd been so set on battling with the Mods, he hadn't looked out for what was in the shadows – or his hotel room.

The couple's bed was in the centre of the room: the set piece.

Ruby had arranged the starkers husband and wife in a loving embrace, with one arm around each other, chaste-like. But the other..?

The husband's hand rested on his wife's right knocker. And his wife's? On her husband's knob.

Their mouths were close. Almost kissing but not quite. This intimacy was denied them (as it is for all whores).

I could tell by the occasional twitch of their muscles that the venom had fully set in. But not death. They were aware. Trapped in their bodies.

'What do you think, dearest prince, of my dolls?' Ruby wound her fingers between mine, drawing me closer. 'This wretched cur and his base bitch thought to make a spectacle of others. But now, by heaven, it is they who shall put on a show.'

Ruby pulled me towards the bed. She paused to lift the discarded gold and diamond bouquetier, which hung on a delicate chain, from the side table, where it lay amongst the wife's sad array of beautiful things that would now never see the ball: a hand cooler of chilled glass, unsullied lace gloves, white satin shoes that looked like they'd never been worn before tonight and a headdress of roses, ivy and lilies of the valley.

Ruby held the bouquetier up to her neb and sniffed. Then she sighed.

I was tripping on the blood. The blue and pink flowers were dripping from the walls. Creeping from the rugs. I was drowning in them. I could even smell them on Ruby's breath. 'Roses, signifying love.' I plucked a rose from the headdress, slipping it into Ruby's long hair.

Ruby startled, as if the tenderness was unexpected.

It was Ruby, who liked to play rough: I'm all about the romance.

It was me, however, who was surprised a moment later, when Ruby pressed a sprig of ivy into *my* hair. 'Ivy signifies faithfulness,' she whispered, before adding, 'let us blood share tonight.'

Blood share? That was...sacrosanct...holy to us, Ruby had said. It was a closeness I'd only experienced once before and hadn't thought I'd experience again. I didn't know what I'd done to earn it, or if the couple we'd stalked had brought it on.

I fairly launched myself at the bed.

Ruby had unwound the wife's hair from its plaits, and it hung in a glossy blonde waterfall to her waist. It mingled with Ruby's scarlet hair, like a meeting of seas, when Ruby leant over her.

The First Lifers watched us with petrified peepers, as we watched them. I wasn't sure who was putting on a show for whom.

I clutched onto Ruby's hand, when she twisted the bird's neck, so we could both latch onto it. Then came the moment when my fangs sank through the creamy skin.

It's all about that moment...when you know you're going to feed. You wait for it. It builds up, whilst your teeth descend. The sensation when the layers of skin break. Then you hit the artery, just before you start to suck. And the blood hits – *bang*.

Ask addicts in opium dens why they go back for more, or crackheads why they beg for the pipe, or...why bloody *ciggies* are so hard to kick.

To a Blood Lifer, take all that and multiply it by...ten, a hundred, a *thousand*...because there's nothing - *nothing* - to compare to the hit of fresh, human blood from the source.

That's honesty for you.

Knowing Ruby was on the other side of the neck - the rose still in her hair, as the ivy was in mine - doubled the intensity.

I could feel Ruby in the pull of the blood: my Author, muse, liberator and love.

I was made to love Ruby. And in sharing blood, we were joined.

Crouching over the body of that bird, whilst her husband impotently watched her being drained (all the time knowing he was next), I near on climaxed.

Of course, that came later.

So what if that's not all I am - *the blood* – if it's not all I became?

You don't get to wrest those precious memories from me. Violate those too.

Honesty - it's a double-edged sword.

You lot are keen as mustard to believe me a *thing* deserving slavery. Now you have the ammunition.

Hate away, darling.

MAY 16

Look, that *honesty* claptrap?

It didn't seem such a good idea this morning when I woke up.

But it was too late. I'd already stuffed my journal into your hands last night.

No wonder you looked so startled.

So I was lying in bed, pulling the covers up to my lobes (like *that'd* save me), whilst I listened to the furious *whirr* of the blender.

I notice you still haven't got any coffee in but...

Yeah, more important things, right.

At last, I couldn't put if off any longer. I built up the bottle to peer into the kitchen.

There you were: high Fendi heels, white frill shirt, with black A-line skirt and scarlet lipstick. Every inch the twenty-first century business woman.

Stuff it – here's to facing the gallows.

I swaggered towards you. 'Alright?'

You blinked at me, before turning away.

Nonplussed, I was expecting a bigger reaction.

But now you were reaching for something dark, which was folded behind you on the marble side. You swung back to me.

I jumped.

Then it was my turn to blink.

My motorcycle jacket.

Intact. Better than: cleaned and mended.

My hands shook, when I took the jacket from you. I turned it this way and that. Black and studded, gold ace of spades. It smelled the same -

felt the same too. A part of me. It took a moment to believe it was real. Then I was excitedly dragging it on; it fitted like a flayed skin. I shrugged my shoulders, running my fingers along the studs. I closed my peepers, breathing in deeply the scent of the leather, as I hugged my arms around myself. When I opened them again, I saw you watching me, with an amused expression.

I attempted to calm myself, nonchalantly leaning against the counter. 'Wankers told me they'd burnt it.'

'They told me that too...until I said, in that case, they'd be next.'

I laughed and then caught myself. 'So does this mean I get to go out?'

'Don't push your luck.'

I realised that for the first time, we were grinning at each other. 'Cheers...I mean--'

'I'd have given it to you last night, if you hadn't stormed in like...'

I flushed. 'About that--'

You waved it away. 'No time. Breakfast.' You turned back to the marble side and continued pressing kale.

I pulled a face, as I settled on a stool. You'd left the *Guardian* newspaper neatly opened, and I considered snatching a nose.

The world outside, however, now seemed so distant and remote I might as well be invisible, travelling in a tandem, parallel universe to every other First and Blood Lifer, who wasn't part of the Blood Club.

I thrust the newspaper aside. Then I spied a book of *Fiendish Sudoku* underneath. I hadn't figured you for a lover of numbers, which are my most constant mates. They sway, sing and surge in multi-coloured matrixes in my mind. Just another pretty snowflake pattern of neurological difference that rainbow brightens this world.

I glanced at the blank squares in the well-ordered grid. '9,3,7,1', I muttered, unthinkingly.

'What?' You asked, without looking round.

'Nothing.'

Then you turned and seeing the Sudoku book in front of me, slammed it shut. You shoved it to one side, as you slipped a dinner plate under my nose instead. The plate was in blue-and-white Willow style but it'd been transformed: Oriental river scenes, bridges and pagodas on islands and birds in flight. Yet each element was isolated from the other and rearranged on the bone china to create something new.

I tapped the plate with my nail. 'My mama had some of this. You know the story?'

You shook your nut, intent on your sodding avocado preparation.

'Two lovers were forbidden to be together. But their love was so... Anyway, on their deaths, their Souls finally came together as these two birds.'

I stroked the pad of my thumb over the two blue birds. I wished I could believe in that humbug - our Souls finding each other after death.

What's the point in torturing myself? I don't. We return to the dirt. All I have are the pictures in my mind.

At last, you turned to study me uncertainly. 'That's wicked sad.'

'Yeah well, it's only a story.' I pushed the grief down, plastering on a smile. You First Lifers aren't the only ones, who can dissemble. I'm done with the cobblers that's *honesty*. You were flicking through your iPhone – *swipe, swipe, swipe* – as if you couldn't make a culinary decision without it: rainbow chard beetroot, mangoes and coconut oil.

You were punishing yourself with perfect examples of grub in its raw, plant-based, sugar-free, gluten-free, *life-free* glory. Food as the new measuring stick for success. *#avotoast! Have a good day!* I nodded my chin at the screen. 'You don't reckon those bints really nosh that muck? It's a diddle. Behind the snaps, I'd wager they're guzzling any old crap. That's the ugly behind the beauty. There's always something beneath the surface.' When you spun round to me, depositing half the avocado on toasted sour dough bread from your Willow dinner plate to mine – *breakfast is served* – I snapped. 'That's it - *I'm* cooking tomorrow. I can order ingredients online. Bloody delicious ones at that.'

You wriggled onto the stool next to me. 'You can cook?'

'I'm over 150 years old. Of course I can cook.'

You still seemed suspicious. 'What sorta..?'

'Meat, chocolate, beer...good old-fashioned grub.'

'Na-ah, no alcohol.'

'A bloke's gotta try.'

At last, you shook your nut. I tried to mask my disappointment, but you knew me well enough by now to recognise it. 'You do breakfast. That's enough. Now I'm gonna be home today on account of I've got no tutes. You gonna be..?'

'A good boy?'

'I was gonna say quiet.'

'Your wish is my command.'

You snorted. 'Since when?'

I'd expected my usual pink Post-it stuck to the fridge. Yet today there'd been nothing.

I'd washed up the Willow plates anyway on autopilot, although I hadn't worn Marigolds – *sod it, bloody sue me*. Then I wandered into the sitting room to find you.

You were perched on the edge of the scarlet leather sofa, your laptop, Blackberry and a sea of documents spread out in front of you on the glass coffee table. You were tapping away, like an angry woodpecker on your laptop – *peck, peck, peck.* Each keystroke an attack. Your expression was so intense, I hesitated to interrupt you.

I shouldn't have worried.

First your iPhone chirped... *What's doing? Uh-hu? Naw, leave it; I got a whole notha...*

Then the Blackberry: repeat above. But this time formal and stilted... *Hello? Yah, this is... Yah, I know...that'd be... I can do that...*

You get the picture.

By the time I'd got your attention, I'd been standing there twiddling my thumbs for too bloody long. Give me some credit though, I'd kept quiet.

At last, you deigned to glance up at me with a harassed frown. 'Yah?'

'There's no chores list.'

Your frown cleared. I could've imagined it but I think your features gentled. 'I reckoned you could have the day off. If you wanna.'

You'd barely made the offer, before I'd thrown myself down on the Sponge chair, bouncing once or twice on the springy foam and hiding my smirk at your flinch. 'I'd bite your arm off.' You looked horrified. Paled. A sizzling shiver of pride tugged at me: *I still had it*. Then, reluctantly, I reassured you, 'It just means I wouldn't say no.'

'Whatever. But I need to--'

'Quiet, I get it. Still...if this is your day off--'

'I didn't say--'

'But you're home? So what happens when your mates come over? *Here, you must try the Chablis...and don't mind the sex slave kneeling in the corner--*'

'When do you kneel?'

'*...I'll just tell him to sod off to his cell, since his existence is challenging your worldview.*'

You took a couple of deep breaths, before firmly clicking the laptop closed. I guess I'm not good at keeping quiet after all. 'It's not a cell,' I hadn't expected you to speak so gently, 'and it's not gonna be a problem.'

'Why?' The idea I'd conjured of you outside this apartment - with friendships and freedom – suddenly bit deep against my own captivity. ''Cos you'll already have me locked away? A dirty little secret? Gagged and hogtied?'

'On account of I don't have any mates in London. Do you always indulge in melodramatic fantasies?'

I shrugged, avoiding your gaze.

'Maybe,' you leant closer (and I didn't miss the way you licked your lips), 'it's *you*, who are into these...kinks. I mean, if you wanna..?'

That's when I was saved by the bloody bell.

When you answered your mobile, I shot out of the chair and dove to the fireplace. I'd have legged it to my cell (and yeah, it *is* a bleeding cell), but that would've been a total retreat.

''Sup Fernando? It's early for you over there. I must be on your mind... The OEB? That's wicked pissa! Hey, you deserve it... Skype me soon and don't work too hard. I miss you, Prof.' My ears pricked up. *Fernando*? *Prof*? I had the flashshot memory of the wall of photos in your bedroom and a certain dark-haired Alpha Geek, who had his arms all over you, as if he was staking claim to a piece of bloody land. I don't know why that made my hackles rise, like a rabid cur. When you ended the call, there was a sudden silence. I glanced at you from underneath my eyelashes. You shifted. 'Look, Light, I was only--'

'I reckon your ringtone's tattooed on the inside of my skull. Don't you have an office to go to?'

'I don't need one; we're in the twenty-first century now.'

'So I'm behind the times because I died a Victorian?'

Your cool gaze seemed to be sussing me out. 'You don't look Victorian.'

'Didn't exactly stay dead.' I pushed away from the fireplace, jumping up to sit on the arm of the leather sofa. I scrutinized your serious features and those intent grey peepers. 'You really don't know anything about us Blood Lifers, do you? How we evolved or--'

'I know enough.'

Surprised, I drew back. 'As in, only good Blood Lifer's a dead Blood Lifer?'

You shot me a sharp look. 'You wouldn't be here, if that's what I thought.'

'Alright then, as in, only good Blood Lifer's one in shackles?'

Your mouth tightened into a thin line. 'And what about humans? Do we come in small, medium or large?'

'In America you can supersize.' I grinned, but you didn't return it: some birds have no sense of humour. Of course, Ruby would've clocked me for that comment. And so would... Christ in heaven that reminded me of what I'd been desperate since I'd woken this morning, fretting about yesterday's entry, to tell you. It's not as if you'd even believe me. Why would you after what I'd written? After the porkies your family have spun to justify our enslavement? To you I'm no different to a serial killer, am I? 'Look, that's not who I am now. I've been on blood abstention for fifty years.'

Your voice was so cold it could've given frost bite. 'Good for you.'

'Not asking for a medal, sweetheart. I just wanted you to know I don't... Not First Lifers. Not for a long time.'

'Makes no difference to me.'

'It does to me. You've no idea how much.'

'OK.' You turned back to your laptop, opening it with an air of indifference. Then there was that blasted *clack clacking*.

I listened for a moment in silence. Then I couldn't hack it any longer. 'What does?'

'What?' You didn't stop typing or look away from the screen.

'Make a difference to you?'

You didn't even pause. 'The profit margin.'

My hands tightened to fists on my knees, as I battled not to spring up and do something I'd regret.

Except that's when the nicotine craving kicked in. An unexpected, powerful burst, which made me want to punch something. Preferably my own mush. At least it'd give me something to do with my hands.

'Bugger it, I need a ciggie,' I mumbled.

'Ya huh.'

I could see the crown of your nut bent over your laptop. 'Just one fag. I'm desperate.'

A small shake of your nut.

'Do you know how long I've been smoking?' I was pacing now. Once I'd thought of holding the ciggie between my fingers and lighting it - not with my beautiful gold lighter because they'd taken that, but with the matches, which you keep for the scented candles - I couldn't shake the image. I needed the nicotine hit. *Yeah, pathetic addict here.* 'Please, you want to see a bloke beg?'

'Hmm, tempting. You're still not smoking.'

'You don't get it,' I pointed at you with an accusing finger, 'you're not a smoker.'

At last, you looked at me. If ever there was a determined mug, you had it. 'And now, neither are you.'

'*I want a sodding fag.*' Something flashed in your peepers; I was walking a dangerous bloody line. 'You know they can't hurt me, right?'

'And how about me? You know what?' You slammed shut the laptop with such force the glass table trembled. 'I've about had frickin' enough.' I backed against the wall; the brocade wallpaper was soft under my fingers. 'I've papers to write, research and accounts to go over before Marlane... *Wait*.'

To my surprise, you snapped the order at me, like I was your trained pup, before striding out of the sitting room. A moment later, I heard the front door *bang*.

Bollocks.

I didn't move a muscle. Frozen. I could take most punishments, only you might as well throw the blinds and candle-like melt me, if you intended to take back my jacket. I hugged the leather to me protectively.

You wouldn't return me to Abona House..?

The breath caught in my throat. I imagined *Sir's* expression, as he pushed his glasses up his neb, when I was redelivered - like rejected goods - in that sodding pine crate. He'd pretend disappointment and disgust in my piss poor performance. But secretly? He'd be delighted because it'd justify doing...anything he'd ever wet dreamed to me.

I began to pant, my nails scoring the wallpaper.

Or you could've gone to fetch your sister..? The older daughter of Cain, with her slave books and helpful tips.

Or to contact your dad on the Estate..?

I screwed my peepers closed, willing away the waking nightmares, as the panic built. 'It's not real,' I breathed, grasping onto reality by my nails, which clawed into the wall, 'not real, not real, not...'

I didn't even know you'd come back, until I heard your voice and by then, I wasn't sure *you* were real. 'Light, *Light*... What the frig are you doing?'

I struggled to focus on you. 'I wasn't... I'm sorry... Please don't...'

When you thrust a blue plastic bag at me, I recoiled.

You shook the bag at me again. I took it gingerly.

I pulled out a plastic packet containing...*one ciggie*?

Confused, I ripped it open. Except when I was actually holding the fag, it was nothing more than an illusion: it was too long and smooth. Artificial.

Dumbfounded, I stared first at the fake fag and then at you. 'So what might this be?'

'Compromise,' you offered, settling back onto the sofa and starting up your laptop. 'It's an e-cig. No smell or risk to me but the same...whatever, to you. What's the problem? I thought you were good at adapting?'

You raised your eyebrow, as you met my gaze.

After the terrors I'd conjured, the fact you'd thought up a solution, as if my comfort mattered (even if only because my whinging was narking the hell out of you), wrong-footed me.

Twice in one day you'd given me back something, which had been stolen from me: my coat and now a way to calm the cravings.

I just don't understand why.

MAY 17

My name is Light, my name is Light, my name is...

When you came home earlier in the afternoon than normal because one of your seminars had been cancelled, you discovered...

Look, all I remember was pulling on those pink Marigolds, as per instruction seven on your Post-it note: CLEAN BATH: WEAR GLOVES – I'M SERIOUS.

The next thing I was coming round, scrunched in the corner by the khazi. My arms were wrapped over my mug. My knees were drawn up under me. My nut hurt at the back, like I'd been smashing it against said khazi. And I was shaking, as if I had no control over my own body.

Yet here's what gave me true pause: *you* were kneeling in front of me. Hugging me to your chest. There was the scent of gorse and sunlight, safe and cocooning. The beat of your heart, even if it was hammering like a steam train. You were tall enough for your arms to wrap all the way around me; strange, I'd never figured on liking that in a bird.

The unexpectedness of your sudden closeness stilled me.

Carefully, I lowered my arms from my peepers. Your hair brushed backwards and forwards against my mush, as you rocked me; I'd been right about its softness.

Reluctantly, I drew back.

'Light? Can you..? Are you..?' You lifted my chin, studying me with intense concern. To my shock, I realised you'd been crying.

You were still waiting for an answer. I hardly knew where I was but I gave a nod.

'Let's see if we can't get you cleaned up.' My nut was hurting worse now; I could feel the blood trickling down my neck. You helped me to my feet, before wiping the back of your hands across your peepers, blurring the mascara and leaving snail-trails across their backs. You looked so...*distressed.* Then your expression brightened. 'I bought coffee. You want regular?'

I could only nod again, numbly.

When I was sunk in the leather sofa next to you, nursing my coffee, with no light in the sitting room but the sea of fig-scented candles, my slave ring was suddenly too bloody heavy.

'What the frig was that about?' You spoke quietly, but I still flinched.

I shrugged, taking a sip of my coffee: *too much poncey cream.* I hoped that by the time I glanced back over the rim, you'd have looked away.

But you hadn't.

'So?'

'I don't remember.'

'Bullshit.'

'It's like I live it but I don't...after.'

Your gaze was cool. 'Huh. You mean *relive* it?'

Embarrassed, I dropped my gaze. 'Yeah, semantics.'

'*My name is Light, my name is Light, my name is--*'

'Bollocks.' I'd startled back, spilling my coffee in a boiling patch on my goolies. 'I mean,' I patted my hand at my crotch, as if this could draw out the heat, 'yeah, I guess I do mean bollocks. So, what else did I..?' It was you this time, who dropped your gaze. 'That bad?'

‘*Pretty leech*,’ you answered softly. I stiffened. I’d guessed it’d been another funfair ride courtesy of Abona. You must know too because *Sir* had called me that when you’d been choosing me, like a new puppy in the window of a pet shop. ‘Look, it’s about your time in Bristol, huh..? When you were trained--’

‘*Trained*, is it?’

‘Cain Company has divisions: Acquisitions, Accounts, Marketing...and then there’s Training. At Abona or the Estate. So you’re ready for clients. I’m meant to know this. I should know this.’

‘Why? Because you’ve gotta know your product?’

‘Yah...I mean...naw, that’s not it.’ You reached over, taking my coffee mug from me, before carefully placing it on the glass table. Then you grasped my hands between yours. It felt...blinding. Unexpectedly your fingers were tracing over my silver ring – S.L.A.V.E – as if discovering something dark beneath bright waters. Your expression tightened. ‘I’ve just spent the last... In there with you, freaking out - bawling and begging – *please...please don’t...please Sir*. Tell me. I have to know.’

So you want to know what *that* meant?

I’m not explaining tonight. I don’t care how impatient you are to learn your family’s business.

You’ve asked though, so I’ll tell.

But I don’t guarantee you’ll like what you hear about your *Training Department*.

If you dig deeper beneath the façade, there’s always darkness. Corruption. Exploitation. Greed for the *profit margin*.

Or most dangerous of all?

An apathetic indifference. It bleeds into everything. Atrocities are committed because of it, rather than some make-believe evil, which is scapegoat blamed for the world's ills. All anyone has to do is open their peepers. Then get off their lazy arses and do something about it.

After all, you saw the lash marks lacerating my skin: was it that easy to explain them away as *motivation*?

But I can't write the memories tonight. I can't relive them, in case... Twice in one day would be too much - for both of us.

Maybe we'll save the eye opening for tomorrow.

MAY 19

I know I promised I'd write down the nasties yesterday, but it was too hard.

I was all set to write: I had the buttery cream of these pages spread open on the dining room table. I'd touched the sun and gone through the daily ritual of counting the Manx, which were hiding in the valleys. I'd sat squarely at the table. Yet, fountain pen in hand, I couldn't put down a buggering word.

I didn't want to remember. Instead, the only thing I felt was numbness. Like death.

But today...bollocks to it.

A memory can't hurt – if only I sodding believed that.

Cold. Black. Silence. I was blind, deaf and dumb.

I drew in panicked breaths through my nostrils: no smell but the stink of leather. I struggled but I couldn't move.

I flexed my fingers: metal was cutting off the circulation around my wrists, dragging them behind my back so tightly my shoulders were wrenched. My legs were bent back, tied by the ankles to my wrists.

Starkers. Chained. Gagged. And in a leather sensory deprivation hood.

I was royally buggered.

Every sensation was amplified because my senses had been stolen: the pain, hunger for food (but above all else blood), raging tempest-warring in every cell, dehydration, waves of dizziness, thundering of my heart and nicotine cravings. I was sweating from them - *sick* with them.

I didn't know who'd captured me or why, only that they were First Lifers and had taken my fangs like bloody trophies. That was the first time you bastards made me bawl like a kid; it wasn't the last. Our fangs aren't simply the method by which we feed. They're our strength – defence - our very evolutionary uniqueness. Our personhood.

Steal them and you steal our Soul.

To begin with, I dreamed up everything I'd do to the wankers, who'd bagged me. Then, as time passed and I grew weaker and more exhausted, all I could think about was who'd come and release me. I was still leery of what these First Lifers wanted, but the fear I'd been forgotten and left to rot was greater.

Daft git, right? What did I know of Cain Company training?

I don't know how long I lay there in that hood. I wept, until the wetness stiffened the leather, making it scratchy over my peepers. Time had no meaning. I had no existence. I was floating in a dislocated world. I lost myself somewhere then.

I left any hold on the thread of reality. I was visited sometimes by my dead papa, who'd hold up a photographic plate to examine, as he praised...*you are a miracle. A human camera. My little Light*...sometimes by my 1960s London Blood Lifer family: Aralt, Donovan or Alessandro...or by Kathy. *My beautiful Kathy.* I never wanted her to leave me, but she faded too.

The hood would always be scratchy after that.

Kathy had been out on the moors under the moon, holding my hand and whispering...never you mind what...but had begun to melt back into the endless void of black, when I startled in terror: something was touching my leg.

It slid down my calf.

I screamed at the shock of it, but the yell was swallowed by the gag.

I was shaking. I'd never felt so vulnerable.

The slide of the freezing chain, snake-like over my ankles, sawed to the bone, as it was removed.

Then there were fingers at my throat...

Bloody, buggering, sodding hell...

The light was so bright in the small cell, when the hood was wrenched off, that I reckoned my retinas had been scorched. I screwed my peepers shut. Tears leaked down their sides.

The smell hit me as hard: an assault of mould, oak floorboards, dust and an intense citrus, underlined with cedarwood - *aftershave..?*

I felt the gag being loosened and taken out; my jaw muscles had been held open for so long I almost begged for the gag to be put back in. I warily moved my jaw from side to side, before opening my peepers again.

For a moment, I still couldn't see. But I could feel a man's manicured hand caressing my cheek. I flinched back.

When I squinted through the painful haze, I barely stopped myself from laughing: a First Lifer was crouched in front of me, considering me like a teenager, who'd been allowed to look after his parents' prized schnoodle for the weekend. With his black framed glasses and tailored grey suit, seeing my captor was like discovering I'd been kidnapped by Mr Poncey Corporate himself, rather than the beasts I'd nightmared in the long blackness. Until he spoke. 'How's it going, leech? You'll make a pretty little whore.'

...*Whore*...?

My insides curdled. My dry throat had tightened, but I forced my swollen tongue to throw back at the tosser, 'Nothing little about me, mate.'

Instinctively, I ducked.

The wanker, however, merely pushed his glasses up his neb and smiled; I noticed his mouth only curled up at the left, as if only half of him shared the joke. 'I'm not your mate; you're nobody's mate, seeing as you're a slave. And me? To you, I'm *Sir*.'

'I'm not a slave. And I never will be – *mate*.' I'd barely finished the sentence, however, before I saw *Sir* reaching for the black leather hood. I could see it looming, like so many more days of torture, towards me. My heart was pounding. I was giving these quick, frightened gasps. *Sir* had only just started to pull the hood over my peepers, when I heard my own tear-filled voice beg, 'Please...please don't...please *Sir*...'

The descent of the hood paused, leaving me in excruciating blackness. Disgusted with myself, I felt shamed. Then the hood was lifted, and I was blinking in the light again.

Just as fast, *Sir* forced open my mouth, pushing the gag back in to my muffled screams, as my jaw bruised. 'Until you learn some obedience, little leech.'

Yet mixed in with the rage, fear and humiliation?

Gratitude.

Because Sir hadn't put the hood on me again.

Sir left me alone after that.

I wasn't trussed up at least, except for my arms. I could sit up and rest against the decaying wall of the...*cellar*..? There was nothing in it, not even a mattress. I had to lie on the freezing floor, with my sore, atrophying muscles. I took to only turning my nut the minutest of degrees, so I could count the manky mould spores, which blossomed black across the ceiling, to play rainbow number games.

Christ knows how long I was in solitary.

There was no window, at least, there had been once, but it'd been bricked up. Now there wasn't even a trickle of daylight - or moonlight - to judge whether I should be awake or sleeping, even under the bright, relentless lightbulb. Normally, the call of the night would've told me, but that sensory deprivation hood had buggered up my senses. The cell must've been soundproofed because I couldn't hear a dickybird.

By the time I heard the locks *clang* open and the *click* of *Sir's* black Oxford shoes, I was too weak to even raise my nut off the ground and could've kissed them; I'm not sure I even mean that figuratively.

'Now don't start and make trouble, and I can get this off you.'

I blinked, hoping *Sir* took that as agreement.

He must've done because he drew the gag out of my mouth.

I groaned.

'There, there,' *Sir* shushed me, as if comforting a kid. He gently massaged my jaw; it felt blinding but sod it, did I hate myself right then. 'Look you, what do you need, little one?'

There weren't bleeding words for what I needed. When *Sir* had first taken the hood off me, I'd have thrown back some defiant response (probably involving his severed head *on a silver platter, cheers mate*), but now I could barely concentrate or swallow, there was only one word record spinning through my brain, 'Water.'

'What do you say?'

Sir's fingers continued their patient massage.

I struggled to work out what he wanted from me. My voice cracked, raspy from disuse, as I managed to whisper, 'Please may I have water.'

'*Sir*.' I don't know why that final step was so hard. I only know it was. Maybe if my imprisoner hadn't looked like such a Mr Poncey Corporate, I would've found it easier. I should've known, however, that it's the darkness underneath you have to watch out for. I hesitated. The moment *Sir* stopped massaging, I knew I'd cocked up. 'Someone's not thirsty today.'

'*Sir*,' and then I added quickly, as if the repetition would help, 'please may I have water, *Sir*.'

'Why are you leeches so stupid?' *Sir's* voice was ice cold. It triggered my fleeing instinct, but I couldn't even crawl away. 'No food or water today. We'll see if your attitude's improved tomorrow.'

Wanker.

I was so bleeding thirsty the next day I did my whole begging routine - *please may I have water, Sir* - with no hesitation.

You'd have reckoned I'd performed the greatest circus trick, the way *Sir* prattled about *good little leeches*. Next up the reward - water in a pipette. *Sir* squirted it into my mouth, whilst he stroked my throat because I'd lost the ability to swallow.

No blood or food. But I guess that would have been greedy, you know?

From then on, I was still chained, but it seemed to amuse *Sir* to tie me down differently each time, like I was a bleeding BDSM doll.

Sometimes it was just one ankle. Others my whole body from my neck downwards - all interlinked - so the smallest move choked me. When *Sir* found me half bloody throttled, he stopped my water ration, until I'd *learnt my lesson*.

As I lay there, hardly daring to breathe, I fantasized that anyone but *Sir* would come through the heavy dark oak door.

I daydreamed Blood Lifers, trapped the same as me but leading a rampaging breakout. Or a stunner of a First Lifer - *Sir's* sister or cousin – would find me and (shocked by *Sir's* cruelty), rescue me.

Occasionally that fantasy ended in my newly grown fangs sinking into the First Lifer's throat... But I hadn't been fed in...I didn't even know. If I'd had the strength, I'd have fed on my own arm.

No one else, however, came through those oak doors. Only *Sir*.

When you're on your tod like that - your whole world revolving around one other person - it makes you dependent. I was reliant on *Sir* for everything, even for releasing my cramping limbs each day.

Sir would unchain me. Straighten each limb. Then rub and massage with surprising gentleness. He'd manipulate me anyway he liked, before binding me up again. Sometimes even more restrictively.

On those days, once *Sir* had left me alone, I'd feel like I'd dived headfirst down the blackest well. Nothing was real.

Other days, however, when *Sir* would free me from all but the lightest chains, it was as if I could breathe at last. I wanted to babble my thanks and

I'd only just manage to keep in the words. I'd still grin pathetically.

Sir would smile, running his hands down the length of my body, before patting me on the nut and calling me a *pretty leech.*

At last came the day *Sir* unchained me altogether, leaving me sprawled in the centre of the cell.

I was leery of the reason for *Sir's* unbuttoned jacket, rolled up sleeves...and the red-and-black hide riding crop, which he'd looped by its handle over his wrist and was tapping ominously on his leg.

'Kneel.' *Sir* stared at me through his thick glasses, as if he believed a month or two under his loving care was enough to break me down to the level of a mutt. *Not. Sodding. Likely.* For the first time, *Sir* frowned. That was dead worth it. Even when he strode behind me and with a heavy swish – *crack* – above riding crop landed hard across my too thin spine. I cringed. But I didn't budge. 'Kneel.' *Crack* – left shoulder blade. My peepers watered. *Sir* had taught me too well about staying still under pressure: *how's that for irony, you sad bastard*? *Sir* marched in front of me, pressing the flexible leather tongue of that wicked riding crop under my chin and forcing me to stare up into his furious gaze. 'You really are a bad, worthless thing, aren't you, boyo? If it weren't for me, you'd be at the Estate. You'd be Mr Cain's to play with - that's *Master* to you. The Estate's not nice like this. Master's not kind. You think your life's hard here? Then you just wait, I say the word and get you sent to the Estate. Then we'll see what you will and won't do, little slave. Now, let's try this again.' *Sir* took one careful step back. 'Kneel.'

I didn't move one sodding muscle.

Then in a whir, as if transformed by my rebelliousness into a shadow man lurking underneath his skin, *Sir* snarled. He hurled the crop aside and leapt at me.

I didn't see the gleam of the shiv, with its curved red-and-black handle, until its point was pressed against my naked chest - right over my heart. I closed my peepers. The point pushed through the skin with a sharp prick.

'*You whore, slut, bitch...*'

I gasped at the pain, shuddering as *Sir* skewered me. And then twisted.

Go on, I thought, *sodding do it. Then I'll be free.*

I opened my peepers, however, because when I was done in, I bloody well intended to stare my killer in the eye.

Shocked, I realised *Sir's* mug was almost touching my own. He was scrutinizing my flickers of expression.

When I met *Sir's* gaze, we stayed like that for a long moment, in a surreal tableaux, whilst his inner demons seemed one by one to settle back into the box, from which they'd escaped, and the feverish fire died down. His peepers were once more cool and clear. The bloke I knew as *Sir* was back behind the steering wheel.

Then *Sir* wrenched the shiv back, and I yelped, plugging my hands over the wound.

'I've decided,' *Sir* pushed up the glasses on his neb, oblivious to the bloody marks, which he'd left behind, 'to let you live.' Such terror and now instant salvation spun me out, until there was nothing left of my emotions but fragile glass. *Sir* was calm again, playing with the crimson shiv, like it was a stress relief toy: maybe that's all I was. 'But it's time you show me some gratitude, isn't it? Seeing as I've saved your worthless life.'

Confused, I didn't answer.

Immediately, the shiv was back, worming its way into the previously burrowed hole, which was still oozing precious blood I didn't have to lose.

In frustration and pain, I scrabbled at *Sir's* hands. 'Yes *Sir*. Yes *Sir*. Yes...'

The shiv was pulled out. More blood lost. This time I couldn't keep my balance, collapsing on my mush.

The clicking of *Sir's* shoes, and then he was gone.

Leaving me, my broken body and my bloody over vivid imagination.

The next time *Sir* came visiting, he wasn't wearing his grey suit jacket, the two top buttons of his pale blue shirt were undone and he'd washed in more citrus aftershave than usual.

I was lying on my side, in the far corner of the cell, enjoying the freedom from the chains for once. When I saw *Sir*, I turned my back on him. I might as well be hung for a sheep as a lamb.

I heard *Sir* settling down next to me on the wooden floorboards. Followed by the sound of something being unscrewed.

Blood.

I was turned round and facing *Sir*, panting and glassy eyed in desperation, faster than I reckoned I was still able to move.

Sir chuckled. He was holding a thermos flask of blood: it was pigs', but beggars can't be choosers.

My gaze flickered to *Sir's* mush, then to the blood and then back again. Sod it, he wanted me to kneel, I'd bloody kneel.

To my shock, instead my thin body was lifted gently onto *Sir's* lap.

I was too caught in the scent of the blood to protest. It filled every cell, craving and hunger-crazed thought of me. The world could've descended into a fiery Apocalypse, and I wouldn't have looked away from that bloody manna. The hunger was worse now the blood was in front of me, than when the starvation had seemed like it had no end.

Sir's manicured fingers were stroking my hair. 'You really were a stupid leech for making me so angry, then I get so I can't help it.' I winced when *Sir* brushed over the injury in my chest, which without the regenerative power of blood, hadn't healed. 'It's not as if I want to hurt you, but you're so bad, you make me do it. But if you've learnt your lesson...' *Sir* dipped his fingers into the thick blood, holding them up in front of my lips.

Smash – that was glass me shattering.

So are these Approved Cain Company Training Methods?

In case you want to rate this one's effectiveness, it stripped away one more layer, infantilising me to a level of dependency, which I felt to my core.

Did I even hesitate to suck the warm blood from *Sir's* fingers, over and over, as evidence of his growing excitement at the suction poked me in the arse?

Or course I sodding didn't.

I was being starved. I sobbed as I fed but I sucked up every drop, licking between *Sir's* fingers, as he shuddered at the sensation.

'There's a good boy,' *Sir* crooned, 'don't cry, I'll make it all better.'

I was nothing but blood: intense, powerful, bubbling and tripping through my damaged body.

I only noticed what *Sir* was cooing in a singsong voice, as a girl talks to a new doll, when he screwed the top back on the thermos. It wasn't nearly enough even for a single feed with my shrunken belly. I could've started bawling, like a real baby, when *Sir's* words penetrated the fog. '...You'll wear this always as a sign of what you are. Who you belong to.' *Sir* was slipping a silver ring onto the finger of my left hand, as if we were in a wedding ceremony. Mortified, I saw the word S.L.A.V.E stood out in hard relief. 'Your new name came to me last night: *slave shadow*. A small 's' because all slaves must know their place. Only Masters have true names. That's who you are from now on. My shadow.' *Sir* patted my arm paternalistically.

For the first time, I felt *owned*. My past had been wiped clean.

I was nothing but property, which could be rechristened.

Sod. That.

'My name is Light.'

'What was that, my pretty leech?'

This time I said a little louder, 'My name is Light.'

I felt *Sir* go rigid.

Then I was tumbled to the cold ground, and he was standing tall above me, that other man fighting for control; I could see the war beneath *Sir's* skin. 'I've just told you, bitch, your name is shadow.'

'My name is... *Oomph*,' a boot to the bloody kidneys, '*Light*.' *Sir* was undoing the heavy silver buckle of his belt, even as I started again, like an incantation, 'My name,' the belt was whipped out of *Sir's* trousers, 'is', he wasn't even pausing to double up the heavy black leather, as he raised the belt high above his nut, 'Light'... *Thwack*... The belt curled around my chest and sides, stinging and welting. I barely drew breath to cry out, before I was hollering, '*My name is Light. My name is Light. My name is...*'

As the belt fell again and again, I never stopped asserting my Blood Lifer identity.

Not once.

MAY 20

You know what I figure? I really am one *stupid leech* not to have seen this coming. One daft mug to have trusted another First Lifer.

You reckon it's easy to flay your Soul's shameful violations to an enemy's kin? To lay bare the tortures inflicted on your body?

Worse, your own black despair?

Yet not once had I thought you wouldn't sodding believe me. That you'd interrogate me instead.

As if I wasn't the victim.

Well, more fool me.

MAY 21

Tonight you said *sorry*.
    I don't know if a slave is required to forgive.

MAY 22

'Again?'

'Huh?'

'An Alex Highbury-Lord dress *again*?' I asked.

You wriggled into this bold check flare dress, like an oversized schoolgirl, pulling it down over your satin pants and bra, as if I wasn't sprawled right there on your white bed. I know slaves don't deserve the luxury of privacy, but I hadn't realised it cut both ways.

Except it was more as if you'd grown so used to me being in the apartment I'd transformed into one of your designer pieces of furniture – or one of your junkshop finds.

You were faffing around with your hair in front of the full-length mirror. Still, I had some sympathy, having spent Christ knows how long getting my pompadour perfect, since the appearance of Brylcreem on my bedside table this morning – the Brylcreem fairy must've visited during the night.

I'd left a list of *essentials* hopefully stuck to the fridge last week on one of your Post-it notes: I guess *black motorcycle boots* don't tick that box..? Maybe you don't want to imply I'll be going out of the apartment...because these white trainers? They're too naff to be seen in anyway.

You stared at me. 'Are you zoo'n' on me?'

'Just saying--'

'It saves time, like, thinking.' You spun round, wagging an explanatory finger at me. 'Einstein--'

'Einstein, is it?' I took a drag on my e-cig.

‘Shut up.’

‘Did I say anything?’

‘Naw, you just do that...eyebrow thing. But I know what you’re thinking.’

I couldn’t help the grin. ‘I should’ve known a slave wasn’t allowed their own thoughts.’

You stepped closer to the bed.

I was suddenly aware how large the bed was. How tall you were. And how bloody scared I’d been for so long. I wanted to curl into a ball but instead I pushed myself up too, e-cig firmly lodged between my teeth.

‘Mouthy enough for a slave,’ I heard you mutter.

I should’ve let it go. You were right. Then again, I’ve never been able to keep my gob shut. ‘Not really a slave, sweetheart.’

You’d already been turning away, distracted by your plans for the day. Now, however, your steel grey peepers lazored back onto me. ‘Bought,’ you paused between each word, as if to ensure their weight sank in, ‘and paid for.’

We were standing dead close.

The fingers of my left hand were curling and uncurling, the e-cig crushed in my other. My skin was tingling, as my phantom fangs itched to descend. ‘Just because you kidnap a bloke,’ my voice sounded calm even to my lobes, when inside the Blood Lifer was roaring end of the world destruction and revenge, ‘take his clobber, starve him, duff him up and sell him to some bird, don’t make him no slave. It makes him unlucky.’

‘And that’s all you Blood Lifers are? Unlucky?’

I laughed...this furious laugh. For once, you backed up a step. ‘We’re many things: lovers, explorers, chancers and *predators* – but right now?

We're the poor bastards, who are being sold by your family as fucktoys and worse.'

I turned away, staring down at the white blankness of the bed.

Why was I risking being this open with a First Lifer? The truth doesn't set you free: it gets you topped.

I'd trusted once before, allowing the truth about us Blood Lifers and my own life to rest in the hands of a human. With what you've promised me tonight, you've earned this memory.

My beautiful Kathy, who I'd hallucinated in Abona's cell. She was the safe place, which my mind fled to because she's the woman I love...*loved*...the woman I loved for fifty years. And now I've lost. Yet I trusted her, and you know what? *She trusted me.* We learnt together, when we met in 1960s London, that our two species could co-exist, without hunting or enslaving the other.

And now I wanted to trust you.

'The Blood Club's exclusive,' you spoke quietly but distinctly. 'Yah, it's unorthodox. But that's why it's special. I'm still learning the--'

'Dirty details? Truth behind the--'

'Business.'

You pulled on your armadillo-embossed platform shoes – that was another inch on me - and marched, *clack*, *clack*, *clack*, to the sitting room.

I trailed after you, hands in pockets, before throwing myself down in the Fjord relax chair. I sank into the brown leather.

You glared at me for a moment - *go on, demand I start the Post-it note chores, I dare you* - but then didn't say anything. Instead you pressed on several computer monitors, which were on a desk next to the wall.

The monitors blinked open on multiple windows, running programmes of complex numbers.

I sat upright. Reanimated.

Bonds, currencies and stock market indices. They whizzed past in choirs, dancing glorious shapes: U.S Treasury bonds, British pounds, Russian T-bills, light sweet crude, heating oil, soybeans, copper, silver and gold.

They spoke in a language of numbers of a whole world, which was still out there and turning. It was so easy to forget that, when I was on my knees scouring.

My world had shrunk. But the real one? Outside the front door of this apartment? It was still vast, infuriating and sublime.

I had to get out. I *was* getting out.

You were as engrossed as me in the screens. You weren't simply watching the markets: you were dipping your toe into the maelstrom and trading via an Internet brokerage site.

'You're a day trader then? Amateur speculator?'

'There's nothing amateur about my trading.'

There was a strange new companionship between us, which was built by the numbers. Foreign to most, yet translated by us both. First or Blood Lifer, numbers are a constant.

Like money.

As I watched you trade, I saw you were right: you were no amateur. You were a bloody genius.

At last, you swivelled on your chair, tilting your nut to assess me. 'Come on,' your smile was gentle, 'wanna see?' I hopped up, diving to your side. 'This must be wicked boring for you.' You waved your hand at the monitors, as if to dismiss them.

'Not when it reminds me of the world. Look,' I sidled closer, leaning against the cold oak desk; it felt good to have its solidity under me, whilst I looked down at you, conquering the Earth through your fingertips, 'you have that tracker, right? And I've been good; I told you everything you wanted to know. So it seems to me--'

'What do you want?'

'To go out.'

'Of the apartment?'

'One night, that's all.'

You stared at me, like I'd demanded to gobble your firstborn (and believe me, that's not my cup of tea). 'Na-ah, not happening.'

'Why?'

'I don't trust you.'

Up front and to the point. I met your gaze full on. 'I'll earn it.'

First you looked shocked. Then...disgusted.

I simply gawped at you, before I cottoned on.

A bloke doesn't like to think an offer of himself (even in misunderstanding), *disgusts* a bint. It bruises the ego. 'I didn't mean...' I wondered whether you were imagining a certain Professor Alpha Geek, in his buttoned up checked shirt; how could a bad boy Rocker *slave* compete with that?

'You're not going out. End of.'

That's what you think.

I relaxed back onto the desk. 'So, this your idea of fun then?'

I swear you blushed. *Score one to me*... 'I like playing with numbers. The risk. You wouldn't get it.'

I grinned. 'Want to bet on that?'

You blinked at me, as if you'd never seen me before. 'London's frickin' perfect for currencies; I'm seeing consistent 35% returns. This year I've already made...'

You clicked a couple of keys, before pointing at a figure, which was so long it barely fitted on one line.

'That's not...in pounds, is it?'

You nodded.

'Bugger me.'

'It's not, like, important,' you shrugged, shrunk into yourself, child-like. 'Daddy says I'll be too busy for it soon on account of I'll be working full time for him. But I'm good at this. It's what I'd do if...' You glanced away, your hands wringing the lap of your check dress. Bloody hell, were we having a *moment*? 'If I had a choice,' you finished.

Sod moments, when the dirty truth of this unequal world we labour in screams to be laid bare - I always was my own worst enemy. 'You're smart. Yet you'd choose to use that humungous brain of yours for nothing but spinning lolly from other virtual lolly..? Globalizing and capitalizing, 'til the world's reduced to a greedy baby bird's mouth begging after investors' gold..? I've seen this before in my first life, and if you think you're exempt from the tempest, simply 'cos you're a Cain--'

You stared at me shrewdly. 'Whoa there. I thought you wanted to go out sometime in your lifetime?' *Score two to you...*

I caught myself, giving an apologetic shrug. 'Right, sorry.'

'So you know,' did you really just stroke the back of my hand? 'I majored in Mathematics. And what excites me? It's not the *gold*. It's the *hunt*. OK, I'm not a heart surgeon, Nobel Prize winner or researcher into tropical diseases. So sue me. This is what I'm wicked good at it. It's me. What have *you* ever been?'

More than you can ever imagine.

That's when I caught a glimpse of the *Fiendish Sudoku* on the edge of the coffee table. You'd been working on a page last night, hissing between your teeth in frustration. You were halfway through the book now, where the puzzles were graded 10 stars. It was taking you the better part of a day to complete one. *What had I ever been*? 'A gambler.'

'What?'

'You like risks? So how about a little bet?'

'Like?'

I swaggered to the *Sudoku*, snatching it up. 'I manage one of these? Then you let me go outside.'

You smirked. 'Trying to prove a point?'

'I thought you liked the hunt – prey's right here.' I spun in a circle, my arms held wide at my sides.

You considered me. 'If you complete a puzzle in less than an hour, then one night this week you can go out for an hour.'

'And if I don't?'

You frowned, as if you'd never considered a consequence for my inevitable failure. 'You're cooking tonight.'

At long sodding last.

I nodded, flicking the book open to the next puzzle. Then nonchalantly as I could, I offered, 'Tell you what, how about we up the ante? If I finish it in less than *half* an hour, I get to go out *alone* for the *whole* night?'

You instantly shook your nut.

'Please?'

'Not happening.'

I raised my arm to hurl that bleeding *Sudoku* against your monitors, which were windows out to a world I couldn't even touch, when something - as if a shard of the old me was fighting its way back (maybe because you'd caressed the back of my hand) - made me lower my arm again. 'Bollocks.'

Defeated, I opened the book at the right page.

'The whole evening,' I heard you say quietly, 'but with me.'

I glanced up, surprised. 'I will earn your trust, you know.'

'But do you trust me?'

'Do you reckon I'd have told you...just...what I have, if I didn't?' Uncomfortable, you shifted, unable to meet my eye. 'Anyway, it's not like I've a choice, is it? You've got my life in your hands.'

You glanced down involuntarily at your hands, as if you expected to discover a doll-sized version of me balanced there. 'If you don't, you're cooking for a week.'

'Suits me.'

'Get started, the clock has.'

28 minutes later...

You stood in the centre of the sitting room, underneath the bright light of the beachcomb chandelier, holding the *Fiendish Sudoku*, as if it might sink fangs into you.

You'd rigorously checked my solved puzzle seven times.

Your mouth hung open, as you gaped between it and me (who was lying full-length on the scarlet sofa, my legs crossed comfortably), like you'd just had the reality of the tooth fairy proven to you. 'How..?'

'I'm good with numbers too.'

I'd forgotten the pure joy of immersion in a puzzle: no room to think or remember beyond its matrix.

'Na-ah, what the frig are you?'

I stiffened. Sticky labels and spectrums from normal to abnormal. You First Lifers are obsessed with rooting out the imperfect (as if perfection is even attainable).

What am I?

That's the question, which has dogged me for over 150 years.

If you meant how had I completed the puzzle so fast..? I'm a savant, you'd call it now.

Everything I've ever seen in this long life I remember, stored like a computer database in my brain. Believe me, it's not a blessing.

And numbers? There's my talent. They're like a landscape: undulating shapes, with their own colours and textures. Some are angelically beautiful. Others monstrous. Yet I'm drawn to the deformed, as much as to the heavenly.

When I was so young I couldn't yet read, I'd hide in the dark underneath my bed because it felt safe, numbers sliding through my mind, like winding silk.

Sometimes I'd lie on the Oriental rug in papa's study at his feet, papa with his clay pipe and crisp sheets of the *Times*, me with the photographic studio's business books.

For years, I hid my secret talent, terrified I was destined for Bedlam. Or worse - that I was possessed. Evil. *Different*.

At night, I'd weep silent tears, as I'd send up prayers to God to take away this curse. He never answered. Yet one day when the truth was revealed, my papa didn't condemn me, he celebrated, calling me his *human camera*.

Photography means *writing in light* in Greek. And so the nickname stuck – my papa's *Light*.

Light's not merely a name, which I took when I was rechristened into Blood Life: it's the name my papa blessed me with before I died. The one that meant it was bloody all right to be *different*.

That's what *Sir* ripped from me. That's why I can't bear to lose it again.

'What am I?' I forced myself to calmly reply. 'One evening out with you better off, that's what I am.'

You looked like you might argue. Then you deflated. 'Later in the week, OK?' At last, a smile spread across your mug, as you studied me with something akin to admiration. You wildly waved the *Fiendish Sudoku*. 'This is wicked pissa! Less than half a frickin' hour. I took, like, two days--'

'Take a breath, darlin'.'

You chucked the book at my nut, and I ducked.

Then we both grinned.

Who cares who bloody scored? I was getting to *go out*; it was like the world had lightened.

That's when the doorbell rang.

I dove into a ball in the corner of the sofa. No one ever came here. *Billy no mates, remember*?

You hunched, guiltily. 'Stay there.'

Back to doggy commands then.

I listened, as you clacked your way to the front door, its *click* when it swung open, and then muted voices – definitely female. Next, two sets of footsteps coming down the hallway...

I tensed, weighing up my options, which were obeying you and remaining curled up on the sofa or making a dash for the relative safety of my cell.

As you and the strange woman strolled together towards the sitting room, I was frozen with the thought: *you meant to sell me*.

To some bint in bondage trousers and bullet belt, more zippers and chains than anything else and graded black hair, which was spiked crimson at the edges, like blood tipped spears.

She was just my type of bird. Except for the way she'd stopped in the doorway and was examining me, as a queen might a traitor, who she found both dishy and contemptible - in the moment before the axe fell. 'It be wearing clothes? It be chug alright but it don't need clothes, you feeling me?'

It?

You hovered behind the newcomer, as if uncertain of entering your own sitting room. I clutched onto my motorcycle jacket; no one was getting that off me without losing something they bloody cared about. 'Marlane, sorry, I mean M.C., I just thought...it's wick raw still and--'

'So? And it be on da furniture..?' I shot off the sofa, my back pressed against the fireplace. The punk smiled. 'Good liccle leech. Dey have to learn dey not people, only property. Dat's why we give dem a new name.'

Marlane..?

Christ in heaven, this stranger was the older Cain sister. The one everybody whispered about at Abona: the spectre in Brixton, just as your dad was the ghoul of the Estate. She was the shadow, who'd been behind the slave books, the bottles and the starvation.

M.C. looked me up and down scornfully. 'Dad would've trained up a bitch alright for you. One dat knew how to behave.'

Your voice was icy. 'I didn't want a broken doll.'

'Or a slave?'

'Well, it seems like I got one, doesn't it?'

'Nah, sis, it don't.'

At last, you brushed past your sister, snatching up a pad of paper and a rollerball, before perching on the edge of the Sponge chair. M.C., however, slunk towards me, which was like being stalked by an anarchist tiger with added attitude. 'The wallad's not kneeling. Kneel.'

Not sodding likely.

'Bad,' M.C. admonished. Now I knew why you spoke to me puppy style. 'First thing you need to understand about Blood Club sis, is dat it be all about image, innit?' M.C. was lecturing you - half-bored, half-matter-of-fact - but she was facing me, her black nail varnished fingers sliding down my chest... 'Dat's why it be unique, safe and guaranteed,'...having a cheeky tweak at my nipples through the thin cotton of my t-shirt... 'But da product? Dat's gotta be perfect,'...around my arse... 'Dat's why dey be sourced from all over da world. Then Yates trains at Abona. Dad on da Estate for da tailored, individualised orders. Specialised shit. And you...'...and then for a wank wander...

That did it. I tried to jerk away, but M.C.'s other arm cradled round, holding me trapped against the marble fireplace.

I stared over M.C.'s shoulder at you for rescue. But you were deliberately scrutinising the notepad, which was balanced on your knee.

I guess it was time I stood up for myself.

Just as M.C.'s black-nailed fingers curled around my jean encased goolies, I whispered close to her lobe, 'A little lower, luv. I think you missed a spot.'

M.C.'s hand froze in its tarantula exploration. Then she was swinging it in a hissing arc - *slap*.

My nut snapped back, hitting the wall. My pride hurt more than my smarting cheek, but M.C.'s spiked bracelet had caught my mouth. I licked at the coppery blood: *waste not*, *want not*.

I'd never seen a punk First Lifer about to explode with fury before. It was fascinating.

'You've gotta discipline da liccle bitches, you get me? Don't you ever..?'

M.C. had taken something out of the pocket of her bondage trousers and was swiping her finger over the display.

Shooting, spearing agony, like a white hot tree. It branched down my spine and then every nerve inside my body, until I was consumed by it.

M.C. played around with the touchscreen.

Yet all I could fixate on was the black logo of the Manx.

I tried to form words, but none would come. My heart was thundering. My palms sweating. Still I didn't kneel (let alone prostrate myself): not to that bint. Not to any First Lifer. Not anymore.

Instead, I braced myself to endure.

I hadn't heard your approach behind M.C. 'Light, go to your room and wait for me.'

I'd never heard you so coldly furious. It was too late now. I assumed you wanted to compare notes on effective discipline measures. And you know what?

It was bloody worth it.

Another swipe of the touchscreen by M.C., followed by the agony falling away, leaving a low level tingling buzz.

I edged around M.C., who sneered at me, like older siblings everywhere, when they've told on you and earned you a spanking. Then I made my escape to my cell.

The last thing I heard before I slammed the door behind me (because I never pretended I'm mature), was M.C.'s disdainful snort, '*Light*? Dat's its *leech* name, sis. Its name be shadow, boy or slave.'

I paced the room, counting each circuit.

Stand, sit, even bloody kneel, I'd start to do one and then freeze.

Permission, I hadn't been given...

Yeah, everything was hunky-dory: I couldn't even take a decision on where to park my bum for fear of getting it wrong because *bad* here. *Stupid. Worthless.*

At last, I risked perching on the edge of the bed, my hands resting flat on my knees, with my palms up, as the least offensive position. Except that's when the traitorous thoughts came burrowing their way in slimy.

OK, so I was going to cop it. Nothing new there.

You'd not...done that before, but it was only a matter of time: you're a Cain after all. Yet you'd sounded so enraged. And you hadn't defended me. Not even when I'd been reduced to an *it*.

That's when the thought squirmed its way in, which wobbled my stiff upper lip: what if my punishment was to lose my name again?

Its name be shadow, boy or slave.

Beat me bloody but don't steal my name. The first time I survived it. The second time..?

That's when my mind went bye-byes.

Silently I stretched out on my back, on top of those Egyptian cotton sheets and then lay there, still as a corpse, staring up unseeingly at the ceiling.

I don't know how long I was like that.

All I remember is your arms wrapped around me - my cocoon – and your cheek against mine, as you whispered, 'She's wrong, I promise. You're Light still. Your name is Light...'

When I blinked, flexing my fingers, like I'd woken back into my body, which after only the briefest break from the fear and anxiety was rejuvenated - like rebirth - you were gone.

But I was back. I'd survived. And I was going out this week.

You have no bloody idea what that promise means to me.

Maybe I'm wrong. Maybe - just maybe - you do.

MAY 23

Last night I saw the outside of this apartment for the first time since you bought me. My first taste of freedom. I earned it.

Ha-bloody-ha now, right?

I intended to write...something...in the early hours and count it as yesterday's entry. I even had the journal spread open...one line...*something*...but I was still too raw.

Instead, I lay back down - motionless - and stayed that way. After all, it worked last time.

I didn't budge. Even when you dragged the duvet off me. Even when you shook me. Even as you screamed my name.

It was only when I heard the front door *bang* that I finally unfroze.

You're home again now but at least you've stayed away from my cell.

Look, I've got to sort out some things. Like how last night could've led to *that*.

If I write it, I'll face it. And if you read it, so will you.

Yet maybe it'll only be part of a story then, and everybody knows words can never hurt them.

It all began with chocolate cupcakes - fancy little affairs - with silver balls sprinkled on the gooey, dark cocoa buttercream, from a bakery with late night opening on Gloucester Avenue.

I dragged you into the shop, like I was a crack pusher and persuaded you to buy a boxful. I tucked them under my arm, before stepping out into the night.

The moon was half-grown; the stars masked behind cloud. I could feel the pull of the night, the coursing of my blood and the predator calling – I was *me* again.

Of course, I still had to ignore the sodding naffness of my white trainers.

Then I felt your hand snake into mine, pulling with proprietorial firmness towards Regent's Park.

You led me on the climb up Primrose Hill, until you collapsed in exhaustion on a bench at a junction of footpaths near the summit. I slid the cupcakes along the bench towards you, like a double agent exchanging secrets, before peering out over London.

I remembered when Ruby and I had stood here - conquerors of our world - the kidsman and his gang reduced to tasty titbits. My chest ached to feel such...*exhilaration* again.

For a Blood Lifer there's nothing like the freedom of the fight, feast and fuck.

Nothing like freedom.

The air was fresher than I remembered. I could see London from here. To the East: pitched slate and tiled roofs, brick and painted stucco, trees and church spires. In the far distance were the towers of Canary Wharf.

Something caught in me, like a photo that's been Stalin-like doctored, when I saw St Paul's. It was the same as all those decades ago but now was framed by black glass. I spun to point it out to you, as if we were no different to the other sightseers, tourists, dog walkers or couples strolling hand-in-hand (rather than Mistress and slave). To explain this surreal feeling of being out of time...to see you'd devoured one cupcake already.

Chocolate crumbs clung to the corners of your gob, as you busily stuffed in a second cupcake.

When you caught me having a shufti, you looked so much like a guilty kid that I couldn't help laughing.

You frowned but then grinned around the buttercream.

I think it's the first time I've seen you unguarded.

For once, you'd let me choose your outfit. I'd picked this silk floral number, which at least didn't make you look like you were planning a boardroom takeover.

Now breathing in the evening air as deeply as me, whilst relishing the last of your second cupcake, I wondered whether this was *your* night of freedom, as much as it was mine.

'It's the quick or the dead around here,' I nabbed a cupcake, munching it in two bites and then sucking the buttercream off my fingers. I caught you having a butchers. Were you flushed? I sucked a little bit harder on my fingers.

'There are no calories in these, huh?'

'Tonnes. Have the last one.'

Your hand shot out, before I'd even finished gabbing. I like an appetite on a bird.

I sprang up again, bursting with the night's possibilities. I sprinted down the hill, diving behind plane trees and playing at the hunt.

'Hey, where the frig are you..?'

'Back in a tick.'

As I ran, I scanned for primroses, even whilst my predator heart screamed at me for the hunt, and my phantom fangs - tiny needle points now - tore my gums, struggling to grow back on the good, fresh blood you'd been feeding me. I imagined the cream flower, with its sun face, tucked in your ash blonde hair.

Primrose Hill is considered a sacred site because of the primroses, which are believed to treat paralysis. Nature always grows its own remedies: maybe it'd only take something that simple to cure our venom..? We're part of nature, no different to the primrose; we're the other side of the coin. Yet I couldn't find a single flower.

Primrose Hill without a single bloody primrose? How can you miss the irony in that..?

At last I gave up the search, stalking a jogger instead. I didn't have the fangs and was decades out of practice. But the instinct? The pull? That's always there: a bubbling, insistent, evolutionary river.

The puffing bottle blond had these iPod thingies wormed in his lobes. I could hear the bass of thrash heavy metal, like a siren's call, after these last weeks of silence.

With an effort, I shook myself, instead working back from oak to oak, until I was behind your bench. Then I slunk to your shoulder.

You were scanning the dark for me, like an anxious parent. You made as if to tap your Apple watch, startling in confusion when you realised your wrist was empty.

I'd argued – begged – for you to leave all technology behind, so there'd be no *chirping*, *swiping* or *Fernando*.

Only us.

I grinned, as I touched your shoulder. I hadn't, however, expected you to squeal quite *that* loudly. Out came your narked face again. Still, we'd drawn too much attention to be comfortable: one bloke with a white knight complex tried to clock me on your behalf. Then there was the kindly dogwalker, who insisted on calling the pigs.

So we scarpered.

Of course that suited me just fine because this was still *your* London. I wanted to explore its other face: the dark and the glory. In the happy bubble of North London? That wouldn't happen.

And one night – that's all I had.

Except as we reached the road, with its boutiques, quiet restaurants and lampposts, which were decorated with homemade signs for book clubs, I realised you were heading back towards the apartment.

I tried to pull my hand free. 'Where are we..?'

'We've been out.'

I set my feet squarely in the universal body language of *I'm not bloody budging*.

You sighed. 'We can't go any further than Primrose Hill on account of then we won't be able to see my apartment. That's, like, my limit.'

'My night, my rules.' I snatched my hand sharply out of yours; you gasped at my strength.

You've not seen anything yet, darling.

You hopped from foot to foot in indecision. At last, you nodded.

When I heard a rattling sound behind us, I waved out my arm, flagging down the black cab. As if in a state of shock at my sudden dominance, you let yourself be hustled inside.

The Sikh cabbie, with a mask of indifference, swung us back into the traffic. 'Where to?'

I slung my arm around your shoulders. 'South.'

We jumped out on a random street, which turned out to be Rye Lane. It didn't matter where we were: it simply needed to be *different*. New to you. Fizzing with the night-time Blood Lifer energy.

If I was only getting one shot, then I needed to make sure it was high dose.

I had a plan (half-arsed but it was all I had), to drag you into the real world of the twenty-first century.

Only when you connected with your humanity and the truth of the dirty, dark but beautiful world on your doorstep, would you understand us Blood Lifers - or be fagged about what was happening to us on a global stage.

Pillock, right?

I've spent, however, my First and Blood Life copping it – once quite literally – because I try to play the hero.

I know you can't figure it: seeing a Blood Lifer in that role. But I have *business* to sort. I've made promises. And I'm enough...recovered to know I will find a way to keep them.

So the plan was to open your peepers. And yeah, I definitely managed that.

You turned round on the spot, bewildered.

I grabbed you by the waist and spun you, as I scented the bus fumes, fresh fish, chicken and vegetables in a kaleidoscope of aromas. A police car - all blues and twos - blared past. A streak of flashing neon in the black. Music boomed from behind shuttered shops. Songs in so many different languages and styles, they melded into one: a babble of noise. Rubbish spilled in stinking piles in the shops' doorways: the ugliness and the grime, which we all dirty ourselves in when we step out into the world.

Blokes in white shirts swaggered down the street, as if they personally owned it. They catcalled to birds, who wore such an array of vibrant costumes, it reminded me of Carnaby Street in the 1960s.

My heart soared, and I let it - just for that second.

There were a multitude of nations on one street: London was no longer a single nation but many. Why not add one more species to the mix? It's not like I don't realise there are those, who'd want to send us *home* too.

Yet this *is* our home. It has been for longer than any of you First Lifers have breathed London's polluted air.

You wriggled out of my grip, smoothing down your hair. 'Where are we?' You asked, as if I'd taken us to the moon.

'The twenty-first century.'

'Na-ah, where are we?'

'Peckham.'

'What the frig..?' You hissed.

'Look, you're barely more than a kid. Why don't you...live?' I strolled away, past cycles chained to lampposts, red-and-blue awnings for Halal butchers, *Afro food* shops, Caribbean vegetable market stalls and fly posted *98p* shops.

At last, I heard the *clack* of your sandals, as you hurried to catch up with me. I smiled.

'These are nizza,' you'd stopped, peering into an African wig shop, as you tapped on the glass enviously.

Each wig was displayed on a mannequin's dolled up decapitated head.

A layered bob of box braids with gilded thread, like a modern-day warrior queen... Ashanti...

Why did I have to remember them – the others? Thorns, waiting under petals to prick me when I dared to forget?

'How about we wet our whistles? There must be a boozer around here somewhere.' A pint and an e-cig - that'd do me.

You glanced around, before true to form, pointing at a long queue, which was snaked outside a bar that was lit up in poncey pink.

The bar stuck out, as some wanker's idea of gentrifying the postcode for the Johnny come latelys. Bints from Essex or Kent, with fake tans and stilettos, were clutching onto spikey haired blokes, just as lushingtons hung onto the barrier, trying to strike up chin-wags with anyone, who'd make eye contact. One pillock was pissing into the gutter. And the worst of it?

A fascist bouncer, (some bird in head-to-toe black), was doing the clipboard business.

I turned away. 'Not my style.'

You seemed to mistake me – no surprise there. 'No worries, I'll get us in.'

'Sorry to pop your bubble...actually no, I'm not sorry, but I don't reckon you can.'

Affronted, you glared at me.

I listened to the crackly vinyl hip-hop, which was bleeding out of the bar, whilst watching a hipster's swagger, as he called out *baby girl* to the clipboard Nazi. She let him through with a brief, shy smile.

Yeah, we weren't getting in.

'My daddy could buy--'

'Money can't buy everything. Hard lesson?' For a moment, I reckoned I'd pushed too hard, and you might actually storm over and brat-like demand to buy the bloody place. Lock, stock and barrel.

Instead, you followed silently at my shoulder, as I led you to a quiet Irish boozer on the corner.

Suddenly I was overwhelmed by the thorn-like memories of my Irish cousin Donovan. They threatened to unman me into poufy tears, before I boxed them deep again. Donovan was not, however, forgotten. I'd raise a pint to him. And when I did? I'd force myself to think about what was still happening to him.

There was a gang of lads, joking around and smoking outside the entrance. They were getting in the last fag before their pint in tribal camaraderie.

That's when the craving hit: I missed my lighter. I slipped out my new e-cig and started to vape. The lighter though...it had this...*feel*.

Yet *you* gave me the e-cig. It's the first thing you ever gave me that's new to this life. The e-cig's beginning to fit in my hand, in the way my lighter always did...and I don't understand it.

I sneaked a glance at you out of the corner of my eye. 'Anyway, I have a rule: no lists. A place has a list – sod it. No one gets to judge whether I should be on or off a bloody piece of paper.'

You nodded. That surprised me.

I pushed through into the boozer: tatty wooden bar at the back, whose shelves were stacked with different brews, spirits and crisps (none of the snazzy alcopops or flavoured vodka rubbish), round wooden tables spotted across the bare floors and emerald upholstered booths underneath the windows. An Irish flag hung limply on the wall; it looked like it'd been hung when the pub had first opened - and hadn't been washed since.

My kind of place.

I strutted to the bar, resting my elbow on it. I was about to order, when I heard...

'Can we get two tonics here, please?'

I caught the barman's arm. 'Hold on, scrub that. Two pints of Guinness, cheers mate.'

The barman, who had narrow peepers and a beard, which was so bushy, it was as if he was compensating for the smallness of his mush, glanced between the two of us. Then he gave a curt nod. The dark liquid began to pour slowly, before settling in the glasses.

I smiled innocently at you. 'My night--'

'Your rules?'

When the Guinness had taken its sweet time, and we finally had two pints with creamy heads in front of us, we inched into a booth. There was a tiny dish of nuts in its centre, as if this was the height of generosity. The window looked out over the street and the station beyond. We could hear the tortured *squeal* of the trains through the glass, and when they went overhead, the whole boozer rattled.

I raised my glass - *to Donovan and the Lost.*

I sensed you watching me, when I took my first sip. My peepers fluttered closed: since Abona I'd been teetotal. It's not like I have to protect my liver. Those degenerative diseases you First Lifers fear? We Blood Lifers have evolved past such anxiety. We regenerate, or for half a millennium at least. It's not eternal life, but I'm a glass half full type of bloke.

Opening my peepers, I smacked my lips. 'Go on then. You do..?'

You hesitated one moment longer, before slurping a good quarter of your pint. 'Keg parties. There were these wicked keg parties back in Boston. Fernando and me would hide all this beer on account of, you know, not being twenty-one yet. If the college authorities came, we'd book it. And this one time?' You leant closer, conspiratorial, 'Fernando invited me to his cuz's house, which he did a lot on account of me having no... I mean, his whole family were out there; he's frickin' lucky. So I was at his cuz's. We were drinking and swimming in his pool, and then the cops showed because of the music. We booked it outta there, over the fence, wearing nothing but...' You snickered, as you took another pull on your pint.

'So,' I played with my glass, twirling it round, 'you and Fernando are..?'

Suddenly you were stone cold sober. 'None of your frickin' business. Now drink up, this little outing is over'.

'Hold up--'

'Naw, I'm done. London's not yours.'

I stiffened. 'The Lost have walked these streets as long as you humans,' I whispered, low and intense, 'which makes them ours, as much as yours.'

I might as well have clouted you. You drew back, with a shiver. 'You hunt here – parasitically. But England? The world? It belongs to *us*. You're just...'

'Parasites?' I offered. You didn't even have the decency to look away.

'These are *my* streets,' you tapped the sticky table for emphasis, in a boozer, street, *postcode* you'd never have ventured into, if it hadn't been for me.

I took a drag on my e-cig. 'Over hundred and fifty years says different, sweetheart.'

You wore that narked expression, which I'd hoped we'd left behind for the night. 'My home. Not yours.'

'Any reason it can't be both?'

'On account of you're...' You stopped yourself, pushing your Guinness away with a jerky shove. Your shoulders slumped. You finished softly, '...not human.'

'Right. Because I'd missed that.' I took a mouthful of nuts, munching thoughtfully. You'd withdrawn hermit-crab like, your hair falling in two curtains over your mug. 'There were humans once, who thought like you, the last time a Blood Lifer had the courage to reveal himself to a First Lifer. It was one of my ancestors. A man of reason, in an age of superstition. He reckoned our two species could live out in the open - side by side - so I was told. These First Lifers? They thought he was the devil.' You'd raised your nut. I could see your peepers - dark grey now - through the veil of your hair.

'What..?'

'They burnt him.'

A train screeched past; the smoke-stained walls shook. The tables rattled, spilling Guinness down the sides of my glass.

You were scrutinising me, as your fingers tore minute strips out of a stained beer mat. 'But you were with a human. Kathy?'

'And that's none of your business.' I downed my pint. 'Let's clear off then. Stop while we're behind.'

You nodded, before downing your own pint. Then you followed me outside. As we waited for a black cab to flag, it started to rain in a fine drizzle; I raised my mush, allowing it to spider web over my skin. It'd been so long since I'd felt the freshness of rain washing clean the air - *life*.

You shivered; this time out of cold, rather than the horror of realising you were sharing this world with us *parasites*.

I shrugged off my coat, holding it out to you.

Taken aback, you hesitated but then slipped it on. You looked dead stunning in it.

When I pressed closer to you, your peepers widened in alarm. 'Trust me?' Then I was gone, into the night.

I was only away for a couple of minutes, yet by the time I'd darted back, that wankering tracker was already clutched in your whitened knuckles. 'You...chowderhead!'

I smiled. 'Sweetheart,' I held up a black leather women's jacket, with studs on its shoulders. 'Swap?'

Slowly, you were calming, as you cast these small, envious glances at the jacket. 'Where the frig did you find that?'

'Getting wet here. Show some appreciation, yeah?'

When you slipped the tracker back in your bag (and I should've bloody known the tech amnesty hadn't included *that* particular device), you shucked off my jacket, exchanging it for the new one with almost indecent haste. It fitted you like a second skin. 'Seriously, where?'

'Nicked it.'

You do a good impression of a ghost.

I took pity. 'Don't have a coronary. I left them the lolly for it; I half-inched the cash from you.' When you were silent, I reckoned I was in for it. Then, however, you laughed - honest to God laughed - and I laughed too. Yet for me it was the absurdity of being tamed enough to break and enter and pay for the bleeding crime out of my pickpocketing. 'What kinda Blood Lifer does that make me?'

'Mine.'

Unexpectedly, you entwined our hands. Our lips were close. I hardly dared breathe.

Then there was a *crash*. A woman's scream. Shouting.

'Whoa, what's goin' on?'

'Don't stare like that. This is Peckham, not bloody Primrose Hill.'

I darted a sideways glance, whilst keeping you shielded with my body.

My fists ached for a barney. But I was here with you. I wasn't free.

A gang of young bloods, in hoodies with purple bands on their arms were banging up some Lewisham bird... *Bitch*, *whore*, *slut*... I flinched, as each verbal assault landed, as painful as every boot and clout. A territorial display in defence of *their manor*.

Too late, I realised we'd been spotted.

'You disrespectin' us?' The leader - a tall bloke in purple hoodie and tight weave - turned to us. You panicked and backed up. The gang, like it had a collective mind, abandoned its last victim, who snatched the chance to pick herself up and limp away. The gang swarmed around us instead. The leader repeated, 'You be disrespectin' us?'

There was no answer to get us out of this.

As the gang swaggered our way, they pulled out shanks, which had been hidden in low-lying branches or stored behind piles of rubbish.

I took a deep breath. And hoped you'd forgive me.

'A bloke who gets his jollies from beating on women doesn't deserve no respect, you git.'

You gasped. There was a silence, in which I wondered if I should've spoken slower.

Then everything kicked off.

The leader shot out his shank at gut level - practised move that - but I dodged, snapping his arm in two places, before round housing him in the chest. Whilst he was coughing crimson, I thrust you into a side alley, flinching when I heard the *bump* as you landed on your arse. Then I stood ready to protect you.

It was sodding smashing not to be the damsel anymore.

My fangs were out of commission, but my fists and feet were still bloody there. The adrenaline roared through me, like a forgotten friend.

I got in a hook to the next crew member's cheek: it shattered. The giant bastard hollered. I knocked his shiv bouncing harmlessly into the red shutter beside my nut, before kneeing him in the goolies. Because street fights? *You fight dirty.* When he went down, the rest rushed me.

I nutted the one in front, booted the one on the right and took an elbow to the throat of the one on the left, who gurgled and collapsed. I bounced on the balls of my feet, flushed with exhilaration. I needed this.

Plus, you kidnap and torture a bloke? He's bound to have some issues to work out. This was better than sodding therapy.

A scrawny wanker pounced on me, waving a samurai sword in my mug.

I went at the samurai sod quick smart with a flurry of spear hands, before he'd even swung at me. He stumbled backwards, as if he'd suddenly grasped he'd only been playing at being the *big bad* with his antique sword and now had come across the real thing. When I landed a strike to his throat, he slid face first into a dirty puddle.

At last, the only member still standing was the leader, even though he was scarlet mouthed and clutching his limp arm. He seemed determined not to lose face in front of the groaning remains of his gang. With his good arm, he struck out.

I grabbed the leader's fist in a wrist lock, breaking each tiny joint in his wrist. He screamed, as he fell to his knees.

I stared down at him. 'Word of advice, mate: don't go picking on strangers. You never know who they'll turn out to be.'

It only took a light push on his forehead to topple the tosser beside his comrades.

Still, there was you to face now.

To my surprise, you were leaning casually in the dark entrance of the alley, watching me. I wondered if you'd given my performance a rating.

I stuck my hands in my pockets. 'I think we'd better...'

'...book it..?'

You dragged me after you down the warren of side streets behind the shops.

It was pelting down now. Even though I was soaked, I was still buzzing from the barney.

At last you stopped, shoving me up against a brick wall at the back entrance to a butcher's.

'Look,' I said hurriedly, 'I'm sorry about--'

'Thanks.'

Questioningly, I tilted my nut. Your lips were close to mine. All I'd need to do was...

You pulled back (of course you bloody did), even if you were still clutching onto me, as if my body was yours.

Because no matter what other nasties you might do with it, you'd never *kiss* your slave, would you?

Then you suddenly hauled me closer, and we were snogging.

At that moment, none of it meant anything.

Slave or Mistress. First Lifer or Blood.

It never does when skin meets skin. It was just Light and Grayse.

So it was a good kiss. To me, it changed everything. But to you..?

'If you would be so kind, some of us are trying to feed in peace.' A nasal but polite Turkish Blood Lifer popped his nut up from further down the alley. He licked down the neck of a twitching First

Lifer bird, who was propped up against a skip; she was probably one of those clubbers, who hadn't made it onto the bouncer's list.

When you shrieked and tried to jerk away, I held you still by the wrist, regretting the bruising but juggling risk and prioritising your life.

The look you shot me, however, told me that you didn't appreciate it.

I shrugged. 'Yeah, my mistake.'

Your peepers were now flint.

I started edging you backwards out of the shadows.

If I hadn't been so – distracted - I'd have sensed this gentlemanly Blood Lifer earlier. Without my fangs, I couldn't take him in a fight. More to the buggering point, I couldn't save *you*. Talk about making a bloke feel inadequate. Now also wasn't the time to give you a crash course on Blood Lifer dinner etiquette.

It seems, however, that our Turkish friend was determined to educate me. 'You know, young one, it is most inconsiderate to interrupt a fellow's kill. I had no intention to do so with yours.'

I spun to you to say...I don't know what. You looked like you might vomit. 'Right, cheers, I'll remember that.'

The other Blood Lifer inclined his nut.

I slipped my arm around your stiff waist, turning you and frogmarching you away from the old git, whilst he set back to his dinner.

As soon as we were safely on a main road under the lights, amidst the bustle of partygoers and the fumes of double-decker buses, you wrenched away from me, like I was toxic. In a way, I guess I am. 'Save her,' your voice was shaky. 'Go back and--'

'She's bitten. Dead already.'

'And aren't you just cut up about it?'

'Hey,' I jabbed my finger at you, 'innocent party here, remember?'

'I was a moron to forget what you are. Why I had to buy you. Marlane told me it was my duty to...that I had to put you in your place fast. I guess I get why now.'

'Grayse...'

I tried to reach out to you, but you only backed away. 'Home.'

It was back to puppy dog orders then? Even after..?

You didn't utter another word on the way back to the apartment. Not a dickie bird. I gave up trying.

Touching freedom and then knowing it was being taken away again, made captivity harder to bear.

By the time we were climbing to your apartment, I felt like I returning to Abona. When I heard the front door being closed behind me and the security system *click* in..? I was hit by a tsunami of panic – heart racing, chest tight and dizzy waves – *no escape, no escape, no...*

We stood in the darkness, until you simply said, 'My bedroom.'

After that moment in the rain - when we'd snogged - I'd reckoned coming back here wouldn't feel the same.

I'd saved your life tonight (twice), although blinkered as you are, you couldn't see it.

You'd kissed me too, let's not forget that.

It's not as if I was mug enough to imagine you'd declare undying love. But maybe you'd *see* me (beneath the sticky labels).

You'd tasted some of *my* world tonight. Maybe that was the problem. I only knew one woman, who'd embraced it. And no one can ever be her.

My mistake.

When I wandered after you into your bedroom, I watched as you stripped out of the leather jacket, which I'd nicked for you.

You stuffed the jacket violently to the bottom of your wardrobe, like it was toxic too. That stung.

Then you circled me, without warning, predator-like. 'Strip.'

I jumped and then stared at you, as if I must've misheard. 'Grayse..?'

You didn't reply.

A sick numbness, like dying from the inside out, took grip, when you pulled the tracker from your tote and swiped it on.

Your sister had bloody taught you how to use the tracker..? And now you were *threatening* me..?

My night, *your* rules?

I still didn't budge.

When I saw your finger descend, however, I hauled off my jacket, tossing it pooled, like a black tar version of *Heartbreak*, on your bedroom floor.

Your gaze was so cold; how could I ever have doubted you were a Cain?

'Everything.' I wasn't in control of my own body, as I kicked off my trainers, stumbled out of my socks and dragged my t-shirt over my nut. Your photos were watching: your smiling, innocent mush, as if you were any other kid. My fingers fumbled with the button flies on my jeans in my fear. I risked a peek at you. You were determinedly not averting your gaze whilst I undressed, like it was some kind of test. *Right, no bloody flinching or trembling*. When I stepped out of my boxers and stood there starkers, except for my slave ring, I found myself staring into the grinning mug of my rival - the Alpha Geek - from his place of honour on the wall. Victorious, he was laughing. Humiliated, I blushed. Would you ever demean *him* like this? What would you do if you knew someone was going to do...this...to your *human*? 'Lie down.'

I lay on my back, with my hands at my sides - palms up - and my legs spread wide apart (as I'd been taught), unresponsive on the white bed. I felt suddenly dead small.

I stared up at the ceiling unblinkingly. If you wanted a fucktoy, you'd have to operate it yourself.

Still in the floral silk dress, which I'd picked out, you settled beside me. Your hair was curling at the ends, as it dried from the wet.

When you leaned over me, I was flooded in gorse and sunlight, but it no longer smelled of escape or freedom - it burned.

First, you caressed the tips of your fingers down my cheek. Only hours before that gentle touch would've given me an instant stiffy. But now? It was as welcome as a nest of spiders.

Your hand ventured lower down my chest, pausing to twist one nipple.

Hard.

My fingers curled and uncurled convulsively. I schooled my features to blankness. There was no sodding way I'd let you see the damage you were doing to my head.

It wasn't like this was the roughest treatment I'd ever received, even as your fist tightened around my flaccid, frightened todger and began pumping it to hardness; Ruby had enjoyed playing games, which had left me sore for days. It's not even as if I'd had much say, being bound by my wrists or the mental bondage of the ties of election.

This, however, *was* different because there wasn't even the illusion of choice.

How was I meant to deal with the fact that the bird, who was using my dick as a dildo, had only hours ago kissed me like I was a free man? Kissed me like she believed my name truly was *Light* again?

If you did...*this*...you'd be completing the process started at Abona.

You'd shatter me into a sex slave for real – *Sir's whore*.

And you? *You'd* be a rapist.

When you leant over me, your hand still working on my todger, I could feel your breath across my mouth.

Your lips were moving closer, as if you were seeking another kiss.

Buggering hell, no...

Your mouth was about to violate mine.

Christ in heaven, if you were intent on fucking me, *please let you not do it with your lips soft against mine*.

That's when I started to shake.

I felt, more than saw, you back off. When our gazes met, I recognised the surprise in yours, as if you couldn't understand my distress.

I reckon it's that more than anything, which did it: I couldn't stop a tear escaping down my cheek.

You studied me for a long moment, before your vice-like grip let go of my prick, and you pulled back sharply. 'I can't do this...' When you stumbled from the room, I heard a door *bang* somewhere - it might've been the bathroom - and then there were sounds like... So I wasn't the only one, who needed to puke. I lay where you'd left me - an abandoned toy - too confused and frightened to do sod all else. At last I heard hesitant shuffling footsteps in the doorway. We stared at each other. 'I'm sorry. I won't...do that again. Get dressed and go to bed.'

This time you couldn't look away fast enough, as I scrambled to pull on my clothes.

And I haven't spoken to you since.

Nothing's ever as simple as a kiss, is it?

MAY 24

'What's doin'?'

I peered out at you from under the duvet and shrugged.

The neon blue ivy was glowing brightly, casting my cell in the role of enchanted forest.

You hesitated on the threshold, toeing the wooden floorboards with your bare feet. I'd never seen you in fuzzy pink pyjamas before: you looked kind of vulnerable. There were bruise coloured rings around your peepers, as if you'd been getting about as much kip as me.

You ran your fingers through your mop of hair. 'So, you wanna watch TV? I've made popcorn.'

In the weeks I'd been incarcerated here, I'd come to reckon you imagined the TV to be nothing but a flat screen on the wall: another one of your designer pieces. More art than function.

I leapt out of bed, snatching the olive branch in both sensory deprived hands.

The lounge was lit by mango scented candles in glowing pools. The furniture was skewwhiff. It was clear you'd been doing your own chores.

About bloody time.

Still, I couldn't help the momentary kick of pride in how much better *I'd* been at them.

You padded over to the sofa, passing me a humungous glass bowl of popcorn.

I pulled a face when I smelled the popcorn was neither sweetened nor salted. Then I carefully perched on the opposite end of the sofa.

The space between us felt like a chasm.

I saw the muscle in your cheek twitch.

'Here,' your hand reached towards me, holding...

Bleeding hell – no - you'd promised.

You were holding the tracker. You were pointing it right at me.

I waited for the pain. But instead there was only something pressing insistently into my palm, your arm around my shoulders and your voice ringing over and over: *Light*, *Light*, *Light*...

I'd been shaking again. When had that started?

I stared down at the object in my hand: the tracker. I nearly hurled the hated thing as far from me as I could. Then it penetrated my fogged noggin, however, that the Manx symbol was missing. I nudged it tentatively with my thumb: there were buttons too, rather than a touchscreen.

'The clicka,' why did your voice have to be so tender? 'For the TV.' You were right. Your arm still hadn't left my shoulder. I didn't shrug it off. I'd dropped the glass bowl. The popcorn had cascaded over the sitting room floor, but you didn't order me to clear up the mess. 'I reckoned you could choose, you know, a channel for us. A movie maybe?'

When did *I* have a choice?

Even my night out of the apartment had been nothing but smoke and mirrors.

For so long, I'd stumbled from grief to grief. Yet now you handed me this gift of choice, as if it was a common penny..?

When I broke down, shuddering with sobs, you simply held me, even though I doubt you understood my tears.

Later, after *you'd* hoovered up the popcorn and brewed me a coffee, you nestled close on the sofa again, resting your nut on my chest. I should've shoved you off - all things considered. But I didn't.

‘What do you remember...’ here it comes, ‘...about the night you were retrieved?’

‘That’s what you’re calling it?’

You glanced at me, two grey lamps in the darkness. ‘Retrieval and Acquisitions Department handles the selection and retrieval of product.’

I bristled. ‘Why not try *captured* on for size? Or here’s a thought, *abducted*?’

You didn’t look away. ‘Where were you?’

‘Bangkok. At a mixed martial arts tournament. If you really wanna know, I was trying to get given a bloody good hiding. But mostly I ended up giving someone else one.’

‘Why the frig would you want..?’

‘The pain,’ I pushed your nut off my chest, before banging my coffee mug down on the glass table – *clang*. I didn’t care that you cringed. I sodding didn’t. ‘If I hurt, I still existed. I was in control. *I* decided if I walked into that cage...but the pain inside? I couldn’t... I can’t...’

‘Kathy?’

‘Don’t,’ I turned to you warningly, ‘you don’t have a bloody clue what it’s like to grieve.’

‘Wanna bet?’

We glared at each other.

You, however, lowered your gaze first. ‘So, what happened in..?’

‘I was being watched. Not like the normal baying crowd. Something or someone else. I was winning most fights, even though I was drunk and swallowed in black. But this night, it was like someone you really didn’t want to notice you, *had*. I’d won the bout, but it’d been brutal. I could hardly stand. That’s what I needed, the bruises and the high. See, I’d just let myself take it for the first half of the match, before I’d Anaconda choked the bastard, ‘til he passed out. Afterwards, I’d sensed these blokes: punk-like in aviator-goggles, red braces, spiked collars and so many tattoos they were swaggering works of art. They were circling the crowd. And I knew, without even questioning the instinct, they were there for me.'

You shifted. You were hiding something. I guess this honesty lark doesn't cut both ways.

'And..?'

'And they *retrieved* me. End of.'

'Light...'

I jittered to my feet, pacing to the fireplace. The aroma of mangoes floated me to warmer, safer climes - to freedom. 'What? You want all the gory details? I took the back way. They chased me out onto the roof. I threw myself down to my Triton.' I paused.

Why the bleeding hell had I mentioned that?

You were assessing me levelly. 'Triton?'

'My bike.' I fiddled with an indigo Italian glass vase. 'She was all I had, apart from this jacket. From my time before. All I cared about. And you lot,' I pointed at you, not caring whether it was fair or not; the grievance had festered for nearly six months and you - a Cain - were in the firing line, 'took it from me. Took *her*.'

I swung away, booting the marble.

I heard your quiet voice behind me, 'They took your bike?'

'Scarlet 650cc twin-cylinder thing of beauty. And yeah, they might as well have done.' I spun the glass vase between the tips of my fingers. 'At first I thought: if I just keep scarpering, everything'll be cool. But then I heard the *roar* of their motorbikes. They were a team. Organised. I couldn't shake the wankers. I wove through downtown Bangkok's traffic jams and onto Wireless Road, pulling my scarf over my gob to stop from choking on the fumes, as I tried not to hit the roadside food stalls. I was frightened by then, which was the first time I'd truly felt anything real since... My heart was shot full of adrenaline, 'cos here were these First Lifers, who seemed to know me. The thought, which fuelled my flight, was the gut awareness there was something dodgy behind the attack. Every time I glanced over my shoulder, I saw red Mohawks swarming after me on black bikes, slashed with crimson. They had the power, but I had a good five decades of riding experience on the tossers. The punks tried to box me in, slamming me with their bikes. I sped up. But there weren't any pavements to manoeuvre on. I reckoned I could lose them in the park. I was wrong.' The glass was smooth under my fingers, strangely soothing. The dark blue was hypnotising, like staring too long into the sky. 'I felt something...hit me. In my right shoulder. It stung. Then everything went blurry. I couldn't see. My hands were falling from the bike and I was too... I heard screeching and tearing, like the Triton was in pain... To crash like that, after all these years...and I was tumbling, thudding along the grass. I was tranquilised, so the pain was muted, but *snap, snap, snap*, I could hear and feel the bones break... My limbs were floppy; the blood was seeping. I must've been a right state, lying there in the dark next to my murdered Triton.' I snatched the glass still between my palms. You were frozen as a statue on the sofa. 'As I blacked out, I remember wishing only one last thing: *please let them take my Triton too*. Yeah, of course they bloody didn't. When you're a slave, you lose everything.'

MAY 25

I guess you never forgot that pink Post-it note, which I'd stuck in potty optimism to the fridge.

The first clue was when I found my white trainers poking out of the rubbish in the kitchen. The second? The pair of brand spanking new black motorcycle boots on the stainless steel counter.

When I hugged the boots to me, like they were my long lost babies, I heard your laugh behind me. 'Wanna put them on?'

Cautious, I dragged on each boot, as if another amputated body part was being reattached. 'The dog's bollocks, yeah?'

You stifled a smirk. 'You coming?'

I hung back. 'Where?' I'd noticed the sheen of black silk, which was coiled in your palm.

You let the silk dangle out, like a shiny snake. 'It's a surprise. You chicken?'

'I'm many things, darlin'. But not that.'

I snatched the blindfold, fitting it over my own peepers. I experienced momentary panic: I was back in Abona. But then it was your hand, pressing into mine and leading me out. I was with you. And I was safe.

Now ask if I trust you?

I heard a *click*. You were taking me out of the apartment again? But I hadn't done anything to earn it this time. I trembled, when I felt the night air on my skin.

We were going down steps... *Here's one, two more, careful...*

Instructions, rather than orders. Protective, as if it mattered whether I broke.

At last, we stopped; the sudden stillness was disconcerting. Then your fingers were edging off the blindfold. I blinked against the dim light.

We were in an underground garage.

You were standing right in front of me; your hands were in your jean pockets. You'd also slipped on the black leather jacket, which I'd filched for you on Rye Lane. The last I'd seen of the jacket, it'd been unceremoniously discarded at the bottom of your wardrobe.

I reached out and stroked your cheek...which was when you stepped to one side.

A Triton.

A sodding scarlet slash of beauty. 650cc Triumph twin-cylinder engine in a Norton 'slimline' Featherbed frame - and my bloody god. I know because it was the exact same model I'd acquired one May Bank Holiday 1964 - and lost six months ago in Bangkok.

For one long moment, I couldn't breathe.

You were assessing me uncertainly. 'You...like it?'

'How..?'

'It turns out money can buy most things. Not such a hard lesson, huh?'

I stumbled to the Triton, hesitating to touch her because it was like touching the Resurrected: sacrosanct. Tentatively, I stroked her, becoming familiar with her lines and curves. 'She's..?'

'Yours.'

It might not have been the same bike, which I'd lost to those hunters, who'd slayed her and tamed me, but she was as close as damn it.

Breath blown through my Soul.

I didn't miss the fact there were *two* motorbike helmets balanced on the saddle. They were both black; yours wasn't even poncey pink. I weighed it in my hands, before holding it out to you. 'Ever rode on one of these?'

'Naw. But...I trust you.'

Our gazes met.

'Right then, hold on tight: this is what true freedom feels like.'

At first, we wove between the London traffic, trapped between the stop and start of traffic lights, caught between bus lanes and wobbly pushbikes.

I was just chuffed to have a Triton between my legs and a bird behind me. I'd had a stiffy from the second I'd seen you in a leather jacket, leant against the Triton and thought - *she's with me*.

As soon as we were out of London though and were tonning it down the motorway towards the coast, that's when I really let the Triton fly.

The engine roared. As I settled over the bike, your arms tightened. There was nothing ahead apart from the shining paths of cats' eyes and three lanes of open road. The night sky above was like polished jet; you were hot against my back.

Abso-bloody-blinding.

One night of freedom – yours and mine – pure and unsullied.

You held onto me, as we drove through the night, in silent communion with the road, until the purple of the sky threatened dawn.

MAY 27

So, I didn't expect this.

I'm back locked in my cell.

On my tod.

I picked up and set down my pen three times – *one, two, three* – before I caught myself in the ritualising. And started to sodding write.

I reckon a couple of ribs are broken. The rest of me's a throbbing bruise, not to mention those three red welts across my back, arse and thighs.

You did hand me some cows' blood, before you threw the lock. The blood was cold, but then what had I expected? I'll mend though: blood is life.

Cheers for that, at least.

This morning I reckoned something was up, when you manhandled me into your bedroom, before I'd been able to do more than pull on my boxers.

I was still wary of that room, with your silent, white bed and the wall of your other, perfect life. And Mr Professor giving it all *don't think I've forgotten what I saw.*

One quiet moment and a match, mate, that's all I'm saying.

There was this single-buttoned suit, pale grey wool and mohair, laid out on the white covers. I glanced between it and your excited mug.

So, it was playing dress ups, was it?

'Guess what?' You grinned, as if I should be as excited as you, even though I wasn't in on your secret. 'There's a business meeting this evening. I was thinking you could come on account of--'

'My dashing good looks?'

'That thing you do with numbers.' I studied you with surprise. You shrugged. 'I thought you told me something like we should use our humungous brains?'

'Listening were you?'

'Sometimes.' I smiled, but the idea I was going out again into the world, where my intelligence would be valued and I'd have a *place*, nearly undid me. 'Also,' you gave me a sideways look, which I didn't miss, 'you need to meet your own kind. And there'll be another...Blood Lifer.'

So that was it then: a meeting of slaves? Maybe you'd erect a pen in the corner for us? And why had you hesitated before you'd said *Blood Lifer*?

I was so lost in my thoughts I didn't notice you drawing my arms into the pink shirt and buttoning it up, as if I was a doll, before threading a floral tie around my neck. Then you started towards me with the suit.

I raised my hand to stop you. 'Don't you reckon I could dress this poncey way, if I wanted? But I choose...' I looked down. The shirt was dead pink; the flowers on the tie frolicked. 'That's the point, right? I don't choose anymore. Whatever you do to me,' ridiculous in my boxers and pink shirttails flying, I banged my chest, like a well-dressed gorilla, 'it's still *me* underneath. Rip out the fangs, turn me into your kept boy, but the predator's still here. *I'm still here.*'

You stared at me, like I'd just savaged your mush. 'I only wanted to do something nice for you.'

I remembered our night of freedom on my scarlet beauty. Nothing but road, roar and revelation. 'You already did,' I replied softly.

'That's private.' You'd paled, as if...ashamed? *Frightened*? 'This? Is business. I need you presentable.'

I snatched the grey jacket from you, knowing I was creasing it, as I dragged it on. 'What you really want is to transform me *into* something nice to have on your arm, when you waltz into your meeting. Use my brains? I should cocoa. Don't worry, I won't show you up. It's not as if this is the first time a bird's done this to me. Humans don't have the monopoly on being controlling bitches.'

Slap.

Shocked, you stared at the crimson handprint on my cheek and then at your hand, as if the two couldn't possibly be connected. Your peepers pricked with wetness, as you chucked the suit trousers at my mug. 'Just put the frickin' things on.'

Then you stormed out – *bang* - there went the bathroom door.

By the time we caught a black cab to Brixton that evening, you were in full on business mode, and I was suited, Brylcreemed and bouncing on my seat with pent-up energy.

All day waiting on the outing, I'd made up for being shirty earlier, with deliveries of chocolate cupcakes (which I'd ordered from that bakery on Gloucester Avenue), bacon sarnies for lunch (you were a convert) and *frappe* (at your request).

I dived out of the cab before you, holding out my hand to help you descend.

You were surprised. Then pleased. *Come on, Victorian here*.

We were in a narrow alley in front of a tall, brick warehouse with depressingly small windows, like a prison. It was tagged with red-and-black graffiti. There was the delicious aroma of fried fish; Jamaican music pulsed through the still air.

I turned to you. 'Now, what's this meeting..?'

The words died on my lips.

Low black motorbikes, with razor red slashes down the side, were parked up in ranks across the street; the vivid memory of their *roar*, whilst I crashed into the arms of oblivion, painted the inside of my brain crimson.

My gaze must've held all the betrayal I was feeling because you rushed to explain, 'They're not here for you, Light, I swear. Look,' you pointed at the sign above the grimy building, which the bikes circled: *M.C.'s Mixed Martial Arts Gym.*

MMA? Was that how they'd discovered me? The network of tournaments, fighters and promoters? My own stupid, death wish recklessness? Sod's bloody law that our two worlds had collided?

At last it filtered into my overloaded mind, who owned the gym.

'Bloody hell, your sister?'

Now I knew why you'd acted dodgy, when I'd told you how I'd been kidnapped. Were you scared of my revenge? Or feeling guilty of your Cain name?

'Retrieval and Acquisitions is Marlane's department. Those punks in Bangkok... They're M.C.'s crew.'

'Wankers.'

'*Don't*,' you nervously glanced towards the silent gym and the rows of black bikes. 'Marlane gets them, like...young. Poor and hungry, she says. It makes them the best fighters, once she's trained them up. She runs these underground tournaments.'

'Underground? Well blow me down with a feather.'

'The core has grown up with her. She's their mentor. And they're family.'

'Her gang?'

You didn't deny it. 'They're loyal. They'd die for her.'

'*Kill* for her? Wait, what am I saying? I imagine they already bloody have.' A kid, with a snarling fighting dog on a too long leash and no muzzle, swaggered past. We edged back. 'Why didn't you sodding tell me?'

'What does it change?'

I shrugged. 'You seen them? Fight?'

You shuddered. 'Na-ah. Not with all that...violence...pain...blood...'

'Give over. You do understand how your family makes its cash? They're not florists.'

Your expression hardened. 'Let's see if we can't get to the meeting on time, huh?'

'Forced labour,' I muttered.

'Work,' you hissed back.

We let ourselves into the warehouse with a security code, riding up in a steel lift to your sister's apartment, which took up the whole of the converted third floor. The lift stank of piss. Before it stuttered to a stop, I couldn't help asking, 'Why's she live here?'

You didn't look at me. 'It's her home.'

Enough said.

When the lift doors clanged open, we were hit by a primal roar of musical rage. An anarchist's mantra, overlaid by a raucous burst of electric guitar and drums, which were duelling with a relentless, driving bass hook.

I couldn't stop the daft grin spreading, as I bounced on the balls of my feet.

You glanced at me, alarmed and then grimaced.

I shrugged. 'It's punk: *Fuck Off.*'

'What the frig..?' You were making shushing motions, casting frightened glances down the hallway.

'Name of the album,' I explained, 'Good Throb.'

'I know.' I hadn't even raised my eyebrow, before you were grinning too.

'Your sister would make one bitch of a Blood Lifer.'

You shoved me back into the manky lift. 'Never let her hear you say that.'

Christ it was difficult to be close to you. The water's muddied now, don't even try and act like it's not.

We battled through the raging, nihilistic explosion of alienation, into the vast open plan but scruffy apartment. Its walls were unfinished brick, which were still tagged here and there with graffiti, and the floors were raw cast concrete. Yet there were goat skin rugs, chandeliers dripping crystals and a drinks bar carved out of natural stone, which was stocked with glistening bottles of booze. The warehouse had been bisected by an immense white cloud, which was pierced with holes, as if the daytime sky had rebelled and invaded the inside.

There were also the same art pieces, mixed in with the second-hand, as you had in your apartment. Except there was a darkness in these, which wasn't there in yours. A baroque chair looked like it'd been singed with a blowtorch. It was beautiful in its destruction.

When we rounded a corner of the cloud divider, there was M.C.: she was sprawled on a blackened chaise longue, in all her tartan miniskirt, fishnets, ripped and safety pinned t-shirt with decorative bloodstains, glory.

'Alright, sis?' M.C. tossed the glossy photos, which she'd been perusing, like she was an editor at a fashion mag, onto the '50s Japanese coffee table. Strike that, like a *porn director*, deciding on her next casting.

Close-ups of starkers Blood Lifers spilled over the coffee table.

Please let there not be one of me...

You nodded over the clash of the music, with a wince.

M.C. stretched, before strolling to her sound system to press it off. The silence seemed suddenly louder. 'You brought it then?'

'He'll behave.'

I put on my most angelic expression.

M.C. snorted. 'You be crazy if you believe dat can behave.' I tensed, when M.C. prowled closer. She met my gaze shrewdly. 'You be in *my* manor now, liccle leech, you get me?'

'Yeah,' *straight face, straight face*, 'I get you.'

Your arm was already around my shoulders, tugging me away. 'He knows what's expected. You set up the table?'

You two First Lifers settled opposite each other across this pale, bone-white table on spindly, skeletal chairs, whilst I - the Blood Lifer - stood behind you, with my hands clasped behind my back. I was the eternal servant: although in my Savile Row suit, I was a bleeding overdressed one. There was a life-size replica of a M16 behind M.C., as if that was what served her.

Suddenly, the surface of the albino table shifted, like a million particles of sand. It reshaped into a 3D projection of the globe. Glowing lights were dotted across its surface, connected by a spider web of threads and photos of Blood Lifers. All projected in a moving display from within.

I blinked. 'Bugger me.'

You glanced back at me warningly.

M.C. smirked. 'It be still bad, I told you.'

'He'll behave,' you repeated, like a ward against evil.

As you and M.C. leant across the table, which was shifting with statistics and the haunting images of the enslaved, I let my mind drift.

I stood ramrod straight, with my chin up, and peepers down: the statue you First Lifers wanted. Yet it niggled - the thought of that miniature globe - as if you truly did have the world in your hands.

Those dots could only be other Blood Lifers like me. My own kind, pet slaves now in rich humans' homes or else earmarked for capture.

When I listened in to the meeting, it was as if you were chin-wagging about any corporate *product* on sale globally, using sanitised business buzzwords to mask the horror, compartmentalizing *Accounts* from *Retrieval and Acquisitions*, so your hands wouldn't be dirtied.

M.C. was fudging and hedging, side-lining you when you questioned her. You were clearly being trained to be the *money woman*. Whilst M.C. was the bitch with the blood on her hands, so you didn't have to be. What are big sisters for?

'£2, 633714327332.34127,' I said absentmindedly, 'you forgot the £3, 327432.34127 at the end.'

Both women were staring at me.

Bollocks.

You'd been working on the numbers for bloody hours, and I'd been shifting about to keep my legs from going numb, daydreaming.

There was a stylised Manx illustrated across the brick wall in creepy graffiti, and I was imagining I was back with *my* Manx cats. Except in the background was the annoying buzz of you and M.C. working on this problem. I didn't even realise I'd solved it out loud.

M.C. sprang up. 'I thought you said you *got* me, liccle leech?'

'Before you take him down...' You were tapping away on the pale table, as if it was a laptop. A figure spread across the surface in tiny black pixels: *£2, 633714327332.34127.*

'How you do dat?' M.C. was still poised to pounce.

'I worked in a bank?' I offered weakly.

You laughed.

After a moment, so did M.C., but there was a nastier edge to it, as she sank back into her chair. 'Well done, sis; only you could buy a blow-up doll and end up with a neek instead, innit?'

I wasn't sure which half of that sentence hurt more.

Your expression stilled. 'Sit down, Light,' you dragged back the skeletal chair next to yours, 'let's see what you reckon to these figures.' I didn't move. You repeated more slowly, 'Sit. Down.'

Finally, what you were offering filtered through to my shell-shocked brain.

M.C. looked as amazed as I felt.

I plonked myself down, linking my hands behind my nut and grinned. 'Alright.'

I felt the most like...a man...Blood or First Lifer....that I'd felt in a long time, sitting there with you at your work. Almost like...an equal.

I should've known it wouldn't last.

When the accounts were finally swiped to one side and a – disgusting - catalogue of Blood Lifers was brought up for your viewing pleasure, I noticed the small Manx tattoo on the inside of M.C.'s wrist, which matched yours, as she leant forward.

The mark of Cain.

I also didn't miss how M.C. lingered over several of the snaps, as if reminiscing or...anticipating..?

When M.C. paused on Donovan, whose dark mop of hair was pushed back, whilst he posed starkers against a grey wall at Abona, I swear the bint glanced at me.

'Da product,' M.C. tapped the table, enlarging Donovan's image. She knew - she bloody *knew* - he was my cousin. 'Thing about da leech be its unique. Secret to most. Dat be its value. All around da world's after unique. In Afghanistan beardless young boys be sold for bacha bazi: fucking and dancing, innit? In India, dey after fair Nepalese girls: only virgins. But a virgin can only be deflowered once. A boy grows up, sprouts dutty hair and becomes a man. A leech? Dey stay a leech always. If dey a virgin, dey heal: a Blood Clubber can deflower dem every night for the rest of dere lives, you get me? No growing up. No changing. What you see, be what you get - forever. *Unique*. Like your boy dere, when da bitch be trained.'

You were squirming in your seat, worse than me. That's when you said something, which knocked me for six, even though it was so quiet I almost missed it, 'When's daddy getting here?'

'Any time, little sis. What's wrong? Missing him?'

If I hadn't been frozen in terror (my hands gripping my seat, so I was close to snapping it), by the imminent arrival of *Master* to the party, I'd have analysed the gleam in your sister's eye.

Suddenly I remembered I was meant to meet another Blood Lifer tonight, like two mutts playing together at the park. My heart fell. The poor bastard must be from the Estate.

The word at Abona was *Master* trained slaves one-to-one for the super-rich, who preferred their toys to be thoroughly housebroken. Maybe the point of this whole exercise was to show me how a proper slave behaved.

Bugger. That.

I was surprised when under the table, your fingers soothed over mine, slipping them out of their death grip.

Or maybe you were just worried about the survival of the chair.

The last time I saw *Master*... Let's say it dispelled my sentimental notions of coexistence. I reached out to him for help, but instead was slapped down so hard I finally learnt the lesson that times had changed.

I'm a product now: that's my value and my life sentence. I'm the hunted. The slave in the new world of the Blood Club.

Unless I find a way to fight back.

You two Cains were chatting away again in low voices: pricings, balances, assets and costings.

I'd gone to that happy place of denial, where I'm still with Kathy out on the moor by the Twelve Apostles; there are sprigs of bracken in Kathy's pixie cut, so she looks like one of the fairy folk and her blue eyes...

He was there. Finlo Cain. Your daddy. *Master*.

Master was standing by the daytime inside the night cloud, which separated this section of the apartment off, like being in the centre of a honeycomb. I could see him over M.C.'s shoulder.

Your nut, however, was low over your work, and you didn't notice.

Master had seemed like a giant, when he'd been behind me, and I'd been overloaded with fear. Yet now I could see he was a short bugger but burly

- gruff looking - with coarse grey hair and a full beard. Like your sister, he hadn't got the memo about it being a business meeting: his clobber was faded blue jeans, thick belt and a tatty black sweater. He wasn't what I was expecting as CEO of Cain Company.

But then when are folks ever what they appear?

Master was silently examining his daughters, as if for flaws. His flint peepers – the same as yours – softened when they scrutinised you. *Master* passed over me, like I was merely another piece of furniture.

I worried at the horn buttons of my suit jacket.

'Well,' *Master's* expression remained hard and impassive, 'what's strange with you two today?'

'Daddy!' Shocked, I watched as you tore out of your seat, knocking it backwards. You flung yourself into *Master's* arms. When you clung to him, he patted you awkwardly on the back. M.C. sprawled further down on her seat, as her and *Master* exchanged a glance, before M.C. shrugged. At last, *Master* prised you away. 'You..?'

'Middling.' I cringed back, trying to avoid notice. 'How's your boy working out?' *No such sodding luck then.* 'I reckoned it not fit. In fact, I thought I may learn this one at the Estate.'

Say something. Please, please, please...

'Naw, he's mint. You were right. He's just what I need to learn about the business, like, hands on.'

M.C. snorted.

Master frowned. 'But a suit? Sitting on a chair?' I leapt up. I may be many things but I'm not a bloody pillock when it comes to recognising other predators. And right then..? I had a hunter's shotgun pointed at my goolies. 'Care you don't spoil it. I admire you,' *Master* smiled at you, almost tenderly, 'what with all these...degrees and the like.

But you're new to my world. I'm putting my trust in you.' You flushed, girlish. That was cracking, that was: you had a bloke in your life already and his name was *Daddy*. Now I understood who you were both knackering yourself for and stamping on your half-formed morals to impress. Who my true rival was. And it wasn't Fernando. 'Trouble maker that Blood Lifer of yours was, oh the neck of him! Do you want to return him and choose again?' I nearly forgot I wasn't truly dead and had to bloody breathe. Thank Christ your face fell. 'No need to make a great fuss girl. It's your goog; I won't take away your plaything. I know you'll train him into a darling slave. You never disappoint me.' Master's smile widened, but you avoided his gaze, tearing at your nails.

'What about me?' M.C. demanded, crossing her arms. 'What if *I* want a goog?'

Master's smile died in the instant. *Note to self: never be on the receiving end of that look*. 'You've already got too much of a feel for the business,' he told M.C. darkly. 'You'd never get a stitch of work done with such a distraction.'

'Where's Captain?' You asked, before M.C. could protest.

Master glanced at his watch. 'The boy has the codes. He'll join us soon.' Surprised, I glanced between you. *Master* allowed his slaves such freedom? When you sat back down, *Master* planted himself at the head of the bone-white table. He swiped until the spiderwebbed globe glowed ghostly with the demise of my specie's freedom, whilst I stood there bloody impotent. 'The latest retrieval..?'

M.C. shrugged, drumming her black-nailed fingernails on the projected world. 'No problems. The product be at Abona now.'

Master nodded.

The way they worked? It was slick. Practised. Informal. I wondered how many years it'd been in the making.

But you? In your business suit, all bright-eyed and bushytailed, looked like you were striving to be initiated into a multinational on Canary Wharf.

Not a Blood Lifer trafficking and slavery ring.

'You still hear from that feller?' *Master* rubbed his hand across the bristles on his chin, as if it was a casual question.

I kept my nut bowed respectfully but bugger me, *Master* had you trapped already.

'Professor Zuniga Sanchez?' You were so proud. So excited. And so blooming naïve. 'Yah, he's still at Harvard. He has a Research Fellowship in Organismic and Evolutionary Biology.'

There went that snort again from M.C.

'Aye, Fernando: the Mexican feller. I wasn't pleased how he was shaping. From what I heard.'

Your gob was gaping. I should've felt sorry for you except...this was Alpha Geek we were talking about. 'What does..? *Mexican*? I mean, what does that even..? And *heard*..? Who told you..?'

'The bettermost people are in Manx,' *Master* continued, as if your views were an irrelevance: *welcome to my world*. 'I'll introduce you to some of them. But not yet. Right now, work comes first. In fact, work always comes first.'

I felt less smug, when I realised you were about to cry. Yet I couldn't even rest my hand on your shoulder to comfort you.

'Good evening all!' I jolted when a young Blood Lifer – obviously this *Captain* – strolled in like he owned the whole apartment and possibly us with it. He had a jaunty peak of strawberry blond hair and a dark blue shirt casually open two buttons at the neck, worn over pressed dun cargo trousers, as if he'd stepped out of a Young Tory Convention (maybe he had, when he'd been elected to Blood Life).

What I couldn't figure, however, is why not one of you First Lifers howled with outrage, when Captain sauntered to a spindle chair at the opposite side of the table to *Master* and threw himself down.

I drew in my breath, shuddering on Captain's behalf. This empathy for other Blood Lifers was new: solidarity in oppression. I tensed, expecting a tech war of three trackers pointed, like lasers, at Captain's boyish self, followed by agonised yowls.

Instead, I heard Captain's drawl, 'It's been a long week: dinners, events, yada yada... You know how it is. So let's make it snappy, yes?'

What the bloody hell was going on?

The humans were looking awkward but...

Oh no, didn't this take the bloody biscuit?

This Blood Lifer wasn't a slave. Nor did you Cains intend to make him into one.

Cain Company, which traded in Blood Lifer slaves, also traded *with* Blood Lifers.

Leech. Bad. Stupid. Worthless. Parasite.

I'd started to believe those words. Yet you First Lifers didn't even believe them. They were merely convenient tools.

If Captain was free and treated with respect for the sake of dirty money, then you truly had been right: everything my people were suffering (and I'd endured), was down to the *profit margin.*

And that was infinitely worse to live with.

Captain must know I was a Blood Lifer: we can always sense each other. I was, however, suited and booted, so how was Captain to know I was a slave, even if I was standing like a sodding choir boy?

Captain still had his fangs and venom.

One bite.

A single bite from him and I'd be free of the whole bloody lot of you. Not you, I don't mean...

And so would the world.

If I could only catch his eye...

Captain looked up and smiled. The baby actually had dimples. I reckon in First Life he'd been a real beta because they're the sort, who christen themselves when they're reborn things like *Captain*, *Ace*, or *Goliath* – the types of nicknames they wet dreamed someone had called them in First Life. Rather than *Carrot-top*, *Loser* or *Shorty*.

I risked a significant glance at *Master*. Then down at myself. Mimed bowing my nut and then took an even greater risk with a nod back at *Master*.

Captain's smiled broadened. 'Cute. I think he's trying to signal me.'

You know the type of silence you want to tunnel away from?

You were suddenly as still as me.

Then M.C. bared her gnashers in what could've been an attempt at a smile but it was one, which said the tiger now had its prey in its jaws. 'Come on, liccle leech, no secrets.'

I knew my peepers were comically large. My mouth was too dry to answer.

'How precious,' Captain stretched back in his seat. I could tell how much he was enjoying my discomfort. I wondered whether he would, if he'd ever felt a bullwhip ripping up his arse. 'I think he's under the misconception I may save him.'

Babe to Blood Life, Captain couldn't have swum these dark waters more than half a decade, yet here he was taunting and tormenting me: 150 years old but a toy to be batted about.

I blinked away tears; no sodding way were they falling.

'So you wanted to meet about..?' Your tone was ice cold.

Captain turned his gaze (and lazy smile), on you. 'He's yours?'

You nodded stiffly.

'He's Plantagenet?'

You shrugged.

'Everyone at the Blood Council was keen as mustard to get as many of those caught as possible. I mean, they're not all Long-liveds but still...what a bloodline. You do know about the bloodline?'

'It be a liccle bitch that ain't got no respect, dat's what I know.'

'Marlane,' *Master* shot M.C. a look. She subsided. 'The boy acts the gor,' Master expanded, 'makes trouble.'

Captain waved an airy hand, as if he was the authority. 'Plantagenets always do. They challenge authority and try to change things with respect to the natural order: our authority and our order, come to that.'

This time *I* snorted and then quickly ducked my nut.

The Blood Life Council. It wasn't a single Blood Lifer but the entire equivalent of Blood Lifer Westminster dealing with the Cains. *Slave trading* with them.

I couldn't point the finger of blame any longer at First Lifers alone.

Blood Lifers aren't the compassionate sort as a rule, but this was beyond anything I'd imagined them capable of. I should've guessed there was a silent partner. How otherwise did M.C. Crew know the secrets of us Blood Lifers: how to hunt, capture and defang us? How had you First Lifers even discovered our existence?

I felt like I would hurl, when I thought about the details Captain must've casually taught you in this room, so *Sir* could train us at Abona: how long it took to reduce us to living skeletons, how taking away our acute senses would mess us up and how to motivate us with blood.

Had Captain looked so cheery then, enthused by his *dinner and events*?

Captain was eagerly passing on the names of the best families to target. I recognised some of them – Sringara, Hardy and Dulcinea. Long-liveds and their authored kin.

Then there were place names and businesses. The wanker even passed over maps with marked locations, along with an analysis of each Blood Lifer's weaknesses. I wondered whether I'd ever get to have a gander at my file; they must've had fun putting together *my* weaknesses.

Then I spotted a pattern. The Blood Life Council was crucifying its political rivals, or anyone with a bloodline strong enough to challenge these newbies to evolutionary advancement.

The sneaky little bastards.

Black betrayal. It hit me, twinned with a rush of rage: a screaming insistence for revenge.

We'd been sold out by our own kind, who were the true puppet masters in the shadows, merely to further their own political ambitions.

And the worst of it? They were so blinkered in their arrogance they couldn't see that they were next. They'd opened the door to you First Lifers, revealed the existence of the Lost and the profits to which we could be turned. Only a fool would think it could be closed again. Once the Long-liveds were tamed, next would come their bloodlines, and then, who would be left? Kids like this Captain? Who did he reckon would protect him, when the *roar* of the motorbikes was at his back?

'You must only take these families,' Captain arched his fingers self-importantly, 'or else you'll risk depleting the stocks.'

Stocks? As if we were fish to be farmed and netted.

And that was it: I bloody lost it.

Captain's smug, red-cheeked mug ballooned, until it was all I could see, as I firework exploded.

I launched myself across the table with its spinning globe of servitude, tackling the wanker and – *snap* – there went the bloody stupid skeleton chair.

Captain tumbled backwards in a flurry of boots and clouts – *crack* - his nut took a blinding bang to the concrete. He howled.

I lifted Captain up by his ripped shirt, before smashing him down again. 'Why, you bastard, why?'

Captain was a bleeding coward; he had enough bottle to send untold numbers of Blood Lifers to centuries of abuse, but I bet he hadn't been in a fair barney in his life. He didn't fight back, even though the little git was the one with the fangs.

My attack was so fast and sudden – *Kenpo Karate, cheers for that* – you First Lifers reacted as if you were floating in space.

I straddled the conniving weasel, getting in as many good ones as I could because I wanted to make this count: for me, Donovan, Hartford, Ashanti, Vesper, even marie antoinette...

White, blinding, shuddering agony.

I collapsed backwards off the now sobbing Captain.

Wracked through every nerve - right to the fingertips and tingling toes - I absorbed the searing pain; I didn't even have the strength to scream. Then it was gone. Instead there was a curtain of black, tipped with scarlet: M.C.'s hair, my brutalised mind supplied.

'Dis be my yard,' M.C. hissed. 'A leech disrespect my yard..? Nah, we be having a boot party.'

M.C. dropped the tracker onto the table, before dragging me onto my knees. She booted me in the stomach with the heel of her foot – Kick Boxing – next my chest – Shotokan– and then with her open hand across my mug – Karate.

Through my bruised peepers, I watched M.C.'s blurred outline pace behind me, before the sudden agony, as she shoved me down onto my mush. She wrenched my wrist and hand up to my neck, like I was being nicked by a brutal copper.

Bloody blinding, she knew grapple holds too.

I tried to roll M.C. off, but she intensified the pressure, until my shoulder was about to pop out of its socket.

I could hear you yabbering in the background, through the haze. When at last I felt you drag your sister off me, I carefully lowered my arm. The joint settled back into place. I panted, before shakily hauling myself up.

Unfortunately, that meant I was staring at *Master*, who was giving me *that* look: the one, which I'd promised I'd never give him reason to direct at me.

Captain was quaking, his bloody stupid hair at all angles, as if he'd just had a wild session of hanky panky; scarlet dripped from his lips. He huddled next to *Master* - gormless prat that he was - as if for protection. He was prodding at his bloodied teeth. 'My fang,' he whimpered, before pointing at me dramatically, his finger quivering. I looked back innocently. 'You broke my fang, you...you...yob!'

I flipped him the two-finger salute.

Captain's cheeks puffed with righteous indignation, as he dived for M.C.'s tracker. M.C. stopped him, however, with a hand pressed to his slight chest. 'Humans only.'

Captain swivelled to *Master*, as if this must be a mistake. *Master* merely patted him on the back. Captain winced. 'It's been a right good meeting,' as Master steered Captain out of the apartment, I heard him placate, 'with your helpful information, we know the best tack.'

Then came Captain's wailed protest, 'But - I mean - this is an outrage...'

'We'll learn the boy, don't you worry.'

Finally, we were alone.

M.C. scuffed her boot against a table leg. 'If it was mine--'

'Well, he's not,' you edged between M.C. and me, 'and he never will be.'

'Whatever.'

I didn't like how M.C. smiled; apparently neither did you. 'What does..?'

'You be a wallad if you reckon dad'll let you keep it, if you can't control da liccle bitch. Dis be a business. We be professionals. Either you get with that or...'

'What?'

M.C. clicked her tongue. 'Are you a Cain or what?'

Master marched back in, before you could reply.

M.C. leant against the graffiti Manx with crossed arms.

'It...' *Master* dragged his thick black belt through its loops - *thwap*, *thwap*, *thwap* - and hurled it onto the white table with a *clatter*. The particles of sand quivered, as the globe trembled and then shivered out of existence. I stiffened. '...needs learning. Or do you want to send it back? Or mark it for the Estate?'

'He's mine,' you clutched my wrist so tightly I could feel blood rushing into bruises. 'No one's... I can do it. I'll train him on account of it's my responsibility. I promise - I'll prove it to you.'

'Don't work yourself into a fidge. I trust you.' *Master's* expression softened. 'Our books on slaves are plentiful. Did you read them?'

'She destroyed dem,' M.C. sneered, 'paper massacre, yeah?'

'It was an accident, like, when I was studying them,' you muttered.

'Marlane, ready us some drinks at the bar,' *Master* commanded.

M.C. looked as if she might argue but then she slouched further into the apartment.

Master slid his hand significantly down the coiled belt on the table, tapping the heavy bronze buckle, before tenderly clasping you by the shoulders. 'Learn it respect. Learn it what it means to belong to a Cain. Or I will.' He kissed your forehead. 'Show me you're still my daughter; I know I'll be fair proud of you.'

Then *Master* too was gone. And that left you and me.

Buggering hell.

You stood, head bowed, staring at that belt, as if it was one of your *Fiendish Sudoku*. You were sinking into black. I recognised the struggle. Except you'd already drowned in the dark.

Your daddy was too overpowering to fight.

Subdued, you reached out a shaking hand to pick up the belt, like it was venomous. You got as far as doubling it over, before not seeming to have the least clue what to do with it. It was a hell of a piece of leather.

I had the sudden urge to make this easier on you. Yet I didn't know where that impulse came from.

I sighed, limping over to the table. 'Get on with it.'

I wrenched off my pale grey jacket, tearing the ivory satin lining. I tossed it over a chair, before bending over the table. I planted my feet firmly a shoulder width apart. Then I rested my forearms on the cool surface, with my fingers splayed. Their imprints ghosted. I raised my nut and shoulders to stare at the opposite wall, so my back arched and offered you the best target (and me the worst bloody humiliation). It wasn't like I didn't remember the position.

Yet I'd come to hope – dream – it never would be for you.

Somewhere in the fantasy, which I'd spun in the long hours alone in the apartment, I wasn't really your slave.

I was simply Light, and you were simply Grayse.

I held my breath, when I heard you hesitantly come up behind me. 'Light...'

I wasn't dropping my kecks. I bloody wasn't. You'd have to use the wankering tracker on me, if you wanted to heap on that added schoolboy shame. And please don't make me count. And please – *please* - don't order me to *thank you* for every stroke. 'Go on.'

There was the *swish* of heavy leather and then – *crack*.

I jerked and gasped but I didn't cry out. I wouldn't give M.C. the satisfaction of hearing me bawl.

I realised, however, that I wouldn't be able to help bucking and squirming because you didn't have a scooby what you were doing, so your aim would be off: too high or too low. That'd bloody hurt.

A second *swish – crack.*

That one got my lower back. I stifled a yelp. My fingers curled.

Yeah, I was right, it did bloody hurt.

Swish – crack.

That third strike stung my thighs. I pulled to the side and then stilled myself with an effort. I could already feel the three raised welts glowing. I waited for the next blow.

Silence.

I clenched in anticipation.

Then I heard the *thump* of something heavy hitting the concrete, before I was gripped by the shoulders.

To my alarm, you spun me round to face you: it was the belt, coiled primeval-like, and it was you, not me, who was bawling.

'Are you happy now? You think I wanted to..? That I like..? Are you soft..?' You pounded your fists against me, and I let you. Then you were embracing me tighter than anyone has since Kathy. But just as fast, you shoved me away, furious. 'You know what? I hope it was worth it.'

So you want to know if it was *worth it*?

My arse hurts, so do my ribs, nut, guts, shoulder, wrist, thighs, back and every single nerve.

Yet the only thing I regret is that I didn't get to rip out Captain's heart. That's why old-fashioned pencils have their uses - at least then I could've staked the bastard.

The thing is, I'm haunted by those I left behind. By the memories of what I witnessed because of Blood Lifers like Captain.

You're a slaver.

Whether you like it or not, blood money buys you all your pretty things. Don't you want to hear how that blood money's earnt?

Then you can judge for yourself if it was *worth it*.

MAY 28

Every day I'd still fantasize someone besides *Sir* would come through those dark oak doors. But the daydreams were less substantial. Nothing was real except *Sir*. The blood I sucked from his fingers. The water (which I could now drink from a plastic cup like a *big boy*). And the chains around my contorted body.

I'd learnt commands for positions, which I could drop to at a word, only needing mild correction from *Sir's* bloody riding crop.

That was my narrowed world – the tiny, damp cell, with its constant overhead light and no demarcation of night or day - and I was slowly losing my mind.

Then came the time I heard the locks and scrambled to *kneel*: my legs spread, with feet together, sitting back on my heels but back held straight, my hands on my knees, with the palms up and peepers downcast.

The perfect little slave.

Yet next there wasn't the *click* of *Sir's* Oxford shoes, rather the *pad* of bare feet...

Shocked out of my obedience, I peeked up.

Another Blood Lifer.

He was starkers too, except for a silver ring, the same as mine. He looked young, like a matinee idol. His shining golden hair was slicked back over the crown of his nut. But with the power radiating from him, I knew he was a *Long-lived*.

Yet somehow there he was, standing scrutinizing me – todger out – plastic cup of water in hand and a bright smile, as if we were meeting over cocktails in a jazz lounge.

He couldn't be real.

I'd finally gone potty.

I started to giggle. Then for one even more barmy moment, my instinct was to holler for *Sir*.

Where was *Sir*? Why hadn't he come to see me today? Didn't he realise I needed him? Then I wanted to hurl with self-hatred.

Suddenly I felt this fellah's soft fingers stroking my cheek; I quietened.

He felt real.

'Are you..?' I managed to rasp.

'Poor little bunny. I heard the new one was all balled up.' The Long-lived's gentle American voice sounded concerned. It was a trick. Another mind-fuck to drag me deeper into bondage. When the bleeder held out the water, I didn't take it. 'Would you like a drink-avous?' He shook the beaker vigorously under my nose.

'No thanks, helmethead, I'm on the wagon-avous.' I replied with exaggerated slowness.

To my surprise, the bloke gave a delighted laugh. 'You slay me!' Then, with a nervous glance over his shoulder at the open door, he dropped to his knee, plonking down the cup. 'Lucky this joint serves an alternative.' The Long-lived raised his wrist to his mouth and bit. He winced, as he worried at the skin with blunt teeth (so I wasn't the only poor bastard, who'd been defanged). He tore a gash in the flesh, just enough for the blood to ooze out. He offered his wrist to me, as he had the water. 'For crying out loud – quick - before *Sir* sees.' I studied the bloke's expectant expression, whilst his scarlet wrist dangled before my mug. This Blood Lifer wasn't my Author or Blood family. Why would a stranger offer me something so intimate?

Impatient, he smeared my lips with his blood. 'Get a wiggle on. You're starved. You sure must've fought *Sir*. Real hard-boiled type, huh? Go on, drink.' The scent of the Long-lived's powerful blood was intoxicating. Trick or not, I was under its spell. The moment I'd licked my lips, it was too much: it hit me, like all of existence fracturing and being put together in the moment. I juddered, my peepers rolling back. Faster than I knew I could still move, I'd grabbed the Long-lived's wrist and was sucking. 'Attaboy'. I was vaguely aware he was threading his fingers through my matted hair, almost as if he knew just what I needed right then. But too soon he was pushing me off. 'Sorry mac, I can't spare anymore yet. On the level, it's not like we're fed much.'

'We?' I was still buzzing from the strength of the Long-lived's blood, which had given me a stiffy. There was no way to disguise it. Luckily, he was politely ignoring my faux pas.

'All the Blood Lifers in this joint – Abona House – that's where you are.'

I began to shake. In all my fantasies, I'd never imagined such a horrific possibility. 'But why? What's the bloody point?'

The bloke looked suddenly shifty, concentrating on licking over his wrist to accelerate its healing. 'For now just drink when you can and get strong. Promise me?'

I nodded, as he passed me the water. This time, I drank it. 'What's your name, mate?'

He didn't meet my eye, as he took the cup back. 'Cupid.'

I spluttered with laughter, but when his shoulders slumped, I was suddenly serious. *Yeah, wanker here*. 'Sorry, I... Your Blood Lifer name?'

'Don't futz around. I can't--'

'Mine's Light.' It was a whisper but it was still blinding to say it out loud.

The Long-lived, however, pressed his palm tight over my lips, like I'd blasphemed. His peepers were wide with terror. 'No, it isn't. I know this is bull, but you'll adapt. I'll help. We'll all help.'

I shoved his hand away, confused and angry. 'Helpful bunch, aren't you? Not like the Blood Lifers I know.'

'Sure, not now we're not,' for the first time, the Long-lived sounded truly despondent.

'How about you tell me your real name? Then I promise I'll eat and drink like a good boy.'

'Stop it, or I'll cast a kitten.'

I shrugged. 'Your choice.'

The Long-lived hesitated, before leaning close and murmuring so quietly I nearly didn't catch it, 'Hartford.'

Then Hartford jumped back, trembling, like he expected to be caught plotting treason. When nothing happened, Hartford brightened. He gave a delighted grin, with a clap of his hands; I understood his wave of joy at the reclaiming of his name after...

How long had he been held here..?

Hartford began singing, "I want Somebody to Cheer Me Up", in a voice so full of jazz soul it lifted me, until I was grinning like a berk as well.

Hartford twirled. He tap-danced. He mimed playing the ukulele.

Bang. Bang. Bang.

Three heavy knocks on the open oak door.

It was like the needle had been lifted off the record - cut dead - as Hartford dropped puppet-like to his knees next to me.

I could hear Hartford's fast, panted breathing. I recognised the fear and understood why: if it was possible to knock with a combination of sarcasm and threat, *Sir* had managed it.

I listened to the *click* of *Sir's* shoes, until their black leather was in my eyeline, stopped in front of Hartford; I was shot with unexpected remorse at my relief for that. I could hear the ominous tapping of *Sir's* red-and-black hide riding crop against his leg.

Why had I incited rebellion? I had a track record for encouraging other Blood Lifers to stand up to their oppressors.

And it never ended well.

The *click* again, as *Sir* strolled around Hartford. 'Knee-chest.'

Bugger it.

Without hesitation, Hartford fluidly shifted onto all-fours, before lowering his nut and chest to the concrete, so his vulnerable arse was left sticking up in the air. He laced his fingers behind his neck.

Swish – the stiff, spring steel rod slashed through the air, whacking Hartford's arse and jarring him forward. I flinched on Hartford's behalf because I'd cocked up, yet the Long-lived was taking the beating. A bloke, who'd blood shared with me. The connection wasn't biological or chemical. But it was a bond.

And now he was getting it - because of me.

Swish, swish, swish - until Hartford was striped with red welts, weals and purpling bruises. His pale skin broken.

I'd have been bawling after the first few vicious strokes, which were much harder than *Sir* had yet laid on me.

Hartford, however, hadn't made a whimper.

At last, *Sir* lowered the crop, *click, click, clicking* back round to the front. 'Kneel.'

Less fluidly, Hartford pulled up his thrashed body to *kneel*. Out of the corner of my eye, I saw him wince, as his arse hit his heels.

I felt even more of a bastard, when I saw the wetness down Hartford's cheeks and realised he'd been silently weeping.

'Thank you, *Sir*,' Hartford said softly.

Sir wrenched Hartford's hair back by the roots and calm as you like, asked, 'Did I give you permission to sing, whore?'

'No, *Sir*.'

'Then why were you singing?' *Sir* shook Hartford by the hair, like a cat worries a rat.

'I'm sorry, *Sir*.'

'You really must be one stupid leech.'

'Yes, *Sir*.'

'What are you?'

'A stupid leech, *Sir*.'

There was no hesitation. No flicker of defiance.

Bloody hell, was this my future?

I tried to shrink into the wall, when *Sir* stepped towards me, the riding crop flecked with blood swinging at his side.

'My pretty leech,' *Sir* crooned, caressing my cheek with such unexpected tenderness, you'd never have guessed he'd just given some poor geezer a hiding, 'did that bitch disturb you?'

I could've laughed or rent the world in two.

Hartford was still kneeling, unable to even wipe away the tear tracks. And I hadn't yet thanked him for the communion of blood.

Time to screw up my courage - and say *sod off* to my pride. 'No, *Sir*, he didn't. Your little leech appreciated *Sir's* kind gift of water and...'

'Yes?' There went the impatient *tap* of the riding crop's leather tongue.

'...for allowing me the company of another leech. But I missed you.'

I held my breath.

Sir settled himself next to me on the damp floor, drawing me onto his lap and petting my hair, as if I (rather than Hartford), was the one who needed comforting.

'*Sir* misses his pretty little leech too. But seeing as I'm awful busy, cupid and the other leeches will show you the ropes. It'll soon be time for you to start earning your keep.' I gritted my teeth. 'Look you, don't worry, I won't overtax your stupid little brain with too much at once.' *Sir* patted my nut, as if my reaction had been worry over Blood Lifer low IQ. 'As you're being a good boy, we'll take it slowly: if you can show me that you can behave.'

I nodded, dumbly.

Sir gave my nut a final pat, before sliding me off his lap. Then he grabbed Hartford by the chin, wrenching his mush up to examine it. 'Tidy, you can still work. Don't be long.'

I listened, as *Sir click, clicked* out of the cell.

I glanced at Hartford, who was shakily hauling himself up. 'Sorry,' I mumbled, 'about...'

Hartford waved my apology away. 'Don't be a sap; we're cool. That was swell - what you said. Defending me to *Sir*. Screwy but swell. You know he could've--'

'Given me a hiding? Like he did you?'

Hartford blushed. 'Yeah. But I'm used to it.'

'Yeah. But I got you into it.'

We grinned at each other for one daft moment like we really were mates. Or brothers.

Until a second Blood Lifer, nothing but a tumble of black hair, dark peepers ringed with kohl and lilac lipstick, stuck his nut in through the open doorway.

For a vomit inducing second, I reckoned yet again I must be barmy because here was the only Blood Lifer, who could call himself family: Donovan.

My cousin.

The last time I saw Donovan was in 1968. I melted his sadistic tyrant of a twin brother – Aralt - under the hot sun, like a candle.

I wondered whether Donovan was one for grudges.

'Hey, stop bugging the newbie,' Donovan called to Hartford, 'and let's split, baby.' *Bollocks, bollocks, bollocks...* I clutched my arms over my mush so Donovan, who was swaggering into my cell, wouldn't recognise my thin form. My thin, defenceless, chained form. 'I wanna--'

'I know what you wanna, baby. But pipe down, you're scaring the poor little bunny.'

'Poor little..?' I could feel them both studying me. Hartford made to block the other Blood Lifer, when Donovan edged closer, but he stumbled. 'What..?' Donovan gripped Hartford by the shoulders, twisting him round and inspecting every inch of his rainbow bruised arse and thighs, before checking over the rest of him, as delicately as if he was a porcelain doll. Then Donovan slammed his fist into thc mould blackened wall. 'I'm wiggin' out... This is...not cool. I'm gonna rip out his--'

'No, baby, you're not,' Hartford calmly raised Donovan's split knuckles to his lips, licking away the blood. It was so gentle, I didn't need to hear any words to know it was love. Even amongst the terror of discovery was a squirming gladness that at least Donovan had found love; psychotic pothead Donovan might've been but lonely too. And it wasn't like I didn't get how he felt. 'Anyway, when will you remember I'm three times your age, mac? And don't need no one fighting my battles?'

Donovan ran his fingers lightly over the weals on Hartford's arse, and Hartford flinched. 'Feels like it.' Donovan crouched next to me. I curled in further on myself. 'Has he always been this bummed out?'

'He was balled up but...' When I heard Hartford's troubled tone, I regretted his concern. Then I wondered where this conscience for other Blood Lifers had come from. *Strangers*, I reminded myself. Even Donovan had been nothing to me for decades. 'He's a swell fella, though. I thought he was, you know, doing better...until you came in.'

Donovan was stroking my back, reaching to pull me up and sooth me, as you would a wounded animal.

I tried to scramble backwards, but it was too late: Donovan had caught a glimpse of my mush.

Donovan transformed in the moment from compassion to raging fury.

Told you about the psychotic, yeah?

Donovan grabbed me by the throat, wrenching me up so far I reckoned my ankle would snap, as it cut against the chain. Then he slammed me against the wall – *oomph* – and all I could do was gasp for air.

It was through the fog of oxygen deprivation that I was aware of Hartford hollering at Donovan and then hauling him off me, although only enough for me to gasp in a couple of delicious lungful's.

Donovan, however, had waved Hartford away, and he'd retreated.

'This,' Donovan's nails dug deeper into my neck, 'is the blood kin, who murdered my twin. As well as killing the only Blood Lifer, who I've ever authored.'

I heard Hartford's shocked intake of breath.

Well, I admit, put like that...

'Come on, be fair, I only killed your brother after the wanker did in Alessandro. Remember him? The kid Aralt authored? He was your family too. Oh yeah, and tried to destroy the world behind your back? Not to mention the beatings and the... I did everyone a favour, mate. And Kira...she was...unfortunate...but she betrayed you. For your brother, remember?'

Donovan's grip tightened. Then to my surprise, he shrugged. 'It's cool. You're right about Kira. And Aralt wasn't my blood brother by the end; he chose not to be. I remember that too.'

Donovan let me down.

Yet before I even had time to collapse, Hartford had me crushed back against the wall. His slight form was like a sodding rhino. I wondered if *Sir* had any idea the danger he was in, if this power was ever directed at him. And then why it wasn't.

Hartford didn't need his venom to take out a First Lifer; every inch of him was a weapon.

I squirmed but I was pinned, like a butterfly. 'Bloody hell...'

'Let me level with you: whatever happened between you and Donovan is in the past. But if you hurt him now..? I'll torture you in ways, which were banned centuries before you were born. Are we clear, little bunny?'

'Crystal.'

Hartford dropped me, and I crumpled to the concrete. When he draped his arm around Donovan, I had to turn away.

My loneliness ate at me.

Yet hearing Hartford's voice, gentle now, I couldn't suppress a smile, 'I need to get to work but I'll be back to check on you soon.'

'Alright, toddle off then, helmethead.'

Hartford gave a delighted laugh.

I glimpsed Donovan's outraged expression, as he was bundled out of the cell and mollified by his bloke.

Blinding.

It was impossible to tell the passing of time in that bricked up, permanently light cell, except by sensation – hunger, thirst or pain – but the Blood Lifers did come back.

Both of them.

They brought another plastic beaker of water, which I guzzled gratefully, whilst they leaned against the wall snogging. I guessed they didn't get many chances, so feeding the sad sod in solitary was like sneaking off behind the bike sheds.

Finally Donovan settled cross-legged opposite and scrutinized me.

I eyed him back suspiciously. 'Alright?'

'What a crazy scene, huh? A real bummer.'

'Yeah, so they caught you too?'

'Man, I was having a blast, running this music company in New York. Not like Advance; I made sure it was managed properly this time. Then these punks--'

'Snap.' Donovan circled my bird-like wrist with his fingers and thumb. Our gazes met, before he glanced once at Hartford, over my shoulder. I didn't understand the seriousness of his expression, before he suddenly bit down on his own wrist once, twice, three times. *Bleeding hell, he was offering..?* 'No,' I spluttered, even as the blood was already trickling down Donovan's forearm.

'My baby isn't given enough blood to share,' Donovan pressed his wrist to my lips, 'but I am. Go on. We're tight, man.'

Tight?

I'd done in both the Blood Lifer he'd authored and his twin brother, yet here Donovan was offering up his blood? All he'd ever offered before was his wacky backy.

I latched on, sucking for all I was worth. Rich. Warm. Blood Lifer. I was singing, soaring, safe in the blood. I never wanted to leave its embrace.

I reckon I must've passed out from the overload because when I came to, Donovan and Hartford were sitting either side of me, chin-wagging. I experienced the first moment of surreal normality since I'd been kidnapped.

'Here he is,' Hartford grinned, 'Sleeping Beauty awakes.'

'Right on, see I've got righteous blood.'

'You're a goof. He's just so starved, poor--'

'Don't say *poor little bunny*.'

'Why? Jealous, *baby*?'

'Just don't call me sodding *shadow* and I'll be sorted,' I licked my lips, settling myself against the wall. 'Cheers, that was--'

'What Hartford did for me.' I glanced at Donovan, but his kohl smudged peepers were carefully lowered.

'How long..?' I caught Hartford's eye. I knew he understood.

'How's a fella to know? No newspapers, radio, calendars...jeepers creepers, no outside world at all. On the level, we don't exist. Except as slaves. The sooner you accept that--'

'I'm not a slave.'

'Oh yeah?'

'I'll never be a slave.' Strange, I meant it, when I said it.

Bloody stupid git.

'Sure, so says the naked man,' Hartford pointed out, 'who's locked up, beaten, starved and at the mercy of his Masters.'

Frustrated, I pushed myself onto my knees. 'That's not what makes you a sodding slave: this does.' I tapped my forehead.

Hartford hastily turned away. But I'd still seen it: the devastation.

I was an ungrateful prat.

Donovan shoved past me, getting in a good elbow. He plonked himself next to Hartford, wrapping his arms around him.

Hartford smiled. 'You sure are a cuddler, baby.' Then, however, he was grave. 'It comes later, the...' He tapped his forehead. 'I've been in this joint... I was the first. Master caught and bagged me, like I was a hunting trophy. And since then? This is my life. It's no line that at the beginning I was just like you.' He shuddered, as if at a horrific memory. Donovan's arms tightened. I wished I had Kathy to hold me. Or even Ruby. Except I didn't - because I'd never inflict this hell on them. I suddenly understood just how terrible it must be to watch the one you love suffer and be unable to save them. 'The First Lifers taught me not to be like you. And now..?' I hated the hopelessness on Hartford's mush. 'I'd have to be screwy to go seeking more pain, when things'll never change. They'll teach you too little bunny. The Cains always do.'

After that, both Donovan and Hartford continued visiting me.

I nurtured the tiny, flickering flame of hope I'd escape my cell and chains. At least I was filling out though and growing stronger, fed by the nourishing Blood Lifer blood.

In between *Sir's* training and the boredom, Donovan and Hartford's mushes popping around the oak door were enough to have me bouncing with something, which I hadn't felt for so long I barely recognised it. The joy of companionship.

I'd only ever had one mate before: Alessandro.

Now, however, I was truly alone. And Donovan and Hartford were all that anchored me.

Sometimes they'd bring water, food (thin gruel and dry bread - these humans had been reading too much Dickens), and depending on *Sir's* capricious mood, honest to goodness blood. At least I got a flask to hold in my own two hands – *all grown up now, see daddy?*

I grew used to us being starkers. Hartford had been right: a bloke can be taught a lot.

Donovan and Hartford would sit side by side with me, waffling on about something or nothing, trying to take my mind off the present. They'd both been through this. They understood how precious snatched minutes of *normal* life were.

I noticed, however, that they returned to work with as little enthusiasm, as I watched them leave. I wondered what they did. But Hartford would never talk about it, even when he appeared beaten, sliced by razors or blackened with blisters.

I became used to Donovan's explosions of impotent fury and Hartford's own weary acceptance.

It hurts thinking of those two, whilst I'm out here. I might be bruised and sore but I'm with you - in the world - whilst they're stuck away in Abona.

One of our favourite games was to outdo each other with our hunting stories.

Because competitive blokes here, yeah?

By the time we were done, we could taste the First Lifer blood warm and feel the cool of the night air. We'd transformed once again into fanged predators pounding with freedom.

'Groupies,' Donovan sighed dreamily.

Hartford shook his nut. 'Jazz babies: now there was a treat! All those blotto dolls in loose dresses, with looser morals, wanting to have a good time. I was in Chicago when it was the hard-boiled gangsters running the cabarets and the dance clubs; now they knew how to throw a party. Later the place to be was New York, where I'd hunt The Cotton Club to the throb of Duke Ellington. Have a smoke. Have a snort. Some skirt up for some nookie and then... Pulse of the blood and the jazz in synchronicity...' Hartford's peepers shuddered closed, as we all licked our lips in sympathetic memory. 'I'd sneak into the Rosewood Ballroom to hear Louis Armstrong play, even when I wasn't on the hunt.'

'Right on, sounds a blast. But you did say *skirt*, baby?'

I saw Hartford bite back a smile. 'What's eating you? There were swanky fellas too, but I was lynched once already,' my mind trapped his throwaway comment, shuddering with shock, 'do you think I'm enough of a goof to have danced the Charleston with a fella?'

Donovan shrugged, sulkily.

'Lay off, baby.' When Hartford swung Donovan to his feet, I cowered back, clutching my arms over my mush.

I reckoned Hartford's true nature had reasserted dominance and a blazing Long-lived was about to show us just what he could truly do.

Hearing only laughter, however, I carefully lowered my arms again.

Hartford was tossing Donovan around the cell in a spirited Charleston.

Suddenly I felt myself grabbed by both hands and dragged into the dance. I tried to protest, thinking they'd forgotten about my chained ankle. Along with the fact I *don't sodding dance.*

They were careful, however, like I was their kid.

I finally twigged they'd been pulling me out of my despair just as carefully.

Maybe rescue *had* walked through those dark oak doors.

My favourite times were when Donovan would risk shutting us in soundproofed, and we'd sprawl together on the cold floor.

Then Hartford would sing.

Nobody knows the troubles I've seen...

Spirituals, gospel or jazz, we were freed on their wings.

Nobody knows but Jesus...

Hartford didn't have permission to sing. It was one of the motivators that right bastard *Sir* held over him, like doggy treats. Maybe Hartford did have some balls left after all.

Nobody knows the trouble I've seen...

There was an intense sorrowfulness in Hartford's tone. Yet there was also a deep hope and faith. I wished I could bloody share it. Even though

I didn't, however, Hartford's strength sustained me. I wondered if that was what being Long-lived truly meant.

Glory hallelujah!

One time when Hartford had limped in, his back and arse bleeding, like he'd been thrashed with something meant for animals (a bullwhip I reckoned), Donovan slammed the door. Then he clasped both Hartford's hand and mine, until we were standing in a Wiccan circle.

Hartford's haunting voice started up... *When Israel was in Egypt's land...* The song suddenly swung into jazz... *Tell old Pharaoh...* I had Hartford wrong, he still had *all* his balls: *Sir* definitely figured himself a sodding Pharaoh. Donovan and I found ourselves impromptu backup singers, with wide grins on our mugs and our fingers entwined... *Go down* (*go down*)... Our bodies swayed... *Moses* (*Moses*)... Our melded voices echoed off the bare walls; we raised them as loudly as we bloody could... *Tell old Pharaoh...* It was the sort of release, which purged the Soul and bonded us as intimately as blood sharing... *Let my people go* (*let my people go!*).

'Even they can't take everything,' Hartford said, once the echo of our voices had died, 'a fella's voice is still his own: *I'm* still me, aren't I?'

'Yeah, baby,' Donovan's grasp tightened, 'always.'

It was Hartford's mellow voice, which transported us to freedom. Even if he'd never done anything else, he did more for me in that, than I'd ever dreamed a Blood Lifer would.

And he *did* do more.

Christ in heaven did he.

It was Donovan, however, who was finally straight up with me about what went on in Abona.

'*Sir's* training you.' Hartford was leaning in the far corner, refusing to look at Donovan. I'd sparked a lovers' tiff. 'He must reckon you're a righteous stud because he's never taken this personal an interest or gone this slow before.'

'Lucky me.'

'No, man,' Donovan shook his nut, 'it's not cool. See, you want to be invisible here. Us three? I guess we're in this cell right now because we don't bow to the man.'

'But why the hell do those wankers even want Blood Lifer slaves?'

'Bread, of course: how much do you reckon they charge each client? They can schedule ten appointments a night, or it'd blow your mind the lolly a whole night rakes in, if the client wants that. Plus some have to because they like to play rough--'

'Pipe down for crying out loud,' Hartford rushed at Donovan, slamming him against the wall.

I was shaking, the world fuzzed to grey. It wasn't as if it was a shock - I knew what I was now. But stated stark like that?

It made it real: there was no hiding.

Donovan squirmed but he couldn't dislodge the Long-lived. 'Hey, don't freak out. You reckon it's better he only learns the truth the first time a cock's rammed--'

Slap. Donovan's nut snapped to the side.

There was a silence.

Then Donovan mumbled, 'I'm sorry. But he has to know.'

'And what am I?' Hartford asked, 'Just a whore?'

Donovan's peepers filled with tears. 'Never to me.'

'And you? What are you Donovan?' I said quietly.

When Hartford pushed himself away, I could see the bruises crescented on Donovan's shoulders. Donovan ran his fingers through his unruly hair. 'Not pretty enough for first choice. Unlike you and...' he glanced at Hartford. 'I'm one of the servants. It's a real drag: we cook, clean, wash...you know, man, run the house and Estate. Then there are others--'

'The Enforcers,' Hartford hissed. I'd never heard him sound like he could stake someone before but bugger it, he did now.

'It's the old divide and conquer trick. Not all Blood Lifers spread the love, they're more into rising up the ranks. Marie antoinette is the worst. This skirt is practically in love with *Sir*. If you're prepared to work for the First Lifers and keep the rest of us in line, *Sir* grants privileges: books, nights outside, even threads. Blood Lifers oppressing each other for an extra shot of pigs' blood a day..? Bummer. Of course Hartford? He's also *Sir's* favourite chew toy.'

'So bloody fight back.' I clambered up, forgetting all caution in my eagerness.

'Says you, who's never even been out of this cell.' Hartford darted towards me, easing me gently back down again.

'But if the others knew--'

'Lay off, what others? Blood Lifers? Who'd be caught as easily as we were? Or the humans?' Hartford spat out *humans* with bitter contempt, before glancing at Donovan, who gave a small nod. Then they both crouched next to me. Donovan clasped Hartford's hand, playing with his fingers; the slap was obviously forgiven. 'Let me tell you a story.'

'I've heard enough of those, cheers.'

'That so? What about how I died?' I shifted, averting my gaze. Us Blood Lifers don't talk to each other about how we died as a rule: it's intimate, like exposing your goolies to another predator. 'Salem witch trials weren't the first of their kind in America. My home town of...' He hesitated, before forcing the word out fast in a whisper, 'Hartford, Connecticut, had that privilege in 1662. All it took was little Elizabeth coming home from her neighbour Goodwife Ayres', taking ill and saying, 'Father! Father! Goodwife Ayres is upon me. She chokes me.' Maybe it was all hooey - or a fever - but whatever, Elizabeth dies, and before I knew it there were accusations of bewitchment from folks I'd considered neighbours and friends. I thought it was just folks beating their gums. Yet up went the gallows in our Meeting House Square, and there were my friends baying for the woman's blood, as poor skirts and fellas were dunked in the pond, as if witches really couldn't sink. Sure I'm a man of god but natural philosophy too, so when I tried to argue against this madness? Suspicion fell on me. When I fought to stop them bumping off the third innocent, my goodly neighbours dragged me from my bed one night into my yard. Then the ring leader – John - a fella I'd known my whole life and crushed on too since I was old enough to realise I felt like *that* about him, demanded I confess. Confess I *danced with the Devil* and spill about my other wizarding collaborators in town. I spat in his eye. So they tied a noose around my neck and swung me from my own sugar maple.' I saw Donovan's hand tighten around Hartford's. 'My Author saved me. He elected me into Blood Life. First Lifers? They'll never save us, my poor little bunny. If the masses discover we exist? There'll be nothing but hysteria and death. That's why I took the name...' I saw the struggle, understanding it properly at last. I didn't push. Frustrated, Hartford shook his nut. 'Because I don't want to forget.'

The next time I saw Hartford, he was alone.

But *Sir* was close on his heels.

Sir wasn't wearing a jacket and his salmon pink shirt was unbuttoned at the neck and rolled up at the elbows. He wasn't carrying that blasted riding crop. Yet there was something about his casual dress - Mr Corporate on a day off - which spooked me, as did the nonchalant way he caught Hartford by the shoulder, giving the tender flesh a squeeze.

Hartford tried to catch my eye, as I scrambled to *kneel*: I understood it as a warning.

Sir barked out, 'Inspect'.

Submissively, as if following a drill he'd done for years, Hartford stood several yards from the wall, leaning his palms flat against it, his back arched and legs shoulder width apart. He glanced over his shoulder at me.

Audience participation was it?

Reluctantly, I pushed myself up and stood next to Hartford, copying his stance. I hadn't realised how humiliating it'd be: staring at that blank wall, with my arse stuck out.

Then I heard one of the sounds no one ever sodding wants to hear behind them, especially if they're standing starkers, hands against a wall, with their goolies hanging free: the *snap* of a medical glove being pulled on.

I reared up, but Hartford snatched at my wrists, yanking me back into position.

I couldn't help, however, having a sneaky shufti over my shoulder, as *Sir* moved behind Hartford.

This was to be a lesson for me then, with Hartford as example.

Were we nothing but poseable dolls?

Sir rested one hand on the pale small of Hartford's back, as if to calm a skittish horse, the other - comical gloved in vivid purple plastic - fondled the Long-lived's goolies, before slipping forward to his todger. A shudder ran through Hartford but then he was still again. Next that purple hand was tracing backwards.

I tried to shove down my stampeding panic.

But then it happened. That thick, dry finger, inched inside...

Hartford's body became rigid. I could hear his panted breaths. Then a second finger joined the first and a third finger decided it didn't want to be left out. When *Sir* crooked them, Hartford jerked, as if jolted by electricity.

Finally, those purple fingers withdrew.

'All in working order, whore.' *Sir* patted Hartford on the rump, almost affectionately. I saw him toss the glove aside, before – *snap*.

That next one had my name on it.

Click, click, click. *Sir* was close behind me; the reek of citrus wrapped me in its choking hold.

I was meant to be showing *Sir* my gratitude. But this..?

I could feel Hartford looking at me. I could almost hear him willing me to just shut up and take it. Like he had. Yet I couldn't figure *why* he had. He was a Long-lived, and *Sir* was only a First Lifer.

'You want to keep those fingers?' I said, without moving, 'I'd think twice about where you stick them.'

I heard Hartford draw in his breath.

But from *Sir*?

Silence.

I tensed. Then I found myself smashed face first into the wall, shattering my cheekbone. My arm was twisted high up behind my back – *pop* – there went my shoulder socket.

Still, a bloke's arse is worth a shoulder if you have to choose.

And I did.

'Look you, my pretty leech, what you don't realise in that stupid, worthless little brain,' *Sir's* mouth was so close to my lobe I could feel the alien softness of his lips, 'is there be two types of clients, see, in the Blood Club. There are those who fuck Blood Lifers for the unique experience. It's like a sex safari. They'll be gentle with you, like I am, even when you're bad.' He shoved me harder into the wall and I gasped, as my cheekbones shifted. 'But the second type? Now they're all about the pain, seeing as you leeches can take it and heal. They pay because they can do such things,' I felt *Sir's* mouth curve into a smile, as I had no doubt he was looking at Hartford, 'that if they did them to a human...well, they'd be monsters, isn't it? Now, who do you think decides which type of client sees which of you sluts?' *Sir* stroked up and down the back of my neck with mock tenderness, teasing the strands of hair.

'Mick Jagger?' *Sir's* grip on my twisted arm tightened. 'Stephen Hawkins? Germaine Greer? Eddie Izzard? Stop me when I get close.'

The punch to my kidneys set off a coughing fit.

'You know I can plug you with something bigger than my finger, boyo. Make sure you feel it.'

I was trembling but I didn't start the tirade of pathetic begging, which I knew *Sir* craved.

Not this time.

Out of the corner of my eye, I saw Hartford straighten. I couldn't understand what he was doing because he never moved out of position without permission.

Then when I realised what was happening, I was cold with choking guilt. I tried, just once, 'Don't, please, don't--'

'Not good enough. You've been a very bad little leech.' *Sir* reckoned I was begging him.

I bloody wish I had been.

It was one shove.

Considering Hartford's strength, it wasn't even hard. But it sent *Sir* stumbling backwards.

Then the two of them stood there: Hartford, stunned he'd dared raise his hand against his master, and *Sir* equally astonished, like a beaten dog had dared to bite back.

I remained with my mug crushed into the wall. I was too ashamed to watch what I'd incited. Instead, I listened.

Horrified, I heard *Sir* stalking Hartford into the far corner - *click, click, click* - never raising his voice or fists. He didn't need to.

'*Sir*, I--'

'Lie down.'

Then there was the sound of a zipper being lowered...

My face against that wall, I heard every moment. Tears streamed down my mush too because Hartford was taking it for me. Again. He'd known he would. He'd chosen it.

I swore then I'd never forget what he'd done for me. Or what I owed.

Hartford was my family now, the same as Donovan; I didn't bleeding care about biology or evolution.

Hartford had copped it in First Life because of his sense of justice. In Blood Life his self-sacrifice was amplified. I was afraid it'd get him done in - unless I saved him first.

I will save my family.

So, you wanted to know if it was *worth it*?

What do you reckon?

Those babes to darkness in the Blood Life Council gave us up to...that.

Give me a hiding every day if you have to. These memories will always plague me. Haunt my waking hours.

But my family are real. They're imprisoned right this moment in that...brothel in Abona.

You know how you earn your lolly now. Has the truth been flayed raw?

Because we sodding were.

So let me ask you this: are all the pretty things you buy worth it?

MAY 30

Last night, you allowed me out for the whole night by myself.

I'm sitting here under the bright sun of the fresco - the Manx watching – as the journal is spread out in front of me on the shining mahogany dining room table and it's like I daydreamed it.

Yet I can still feel the night burning in my gut.

When I'd woken up, fluffy-headed under the duvet, I'd noticed the journal had been moved from the corner, where I'd hurled it. It'd been tidied back onto the crochet lace bedside table.

As if it was important.

Maybe you'd had a butchers? Because you decided to let me out that night, with the promise of no cameras or handholding. And the symbolic turning off of the bastard tracker.

Free. Even if it was only for one night.

I don't have to tell you what happened.

But me and you? Whatever *this* is...Stockholm Syndrome or...

Last night, however, you gave me back something, which I'd reckoned lost: I was a true Blood Lifer, alone again in the world.

I prowled the black, under the wide, white moon, led only by my blood. I was exultant in my anonymous freedom, camouflaged once more in the warm night dark.

Gangs of blokes wandered the vomit splattered pavements, searching out strip clubs or brothels, kebabs or cheesy chips, cocaine or cabs home. Cruisers were hanging around a public khazi; I glimpsed a couple shagging against a wall in the shadows of an alley. Junkies slumped in self-induced trances, or crouched in payphones inhaling crack pipes. One bint, who was off her nut on ketamine, drooled and dodged honking cabs.

This was London.

My London.

Where no one knew or cared who I was and I was safe even in the darkest of worlds.

I slipped your iPod out of the pocket of my jacket, worming in the earbuds. After all these months of sensory deprivation, it was blinding.

But your taste in music? It's so bland it may as well be white noise. What you need are the greats: Billy Fury and THE FOUR JAYS, Jimi Hendrix and The Sex Pistols.

So I'd uploaded them.

Because your passwords..? They hadn't been difficult for a bloke like me to memorise from a glance over your shoulder.

In the dark, I put on The Rolling Stones. It was like coming alive. Around me, London took on a psychedelia - a clash of experimental chaos.

I ran and ran and... *Alessandro.*

My hands curled into fists, as I jumped benches and scaled walls.

The music spun me back to the summer of 1968, when I'd discovered my Blood Lifer family. The Stone's *Their Satanic Majesties Request* had been Alessandro's favourite in his obsessive vinyl collection.

Alessandro was my mate: my first and only.

Yet I bloody got him killed.

I stopped running, panting for breath. I rested my forehead against the cool brick of an alley.

See, there's the problem: the last time I played at hero, someone else paid the price. I tried to be the leader and I cocked it up; I'm scared I will this time too. I incited the innocent to rise against his tyrant of an Author.

I incited Alessandro to his death.

Until I met Hartford and Donovan, I was alone.

With Kathy I was always a Blood Lifer in a First Lifer world. Now I have mates again – *family* - and I can't bugger it up.

When the otherworldly harpsichord started of "In Another Land", I forced myself on towards a park, which was dark with leathery-leaved plane trees.

When a desolate wind swept across an empty plain on the track, I felt it keenly - the loneliness and dislocation. It plunged me back into the despair of Abona. Then began the drumbeat. Like a heartbeat. A coming alive.

I was sprinting now, desperate to reach those trees, with an animalistic instinct for shelter and panicked flight.

And that's when I thought of you. And I calmed, slowing, until I was jogging again.

In this strange, new world I'd found myself in, yours was the only hand I'd had to hold. I'd reckoned it'd been proprietorial. A sign of ownership. That I wasn't the nancy boy type to need hand holding. Only maybe the truth was *I did.*

Maybe the truth was *you* did too.

Once, when I was visiting London from our home in Watford with my papa, I let go of his hand. I didn't realise it straight away, but it was nearly the end of me.

By letting go, I risked losing everything.

We were on Regent Street outside Bassano's, surrounded by a gaggle of grave men in overcoats and sober suits, with side-whiskers or neat beards, which ran under their chins, who were debating the relative merits of using paper or glass negatives.

Paper had revolutionised the photographic process by producing not one negative but hundreds: multiple identical twins. A man's youth enslaved for eternal parade.

I half-listened, restlessly shifting under the molten summer sun. Sweat trickled under my collar.

Papa was extolling glass coated with collodion (gun cotton dissolved in ether). It sharpened the prints to mimic real life: photography not as art. But truth.

Folks were passing in and out of the studio in a steady stream to record forever the rites of passage: a nurse with a babe in arms, who'd achieved the feat of sitting unaided and a lanky youth (not much older than me), who in his shiny new suit was celebrating his first job.

Then my little fingers slipped out of papa's larger hand in the heat of his debate.

And I was free.

At first, I stood there, obedient. In these London expeditions, I was papa's joint explorer. Today, however, in the height of the afternoon sun, I was narked because papa had insisted on holding my hand, like I was not yet in breeches.

Papa had blamed *the Season*, saying he didn't want me to be *swept way*. Yet I'd also heard him muttering to mama his promise to keep tight hold of *precious Light* because kids were being snatched for *unnatural crimes*.

When I'd asked papa about it, however, he'd blushed in a way I'd never seen before.

Papa had always urged me to seek out knowledge. To question everything. And what I'd learnt that day was all adults had secrets.

I stared around at the thronging street.

It was terraced and stuccoed, with parades of shops. Tides of carriages washed down the dusty, wooden thoroughfare, rattling and clattering; their panels glittered and the flanks of their horses gleamed. I caught glimpses of golden tresses, lilac muslins and cravats in the cushioned interiors. Blokes, birds and kids of every class and type - duchesses, foreign counts and schoolboys - chattered, laughed, lounged and ebbed and flowed along the street, free to explore its delights.

I peeked once more up at my papa, who was still intent on his debate. He hadn't cottoned on that he'd broken his promise to keep hold of his *precious Light*.

Then I melted away silently into the crowds, allowing them to carry me along. I figured I could sightsee and be back before papa even missed me.

I was heady with the excitement of Regent Street. I've always wanted *more* – more than childhood. London. England. The world. First Life. My own skin. Ruby. More than... Sometimes I don't even bloody know.

Then, I thought Regent Street was it, with its fancy shops and temptations.

I wandered from glass-plate window to glass-plate, passing footmen leaning in the stores' doorways. I gazed at the rich, paisley patterned shawls, tiered cape jackets and ribboned or feathered bonnets on pegs, before resting my fingers against a confectioner's window. My stomach growled at the glorious sight: piles of buns, cakes, bon-bons, jellies, preserves and round, glistening barley-sugar cages. I forced myself away from the delicious treats, jostled as I tried to have a gander at the itinerant vendors, who were calling out to passers-by in jovial patter, their wares laid out on the kerb: prints, stain-cleaning pastes and mosaic gold chains.

Fascinated, I was listening to an Italian boy grinding a piano organ, when I noticed a dealer hawking spaniel pups at the lamppost. He had one of the tiny things captured in his colossal, weathered hands, and it was kicking its front legs piteously.

I struggled through the crowds, weighing up papa's reaction if I returned with one of the back-and-white bundles with dark, sad peepers stowed in my pocket. The dog could be my mate: I didn't have one of those. I only hesitated because papa might drown it; I wasn't sure - for the first time - if I trusted adults anymore.

That's when I felt the fingers curl around my arm.

I stiffened. 'Papa..?'

'That's right, my pretty little boy. How bad you are for running off.' Terror, like I'd never experienced before. *That wasn't papa.* Too nasal. Too harsh. The bloke smelled wrong too: mildewy. And the hand was huge in a too neat glove. I tried to wrench away, but the man's grip tightened... *Snatched for unnatural crimes...* I swung my fist, catching the bastard a hook under his bearded chin. 'You wretched rat!'

The man, who wore a seedy linen suit and whose oily hair was smartly parted (at least I'd knocked off his top hat), caught my two wrists in his one strong hand. Then he hauled me up by my middle; my legs kicked ineffectually. He snatched up his top hat, ramming it back onto his nut.

The spaniel seller sniggered, as if this was all part of a shared adult joke.

Hot tears sprang into my peepers. Why couldn't he see – why couldn't everyone see – I was being kidnapped?

'Papa! Papa--'

'Shut up, you little...' the bloke hissed, squeezing me, until it was painful.

Still I didn't stop hollering, 'Help! Help! Papa--'

At last, thank Christ in heaven, a gentleman in quilted overcoat, who was resting on a fancy silver walking stick, tapped the wanker on the shoulder with an imperious knuckle. 'See here, my good man, what is this rumpus about?'

'My papa--'

The tosser slapped his hand over my mouth. Then his wily mug smoothed into an expression of utter consternation. 'Such a wicked lad. Incorrigible. The worst of liars. A runaway.'

At once the kindly gentleman's concern transformed into a stern frown.

I wilted. Because wasn't the wanker right? I *had* run away. This was my fault.

I stopped struggling, although I couldn't stop the tears, which were now mostly of shame.

This seemed to confirm what the gentleman was looking for because he gave a curt nod. 'My apologies, sir. But you hear such things just now. I was only doing my civic duty. Still, boys are cunning creatures. Quite despicable. I hope you don't intend to spare the rod?'

The kidnapper's mouth slid into a nasty curve of a leer. 'Have no concern on that head, sir.'

I lay limply in the man's arms, as he dragged me off Regent Street, further from my papa and towards Piccadilly, on a long, ugly road.

It was as if every step, I was lost a little more to a darkness, which I hadn't known existed until that moment.

I'd wanted *more*: knowledge and the adult world.

Well, looked like I was going to bloody get it, didn't it?

We passed a dark livery, coming to a brick and tile Stuart house, which was attached to it.

I could see pale kids (boys the same as me), peering down out of the windows. The terror returned: once I was trapped inside that Stuart house, I wasn't getting out again.

'Home sweet home. You're to be my bitch's shadow.' The kidnapper was stroking my hair, like I was his doll.

No one had ever touched me in quite that manner before: it made me shudder. So the next time the kidnapper's hand moved down to my mush, I turned my nut, catching his fleshy palm between my gnashers. And *bit*.

The bastard let out a roar, like a bull, as he shook me. But I wouldn't let go. He dropped me to the muddy pavement, clouting me, until I saw stars. Gasping, I legged it.

There were a few steps of intoxicating freedom. Until the tosser tripped me.

The man boxed my ears, as he hauled me inside, still fighting for all I was worth.

'Let go...'

My kidnapper threw me to the tiled floor, and I hit my knees hard.

When I looked up through my tear blurred peepers, I thought for a moment I must be facing a looking glass, except...this other boy was dressed in a flimsy cotton shirt. And no kecks. His peepers were rimmed with kohl and his lips tinted with rouge, like some beautiful boy-girl. Except one of his peepers was purpled and he was ghost-white.

He was some posh gentleman's fetishized fantasy.

Shocked out of my own distress, I pushed myself up, as I stared at my twin, whilst he studied me.

'Look what I've found, my little bitch, a twin Mary-Ann for you. Your shadow. The punters'll pay a pretty penny for the two of you together. You train him up good and quick, you hear?'

I knew *bad* things, *immoral acts* and *unnatural crimes* were going to be done to me, even if I didn't know what they were.

I tried not to show my fear, yet I knew I was trembling.

'Those threads? Kid like him? He's not workhouse or off the street. No foundling or orphan.' I don't know why I was surprised by my twin's soft Spitalfields accent, as if I was expecting to hear my own voice reflected back at me. 'So where'd you get this one from then, Mr Dabs?'

Smack - I flinched, when Mr Dabs clobbered the boy in the mush – *smack* - before copping him a mouse in the other peeper. 'Never you mind where. He's mine now.'

I bristled. 'My papa--'

'Ain't your papa now. This is your home.' I gazed round at the low-ceilinged room, which was hung with heavy purple drapes and had a tatty chaise longue and oak cupboard. 'I'm your papa and you...have been very naughty.' When he shook his sore hand, I was dead proud of the inflamed scarlet bite. 'Little bitch, fetch the cane.' My insides froze. I stood still though, whilst the other boy reluctantly opened the cupboard. When my twin pulled out a long rattan cane with a crooked handle, which looked like it could thrash you half to death, I took a step back. 'You, brat,' Mr Dabs pointed at the end of the chaise longue, 'lower your breeches and bend over.' When I didn't move, Mr Dabs sucked his yellowing teeth in irritation. The other boy was holding the cane, like it was loathsome even to touch, which told me he'd often felt its bite. Our gazes met; there was something dark and questioning in his, which I didn't understand. But he didn't hand the cane over to Mr Dabs. 'Come on, little bitch, or do you want a thrashing too?'

My twin startled, yet he still hesitated. Then I could see it: the moment he came to a decision. He squared his shoulders. Then he gave me a cheeky half-smile, before he brought down the cane in a full swishing *crack* on Mr Dab's sly mush.

Mr Dabs howled and crumpled.

'Scarper!' The boy yelled, grabbing me by the arm and dragging me to the front door, 'Go on then.'

Shocked, I stumbled out into the light, expecting to see my twin behind me.

But he was slamming the door...imprisoning himself with the enraged Mr Dabs.

I legged it as fast as I ever had, back to Regent Street and Bassano's. And back to my distraught papa, who furious, grabbed me sharply by the shoulders.

When papa caught sight of my swollen mush, however, he clasped me close, whilst I wrapped my arms around his waist. I no longer cared how much of a baby I looked, as I sobbed.

'You let go, Light,' papa said softly, allowing me to hold onto him, as the tears fell. 'You let go of my hand.'

For me, that afternoon on Regent Street was only a brief glimpse of a dark world, before I twisted away.

I don't reckon, however, that my rent boy twin ever escaped. As if he were my whipping boy, he lived out my planned fate.

That memory didn't come fresh re-lived to my mind, until I was slouched last night on a bench in the park under the plane trees, the scruffy crows shuffling in the branches, opposite a rainbow-bruised tramp.

I thought of holding your hand and that sparked those past ghosts.

All right then, so maybe my whipping boy lived out his First Life longer than I survived, although for his sake, I hope he didn't. His best prospect was to have ended up as some rich man's toy.

I guess that means I truly *am* his twin now, doesn't it?

When the spotters came hassling to register me as homeless, I dived over the fence to find a 24 hour café.

I hunkered down over a coffee with the cabbies, blood-splattered butchers from the markets, rickshaw drivers, whose vehicles were abandoned half-on, half-off the pavement outside and the ropey looking hookers, who were knackered from a night of sucking and shagging. Outside a noisy street cleaner swept past, clearing away London's detritus: pig heads, sycamore leaves, coffee cups, chip cartons, chewing gum and ciggie butts.

I'd bought myself a fag at a convenience store but threw it in the gutter after one drag. It felt wrong in my hand.

Your e-cig it was then.

I puffed and drank and in that café of night walkers, I thought.

I knew I should return to you. I could feel the pull of dawn and could see the purple bruising to the night sky, which warned of the rising sun.

Yet I was crippled by sudden desperation.

I smoked my e-cig, as if stuck to that plastic chair, like I'd never get my arse out of it and back to you, even if the sun's rays shone clear through the glass and melted me to the seat.

Haven't you ever wanted to end it? No memories to haunt. No guilt. Nothing to strive for or endure? But I made a promise to Kathy before she died that afterwards I'd live.

Kathy had dementia, but the promise came early on, when we weren't lost to each other. It looks like a bleeding stupid thing to have done now. But then you didn't think you were condemning me to eternal slavery, did you, my Moon Girl?

Just an eternity alone because that's the thing about you First Lifers: you age and die. Yet you reckon *you're* the superior species..?

Evolution wouldn't agree.

Kathy left me alone in the dark, and I'm still here.

Crawling out of the black, Kathy once told me, would be my redemption. I never thought redemption would be this much of a bitch.

Then I remembered you needed me to hold your hand too, downed the dregs of my cold coffee and scarpered, the dawn at my back.

When you swung the apartment door open to my banging and hauled me in by my jacket, you were pale and anxious, wearing those fluffy pink check pyjamas, which were never a good sign. 'Where the frig have you been? I thought you'd forgotten the dawn.'

I started. The only other person, who's ever cared enough to say that to me - *don't forget the dawn* - was Kathy.

'I never forget the dawn, darlin'. It just forgets me.'

We looked at each other. Then for the first time burst into exhausted, overstrung giggles.

Strangely, returning now didn't feel like giving up my freedom.

As I lay in bed, I remembered the bottle of my little whipping boy twin, squaring his shoulders and risking everything for another boy, just because he had a proper home and a papa.

That was when I knew I was ready to be the leader my family needed.

Please don't let my fingers slip out of your hand. Hold on.

JUNE 3

‘This is... The blood and...I’m gonna... Like are you sure you wanna..?’

‘Only way I’ll learn.’

You clung to my hand, as we ducked through the dark, dusty gym, which stank of sweat and rage. We wove between the baying mob, who were circling the cage. They were high on violence and pain.

My guts did a dance, when I recognised a red Mohawk. The bloke swivelled his nut, his manic gaze locking onto mine, before he knocked the shoulder of his mate, who was fly-eyed in aviator goggles.

They both scrutinised me.

Then they were swarming all over me, their large hands clamped front and back around my throat.

I just had the time to notice the Manx cat tattoos on their knuckles, before Mohawk’s grinning mush was pressed right into mine.

‘M.C.’s my sister,’ I heard you snap, ‘he’s my...’ *This’d be interesting*. ‘...He’s mine.’

Mohawk and Aviator’s grips’ tightened. Then, however, as if by telepathy, they pushed back, setting me free. They made the mocking universal gesture for *after you*, towards the cage.

When I sensed you holding back, I made an effort to straighten my shoulders – *not intimidated here* – and pushed forward by myself.

The huge brawler in the cage was stripped down bare chested to a pair of shiny scarlet

Kickboxing shorts and hand wraps. Spider webs inked every inch of bare skin. His mush was a work of sodding art: swollen and bleeding from his gob and broken eye socket. Yet he was still punching.

He was a slugger, slow but powerful.

Thing was, he was being taken apart. Toyed with – by M.C.

In red sports bra, shorts and hand wraps, in the close heat of the dingy gym, M.C. was sweating. The only mark on her, however, was the blood on her lips from a hard hook.

Two jabs and then a cross. M.C maintained her distance, wearing the poor bastard down. He was bobbing and weaving, finally reduced to covering up. M.C. hopped on her front foot: the flying punch caught the punk to the side of his nut. When he stumbled back, M.C. pounced, with elbow strikes to his chest until he bled, followed by a spinning back kick to his chest and a hook kick to...his groin..?

So there was no such thing as illegal blows? No ringside doctors, rules or referees?

This was survival of the fittest: of course a Cain was at the top of the pile.

I could tell M.C. was an out-fighter. And me? In the ring, I'm a swarmer. You know what that means? In a fair fight, without the wankering tracker in M.C.'s hand, *I'd* win.

Not like it'd be fair though because M.C. would fight dirty.

Yet here's the blinding part – *I fight much dirtier.*

Back in the 1880s, when I was still an amusing bauble for Ruby and my love for her was as intense as a living fire, Ruby would insist I enter no-holds-barred, Greco-Roman challenge matches. The matches were all the rage in the music halls. I'd always win. See, I've been playing at this a long time.

When Ruby and I would get back to our crib, we'd have a wrestling match of our own. Except this time it was Ruby, who'd come out on top.

I prowled around the cage in the shadows, studying M.C.'s strengths and weaknesses, as she in turn stalked the inked punk.

When M.C. knocked the slugger stumbling to my side of the cage, a tear of his blood splattered my cheek.

Just for a moment, M.C. caught my scrutiny. Her blazing peepers narrowed. Then to my surprise, she grinned.

Not looking away, I steeled myself, before licking the blood from my cheek. I juddered with the high of human blood.

M.C.'s grin died. In a blur, she gripped the punk, wrapping her legs around him, before grappling him face down onto the matt. Yet she never looked away from me.

M.C. manipulated the brawler like a chess piece. She placed his body into omoplata - shoulder lock - using her leg; she pressed his elbow joint as well. When the punk howled, I winced. If he didn't submit, his shoulder would... *Pop*.

The poor git was frantically tapping out on the mat, but M.C. wasn't letting go. Even her Crew had fallen quiet at the bloke's screams.

At last, M.C. released the pressure, only to wrap her arm around the brawler's neck in a blood choke: the geezer went limp.

Checkmate.

M.C. threw her crushed opponent down to silence, in that crowded gym. Still her deathly cold gaze never left mine. Blood smeared on her lips,

M.C. stood over her prey, roaring in victory, like a tiger after the kill.

'Did you get what you needed?' Your whisper was tense but determined, your hand slipping into mine.

'Yeah,' I still didn't lower my gaze from M.C.'s. Never again. Never bloody again. 'Oh yeah, I got it.'

JUNE 6

It's black outside, yet you're still not back.

I'm scribbling this in the shadows of the lounge, my arse numb on the log bench, because what's the point in lighting your mango or fig candles tonight?

Just come home, darling.

I was cooking up this cracking stir-fry.

It was a compromise, the best of both worlds: your plant-based, gluten and sugar free purity, melded with my taste explosion of hot chillies, ginger and garlic (that's another one of those bollocks vampire myths because we can munch on garlic until we sweat the stuff).

Your range had never been so splattered with cooking sauces, which were spitting from my wok, whilst the dazzling white sides were littered with wooden spoons and chopping boards that were bright with curling vegetable parings, as if a sentient being lived here. Rather than an automaton.

I hummed The Stones as I stirred, wrapped in your red apron. When you pottered into the kitchen in worn jeans and ivory cashmere, I smiled. You slipped your fingers over mine in sync with their rhythm. 'Grub'll be up soon.'

You nodded.

A wave of gorse and sunlight washed over me, as you pressed closer. 'What's that perfume? It smells like...'

When you drew back, I bit my tongue. *Stupid bugger, aren't I?* 'Fernando chose it because it smells like gorse,' you were shifting a wooden spoon on the marble top, as if to distract yourself. 'It reminds me of home – Mann - on account of the gorse on the Estate. Fernando reckoned it would. He's wicked clever like that.'

I'd stopped stirring; I could smell the chillies catching.

Fernando: of course that git had bought it for you. Considerate, perfect First Lifer Fernando.

Your virtual world, with virtual mates and mythologised semi-boyfriend is easier to face up to than the real one. That makes *you* the unreal one, princess.

I stiffened. 'What I can't figure is why you're more trapped in the past than I am.'

You backed away, before pulling out your iPhone like a shooter. 'You know what? If I'm, like, wicked fried on account of being *trapped* in the past, why don't I just stay there?'

You touched the screen, and there he was: Alpha Geek in all his miniature buttoned up glory, grinning that goofy grin. It made me want to whack your mobile with the wok.

Still, I didn't do that, so...progress.

'Great Scott! I do declare, Grayse Cain, twice in one day! What's doin'?'

I hated the way you smiled. 'Nothin', just wanted to see you.' You glanced significantly at me, before waltzing out of the kitchen.

'Hey, grub's up soon...' I called after you.

No response.

Of course not.

Earlier, I'd perched on the sofa, your laptop open in front of me on the glass coffee table, having a gander at some schematics.

The Internet's a bloody miracle: a democratization of info, which The Man can't pull the plug on. Or own. Finding what I'd needed had been a piece of cake.

After, I'd tried for the more lawful route, digging into protection against slavery, to build a case for our freedom. But here's the thing: humans are sneaky bastards.

'The Vienna Declaration,' I'd clicked on the link excitedly, 'and Roman Statute go on about sexual enslavement but...'

'Yah?' You'd been sprawled in the Fjord Relax chair, painting your nails sexy in scarlet.

'They're on the basis of '*human* rights' or 'crimes against *humanity*'. Look at even the term *human* trafficking. United Nations Global Initiative to Fight *Human* Trafficking. Council of Europe Convention on Action against Trafficking in *Human Beings*--'

'Whoa rant boy, so what?'

'So,' I'd stabbed an accusing finger at the screen, 'don't you get it? It's not *Blood Lifer* trafficking, is it? Every single sodding law on trafficking and slavery is worded to exclude any species but humans. You lot can do anything you bleeding want to us.'

Our cherished invisibility had left us vulnerable to exploitation. By staying Lost, we'd condemned ourselves to slavery.

'Naw, don't *you* get it? You reckon you're so frickin' good at hiding? Safe before us Cains? You think the powerful men, who drew up these laws didn't know about you? Why do you reckon they were so careful to assert *humanity* in each law?'

Shocked, I'd realised you were right. Trust a First Lifer to think like a First Lifer.

I pretended to be busy with the Willow plates, plonking them next to the range in preparation, when you strolled back into the kitchen, dropping the mobile onto the stainless steel counter.

'I'll lay the table,' you said softly.

I nodded.

Then you were gone. But your phone lay there - whispering devilment. Or that's the story I'm going with; although Mr Professor risked...everything.

Snap. I'd gripped the wooden spoon so tightly, it'd broken. I tossed it in the rubbish. Then I turned back to the phone.

I was going to do this; I was the leader now.

I pressed on Skype.

Alpha Geek's mug was a picture when he caught a butchers of me in your kitchen. His first reaction was still that charming *let's work this out together* smile, but I wasn't buying it – *he was pissed.*

I made sure Fernando had a good view of the two plates laid out next to the hissing wok in domestic harmony behind me, whilst I was snug in your cooking apron.

Fernando's smile faltered. 'What the frak..?'

'Sorry mate, must've...you know, by accident.'

'So, who are you again?'

It was like two stags at bloody mating time.

I leant casually against the counter. 'You're that professor bloke? The one Grayse used to know--'

'And that makes you..?'

'She hasn't told you?'

‘Where is she?’ Fernando’s dark peepers were flicking side to side in frustration, as if he could see outside the limits of the screen. ‘Are you..?’

‘We’re about to nosh here, so it’s not a good time. Look, this is embarrassing. Maybe she should--’

‘It’s OK, I get it.’

The screen went blank.

I let out a deep breath. That’d been my first contact with a First Lifer, who hadn’t known I was a slave, for six months.

And it’d been blinding to play him.

I began to hum “In Another Land”, as I gave the last few stirs to the meal; it smelt like a rock band kicking it at Glastonbury. I was ravenous. ‘Oi princess, it’s--’

In a furious whirr, you slammed into the kitchen, shoving me across the stainless steel counter. The shock shuttered my mind into shut down.

I caught glimpses of your flushed, raging mush... *I know what you did...* Your grey peepers were so cold I don’t know why I ever reckoned you were softer than your sister... *You’re meant to be a secret...* I stayed down, but you kept advancing... *How could you do something so bad? I trusted you...* You were standing over me... *Fernando tells me everything; he’s like my brother...* Your mouth was twisted and hard... *I have a Blackberry too, or are you that stupid?*

Bad... Stupid... My body contorted, as a bullwhip tore the skin afresh in searing slashes, whilst I writhed - *count, my pretty little leech.*

‘Bad... Stupid... Bad... Sorry... Yeah, I’m bad. Sorry... Sorry,’ I mumbled, my nut turned away and my palms splayed on the counter. At last, my distress seemed to break into the red rage, which was fuelling your diatribe; you reached out towards me. I screwed me peepers shut. I deserved a clout but stuck in the grey area between Primrose Hill and Abona, I still panicked. 'Sorry, sorry, sorry, sorry...'

You hastily withdrew your hand, backing across the kitchen. 'What was all that about?' You sounded calmer. I risked opening my peepers. Then I pushed myself up. My tooth hurt from where it'd banged the counter; I could feel the fang growing through behind it. I had a quick shufti at you leaning with your arms crossed in the doorway. 'Was it a message? A way to escape?'

Shocked, I stared at you. 'Not bleeding likely.'

'Then what? What were you thinking?'

'That I didn't want you to leave,' I couldn't quite get myself to add *me* but I knew you heard it from the way you blushed, 'or go to America and send me back to Abona.'

When you surged towards me, I couldn't help flinching. You stopped mid-step and flinched in response. 'That'll never happen. I promise.' I still, however, couldn't meet your gaze; I couldn't make myself believe it either. Suddenly I realised the kitchen was hazy with smoke: *my stir-fry*. Coughing, I dived for the range, twisting it off. We stared at the blackened remains sadly. My stomach rumbled. You spun away, with a flick of your hair. 'I'll eat out.'

A few short steps and – *bang* – you were gone.

You still haven't come back. It's very late.

I reckoned I'd sit here and wait up for you. But then it's not like I'm your...*anything*...is it?

I wish you'd come back. It's silent here and I'm...a muppet, all right?

I need you to understand.

JUNE 8

You insisted your sister had booked it. But you still didn't stop the bint she sent from waxing me full body and privates smooth again. It's part of the Blood Lifer regimen, like polishing and waxing your prized motor.

And it bloody hurt.

At least she was professional, using this bubble gummy soft wax on my danglies and other private places.

Not like the Doctor at Abona.

It's not as if I had any choice in it though: my body's not my own any longer.

And isn't that the bleeding point?

JUNE 9

I swore I'd explain everything. But not tonight. My jaw and fangs ache. My wrists are purpled with bruises. And I'm lying on my stomach on top of my duvet, as I write this.

I'm trying to figure out how I got from Amy Winehouse to risking a promise, which would mean casting my lot in with you alone.

Either I'm right to trust you. Or I'm the biggest bleeding mug of them all.

On my knees this morning beside the coffee table, I had your vases ranged for dusting with the special pink cloth, which you'd marked in the cupboard. Your indigo Italian glass vase was up next for the once over. I'd worked out your high-tech sound system and was humming along to a music channel.

Then it'd started up – that song, which had thrown me right back to the moors, the sobbing grief and death of everything, which was good in my world. Immersed in the soulful pain of Amy Winehouse's "Back to Black", I'd found myself on my knees, singing along.

Kathy: my love, my Moon Girl, whose Soul snared mine; I'd been enraptured by every word, which she'd sung up on stage.

Yet after we'd escaped together from Ruby and the rest of my brutal family, Kathy had learnt the truth about me - and she'd never sung again.

The truth silences you.

In the early stages of the cruel dementia, however, which stole us from each other, I'd once found Kathy in our room, swaying to "Back to Black", as it played on the radio. She'd been mouthing the words. For one glorious moment, I'd hoped she'd sing again, transformed to a ghost of her youth's transcendence.

But hope's the killer.

When Kathy died, I'd buried her at night out on Ilkley Moors.

As I'd uprooted the scented heather, I'd been assaulted by images of Kathy's dad's skeleton, rotted down to nothing but bones and rags. Burying that bastard on the moors had been the greatest proof of love, which Kathy had ever asked from me.

Yet as I'd dug out Kathy's grave in lonely vigil, I'd been raging. But there was nothing to face. No enemy but death. And that wanker wasn't hanging around for a barney.

I'd whispered the lyrics to "Back to Black", like a eulogy, as I'd laid Kathy's body gently into the boggy grave. Then I'd tipped the soil back over her, starting at her feet and delaying the inevitable moment, until finally even her face had been covered, and she'd been lost to me - irrevocably and eternally.

As the last earth had fallen, crumbled between my fingers, I'd broken down, weeping until the world had blurred to nothing.

Kathy had freed me. Yet now she was gone. I'd been alone and desolated: there was nothing left. I'd promised Kathy, however, not to meet the second death. My only plan was to flee the pain. I'd scarpered on my Triton before the daytime carers or cops.

I never intended to come back to England. Not after Kathy.

150 years of loneliness, obsession, rejection and betrayal. Yet nothing has come close to the agony of that moment.

Then again, I'm only a slave, and we don't *feel*, right?

I realised I hadn't heard the *click* of the front door, when I glanced up, and you were standing there.

You were leaning against the wall, with a thoughtful expression, as you watched me on my knees, dusting cloth in one hand, glass vase in the other and tears in my peepers, whilst I sang along to Amy Winehouse.

I must've looked like a right berk.

Abruptly I shut up.

You dropped your tote, shucking off your charcoal jacket. 'I reckoned I'd work from home; I've got tutes this afternoon.'

'You back for dinner then?' I managed to ask, placing down the vase and hastily wiping at my peepers.

'Eight OK?'

Now wasn't this domestic?

I nodded.

'I've gotta go out after. Marlane wants me to work on some project.' You started to sit down on the Sponge chair but then popped up again. 'He's not a bad guy, you know.'

Had I missed half a conversation? Then our gazes met, and I knew *exactly* who you meant. 'Fernando?' It was like sucking sodding wasps.

'Professor. And yeah, he worked his ass off for his fellowship at Harvard.' Why were you so agitated? Wringing your hands and pacing up and down, until I felt dizzy just watching? 'He helps out his family. He was wicked kind to--'

'Got it, right, decent bloke.'

When you stopped dead in front of me, I wished I wasn't still on my knees, like I was ranked ready to service you, which was both disturbing and hot.

'We're not... I mean, yeah, we dated for, like, all of two seconds. But now we're... Fernando's my best and only friend. So don't frickin' screw that up for me because you're... OK?'

Then you marched into the kitchen, and I could breathe again.

It was nearly eight o'clock. The apartment was thrumming with the psychedelic dream world of the Beatles, sighed with the rich aromas of fresh pasta, beef, ham, wine and grated Parmigiano and glowed with every candle I'd been able to unearth, like the stars had descended to burn amongst First and Blood Lifers alike for one night only.

Buggering hell - "Lucy in the Sky with Diamonds" - took me back to the summer of 1968 and the buzz of Carnaby Street, when First Lifer creativity forced me to question the fundamentals of Blood Lifer belief. No longer could I hold the comfy notion that the Lost were the superior species feeding as evolutionary right on the weak. Instead we were only another creature, one step alongside you humans. Who bloody knew which one of us was the apex? It was a summer of obsession, caught between two women: the Blood Lifer Ruby, who'd authored me and the First Lifer Kathy, who freed me from Ruby's control.

I chose between two worlds that summer. At least it was a *choice*.

Now my life has narrowed, until there are no choices. Only obedience.

Survival though, that's a choice. *Adapting*.

So how can what I'm feeling be..? I'm waiting for you to come back to me, and my Soul's sodding soaring. What is this? No different to marie antoinette and *Sir*? And I bloody pitied her.

It's all right, I'm not a total pillock; I know you don't want me, not like I want you: equal to equal.

I've already had that with one woman. Maybe to seek it with a second is chasing shadows.

When I heard the front door open and shut with a *click*, I darted out of the dining room and swung you round the hall.

You were stiff as a marionette.

Then as I twirled you round to Lennon's joyous nursery rhyme, you relaxed and laughed, throwing down your tote, before clasping your hands behind my neck.

I spun you, as one drug fuelled summer back in the 1960s Donovan had once spun his groupies.

'How's my Sun Girl?'

You laughed.

Your nose suddenly wrinkled. 'Is that lasagne?'

'Yeah, that alright then?'

You grinned. 'It's mint.'

I grinned too, as I danced you into the dining room.

When you dragged back against me in shock, I let you pull out of my arms. You stared around at the piles of Marzolino and Pecorino sheep milk cheeses and honey on the salvaged wood sideboard, which were next to Willow plates of biscuits and cakes: a dark chestnut castagnaccio, littered with nuts and raisins, almond cantuccini and fiorentini.

You twisted to me. 'You baked these?'

'Told you, 150 years is a long time to--'

'Bake?'

'Gotta do something.'

'You're not--'

'What you expected?'

You laughed again. The Manx watched from their hiding places, behind the oak and holly bush; the sun beat down, even though it was night. You fell into your seat with a sigh of delight. 'I love lasagne. And this is just right for...' I was settling into my chair, glad I'd bothered to lay the posh candles - their flames flickering like fireflies - when I noticed you were peering at me suspiciously. '...Florence. How'd you know?'

Confession time.

I squirmed. 'There's this bird in a photo in your bedroom, who I guessed is your mum. In the background there's Brunelleschi's Dome. So, Florence. Plus you've got that Italian glass vase.'

I remembered strolling those piazzas with Ruby, under the velvet black of a Tuscan sky.

You'd forked some pasta. Creamy béchamel sauce was seeping off one end. 'You've been then? Florence?'

'Not for over a century. But the beauty of that city doesn't change,' I took my first meaty mouthful. 'Ruby and me took a Grand Tour, of sorts.'

You sucked the pasta off your fork: from the orgasmic expression on your mush, I figured it was good. 'So, maybe you can do, like, more of the cooking?'

I raised my eyebrow. 'Anyone would reckon I was your slave.'

You flushed, hurriedly munching another forkful. 'Mummy would talk about it – Florence - but I've never been on account of the studying. And mummy...' I'd wondered where *Mrs Cain* figured in all of this. No way was I daft enough, however, to go prying into that dark family closet. 'She died. So Daddy sent Marlane to work in London on account of she was sixteen, and he wanted her to make it herself. Prove she could run that wing of operations. I wanted to stay in Mann with daddy, but he was like, *na-ah, you'll get in the way*. So I had to go and live with this aunt I didn't even know in Boston.' You finally glanced up at me. 'Lucky me, huh?'

'Considering what I know about the rest of your family, I'd say yeah.'

You bristled. 'It wasn't always... Marlane and I would go riding on the Estate. And mummy would cook these wicked frickin' meals like...uova frittellate o affrittellate: fried eggs with black pepper, bacon and--'

'Spinach, I know: it's next. So come on, eat up.'

You gaped at me. It was priceless, until... 'Na-ah, how'd you really find out?'

I stiffened. You'd transformed from warm to icy in a single mouthful. Every emotion amplified? That's obsession for you. 'Look, before you freak out, I did recognise the photo. But the food?' I fiddled with my knife. 'I caught a butchers of you online to your sister. About how you missed your mum's meals.' Your expression had tightened into sudden fear. 'I wasn't snooping, I swear. I just caught it over your shoulder--'

'Arc we..?' You stared round: at the red candles, cake and biscuit laden sideboard and layers of Parmigiano topped lasagne in front of us, as if only just swimming awake. 'Are you..?' I blinked at you in confusion. 'You're not my boyfriend.'

Any colder, you'd have cryogenically frozen my bloody balls.

I struggled to answer, as my fingers curled around the polished edges of the table; my slave ring was bright under the candlelight, 'I think I've got that sodding clear, cheers.'

'You can never be my boyfriend.'

'Again, thanks for the clarity, but not a problem.'

There was an awkward silence. Quickly, you leant forward. 'Then why..?'

Frustrated, I shoved away my plate. 'I wanted to do something nice, alright? Cook your favourite meal. Because you saved me from *that place*. And a fortnight ago you didn't...when you could've...' I remembered lying starkers on your white bed. Your caress on my cheek, chest and lower... But you'd stopped: you'd *made* yourself stop. If anybody knew how hard that was, it was me. You'd chosen to defy your family and your training to give me back myself. I wouldn't forget it. 'Sorry, you hate it.'

When I banged away from the table, you caught my hand between yours. 'I don't hate it. Please, can we eat now?' I sat back down slowly, picking up my fork. 'Light?'

'Yeah?' I asked, before stuffing in a mouthful of mince and ham.

'Don't go catching what I write again.'

I gulped the food at the hardness of your tone. Then I grinned. 'I wouldn't dream of it, sweetheart.'

Later, when you'd left for your night project, I was still buzzing, bustling around the kitchen, banging cupboards open and closed, as I piled away washed up coffee cups, foiled the remaining castagnaccio in the fridge and stacked left over cantuccini and fiorentini into a red-and-black biscuit tin. When I heard the front door *click*, I didn't even turn from the counter. I smiled. 'In here. What? You too tempted by my delicious treats to stay away?'

'Not me, liccle leech. But I reckon you got dat proper right about my sis.' *Bollocks*. I twisted, but M.C. already had her arm around my throat. When I struggled, M.C. crushed me against the marble counter, sending the Willow plates – *smash* – to the tiled floor. The fight went out of me then. Two birds. Souls broken apart forever. 'Why don't you seckle?'

M.C. shook me again for good measure. Then she hauled me through to the sitting room.

This had to be a setup: M.C. sends you on a wild goose chase, so she can get up close and personal with yours truly.

The only thing I couldn't work out was *why*.

When I saw the neat man with silver beard, in a long woollen coat, who was carrying a black medical case..?

That's when I got the collywobbles.

I clutched hold of the doorframe, digging in my nails. I heard the Doctor chuckle behind me.

'They always try this on, don't they?' The Doctor sounded so genial, like he was here to check a brat's temperature, who merely needed to be coaxed to take their medicine with strawberries and sugar.

'Dey don't like it, innit? Know what else dis wallad don't like?' The agony frying my nerves dropped me to my knees in a mad surge of Schumann's *Piano Trio No. 3*; I was falling deeper into the fairy tale. At last, M.C. took her finger off the touchscreen. 'On da chair.'

I tried to stand but felt like my bones had been melted. Refusing to look at either of the bastards, I crawled to the Fjord Relax chair, hauling myself up onto it by my arms; I do realise the irony because any second now I would be anything but relaxed.

M.C. grabbed my wrists, binding them with the red nylon rope, which I bloody hated: what was it, on bulk discount? She strapped my arms close to my body and then all of me to the sodding chair.

I guess they really needed me to stay still.

As M.C. worked on tying me down, the Doctor was busy laying onto the coffee table his grisly work tools: curved extraction forceps, brushed satin stainless steel scissors, orthodontia pliers, an ominously large pile of gauze and a pair of steel dental retractors...

I shuddered, struggling to control my shallow, panted breathing. But I'd been through this once and nothing that'd been done to me had touched this sacrilege: fangs are a Blood Lifer's proof of evolution.

At last I understood why M.C. had made bloody sure you weren't here to witness this abuse.

I couldn't help the tears forming.

The Doctor soothed his hand over my forehead, as if I was his patient, rather than his victim. 'Now, now, come on, be brave; there's a good chap. It'll soon be over. You know the drill: open your mouth.' I considered keeping my lips clamped shut, but that'd only earn me another dose of the wankering tracker. Reluctantly, I opened my gob. The Doctor shoved in the retractors, winding until my jaw ached. 'Has he been a good enough boy for anaesthetic...this time?' The Doctor gave a bright smile, which didn't reach his peepers.

I stared up at M.C., as if at an executioner. Her expression was hungry and hard. It didn't surprise me, when she shook her nut.

'Shame,' the Doctor purred. Then he spread heavy green plastic sheeting over me and the chair because God forbid my blood stain the furniture, before he selected the steel forceps. He tested them a few times - *the sadistic tosser*. Finally he was all I could see, as he stood close, tapping my canine. 'Fangs out.'

I could feel my fangs shrivelling back inside my gums, like a bloke's goolies when he sees a mate taking a boot to the privates.

My half-formed fangs shot out, as the Doctor grabbed me by the hair with one hand and gripped the first fang with the forceps, ready to wrench.

I closed my peepers. I tried to hold still but I was shivering.

'What the frig are you doing?' *You*. My saviour. My Sun Girl. *Thank you, thank you, thank you...* And you were dead pissed. 'I said...'

The Doctor didn't even remove the forceps from my fang. In fact, he twisted.

I let out a distorted holler.

Before I knew what was what, the Doctor was sprawled face first on the wooden floorboards, his tools clattered with him.

'Out,' you barked, 'Get your damn asses out of here. Both of you.'

M.C., for the first time, appeared flustered. 'Sis, the Doc's safe. He's gotta remove the liccle leech's fangs before--'

'Get the hell out of my apartment.'

'Alright. But I be telling dad dat you ain't following care instructions. You reckon he be letting you keep an untrained bitch with all its fangs?' The Doctor shuffled – limping - out of the apartment in front of M.C., casting obsequious, apologetic glances at you. M.C., however, threw back, before she slammed the front door, 'When it be mine, I'll do more than defang it, you feel me?'

Then you were a blur: flinging the plastic sheeting off me, unwinding the ropes around the chair, ripping at the knots around my chest, arms and wrists and then dropping to your knees next to me. You rubbed my bruised wrists, which were encircled by a deep purple line, before lifting each to your lips and tenderly kissing them in turn.

I held still in case somehow I broke the spell.

My fangs were out, for the first time since they'd last been ripped from my gob; it felt blinding. Yet I also knew how you felt about my Blood Lifer status: this *parasite*.

I began to pull them into my gums, but when you knelt up and gently removed the dental retractor, you didn't recoil.

Gasping with pain, I stretched my jaw. I was still only half a Blood Lifer: my venom wouldn't function until the fangs were fully regrown. But you hadn't let the Blood Club take them again.

You'd saved me.

Now I had to save the others.

You were stroking the back of my hand. 'I...decided I wanted to be here tonight more than work.' Your peepers were bright with tears. 'What if I'd chosen work..?' Those tears were for me. Deny it all you like. Call it a non-date. I don't sodding care: you couldn't let them do that to me because...*we both know why*. 'Tell me,' you begged, 'everything they did to you.'

Finally, I retracted my fangs and then, even though my wrists throbbed, I took your hand because you looked so bloody defeated. 'Nosey bugger. I thought you were reading my journal?'

'The truth.'

'It is the truth.'

'I need...the worst.'

'It's not enough?'

You examined me with an intense gaze. '*Family*? *Promises*? There's a whole notha buried story going on. And I wanna know.'

I tensed. *You're no daft bint, are you*? 'If I tell you...will you let me go?'

You snatched your hand back from mine in shock. 'You wanna leave me?'

I shoved up from the chair, still unsteady but unable to stop my agitated pacing. 'I want to be *free*, sweetheart.'

'Then *no*, Light,' your voice had hardened, as you too pushed yourself up, your arms firmly crossed. 'If freeing you means I lose you, then frickin' no.'

I was breathing too rapidly. 'OK then, how about this: loan me out...just for...buggering hell...for a bit? I've got business, right?'

'Business?' You stared at me blankly.

'I'll write it. The worst of it. What I've promised and left behind. I write it. You read it. Then you'll understand why you need to let me go. Even if I have to come back to you.'

So, I promised to explain. Write the worst. Tomorrow then.

JUNE 10

I'm writing this so you'll let me go and I can do what has to be done.

It's been so long since I last cared for family. I've almost forgotten what it feels like.

You want honesty and truth? Yeah well, they're for folks, who reckon they can control a black and white world, where transparency can save us all.

Sod. That.

There's no such thing as an honest fact, statistic or spoken word: *everything is spin.*

Yet you want to know what I witnessed at Abona? The worst?

If I tell you, you'd bloody better let me rescue my own from their bonds.

Then I'll bear witness.

The next time the dark oak doors opened after *Sir* had...hurt Hartford at the inspection because of me, I'd scrambled to *kneel*, not yet knowing what I would say to either Hartford or Donovan.

Donovan was easier. He'd lay into me: I could live with that.

Hartford? *Sorry* didn't exactly cover it.

When instead a cold steel leash was slipped around my neck, I glanced up, startled.

It looked like my problem was solved. A Blood Lifer, who I'd never seen before, was wrenching off my ankle chain.

I flinched, quailing back from the tall Ghanaian (a warrior queen with layered box braids, which blazed with gilded thread).

She regarded me fiercely, as she clutched my leash.

'Where's Hartford?'

The warrior queen's peepers narrowed: *wrong question...* 'Don't disturb!'

'I said, where's--'

The Blood Lifer yanked on the leash. Unprepared, with my wrists still crossed at my back, I fell on my mug. I blinked back the pain. 'I just wanna know that Hartford's--'

'Aba! Cupid be in slave quarters because of you, wicked boy, after the big man's dirty blows.'

I braced myself with my hands. 'Right, get that. Is he..?'

'He'll live. Up, obroni.'

'Obroni – white man then, is it?' I pushed myself warily to my feet. The steel around my throat made it hard to swallow. 'I prefer Light.'

'Your name be shadow.' The warrior queen's gaze was assessing, but I saw a flash of fire in her peepers now too.

'The wankering First Lifers can tattoo *shadow* on my bleeding arse: I'm still Light.'

At last the Ghanaian grinned: night transformed to day. 'Challey, you be fine.' When she slouched closer, I tensed, but she only loosened the collar; I'd known the bint had it too tight. 'They call me cocoa. If the white men in this time be not so ignorant, it could also be *gold* or *kola nut*.'

I laughed. 'So what do I call you then?'

'Ashanti. My house fought you obroni, men and women on the battlefields. My people will not be forgotten.'

'Good on you, luv. Now,' I pulled at the metal collar, 'what's this all about?'

'You vexed big man, so he wants me to show you. You sabe?' I was beginning to; I couldn't stop the shivers shuddering through me. 'Now we walka walka sharp sharp.'

Ashanti tugged on my leash, forcing me to trot after her.

When I reached those oak doors, however, I hesitated. Then I pulled back, with a shake of my nut.

It should've been everything I'd fantasized about: escape from that cell. But it was *my* cell. I knew it. Every inch. I'd counted the bricks, the blossoms of mould and whirls of dirt: I'd named them. I knew the feel of each patch of cold, bare floor. Inside, I'd only had *Sir* to brave. But outside..?

I had the whole of Abona House.

Suddenly, I couldn't breathe. My chest spasmed, as I clutched onto the doorframe.

Then Ashanti was holding me tight, her lips close to my lughole. 'Advise oneself, boy: you must not act as if not right,' she tapped her forehead, 'out here in Abona. From today onward going, you be an ashawo for the First Lifers. Are you a pikin to need slaps?'

'No,' I whispered.

Ashanti let go of me.

Ashawo – slut.

Ashanti was right: I had to pull myself together.

I forced myself after Ashanti down the narrow corridor. It became clear I'd been locked away in an adapted cellar; when we passed rows of identical doors to mine, I wondered how many other poor bastards were chained behind them.

At last, we climbed a mahogany spiral staircase to a warren of rooms, which must once have been servant quarters in this great house. And now, with no hint of awareness of irony, were the slaves'.

There was a kitchen, with Blood Lifers working like ants, who didn't even spare me a glance. I hoped I'd see Donovan. But I didn't.

Donovan had always waffled on about the other Blood Lifers, who helped him run Abona. Before it'd felt like a dream: now I was confronted with the reality.

And it was terrifying.

I had the sudden urge to hide under the huge oak kitchen table. Then I remembered Ashanti's *slaps* and resisted.

Ashanti pulled me on, passing poky bedrooms with stained mattresses. There were no blankets or privacy. It was still a step up from my cell. The rooms, however, were empty. It wasn't hard to work out where the remaining Blood Lifers were.

'Am I..?' I couldn't quite get out the words.

It wasn't easy to ask some Blood Lifer bird you'd just met, if you were about to be buggered by some sweaty sex tourist.

Still, Ashanti got it by the horror in my peepers, when she continued to lead me upwards towards the main house. 'You be trained slowly slowly. From the first beginning, you watch. Then you help with appointments. Then...'

Yeah, *then...*

When we stepped off the spiral staircase out of the slave quarters and into the front of house for the johns, it was like we'd travelled to another world.

Creepy-crawly motifs swarmed over the embossed wallpaper and chaise longues were richly upholstered with orchids. Butterflies and moths alighted in felt, wool and satins on patterned neo-baroque floor lights and brocade sofas. A vast golden chandelier was suspended from the high ceiling, like a burning sun.

These First Lifers had recreated a slice of the daytime world amidst the night, like fish and chips served on the Costa del Sol. Yet it was a fake, just like whatever they reckoned they were getting from us. Nothing but smoke and mirrors: in here we were no longer the Lost.

I peered down the stairs, which swept from this floor to a humungous entrance hall. It was typical of First Lifer drama, where members could gather on the chessboard marble floor and look up, the better to enjoy what was on offer, before they made their choice.

I could also see the high front door.

My heart bloody hammered. I'd never been this close to escape before. The upper floor of the house was empty. Apart from Ashanti and me. If I could just get her to let go of the leash...

Ashanti, however, hauled me to the first door on the corridor. She slipped aside a discrete peephole. When she gestured with her hand, I bent down and squinted.

Purple - walls, ceilings and floor. Lights inlaid into the deep purple velvet, like night-time stars and they – a paunchy First Lifer and a Chinese Blood Lifer, who was so tiny she was almost buried underneath the man's folds – were floating amongst them.

I drew back sharply.

When Ashanti tugged me on to the next door, I shook my nut.

Ashanti sighed. 'Challey, at least you can do this. Big big trouble you don't. Big man says--'

'No chance.'

Ashanti dropped my leash and walloped me across the cheek with her open hand: I guess she had warned me about those *slaps*.

When Ashanti didn't pick up the chain again, however, my fingers curled into fists, as I tried not to draw attention to it.

'Don't bring yourself!' Ashanti snarled. 'My alomo be through that door with an American man. Don't you think I want to finish him? But Master, he mighty.' She glanced nervously up and down the hall. 'You will make big big palaver here.'

'I'm sorry your girl's--'

'Pshaaa! You are serious, boy. What do you know about the bond of house? Have you authored? Got a life born from your fangs?' Ashamed, I looked down. Where had the Plantagenets been for the last five decades? Yeah, that's right: *I'd murdered two of them*. Then I'd hidden, to live out the span of my lover's human, frail life. I don't regret it. But Ashanti was right. Who was I to speak of *family*? 'You be moons older than I. But where be your elected? Adjei! To my mind the First Lifers use your house against you: behave or they retaliate with dirty blows to your elected.'

...Or the one you love...

I understood now why *Sir* had such control over both Hartford and Donovan. For once, my loneliness gave me an edge: I didn't have anyone to hold over me and use to pull my puppet strings.

You're only as strong as the weakest link in your chain. Even if Donovan and Hartford were now bonded to me, *Sir* didn't know it. I was still a chain of one link.

A chain, which was still not being held.

I risked a glance at Ashanti, who appeared lost in her thoughts and then back at the stairs. I didn't know when I'd get another chance.

So I took it.

I was surprised I had so much strength left in me, but I was aided by terror and a bubbling sublime excitement, which I always get from a caper, as I launched myself down those stairs. I couldn't even feel Ashanti behind me. I lunged into the cool hallway, my bare feet cold on the marble, as I sprinted for the front door. It was bloody big.

And it was locked.

Letting out a hiss of frustration, I booted at the door; the slam echoed through the halls.

The high, blinded windows. If I could only...

In the moments, however, that it took me to turn, a dozen Blood Lifers had materialized, as if out of the creepy-crawly wallpaper. They began circling me, like sharks scenting blood. The funny thing was the bleeders were wearing random threads: tight shorts, bra and knickers, ripped jeans and one had on just a stripy scarf. Each also clutched a weapon: cudgel, knuckleduster, baseball bat or strap curled around meaty fist.

The Enforcers.

It'd been a test. The whole bloody thing: the empty house, route to the front door, Ashanti leaving the leash loose and these tossers being convenient-like to take me down.

I guess I failed, by *Sir's* reckoning. His lesson? That there was no escape. But *Sir* was wrong - no matter what he did to me now - and I'd prove it.

I expected one of the bruisers to get stuck into me but instead I heard footsteps on the stairs. The other Blood Lifers stilled deferentially, as if awaiting their Queen Bee. I took a gander, and there she was: this Blood Lifer in pale pink silk ball gown, her strawberry blonde curls piled on top of her nut in a pouffe - the detested marie antoinette.

When antoinette advanced towards me, a black blindfold dangling in one hand, I backed up against the wall.

Antoinette frowned, like you would at a lad, who'd been caught filching from his mama's purse. 'Where are you going, mon Ganymede? To make yourself a pair of running hands so?' Her light Parisian voice spoke of summers idling resplendent in the gardens of the Chateau de Versailles and nights fleeing from the masses and the guillotine. Antoinette was bloody making up for that social reversal now. 'I hope you understand how ignoble and impure a deed this was? Most evil and contemptible, when Monsieur put his trust in you, n'est-ce pas?'

I spluttered with laughter. 'Sod off.'

I expected a clout.

Instead antoinette seemed saddened, before gesturing at her acolytes. 'Monsieur furnishes us with fair reward for our obedience; every one of you will receive an additional ration of blood for your help with this wrongdoer.'

The Enforcers bowed their nuts towards antoinette, as towards a god.

How long would I need to be shut up in this madhouse, before I too bowed to this aristocratic bitch in order to earn an extra mug of pigs' blood?

'But you, catamite?' Antoinette poked me on the chest with a perfectly manicured finger. 'You have yet to learn Monsieur's lessons. Maybe you're simply lacking in brains?' She arched her eyebrow.

'Again, sod off.'

'Mon dieu!' Marie antoinette clapped her hands together sharply. 'That is it, you are done. Put this on and follow me tout de suite.' She pressed the blindfold into my hands. I hesitated but when I read the challenge in antoinette's peepers, I reckoned the only two choices were to wear it or to take a hiding and *then* wear it. I chose the first option. 'Bien.' I felt slim fingers clutching my bicep, before I was dragged across the marble floor. 'Down. Steps. Stop. Turn.'

More doorways and steps, until finally I was pushed and manipulated (but this time by someone else's hands, which felt strange, as if they were wearing latex medical gloves), onto my stomach on an examining table. I started panting because nothing good ever comes of being strapped face down to an examining table.

When I felt a third pair of hands (and these I recognised as *Sir's*), start tracing circles on the middle of my back, as if soothing an animal, I nearly bit my own tongue off to stop myself from whimpering apologies.

'I saved your life, little one,' *Sir's* fingers were still tracing circles, but his nails were digging in now; held down as I was, I couldn't flinch away, even when *Sir* gouged into the flesh, 'but seeing as you're still too stupid to show gratitude, I'll have to teach you what happens to bad little bitches, who can't be trusted. Now you'll have to be tracked. You don't realise how lucky you are, seeing as I'm personally paying for this. It's only because you'll be such a good whore that I don't make an example of you, unlike other leeches...' His hands paused, as if suddenly aware of the bloody tracks, which they'd flayed on my skin, before smoothing tenderly over them. As if regretful. 'I tried to be gentle with you, my shadow. How's it my fault if I give you a chance to prove yourself, and instead you disappoint?'

Sir was stroking my spine, all the way up to my neck.

Furious, I still couldn't stop the traitor tears welling of hot shame. I can't explain it, except that after so many months of babied dependence, all I wanted was for *Sir* to take me on his lap and comfort me.

It shocked me how much *Sir's* cold disappointment kicked me in the gut. How much I figured I deserved punishment, especially if it'd earn me *Sir's* approval again.

'So has he been too bad a boy for anaesthetic?' A second voice, which I reckoned belonged to the hands in the latex gloves.

'He's a very bad boy, Doctor. No anaesthetic.'

I didn't care what they were chin-wagging about, I wanted the sodding anaesthetic. '*Sir*--'

As soon as I opened my gob to beg, however, a steel gag was thrust in and tied at the back. Then the Doctor examined with careful, light touches, the place on my spine, into which *Sir* had burrowed his nails.

When the cold scalpel sliced deep into my spinal cord and the bundle of nerves, which connected my brainstem to every other nerve in my body, I screamed.

Yeah, I sodding screamed.

At some point, I passed out.

I came to, with a jet of ice cold pressurised water in my mush. Gasping, I flopped around like a landed fish. This phantasmagorical music - a wild fairy tale of battling violin, cello and piano – was playing somewhere.

Hardly conscious, shivering as I was sprayed with freezing water, I remembered the winter Ruby had played this record in Berlin - *Piano Trio No. 3 in G Minor* - twirling round and round in a blur of red, lost in its madness.

Suddenly the water was switched off. Disorientated, I blinked.

I was on the soaking floor of a vast, windowless wet room, which had examining tables alongside one wall (I reckoned I'd been strapped onto one of them for my impromptu spinal surgery). There was orthodontic and surgical equipment on stainless steel trays and a record player.

My back shot sharp branches of pain through the rest of me, whenever I tried to twist and see what had been done. I glared up at *Sir*.

Sir stood – jacketless - his pink shirtsleeves rolled up past the elbow, holding nothing but a little touchscreen device. There was a black cat icon on it. When he saw he had my attention, he smiled. 'Welcome back, boyo. Look you here,' he shook the device, 'I now control you.'

I glowered at the barmy bastard.

Sir's smile faded; there was a manic gleam again in his peepers. 'A tracker's been buried deep in your nervous system. Firstly, with this I'll always know where you are.' I'd botched up any escape plan. I could never hide in the shadows again. Cornered, I crawled to the far side of the wet room, still dripping with the cold tears of water, cowering in pain and confusion. *Sir* laughed. 'There's a good boy, you're understanding at last. And secondly?'

Sir swiped his finger over the device and I howled.

Fire raged down every nerve in my body. Schumann's wild carnival danced in my mind, as I curled up on myself, trying to escape something, which I no longer ever could: because it was inside me.

Impotent, I wept.

At last, the pain ended.

Shakily, I looked at *Sir*.

'Secondly,' *Sir* repeated calmly over the music, 'you can be disciplined without marking.' When *Sir* held up the device, I couldn't help wincing, as his finger hovered over the screen. 'Let's start training.'

Then the agony exploded.

Afterwards, when I felt like my organs had been electrified, my bones charred and I ached from thrashing in the throes of that bastard tracker, I was lifted by the traitor Enforcers back onto the examining table.

Then the Doctor – a tidy little man, with forked silver beard – took far less care than I'd bloody have liked, waxing me head-to-toe.

I yelped when he did the small of my back and my pecs. When he got to my goolies - weak as I was - I nearly scrambled off the table.

The Doctor pressed me back with a gloved hand. 'There, there, be a good boy. You don't want me to call *Sir*, do you now?'

I hurriedly shook my nut. I was certain I'd be fried to nothing, if *Sir* used the tracker on me again.

'Anyway,' the Doctor was continuing chirpily, whilst he applied the wax and - *rip* - *buggering hell.* I bit through my lower lip, sucking on the blood to stop myself from yelping, whilst the Doctor pulled the skin taut on my privates, as he worked on them – *rip*. 'You want to be all smooth and pretty for your clients, don't you?'

I'd rather sink my fangs into their throats and devour their warm blood.

I spent the next hour happily imagining different dismembering methods for the Doctor, *Sir* and the Blood Clubbers, so I wouldn't have to deal with the reality of being transformed into a fetishized toy.

At last, I realised the *ripping* had stopped. Someone was standing over me. I opened my peepers.

Marie antoinette was scrutinising me with a smug smile. 'Monsieur has taught you lessons, yes?'

I stared antoinette down in silence.

Antoinette's smile wavered. 'Je veux dire you've seen the urgent necessity of reforming?'

'Sorry, luv: I'm unreformable. You're the bitch playing traitor.'

Antoinette stuck her nose in the air. 'Au contraire, you silly boy. I serve Monsieur. And you? Despite the violence of your utterance, you will come to understand. Maintenant: up. You will see what comes of the truly unreformable. Then maybe you will not wish to be counted amongst their number, n'est-ce pas?'

When antoinette led me with stumbling steps to a silent troop of Blood Lifers at attention in a tiny courtyard, Donovan broke ranks to clasp my hand. I could tell he was scrutinising my now hairless body for bruises, burns or blood, like he did with Hartford but – *cheers, tracker* – there were no marks to witness my ordeal.

Me? I was lost in the feel of the pure night air. Fixated by the patch of black and piercing stars; they weren't like the false ones inside the brothel, which were as fake as everything else in that commodified harem. I was flying from the sensation of being outside for the first time since my kidnap, which meant I didn't look down.

Until I heard the groan.

I doubled up, puking violently over the grey face of Abona.

Donovan gently patted my back.

A...something...Blood Lifer...a bird once...had been hammered crucifixion style to the ground, with nails through her wrists and ankles, or what was left of them.

She'd been positioned in the shadow of Abona but just enough so the sun would melt her skin candle-like. Flay her. Blind her peepers. Boil her tongue.

That happened to me once and let me tell you, it's not something you ever forget.

I wiped the flecks of vomit from my chin, as I straightened. I couldn't figure out how the poor bird hadn't copped it. Then I caught a shufti of a thin tube, which had been slipped between her lips: *the sadistic bastards were force feeding her blood to prolong the agony.*

Melt her in the day, heal her at night. And repeat...

Donovan must've seen the terror in my expression because he grasped my arm. 'Chick tried to escape,' he muttered. Then he met my gaze. 'Hartford says to be cool about... I mean, when I heard the Enforcers had taken you, I was wiggin' out. And now Vesper...'

As if by voicing the name, Donovan had set it free; *Vesper* was taken up and murmured around the ranks of still Blood Lifers, who were bearing witness to her mutilation – *Vesper*.

I knew it must be her true, Blood Lifer name.

'Vesper,' I breathed, adding my voice to the many.

Guilt wormed at me: *Sir* had made the example out of her. Instead of me.

I sent up the silent promise that if I had the chance, I'd rescue Vesper. I couldn't continue my life with her like this: flayed every sunrise for the very same crime I'd committed. It was like a nail in my guts.

No one else tried to escape after that. Even me. I guess both Hartford and marie antoinette were right: *Sir* had taught me my lesson.

'Come now, mon Ganymede,' marie antoinette's pink silk swished ahead of me, down the purple corridor, her curls swaying high on her nut, 'Monsieur wishes to furnish you with most important information and quite the opportunity.' Her hips swayed with self-importance.

The strains of Supergrass' "Sun Hits the Sky" bled through the dark door at the bottom of the hall. I clenched my sweaty palms. Antoinette knocked, before pushing open the door. She gestured for me to enter ahead of her, as if I'd been summoned to the Headmaster's office for a caning.

I edged into *Sir's* study.

Sir was poised hawk-like in front of a bank of monitors. The monitors held multiple screens of what looked like every room on the estate: punters getting suck jobs or buggering Blood Lifers on four-posters, empty hallways, the kitchen, slave quarters, cells (and I'd been right, there was another poor git down there, convulsing in a sensory deprivation hood), woods, what looked like a stable and...*the front door*.

Sir must've had eyes on my escape the whole bleeding time; I wouldn't be surprised if he'd had popcorn. *Sir* straddled those screens like a twenty-first century god.

When *Sir* looked up, he gave a tight smile.

I dropped to *kneel*.

As the electric guitar started to weep, *Sir* muted the music.

I was suddenly too aware of my own breathing and the *rustle* of antoinette's ball gown, as it brushed past me snake-like, when she stepped around me to *Sir's* side.

'Has my pretty leech been a good boy this morning,' *Sir* asked quietly, 'or is he still a mouthy brat?'

'Hmm...' I held my breath. Bugger it, did this one savour the power she cradled in her soft hands.

'He has learnt his lessons, Monsieur. Not a word spoken.'

I tensed when I heard the chair *creak* and the *click*, *click* of *Sir's* Oxford shoes.

Then *Sir's* fingers were in my hair, petting me. 'See you, my little one, why I had to be so harsh? I only do it to help you, seeing as you're so stupid you won't learn any other way.' He was still stroking my nut, twisting the strands of hair. I couldn't stop myself from leaning into his touch. 'Marie antoinette here is my trusted lieutenant.' Confused, I glanced at antoinette, who was blushing. She would've been fanning herself, if she'd been able to – *daft bint*. 'You too can be promoted. A lieutenant like her. I'd be proud and wouldn't be disappointed in you then, see?' I stiffened. So that was why the special attention? To mould me into the one thing I'd never become? 'If you behave and are obedient, I'll protect and care for you: blood, water, food, clothes and time outside.' *Sir* gripped my chin, forcing me to meet his gaze. Bloody hell but it was hard to mask what I truly felt. How much I wanted to tell him to shove his offer. 'What do you want, my shadow?' *Sir* traced my lips with his thumb. *If I had my fangs, it'd only take one small bite...* I must've let some of the thought flicker across my mug because *Sir* snatched back his hand. Trying to regain his composure, *Sir* threw off his jacket, tossing it to antoinette, before turning back his sleeves. Then he ran his fingers through his hair, as if psyching himself up for something. 'Well, my pretty little whore, ready are you to rise up the ranks?'

Marie antoinette boiled the water. *Sir* tipped it into the stainless steel thermal jug. Then I was told to follow *Sir* out into the grounds, by the light of his swinging torch.

I was trotting over sharp gravel, which sliced my bare feet, but the night sky was above me: I was outside in the wider estate. I should've been fizzing with elation. But nothing ever came free at Abona. Everything was a lesson. I warily eyed that jug in *Sir's* hands.

We'd passed kitchen gardens, an ice-house and a horse pond with sleeping koi. I hadn't realised even from the monitors how massive the estate was, yet we'd only walked through a tiny portion of it: us slaves were buried and alone. I wrapped my arms around my naked chest, shivering as the breeze cut me.

When we reached a neo-classical stable block, *Sir* slowed.

I could hear soft, anguished voices inside.

Christ in heaven, no...

I took one step back.

At *Sir's* warning glance, however, I followed him through the black entrance.

At once, the voices stopped.

Donovan was manacled to one side of a horse stall, his wrists stretched above his nut. On the opposite side - facing him - was Hartford, who was manacled just the same. Their distress was so palpable, it was a living entity, alive with us in that stall. It was suffocating.

When *Sir* strolled towards Hartford (who hung unmoving in his chains, with his peepers downcast), it was Donovan, who frantically started begging. '*Sir*, I'm sorry, sorry, sorry... Please, I'll be good... I'm gonna be good... I've learnt my lesson.' It was a shock to hear Donovan reduced to such desperation. 'I'll do anything, just...hurt me, please? Punish *me*.'

'Punish you? I am.' I couldn't stop staring at the jug hanging in *Sir's* hand. *Sir* tipped back Hartford's nut gently. 'Open your mouth.'

Hartford was trembling but he dutifully opened his lips. Donovan glanced with his tear-filled peepers at me - the kohl smudged down his cheeks - as if somehow I could stop this. I wished I had the same bottle as Hartford. But now that tracker was implanted in me..? I had to be a good little puppy. 'You gave water without permission to that bitch, who's pegged out in the sun. So now I'm giving *your* bitch water.'

'No...' Even as I hissed it, it was too bloody late.

Sir had flipped open the funnel on the thermal flask, jammed it between Hartford's teeth and had begun to pour.

I watched in horror as the boiling water gargled down Hartford's throat, *Sir* ramming him in place with a knee against his chest, whilst his other hand jerked back Hartford's angel-gold hair.

Donovan was weeping, banging his nut rhythmically against the wooden stall, wrenching his wrists bloody against the manacles.

I was frozen. Then I shattered.

Hartford's fingers were clawing, until the nails bled, at the stone stable wall behind him. His back arched rigid. His streaming tears, however, were silent; even when *Sir* flung down both the empty jug and Hartford in the same movement, Hartford didn't make a sound. *Sir* had stolen the very last shred of him.

His voice.

Sir wiped his hands on his trousers, before tossing me a set of keys, which I caught in a dazed fog. 'Undo the bitches and bring them back to the house. You've made me proud shadow - that was a lovely job. Extra blood ration for you tonight. You've earned it.'

Sir patted my rump as he left.

Donovan was breathing hard. I'd never seen anyone look at me with such hatred before.

I paled, before scrambling to release Hartford. As soon as the chains clanked to the dirty floor, he curled into a silent foetal ball, his slim shoulders shaking in pain and grief.

'Baby,' Donovan called softly, 'baby, I'm here...'

It was like Hartford hadn't even heard him.

Nervously, I edged towards Donovan to unlock his manacles. The moment they fell from his bruised wrists, Donovan's hands were around my neck, as he knocked me back amongst the straw. 'You...*Judas*...After everything, man, an Enforcer..?'

'I promise,' I managed to gasp, 'I won't ever be one of those collaborators. I'll stop *Sir*...somehow...I'll...do something...'

Donovan's grip didn't loosen. 'You can't. There's no way, there's just no--'

'Let me worry about that. Hartford needs you right now, yeah?'

Donovan shuddered, as with an effort, he pushed the psychotic back into its jack-in-the-box. His fingers eased away from my throat. Then he nodded, pulling himself off me. But he turned at the last moment to wallop me in the guts, which all things considered, I deserved.

Donovan dropped next to Hartford. He made several attempts to touch him but each time backed off, helpless in the face of Hartford's torment. Finally he curled around him, as if they were little kids hiding from the world. It was so intimate I was ashamed for witnessing it. Donovan pulled his lover closer but he didn't say a word: there was nothing to say.

The silence in the cold of that stable was scorching.

It wasn't long afterwards that I saw my chance to keep my promise to do something. To stop *Sir*.

To save us.

At least, that's what I *thought*.

Hartford was still unable to speak. He huddled on a corner of mattress, lost to both Donovan and me; he was unable to swallow either water or the blood, which we both gnawed from our wrists. It seemed so silent without his cheerful nattering or bursts of song.

Sir had stolen Hartford's heart and Hartford from us.

Then all of a sudden marie antoinette was chivvying us out in rows onto the lawns of the walled garden, clapping her hands, like it was bloody Christmas come early.

'*Master*,' Donovan had just been able to mutter, 'Finlo Cain: the owner, man.'

I tensed.

The Estate.

How many times had *Sir* held that fear - the monster under the bed - over me?

Yet what if it was all a bluff?

I knew what Hartford thought. After the way he'd been lynched and then the abuse he'd suffered at Abona at the hands of First Lifers, who could blame him?

Yet I'd seen the other side of humanity for five long decades; I'd lived amongst you. Kathy had shown me the very best of First Life.

The owner had to know what we were. How we were used. That didn't mean, however, he knew what was truly going on in this Bristol house, behind the grand façade and Egyptian sheets, which the Blood Club never saw.

What happened to us in the stables - or Vesper crucified out in the sun.

I guess I wasn't yet ready to believe that.

'Inspect,' antoinette trilled.

I stood to attention on tiptoe, like the others, with my legs spread and my hands clasped behind my nut. My back was arched: my intimates ready for the owner's pleasure.

I could hear *Sir's* voice, charming and calm, like it always was with other First Lifers. Then this other older, gruff one, behind me – *Master*.

They were moving up the row: pausing, commenting and touching.

My breath quickened. Guilt-soaked from having been moulded by *Sir* into an unwilling Enforcer, I knew I was going to risk it – for Hartford, Donovan and myself. For bloody all of us.

Master was behind me. I flinched when calloused fingers traced down my spine. 'Is this the goog that needed learning with the tracker?' A deep Manx growl.

I felt *Sir's* caress on my shoulder. 'But he's a lovely job now. The waiting list for him is already a show--'

'*Master*,' I wet my lips. A ripple had quivered down the ranks of slaves when I'd spoken, which was then followed by a dead stillness. 'Please help us. You need to know what's--'

'Did that stupid slowan of a slave just address me?'

Bugger it.

'Sorry, Mr Cain. I'll--'

'100 lashes with the bullwhip and I want it scrooging, screwed up and chiming like a foghorn, so it learns never to address a First Lifer again.'

I tried not to quake, as I remembered Hartford's bleeding back and his arse torn up by the bullwhip.

I felt *Sir* and *Master* move away, dismissing me and my pointless outburst.

I was a mug.

50 years too long spent amongst First Lifers had made me soft. Hartford had the right of it. These humans knew the darkness at the core of Abona. And they didn't sodding care. Just because we weren't the same species.

At last I truly got that we were on our own: there was no one to rescue us but ourselves.

Before they turned back towards the house, I heard *Master* say (deliberately loudly I was certain), 'And if you can't learn that bad leech? Mark it for the Estate.'

Sir had hung me in chains by my wrists from the ceiling of the stables. My shoulders were wrenched, as my toes struggled to touch the dirt floor.

Crack – I gasped and writhed, as the tip of the red nylon bullwhip bruised and lacerated a strip across my shoulders: it felt like I'd been burnt by a branding iron. My muscles were cramping.

At the start of the punishment, *Sir* had forced me to *count, my pretty little leech – crack - one, thank you Sir – crack - two, thank you Sir* - but I was long past being able to form words.

Crack – I screamed, as the whip seared my arse; I could feel blood dribbling down my thighs.

Crack – another sharp slash where my arse met my thighs (and didn't that sodding hurt).

Crack – Sir caught my legs.

I buckled, *chiming like a foghorn*, just as *Master* had requested.

I realised now how easy *Sir* had been going on me, as I'd guessed when I'd seen him laying into Hartford with the riding crop.

Crack, crack, crack... I swung side to side, squirming ineffectually. My mug was wet with tears. My throat hoarse from screaming.

As the lashes fell, I hung onto the memory of Hartford's strength.

Let my people go... I sang the song on loop in my mind. Whilst my body continued to shudder under the whip - my peepers flickering shut - my dry lips formed the silent words... *Tell old Pharaoh...*

In my agonised, befuddled brain, I was united in the darkness with Donovan and Hartford, leading them out into the tunnel of black - *crack* – my striped, bleeding body, shut down...to freedom...

To let my people go.

All right then, so I've written, and now you've read.

My witness and promise to *do something*. To save them - my family.

That's my business. It's why I have to go. Please give me that.

Let me go.

JUNE 13

I'm not sure why I'm writing this. If you'll read it.

Donovan says this whole slave journal is *grotesque*. He wanted to burn it sacrificial, when he rifled it out of my leather rucksack earlier.

Except Donovan doesn't understand I was never writing it for my Mistress. You got that, right?

It kept me sane, amongst the waking nightmares and terror of being bought by *Master's* daughter. It was a way to say what I thought. Unfiltered. To be a Blood Lifer, without the conditioning leashing me with fears. To tell you what I was, without having to talk because you were Mistress and I was slave.

But how can you truly get it? When you're still trapped in the spider's web of lights, which span the global empire of Cain Company?

'Mr Yates was down Bristol. Not me,' you'd argued, even after I'd flayed my Soul raw. 'Cain Company established, like, the broad strategy. But Mr Yates was on the ground. There were no casualties reported. In fact, there were higher efficiencies and productivity--'

'Do you ever stop and listen to yourself? Whatever happened to *the buck stops here*?'

'Na-ah, that's not fair. You Blood Lifers are dangerous. And Mr Yates found a method to--'

'Break us?'

'Control you - on account of that was his frickin' job. Not mine.'

'Whatever helps you sleep at night, princess.'

Still, you let me go.

And now I'm... No, not free. I'm not some daft muppet, giddy on the first piss poor sips of freedom. I'm still tracked. Maybe you know where I am right now. If you wanted, you could press a screen and M.C.'s punk crew could retrieve me in...what's the boast? *An hour*?

The thing is, that means I'm endangering the others. And it all comes down to *family*. I get that now. It's everything the Blood Club tried to strip from us at Abona.

Not home but *love*.

Yet the bloody irony of it? In that hell, I'd found love of my own kind for the first time since I lost my own family - an uprooted and unwanted orphan school kid.

I haven't forgotten I'm only on loan. Just give me a bit more time to settle this fledgling family of mine, before I leave it for servitude again.

I've set my family up in an abandoned 1930s council house; even as squats go, it's not much cop. There's a ratty sunken sofa, boarded up windows and stubs of candles in each room. I brought sleeping bags. It's better than the overcrowded slave quarters.

The others could go anywhere. Become the Blood Lifers they once were (at least as much as that's possible with partially grown fangs). Yet something's holding us together. Trauma. Family. And a promise about a girl.

I won't say where we are. Even that's too great a risk. I imagine your sister and dad are tearing the world apart to find the escapees.

Too bloody bad.

Moses has led them to the Promised Land.

Even if it does look suspiciously like a squat.

JUNE 14

My crimson ghost flew me on its twin-cylinders down the motorway to Bristol, as soon as I'd picked up supplies.

Number one had been some threads: I'd remembered Donovan had been into Mod stuff, so I'd selected an indigo crushed velvet suit, but I'd had to take a stab at Hartford's cool cat jazz style.

Number two had been a pocket torch green laser - a dead nifty piece of kit.

See when you'd reckoned I was obsessing over legalistic definitions of slavery - as if the Law would ever get us out of this - I'd actually been researching ways to disable my tracker (and before you throw a wobbly, that's a no-go).

Why?

So I could mount a rescue on Abona House.

I never forgot my family, not for one sodding second. Like a game of chess, however, I had to plan my moves.

A few little porkies don't obscure the greater truth. Or maybe I was right before: there's no such thing as *truth*, only what we want.

And I wanted to break into Abona, which made the Internet my best mate. There's nothing you can't learn, if you dig deep enough. So, I learnt I needed a green laser.

When I reached the first CCTV camera, which was on the roof of the low stable block, I steadied myself. I was swamped by memories of the *crack* of the bullwhip and Hartford's silent agony, as *Sir* tipped the boiling water. Then I lifted my laser; I directed it to the back of the CCTV's light bulb, which created a super bright spot on the camera's sensor. It was blinded. After a few seconds, the circuitry melted. The camera blinked off.

I darted towards the house through the humid evening, knocking out each of the cameras as I went. I knew the fact they'd been tampered with, would be alerting the Enforcers to the presence of an intruder. Maybe even *Sir* would be watching, spider-like behind those banks of screens, as one by one they faded back to black.

This was a snatch and grab operation, however, I'd be in and out for my family, before *Sir* knew what had hit him.

I'd memorised the security codes, so breaking in to the slave quarters was easy. I'd discovered the codes the same day I'd read the messages between you and M.C. about your mum.

Remember Florence and our non-date? I swear I wasn't *snoopin'*: I was spying.

The kitchen heaved with Blood Lifers.

My stomach churned. I was starkers, so I could weave in and out, as anonymous as the other slaves. I kept my nut bowed, hoping I wouldn't be recognised.

Then I spotted Donovan. He was slumped by the industrial refrigerator, sorting out ranks of blood bags. He looked knackered. Thinner than when I'd left. I had a feeling I'd got here just in time.

I slipped behind him, tapping his shoulder.

Donovan didn't look round. 'Don't bug me, I'm counting.'

I tugged on Donovan's hand this time.

Irritated, he swiped at me, but when he caught sight of my mug, he yelped.

I bundled Donovan out into the corridor, before he could draw any more curious glances. 'Where's Hartford?'

'In our room. He's...recovering. You're blowing my mind, man... What happened? That skirt returned you?'

'Thanks for the vote of confidence, mate. This is me *doing something*. You and Hartford are getting out of here. Right now. With me.'

I made towards the bedrooms, but Donovan clutched my arm, hauling me back. 'First you tell me how you're gonna do that because it didn't exactly work out last time. You don't..? And I'm not riskin' my baby.'

'Fair enough. CCTV's down, I've discovered the security codes and know the routes outta here. I've also arranged a place to lie low after and supplies. Good enough?'

A slow grin spread over Donovan's mush. 'Right on.'

We found Hartford sprawled on his stomach on a dirty mattress. His back had been carved into pretty patterns in shallow cuts by some sadistic john: yeah, dead *exclusive* the members of this Blood Club of yours. 'Hey baby,' Donovan whispered, 'wake up.'

Hartford weakly turned his nut towards us. When he saw me, however, he scrambled up and threw himself at me, clasping on limpet-like.

Then I realised he was weeping.

I prised Hartford back. 'Hey, helmethead, what's with the..?'

'You'd got out, mac; you don't need to act hard-boiled with me. Now *Sir's* gonna--'

'I'm not a slave here again, you nitwit; I'm the bloody superhero. And you're getting out now too.'

Hartford took an immediate step back, before glancing at Donovan, who nodded encouragingly and whispered, 'It's cool; we'll be free.'

I hadn't expected the cold fury in Hartford's gaze, as it swung to me. '*Bull.* We'll be crucified. Melted in the sun. And you? Poor little bunny, why did you ever come back to this joint, for crying out loud? Are you screwy? And don't give me a line. Level with me.'

'To keep a promise,' I answered softly, 'and save my family.'

When Donovan gripped Hartford by the shoulders, I reckoned he'd find himself tossed across the room, but Hartford allowed it, trembling in shock and confusion. 'Is this what you want your life to be? Forever?' Donovan traced his fingers through the bloody swirls, which were carved on Hartford's back. Hartford winced. 'Let's split, man. We can be together.'

At last, Hartford nodded, hooking his arm around Donovan's waist. Turning to me, however, he insisted, 'Not without Ashanti.'

'No deal. We have to go now or--'

'Let's ankle then. But we're taking Ashanti.'

Bloody. Hell.

The Enforcers must've been alerted that the CCTV was down, and Hartford was right: if they caught us, being pegged out in the sun would be the least of our torments. 'If we do that, I can't guarantee to get us out...so bugger it all...why?'

Hartford gave a small smile, as he limped to the door. 'She's family.'

Christ in heaven, what could I say to that?

Ashanti, however, wasn't in the kitchens, bedrooms or the cellar. As we searched the warren of corridors with mounting desperation, it became obvious the CCTV alarm had been well and truly triggered: an Enforcer in stripy scarf or lacy knickers would shove past us, clutching cudgels or canes, as if they were on their way to being skinned alive. I'd drop behind Donovan and Hartford, and because the Enforcers were in such a tizzy, they wouldn't notice me.

That is, until Miss Guillotine dodger herself appeared.

'*You*, mon Ganymede..?'

Marie antoinette had bustled down the corridor in her silks, wringing her soft hands together. We'd fallen back, but this time antoinette had stopped. She'd assessed our little huddle suspiciously, before pushing Donovan aside, as if parting the Red Sea, to leave me in all my glory.

I'd shrugged. 'Alright, luv?'

So now antoinette was staring at me, like I was a sodding ghost. I wondered (for one barmy moment), whether I could get that one to stick.

'This....' Antoinette struggled, before rallying, '...savours of evil and bloody deeds. A corruption of Monsieur's noble lessons--'

I snagged antoinette by the throat, slamming her into the wall. When she squeaked, Hartford laughed: I wished it was a sound I could hear every day. 'See here's the thing: I've never been one for lessons.'

'Au contraire, Monsieur *knows*, silly boy. He will teach you...'

'Her pocket.' Donovan dived for antoinette's ball gown, pulling out a tiny device, which was transmitting.

Hartford paled.

When antoinette smirked, I lowered my mug close to hers. 'I know I should feel sorry for you.' Antoinette's smug smile died. 'But I don't.' Then I nutted the bint. She crumpled in a pile of curls, blood and silk. 'Right then, we're scarpering. Now.'

Hartford, however, grabbed my hand. 'But Ashanti--'

'We can't help her. And if we stick around any longer, we won't be able to help ourselves either.'

'Vesper,' Donovan suddenly exclaimed, 'her courtyard. Ashanti's in charge of feeding her.'

'One last chance,' Hartford begged. I felt a right bastard. 'We'll blow if she's not there. Please?'

I could've turned sodding cartwheels, when we dashed into the courtyard, and there were those black braids, bent over the crucified body of Vesper.

Ashanti startled, when Hartford yanked her up. 'We've gotta leave this joint. Light's come to rescue us.'

Ashanti, however, only assessed me coolly. 'How! That obroni? From the first beginning he be a confusionist. Big palaver. How I trust him?'

'Then trust me,' Hartford pleaded.

Ashanti gestured down at Vesper. 'Look what big man--'

'I thought you were a warrior?' I raised my eyebrow.

Ashanti bridled, her lip curling. 'Challey, when we be free, I show you.' Then her expression darkened. 'But my alomo be with an American man. How we get her?' The silence in the courtyard was broken only by Vesper's raspy breathing. Slowly, Ashanti looked between the three of us. 'Adjei!' She stalked towards me; we didn't have time to find out first-hand just how good a warrior she was. Hartford, however, stepped in front of me; the pressure from his slim hand was still enough on Ashanti's much broader shoulder to stop her. 'I won't leave her.'

‘We’ll come back,’ Hartford twisted to me, with such naïve hope in his peepers it tore my heart bloody, ‘save her. Save everyone.’

What was I all of a sudden? *Sodding Spartacus*?

‘You promise, boy?’ Ashanti demanded.

I sighed, my mouth dry. ‘Yeah, I promise. Now let’s get a wiggle on or...’ A groan from behind me yanked the nail, which had been lodged sharp in my guts; I’d never forgotten my promise to Vesper. Ashanti watched me questioningly, as I stumbled to Vesper’s side. I fell to my knees next to what had once been her mush. Vesper was trying to focus on me with her half-blinded peepers; only the palest hazel remained flecked in her irises. I wrestled to rip out the damn nails in her wrists first, but they were lodged so deeply her muscles and ligaments pulled away fibrous in my hands. Vesper’s breathing became more rapid. ‘Sorry...sorry...’

Cursing, I fought at the ones in Vesper’s ankles, but when there was the sudden *snap* of bone, I fell back horrified.

Then I heard - soft but hoarse - with a distinct Catalan accent, ‘Kill me’.

That was all. Hopeful and determined.

When I met Vesper’s pain-wracked peeper’s, I found I couldn’t say anything.

Instead, I nodded.

I could feel the others behind me, watching. Then Ashanti’s hand was on my shoulder, squeezing.

Taking a breath, I lightly clasped Vesper’s fingers. They curled into mine, before I fixed my other hand around what remained of her stringy neck. Christ in heaven it was hard but I kept smiling at her. I never broke eye contact - not once - as I choked the life from her.

Strange, I've done in my fair share of Blood Lifers, but that one was different: it felt like a gift.

I pushed myself up. 'Right then, let's--'

'Look you, you've gone and broken my doll. I say you leeches want *your* chance in the sun, isn't it?' *Sir*, his arms crossed, was standing in the arched doorway to the courtyard. Hartford dropped to his knees, his puppet strings cut. But the rest of us? We remained bloody standing. If anything, Ashanti raised her nut higher. That made *Sir's* mouth twist into a frown. When *Sir's* scowl settled on me, it was as if he couldn't decide between shock, outrage and delight. 'My pretty little leech returns to me? What? Did my shadow miss me?' Then his tone hardened. 'Mr Cain will have you for the Estate now, see if he don't. I can't keep a Lieutenant by my side, who makes trouble.'

'I don't need you doing me no favours, mate.'

There was only one expression on *Sir's* mug now: fury. 'Whore,' he pointed at Hartford, who was still in *kneel* and trembling, 'inside.' Hartford began to rise but then sank down again. Frustrated, *Sir* stormed closer. 'Inside, bitch.' This time Hartford didn't move. *Sir* pushed at his black-framed glasses, before glaring around at us significantly. 'The Enforcers will be here any minute.' Then *Sir* was suddenly all silk and sweetness, as he stroked Hartford's slick of golden hair: he'd transformed into the bloke, who I'll admit I'd come to need in those long months, when *Sir* had babied me to dependency. 'Obey me now. And I'll remember it.' *Oldest trick that is, attacking the weakest link*. 'You won't be punished by the sun, I promise.' When Hartford still didn't budge, *Sir's* caressing hand tightened, before he wrenched back Hartford's nut.

At once, Donovan and I dived for *Sir*.

Electrifying fire burst through me, burning me up from the inside. I whined and dropped to the grass, rolling side to side. My back arched. My nails scrabbled at my own mush, as if I could scratch the pain out of me.

Donovan was hovering over me, uncertain and freaking out, darting fearful glances at the device *Sir* was now holding because he'd never seen the tracker before.

Through the grey fog of my own suffering, I realised it was Ashanti, who was stalking *Sir*.

Sir was so into the floor show that he didn't grasp he'd transformed into prey, until Ashanti was twisting his elbow back. Then the bone was breaking – *crack*.

With a holler, *Sir* dropped the tracker.

Ashanti kicked the wankering thing to Donovan, who jumped on it, smashing it into tiny shards of metal and plastic.

At once, the searing burn stopped. How had those fragments held such power over me?

Sir had backed against the courtyard wall, nursing his bent, limp arm.

When Ashanti met my gaze, I nodded my thanks.

Then Ashanti launched herself full fighter mode once again at *Sir*, clouting him across the mug, which broke his front tooth and stained his gob red: *at least the bugger partly learnt what it was like to be defanged.*

Sir didn't flinch, beg or even fight back. I couldn't suss out, however, why Ashanti was just standing there, as if she was hugging the bastard. Then I heard a strange gurgling noise and I knew - *I bleeding knew* - that somehow *Sir* had murdered her.

Ashanti was Hartford's family, which made her *my* family too; as tears pricked my peepers, at last I got that.

Donovan tore to Ashanti, carrying her still body away from *Sir*, who was grinning manically around his crimson lips.

When *Sir* spat out a fat globule of blood and shattered teeth, I realised dully that his hands were stained crimson as well. Then I spied the red-and-black handle of *Sir's* shiv, which was stuck deep in Ashanti's chest – through the heart.

Of course Captain had trained these First Lifers in that weakness too.

I struggled to crawl, my limbs still fizzing with damaged nerves, to where Donovan was tenderly laying out Ashanti. Over her corpse, Donovan looked at me, his cheeks wet.

It was Alessandro all over again: another Blood Lifer shanked because of me.

I turned when I heard Hartford slowly stand. All this time, he'd never risen from *kneel*. Hartford didn't even look at Ashanti. Instead he advanced on *Sir*.

Donovan made to rise to follow him, but I caught his arm and shook my nut. 'Some things a bloke's got to do on his own.'

For the first time, *Sir* backed away, his remaining good hand, which was gory with Ashanti's blood, pressed against the courtyard wall, until he was trapped in the corner. 'Kneel,' he blustered, 'down.' *Sir* could see in Hartford's peepers at last, however, what he was. What he'd always been. And what *Sir* could never truly tame. It'd only ever been buried out of the need to protect Donovan: his own love used as a weapon against him. But now Hartford had been freed - he was a

Long-lived. *Sir* had unleashed him. 'Cupid...bad boy--'

'My name is Hartford.'

Hartford launched himself at *Sir* and in the hush of the courtyard, as Donovan and I grieved over the fallen body of Ashanti, he tore that bastard limb from bloody limb.

Who needs fangs when you've got murderous grief? It was every one of my revenge fantasies come true. It was...justice. Blood Lifer justice. Not your human law.

It felt like absolution for us all.

JUNE 15

Hartford's still grieving; I had to tumble him out of his sleeping bag to get him up tonight. He's squiffy half the time on the booze, which Donovan brings him. It's not like I can give him a hard time. He lost Ashanti because of me.

I may be head of this screwed up family of misfits (and don't ask me how *that* happened; it seems some of the Spartacus rubbed off during the rescue), I'm still not telling a Long-lived what to do. Hartford was locked up for so long it'll take time for him to cope with walking in the world again.

I know I did.

Yet when Hartford does, he'll soar above it, like a bleeding butterfly.

Now Donovan? He's already strutting his stuff. He sprawls on our ratty sofa, as if it's luxury leather. Or swings back to the squat with cardboard boxes of take-away: Chinese, Indian or battered cod from the chippy. He buys our blood from a range of butchers, so we can't be traced. Then we feast. I've never seen Donovan happier, than when he's watching Hartford drink the blood, which he's provided unrationed.

We don't have our fangs back yet, which means I know Donovan can't also be feeding on First Lifers. Do you reckon, however, that I'd restrain him? Donovan's earned the right to stalk the night unfettered.

Maybe I'll persuade them to blood abstain, like I do. After all that time on pigs' blood, it'll be easier than the struggle I went through, cold turkey.

Here's the thing though: I made a promise to rescue Ashanti's girl. To rescue every last one of them at Abona. And I'm a man of my word.

Sir's dead.

But you Cains? The Blood Club? It's still delivering strong *profit margins*.

If I save one slave, another will simply be hunted to take their place.

Plus the specialist, individualised market, which nets the billionaires? That's buried on the Estate. With *Master*. As long as he's training Blood Lifers *good and proper*..? None of us are safe.

We can't run forever.

We either stand and fight now. Or First Lifers will become the apex predator.

The only question left is: will you help us? Or your family?

JUNE 16

'*Don't*,' Donovan clutched my arm, his nails scoring into my flesh. When I met his gaze, I recognised the pain in his peepers but hadn't expected it. 'Please, man, we'll find a way.' He glanced back at Hartford, who was still wormed in the blue sleeping bag, only his tufted blond hair - no longer a sleek helmet - visible. 'Not Hartford. He's done. My baby's given enough. But you and me?' Donovan licked his lips nervously. 'Whatever this suicide mission is? Rescuing Ashanti's chick? Then we'll--'

'It's the bloody tracker,' I pulled Donovan's fingers away from my marked skin, playing with them between my hands soothingly. 'If I don't go back to Grayse, she can track me. To you. I'm not gonna risk that.'

'Then we split,' Donovan was rigid - so bleeding tense - yet I didn't need that to know how much his offer was hurting him. How much he was prepared to sacrifice for me. 'We run together. Leave Hartford behind. Then at least he's safe, yeah?'

I tried to smile. 'Cheers, mate. But I'm not running. And as I told you before, Hartford needs you.'

'Not cool,' Donovan burst out, 'I won't let you be a slave, whilst we're free.'

I gripped onto Donovan's hand more tightly. 'We don't have a choice.'

JUNE 17

So now I'm back here at Primrose Hill – your S.L.A.V.E – are you happy now?

Business is sorted. Loan paid in full.

When I arrived this evening, you were out.

I had a shufti around the apartment, stroking each of the Manx because it'd felt like I'd abandoned them but now I was...home.

I'd only just strolled into the sitting room, sprawling on the scarlet sofa, when I heard the *click* of the front door.

My first instinct was to run, like some lovesick puppy conditioned at the sound to hump your leg. With an effort to look cool, I restrained myself.

I hopped up smartish, however, when M.C. mooched in ahead of you in studded tartan and denim, a messenger bag glittering with skull-and-crossbones slung over her shoulder. I only caught a glimpse of your pale mush behind her, before I had a mug full of enraged punk, pressing me down onto the sofa by the front of my t-shirt.

All right then, consequences time.

I'd reckoned at least I'd get to talk to you first. But life's a bitch like that.

I hadn't expected your voice, cold as bloody ice, from behind M.C., 'Don't touch him: he's mine.'

The pressure on my front eased. M.C. scrutinized me. 'It be proper booky. Dis liccle leech's cuz and its bitch done run.'

'My Blood Lifer doesn't know anything. I've questioned him, remember?'

'Dat's what it says. But if it gets worked--'

'Na-ah,' you insisted. I heard you step closer, as M.C. shook me once more, before standing. I let out a breath, unbunching my hands, which I'd unconsciously fisted into the sofa.

'Problem be I don't have a scooby where you've been hiding da liccle leech, innit?'

'It was a punishment.' I noticed you looked as if you hadn't taken a kip since I'd left and your black A-line shift was crumpled. 'He was locked in his room on account of I'm training him now, like daddy wants.'

M.C. sucked on her teeth. *Yeah, she wasn't buying it.* 'Dis leech at Abona says it saw your bitch dere day of da escape, when Mr Yates was messed up big time. Why'd it say dat?'

My heart was bloody galloping the Grand National.

'That's fried. Maybe the slave's trying to shift the blame onto someone, who's not there to be disciplined? Or avoid trouble for themselves? What's the CCTV show?'

I flinched, when I realised what this would mean for marie antoinette. Then I remembered how she'd bustled to boil the water for *Sir* and I didn't feel half as bad.

'CCTV was down, innit?' M.C.'s gaze flickered to mine. 'Don't worry, sis; my crew be retrieving da bad leeches. And then..? It be a boot party.' M.C. wasn't reassuring you, she was threatening me. Then she smiled. 'You saying dis liccle leech's trained?'

'Naw...I mean...yah...but only...'

'Kneel.' I slipped to my knees next to the glass coffee table at M.C.'s command. I hoped you understood the game I was playing. 'Looks like da liccle leech be learning,' M.C. sounded proud, as if her kid sister had passed the first grade of *Mistress School*, 'but da dutty bitch was on da furniture. Dere's disrespect big time.' *Thwap – thwap – thwap*. I knew without being able to see that M.C. was pulling out her studded belt and lobbing it to you. 'Gonna learn it?'

'Later,' you replied briskly. I hoped that was you catching onto the game and not a promise, as you tossed the belt – *thump* – next to me. I forced myself not to sneak a look at it. 'Now, let's see if we can't get *my* training done. It's late.'

I glanced from underneath my eyelashes, whilst you both settled on the sofa. M.C. took out a laptop from her skull-and-crossbones bag. I let myself sink deeper into my thoughts - safe in them - as you threw figures back and forth. The numbers swirled radiantly.

Donovan and Hartford were free.

They'd look after each other: I'd made them swear it, until with a laugh, they'd insisted they weren't kids.

I was a slave again but I was alive, whilst *Sir* was dead.

Count your blessings and all that.

'Da Blood Club's a product business, you get me?' M.C.'s lecturing shocked me back to my body. I was numb with holding still so long, kneeling at your feet. *Product business*? 'Every product business uses da Internet to cut costs, keep stock of inventories and customers' needs, desires and shit.' You were scribbling away on the pad of paper, which was balanced on your lap. I gritted my teeth. M.C. had pushed her laptop back into the messenger bag and was lounged amongst the sofa cushions. 'It be costing more to tailor da product, but dat's what makes you unique. Dat’s da premium return. Da big cash.’

‘At the Estate?’ You paused, pen poised.

‘You be proper learning. Internet teaches us da personal needs of da private sales. Dad conditions da leeches to meet da needs.’

‘Needs?’

‘Anything Blood Clubbers ask for? Dey get. Dad’s da best. Don’t worry about it, sis; you don’t--’

‘But I want to understand. You were right: I’m a Cain. I know that now.’

Bloody hell, I hoped you *were* acting.

‘You’re gonna make dad proper proud.’

I shifted on my painful knees and then froze, when I realised I’d drawn M.C’s attention. ‘I be letting you deal with your liccle leech now. Alright sis, see you tomorrow.’ M.C. pointed at her studded belt, which still coiled darkly next to me. ‘You don’t be needing to give dat back ‘til den, innit?’

I forced myself not to watch, as you walked M.C. out of the apartment.

I was suddenly nervous to be alone with you.

I’d come back, but so much had changed. I didn’t know what I was to you: more or less than the non-boyfriend, who you snogged when the need burned.

Whether you were now firmly back under the wing of your family, and I was nothing but a *product*, belonging to the daughter of Cain.

You paced back to the sitting room, skulking in the doorway.

No way to read that then.

Still, you hadn’t gone for M.C.’s belt, so if I was going to take a punt...

Bugger this.

I launched myself at you, sweeping you round, as you yelped in surprise.

Then you clasped your arms around my neck and held on, repeating my name, as if I'd vanish in a puff of smoke if you didn't. 'Light, Light, Light...'

At last, I let go.

You stepped back, looking suspiciously like you were wiping wetness from the edges of your peepers. 'Do you know how many lies I had to tell?'

'Not as many as I've told.'

We stared at each other, before I dropped my gaze. 'Cheers, for... It's done. They're--'

'Yah, kinda got that.' I hadn't been prepared for the bite in your tone.

I flushed. 'A bit more acid in that, sweetheart; you didn't quite melt me.' You pushed past, but I pursued you, confused. 'What's..?'

When you swung back, I realised just how poorly you looked. 'Are you..? Has all this...been about nothin' but *surviving*?'

'I'm a slave,' I explained, 'everything's about survival.'

'I thought you trusted me?'

'It's not about trust.'

'It's like...making me feel...manipulating me into helping you? What I wanna know is if you *used* me to free your family?'

The instant denial caught in my throat. Porkies wouldn't work. Not when your flint peepers were considering me so intently you were flaying me raw. 'Wouldn't you?'

I saw the hurt flash, before you buried it. 'You know what? Yah, I would, so I guess I can't blame you. But it doesn't make it right.'

'Neither's kidnap, torture or rape. That never stopped you lot. It never stopped--'

'It did,' you said quietly, 'I stopped. I...' Then you were legging it from the room – *bang* – there went the bedroom door.

Abso-bloody-lutely blinding: not one night back and I'd botched things up.

Sighing, I collapsed back onto the sofa. My leg knocked against M.C.'s skull-and-crossbones bag.

Now wasn't that interesting?

Remember how I told you it wasn't *snoopin'*: it was *spying*..?

I glanced at the door, but the apartment was quiet, lit not by the salvaged chandelier but rather by fig and mango candles. I relaxed into the exotic aromas, as I sneaked my hand inside the bag. I slipped out M.C.'s laptop, before balancing it on the coffee table. I flipped it open – M.C. hadn't even shut it down. I clicked through her browsing history: punk music, motorbikes and finances.

Then I opened another section, marked *Blood Club*. I was immediately plunged deeper into the Internet.

It was when I came to a sequence, which included *onion* that I hesitated.

I knew this would lead to the Tor Network: a hidden network of encrypted websites on the Dark Web, which like an onion, had many layers. Deeper and harder to find. Anonymous too, so they said, for its users.

So I figured, if you were selling slave Blood Lifers, where better to advertise?

At its best the Internet can emancipate the individual, yet here it was at its worst: enslaving a species.

My finger hovered over the link.

I remembered M.C. flicking through glossy photos of starkers Blood Lifers - the same ones she'd flaunted, projected on the dining room table.

Now I could guess why they'd been taken. After all, this was a *product business*, and you used the

Internet to make sure you were meeting the customers' *needs, desires and shit.*

I clicked and waited, impatiently bouncing my knee as the website loaded slowly, and the information was bounced around the globe.

Buggering hell...

I clutched onto the sofa to stop from cursing. I glanced back at the doorway: you were still in your room.

There was Hartford, strapped to one of Abona's four-posters, his back, arse and thighs striped and bleeding. Underneath was written every fetish I'd ever heard of. And a few I hadn't. The prices were eye watering. Then there was photo after photo of the things, which Hartford would never talk about. Now I understood why: I wished I didn't. I clicked on as fast as I could.

Then I stopped. Everything stopped. Even my sodding heart.

You were planning to sell me.

Because there I was: at *Sir's* feet and again at *Inspect*. Dazedly, I read the list of kinks, which I could be trained in (if my new owner wished), whilst at the Estate.

I don't know how long I was staring at that screen, lost in the terror of it. When I looked up, you were at my shoulder, studying the screen too. And frowning.

I scrambled away from you. Startled, you reached out to me, but I held you back. 'Why? What have I bleeding done to...deserve that?'

I didn't understand the way you hesitated, as you twisted back to the screen.

You looked like you were ready to puke, once you'd scanned it. The snaps didn't seem like they were doing it for you. 'You've got it wrong. I wouldn't ever let them do that. No one's having you but me. No one's touching you but...' You looked away, pink creeping up your neck. 'I didn't even know--'

'You never do, right? But that's what your daddy's planning for me and all the other *products*. How can I do nothing when... How can *you*?'

Frustrated (and I didn't know at which one of us more), I shoved past you, slamming into my cell and crashing shut the door.

Except it's not a cell (I've felt that for a long time). It's just stuck in my throat to write anything else. You've given me sheets, which are as soft as your own, this nifty crochet bedside table and the neon blue ivy, so I can tell between day and night.

Yet even a palace is a cell, without true freedom.

I know now that whilst the Blood Club exists, I'll never be free: of fear, guilt and this consuming desperation to help...all of them.

The Lost.

We're not slaves. We're the next evolutionary step, with as much right to this world as you.

The only thing I can't figure yet is how to cut off the head of the snake: the Estate itself.

I threw myself onto the bed on my stomach. When I heard shifting footsteps outside my door, I tensed. But you didn't come in. I breathed in deeply the scent of gorse and sunlight.

No one's having you but me. No one's touching you but...

What the bloody hell was that? I've had my fill of possessive love. I know I'm an obsessive git myself.

But whatever this is between us..?

It wouldn't win the medal for healthiest relationship of the year.

It's controlling and destructive. And I've already had that with Ruby, cheers – didn't end well.

Not to mention, I'm not your *boyfriend*, remember? Can *never* be your boyfriend?

Now isn't that a ringing endorsement?

I'm sorry I let you think I used you to free my family. It's not that it's untrue - especially at the start - yet the feelings part of it..? I didn't figure on that. Bloody daft falling for the bird, who owns you.

I'm not free to love because when you're a slave, nothing can be a true choice. It's always forced: out of fear, conditioning or survival.

If I was free..?

I hate myself for feeling like this towards one of you Cains. I'm a bleeding wanker for wanting you to love me back - just a little bit - when all I am to you is something to be owned and touched.

No one's having you but me. No one's touching you but...

It's all right. I get the message.

JUNE 18

The look on your mug when you stormed out of my room this evening, brandishing my journal like a bloody grenade, I reckoned you were about to rip my throat out with your bared gnashers. 'So you wanna be with your *family*? Not me?'

I backed into the kitchen, bumping into the stainless steel counter and scrabbling for purchase on it. 'Hold your horses--'

'Ya huh!' You slammed your hands down either side of me on the counter; one still clutched the journal. 'You *get the message*?'

I swallowed. 'Don't I?'

You lowered your lips close to mine; your ash blonde hair was a soft veil across my cheeks. 'What do you reckon?'

'I dunno.' My peepers fluttered closed. Our lips moth-touched.

Then suddenly, you were gone.

My peepers snapped open. I met your frustrated ice gaze.

You stood rigid, with your hands on your hips.

My burgundy journal had been abandoned on the counter; its spine was dented. I don't know why that hurt so much.

Your voice was low and sharp, 'I don't care if you are 150 years old, you're still a chowderhead.'

'Fair enough.'

'Because I guess what you're missing,' you continued, your stare so intense I pulled my leather jacket tighter around me, 'is you may not be free to love on account of being a slave, but *I'm* free to love whoever I frickin' like. Don't you dare say that's not loving you back.'

I gawked at you. It's not often I'm stunned into silence, so I've got to give you credit.

Before my overloaded brain rebooted, however, you were back to business again, as if you hadn't just used the '*L*' word for the first time. You pulled out your mobile, flicking through screens. 'So I've been thinking about how to bring down that sick website. I had this tute about ways the Internet can be used to compel companies to behave better--'

'Hang on a tick,' at last, my dazed mind cleared, 'we're not only yakking about taking down a website. If we do this, I'm going for the jugular: the whole slavery Empire.'

'I know.' You sounded quiet but determined. 'This is the twenty-first century though. Everything doesn't need to be...fangs and fists.'

I smiled. 'Does this mean I'm doing the whole Spartacus thing with or without you?'

'With.'

You grasped my hand. 'Landmines were banned because of an Internet campaign, you know.'

'I'm not sure we have the same sympathy factor. Plus the Internet's not such a bastion of good, when the most searched for three letter word is *sex*, not *god*. I'm not throwing stones here because I'm all for porn me, but it's both why and how M.C. used it to whore us.'

'How about,' I could feel you instinctively pulling me away from the counter, closer to you, 'we see if we can't simply get the info democratized? Let the world know--'

'What? Turn the Lost into a protected species? Like endangered Bengal tigers? Because that worked out so well for the other apex predators on this planet besides you First Lifers.'

'We wouldn't--'

'Because the first use you found for us wasn't as a nifty fucktoy? What's next? Eternal organ donors, whose organs always grow back? You can bet someone'll justify that. Military's controllable super soldier? Zoo exhibit? Safari trophy?' I'd wrenched free from you and was pacing the kitchen. 'Or then there's the expendable worker wherever jobs are deemed too dangerous to risk breakable humans: on sea-beds, oilrigs or down mines...' I waved my hands above my nut, as if a rocket shooting into space. 'The perfect astronaut, 'cos we won't cop it before the end of the space flight.' I jabbed a finger at you. 'That's if you don't exterminate us in a single mass genocide or drawn out, desperate guerrilla warfare, in some terror-stricken kneejerk reaction.' I stopped, leaning against the marble counter. 'Yeah, let's go with your option.'

You pouted...actually bloody pouted. 'So we don't tell the world. Only the site on the Dark Web.'

'You're saying the only tossers we'd tell would already be Blood Club members?'

'We could redirect consumers to the conditions behind the trade. No one'll be blind to it.'

'Or think we're pretty, vacant toys, born to be slaves? Bloody cracking.' We grinned at each other. Then my grin faded. 'I don't want to be the one to throw a spanner in the works but I'm no hacker. How about you?'

You shook your nut.

Disappointed, I deflated. 'That's that, then.'

'There's Fernando.'

Of course there was. Mr Alpha Geek himself: he probably hacked into the US Government and Space Command to search for evidence of extra-terrestrials on his evenings off.

I stiffened but bit back my pride. 'King of the Hackers, is he?'

I hope someday other Blood Lifers appreciate how much saving them has cost me.

'He calls it ethical hacking.'

'I couldn't care less what label he sticks all pretty on it, if it works.'

You brandished your mobile, holding it between us. You touched the screen and after a moment a check shirted Fernando - chirpy in some kind of tech lab, which was flooded with enough sunlight to make me automatically recoil - pinged up.

Fernando sprawled in his chair. His white-toothed grin was so wide it looked painful. 'Hey Grayse Cain, my favourite Manx, 'sup?' Then I sidled sheepishly closer to you, and Fernando caught sight of me. His smile narrowed. 'What the frak is *he* doing there? You said--'

'I lied.'

When Fernando tensed, I almost felt sorry for him. Almost.

'Are you..?' Fernando twisted away to face a wall, which was tacked with posters issuing safety warnings in urgent red, whilst stick men acted out scenes of biological terror, as he muttered, 'Is he forcing you to..?'

'Naw,' you quickly reassured, 'he's not... That's not what this is.'

Bloody hell but did the bloke look betrayed. 'So, you two, you're..?'

Good question. You glanced at me, and I studied you. *Your call*.

The silence was dragging on uncomfortably.

At last, you smiled at me. 'It's complicated. But yah, we are.' I could've run laps around the bleeding kitchen. I contented myself, however, with grinning back. The Professor might've been able to give you the family, Harvard and the *day*. But you'd still chosen me. 'There's a whole notha nightmare goin' on here. It's a secret. For now. We haven't told anyone else. We're trusting you.'

Fernando nodded. Yet I recognised the pain in his dark peepers. I don't reckon you have an inkling how in love the Professor is with you. 'Is that all? Because I've got work...'

'You're this important Professor of Evolutionary Biology and whatnot then?'

'I specialise in Mathematical and Computational Biology, primarily evolution, yah..?'

'That so?' Alpha Geek might've lost in love but he'd think he'd won the lottery when he hacked into the site on the Dark Web and discovered an entire evolutionary branch of biology lost to humanity.

Fernando swung back to his lab, panning his phone, so we could see the ranks of high-tech gadgets and humming screens. 'Plus I get to play with nizza computers all day, so I'm happy. Talking of which, this rat has to get back to his race, so--'

'Fernando, we need you. This is wicked serious, it's--'

'Whoa, what's goin' on?' Fernando glanced between us, gnawing at his lip, the picture of concern: *the perfect wanker*.

'You hack, don't you?'

'You wanna say that a bit louder – unencrypted - just in case the FBI aren't monitoring?' The screen blurred, as Fernando waved the phone in his agitation.

'Paranoid much?'

'Come on Grayse, you're killing me here. I can't risk nothin' now I've got the Research--'

Frustrated, I snatched the phone. 'Wink, wink, ethical hacking; we got it. Will you help us?'

Fernando only wavered for a moment. 'I'm sorry, I can't--'

'Open your peepers and do something about the world around you for once in your life.'

'Goodbye.'

'No, wait,' Grayse grabbed the phone back, 'ignore Light. He's a...' Exasperated, I scuffed my heels against the white kitchen units but stopped at a glare from you. 'Don't do it for Light, do it for me.'

Fernando's look was hard. 'You always were good at twisting the knife.'

'I was wrong. Don't do it for me. I'm gonna send you links to a website on the Tor Network--'

'Whoa, what the frak are you doin' messing with that?'

'I told you it was serious. Just look at it and know what you're refusing to bring down before you pussy out on account of your Professorship.'

Fernando flushed. 'It's not like that.' Mr Perfect wasn't looking so bleeding perfect anymore.

In fact, neither of you could meet each other's eye.

'You'll see,' you were quiet, thoughtful-like; it took me by surprise, 'something wondrous, which you'd never imagined possible. But also in such danger that I promise, when you do - like Light said - you won't be able to do nothing on account of I know you're a better man than that.'

Shocked, I glanced at you. We were *leeches* and *parasites*. But now we were *wondrous*..?

Moreover, I was right about something..?

Fernando swallowed. Then he nodded, before he blinked to black, as he cut the connection.

You breathed out, still staring at the blank square. 'What if he goes public? Fernando's all into info belonging to everyone, you know? It's what hackers do.'

I shrugged. 'Then he goes public. Look, it's pointless taking down Cain Company, if the trade's still out there, with eager consumers. All we're doing is creating a vacuum for the next slave trader to step into your dad's shoes. Then who knows, they could be sodding worse. We can't get the genie back into the bottle. But we can smash the bottle.' I'd known since the long nights squatting with my family, when I'd been psyching myself up to return to you, that I'd only completed part of what I'd sworn that day in Abona: to rescue Ashanti's girl and every other enslaved Blood Lifer. To save my race itself. That was the promise, which I'd secretly made to myself. To keep it, however, meant facing my greatest fear: *Master* and the Estate. Of course, I hadn't yet told you; I reckoned that was a drink and sitting down type of conversation. 'Would kill for a coffee right about now.'

'Shame I'm not your slave then, isn't it?'

Right, figures.

We settled on the sofa, your nut resting on my shoulder, which felt like it fitted. I sipped my coffee in silence, building up my nerve. Tentatively, I stroked your soft hair. You allowed it.

I could get used to this.

Except, I couldn't allow myself that luxury.

What you'd said: *complicated*? Wasn't that the understatement of my second life? Still, you'd told Fernando we were...something. As far as we went, that was the clearest it'd been stated. Yet now I had to persuade you...

'You've gotta send me to the Estate.'

You shoved yourself off me with comic speed. 'Are you zoo'n' on me?'

'Dead serious.'

'Na-ah, not happening. You've only just come back.' You didn't add *to me*, but I heard it; I'm sure I did.

'The website. It's not enough.'

'What will be for you, huh?' You snatched my mug, slamming it down onto the coffee table with an ominous *crack*; black seeped down the edges, pooling at its base in a dark sea. 'What is it with you and this...hero complex?'

I laughed but I knew what a bitter sod I sounded. 'I'm not a bloody hero, just a bloke with a promise to keep.'

You stared at the dark puddle of coffee, rather than turn to me; you traced patterns in it with the pad of your finger. 'You're soft if you reckon you can survive...as you are...if I send you to the Estate.'

'But that's the belly of it, don't you see? We're only pissing around the edges here. But the Estate? That's the true blood and guts of the operation.'

'Why do you think I don't wanna..?' You twisted back to me. '*I'll* go down Mann, see what daddy's--'

''No good. They're only letting you in on the sanitised face of the company. If I go, then I'll see the worst. Much as that gives me the collywobbles, I'll be there undercover. I can remember things: human camera here. Trust me, it'll be alright.'

'Naw, it won't be.' Your voice was dead small. 'What if daddy...breaks you?'

It was hard to shake the memory of *Master* behind me on that inspection line, his calloused fingers tracing the small of my back... *100 lashes of the bullwhip...* I forced you to meet my steady gaze. 'Not gonna happen, darlin'.'

'You don't know my daddy.'

'You don't know me.'

We stared at each other for a long moment, before I started backwards, as you launched yourself at me.

Then you were hugging me, like my death sentence had just been announced.

Maybe it had.

Gently, I patted your back. If I allowed myself to wrap my arms around you, I might not be able to let go. The feel of your warmth melting into me, made it even harder. 'Ring your sister; it'll look better non-direct like. Tell her the training of your leech is going well but it needs something more.'

You gazed at me through wet peepers. 'What? Now?' Your arms tightened around my middle.

I nodded. 'You gonna be OK with the acting?'

You sniffed. 'Trust me, I can act.'

Yeah, that's what I'd figured. Still, you didn't move.

'Any time now, sweetheart.'

'Light, please...'

'I'll take a gander, plan the caper and then come back to you, the same daft wanker of a Blood Lifer as I ever was. I promise.'

Reluctantly, you rang M.C., never taking your gaze off me, nor letting go with your other arm; it felt like you were telling me that you'd be with me, no matter what happened next.

That meant the bloody world to me.

''Sup Marlane?' You still didn't look away from me, stroking my side. 'Sorry, M.C., I get you. What's doin'? Well, I've been training my leech on account of that's what daddy wants, and you were right...they need disciplin'.' I was unable to hold back the shudder, when I heard M.C's tirade on the other end about the bastard tracker. You held the mobile pointedly away from your lughole, however, before leaning in and kissing me softly down my neck. Then I shivered for a whole different reason. Finally, you held the iPhone back again. 'So I'm wicked busy with my course and... You think that'd help? But a whole month?' My stomach cramped. *A month..?* I'd reckoned on a week, maybe a fortnight if I was unlucky. I didn't know whether I could hold out under *Master's* loving care for a whole month. You were looking uncertain, however, so I forced myself to smile and nod: this was our only chance. 'Don't take his fangs though.' Why hadn't I thought of that? 'Leave it 'til after, then I can watch. It'll be, like, informative...' I heard M.C. snort with laughter. When your gaze met mine, I saw the apology in it. 'Just remember it's still mine M.C.; I want the promise that after a month, it'll be my toy again.'

When you finally ended the call, we sat for a long time in the dark of the mango scented lounge. The candles were sharp pricks of light amidst the black. The spilled coffee was now nothing but a congealed stain, sticking the cracked mug to the glass; its bitter aroma soured the mango.

We didn't say anything because what more was left to say?

All right then, I guess it's time for me to be learned.

AUGUST 27

Well, it's been a long time, hasn't it? Bloody longer than the four weeks your sister promised. A long time since I've been myself enough to write in these buttery cream pages. Or even to know my true name.

My name is Light. Light. Light. Sodding Light...

I must've given you a right fright. For that, I'm sorry. Sorry I lost myself in the dark, letting myself sink into its safety and hide the last kernel of my Soul so deep no one could hurt me anymore. I'm dead sorry I couldn't fight my way back to you sooner. Most of all I'm sorry you were right: cocky wanker that I am, I didn't know *Master*.

And Christ in heaven did he break me.

Yet I still came back to you because only you were real to me.

There are things I'll never tell you - or anyone – about that month on the Estate. Methods of training. But others? I owe you an explanation for why I returned to you marionette-like: *learned*, as *Master* said. We got into this together. You deserve to know what went wrong.

I underestimated both *Master* and M.C.: their creativity, cruelty and the added skill of the mind fuck - you never truly submit until your mind's in bondage. That's where they succeeded. And *Sir* failed.

So, Cain reputation well deserved.

Maybe one day soon I'll feel strong enough to give you that explanation. Then you'll understand.

SEPTEMBER 2

There's no darkness conjured in Blood Life that humanity didn't invent first.

When I lay starkers, except for my slave ring, in the pine crate at the Cain Estate, the red nylon ropes were roughly dragged from around my bruised throat, wrists and ankles.

I blinked up at the crystal star above me; the chandelier scrolled with letters. Dazed, I spelled out C – A – I –N: your name amongst the constellations.

Here at last facing my worst fear at my own insistence, I steadied my breathing, before I was yanked out onto the black terracotta tiles. I instantly went to *kneel.*

Master's worn jeans and muddied work boots, which stank of garlic, were within licking distance – I hoped he wouldn't take that literally.

'I hear my daughter's not pleased at the way you're shaping, boy. I reckon you're not fit, but she wants you trained.' I remained motionless. We'd decided I'd play this, as if you'd already partially broken me, but I still had some spirit left. *Master* was most likely to buy that charade. 'I haven't forgotten the neck of you at Abona. Don't worry, I know the bettermost way to learn you. And I will, I promise.' I didn't bloody doubt *Master* would try. 'Mr Yates was soft on you, blinded by his favourites. I have no favourites: leeches be nothing to me. I will learn you respect. Do you understand?'

'Yes, *Master.*'

There was a silence. I'd surprised the wanker. Maybe I'd better pull back on the compliance.

'You're a goog. Good for nothing but pleasure. You obey and serve.'

'Bugger that.'

I glanced up, meeting *Master's* gun metal peepers, which had darkened with outrage. I couldn't help flinching, when *Master* tapped the brass buckle on his heavy leather belt and then held up one finger, as if counting.

Not a good sodding sign.

Still, I shifted my shoulders: I had to get the act just right. 'Something wrong, mate?'

Master tapped the buckle on his belt again, lifting a second finger – two. 'A slave doesn't swear. It also doesn't address a First Lifer without first requesting permission: ask, '*Master*, may I?' Was 100 lashes of the bullwhip not sufficient to learn you?'

'Yes, *Master*. But I didn't know those rules, did I?'

'You'll be punished for not obeying rules you do know and punished for breaking those you don't yet know because they've still been broken.'

'That's not fair.' That bleeding tapping again and another finger – three. 'What did I..?' More tapping and another finger – four. I opened my gob again but then snapped it shut. I hesitated, before forcing myself to ask, '*Master*, may I?'

The sod actually smiled. 'No, boy, you'll follow me to my private rooms for your training.' I started to stand, but *Master* shoved me down to my knees. My kneecaps hit the tiles. Hard. I bit back a string of swear words. 'Crawl.'

Bloody buggering hell...

Master met my stare challengingly.

We Blood Lifers were nothing to *Master* but playthings to be brutally broken. *Master* truly wasn't like *Sir*.

I'd better be bloody careful: this was now about survival.

I dropped my gaze. As soon as I heard the *clump* of *Master's* boots, I crawled behind him, cautiously glancing around to memorize the route.

We'd been in the humungous main reception of a neo-Palladian mansion, which was decorated to the luxurious tastes of the superrich, in contrasts of light and dark: white chairs, silver brocade chaise longues, black rugs and an ebony table, which ran the entire length of the room, like an altar waiting for its sacrificial offering. The fireplace was white stone and the wallpaper was black baroque, which reminded me uncomfortably of Abona.

Master drew me on hands and knees through a high atrium, which was embellished with gleaming Doric columns, sculptural chairs that were cast in solid aluminium and a 20 ft. high mural of a Manx cat. The Cain logo wasn't calming (like my cats back home with you), but intimidating - meant to impress with its power. It was surreal, like being steered through fairy tale props.

Is that all us Blood Lifers were to you First Lifers? Mythical fairy tale creatures? And is that what this Estate offered to the billionaires, when they stepped off the private helipad?

A natural history museum, where you could buy one of the exhibits?

Master led me up a sweeping black staircase and then down corridors of endless bedrooms, until at last we were in an entirely separate wing of the Estate. It was focused around a bare, circular hallway, with oak floorboards.

My knees were sore.

Master hadn't slowed the pace or glanced down at me once. The upside, however, was I'd manged to have a good shufti around.

One heavy door was closed, which I was immediately leery of, when the others stood open. A quick gander at the open rooms showed a couple of bedrooms, a bathroom with opulent claw-footed bath, a vast pool room, a library that a Victorian gentleman would be jealous of (including me), and a traditional snug, complete with roaring log fire - despite it being a cool summer evening - and antique brown leather sofas.

This was the guts of the home, where *Master* lived and worked: where I was his slave.

I followed at *Master's* heels into the snug. The smoke from the fire stung my peepers. Arts and crafts cushions were scattered over the sagging sofas and on a high-backed armchair. An Oriental Victorian rug was thrown over the floorboards to the relief of my knees. Gold framed portraits of Cain ancestors (I'd wager), were hung on the walls.

This was the rotten heart of the Estate?

It was so...cosy. Not the torture chamber, which my overactive imagination had built up.

I relaxed.

Until *Master* stepped around the sofa and crawling after him, I saw the cage.

I nearly backed away, until I remembered this was my own bloody stupid idea.

Master slapped his thigh lightly. 'Heel.' Biting my tongue to keep from mouthing off, I shuffled closer to the metal cage, which was in the corner of the snug, facing the white wall. It was large enough for me to sit up, with my neck bent or curl on my side but not to stand. There are many ways to reduce a man, thin layer by thin layer, like peeling an onion, until there's so little left you control it all:

take away his right to be viewed as more than an animal and you peel away yet another layer. When I crawled into the cage, *Master* slammed the door, padlocking it. 'Good boy.'

I watched, as *Master* marched from the snug – *clump, clump, clump* – and then I was alone.

At first, alarm clawed at me, basic and primal.

I tried wriggling my hands through the bars to test the extent of my entrapment, but their backs became stuck halfway at the knuckle. I spent an anxious couple of minutes wrestling my hands back in, scraping the skin off them.

I couldn't see anything beyond the tired back of the sofa and two corners of white wall: I guess that was the bleeding point. It soon became mind-numbing. It also gave me too much time to think: like how I now got the misery of zoo animals.

Master hadn't told me what I could and couldn't do. It was both boredom and exhaustion from the long, painful ride in the pine crate, however, which made me settle down awkwardly on my side and fall into an unsettled sleep.

Until, I was shocked awake again.

'Kneel.' *Master* was glaring down at me. I'd been locked in a sodding cage. Sleeping. *What the bloody hell could I've done wrong..?* Yet I still found myself watching *Master's* fingers in panic, as I pushed myself stiffly to a cramped *kneel*, in case they moved towards the brass buckle on that bastard belt. Then I caught myself: *how had I fallen under Master's control so fast*? I had to act the part of the good little doggy. But somehow the act was feeling more and more real, every second I huddled in that cage. 'You, boy, were lying down.'

Confused, I nodded.

No, no, sodding no...

Master tapped the buckle on his belt, before raising a fifth finger – five – until his whole large hand was spread wide. 'You always answer a First Lifer in words.'

'Yes, *Master*.'

'Good, you're learning. A slave never lies down, unless told a position or given permission to sleep.'

I tried not to squirm or scream. Instead, I simply said, 'Yes, *Master*.'

Master stroked his neat, grey beard. 'So you deserve punishment?'

My guts twisted. The bastard was manipulating me to agree to my own punishment. I attempted to stand but bumped my nut on the bars. 'I'm not a bleeding psychic, you know.'

This time when *Master* tapped the buckle, he held up two fingers on his next hand – six and seven. Then he unpadlocked the cage with a *clang* but ominously without a word.

I hurried to crawl after *Master's* stiff-backed figure.

We were out into the bare hallway. *Master* was unlocking the one closed door. My stomach dropped, when *Master* swung open the door and announced, 'The training room.'

Because here it was: everything my imagination had spun when *Sir* had held the Estate over us leeches as the ultimate threat. The reason this final step had taken me so long. The darkness at the core of the Cain Company.

The torture chamber.

The walls, floor and ceiling had been painted black, like we'd been sucked into a void. The room was lit by a clinical spotlight, which *Master* clicked on, as if over a medical procedure. One entire wall was laid out in neat ranks with canes: loopy, rattan, bamboo, Singapore judicial, old-fashioned crooked handled (like they'd thrashed me with whilst at orphan school), and dragon canes, with which I hoped never to be thrashed. Then there were crops, oiled belts and straps (including wicked prison straps), tawses, both double and triple-pronged, paddles with holes in every shape and size, which hung from D rings, in thick birch ply, leather or rubber. And the whips..?

Let's just say *Master* liked his whips.

Against the wall next to it was a frightening array of fresh switches and birches in tall vases of water, as well as banks of cupboards with shallow drawers: my mouth went dry, when I couldn't help imagining what was inside those drawers.

Except for a Blood Lifer? All that could be a bit of rough foreplay, right?

But that wasn't all there was in the training room.

A St. Andrew's Cross was bang against the far wall and then spaced out, as if they were workstations: a black spanking bench, a birching horse, a padded examination table with stirrups, a low whipping bench with leather straps and chains and hooks hanging at points from the walls and ceiling. A triangular log of wood, which looked dead sharp, was in the corner. It was, however, what dangled on the opposite wall to the canes, which spooked me.

At first sight, it looked like a cross between a hardware store and the torture chamber, for which I'd taken the training room. That was before my brain, however, had thawed enough to look more closely... Shackles, leather restraints, harnesses, straitjackets and gags. Sex and bondage toys... No, scratch that, every BDSM wet dream.

That was it, I was scarpering.

It seemed, however, that *Master* knew me better than I did because before I'd done more than push myself up, he'd enveloped me in his bear arms. 'Shh boy, you need this to learn you.'

Sod. That.

I thrashed back, smashing the tosser clanging into his own torture devices. *Master's* mug transformed into grizzled fury.

Buggering hell, I was in for it now.

I dashed for the hallway.

White hot fire, like a snake of acid, curled down my spine and hissed into my arms and legs. I screamed and dropped to the floorboards. I curled in on myself, rocking in misery.

I was only faintly aware of *Master* in my agony, as he stood over me, holding something in his hand. 'You are a stupid slowan. You'll be strung-up and chiming out a good while, a bad boy as you are. This,' *Master* waved what I realised too late was a wankering tracker, 'was set too low before, for a leech such as you. But you'll feel it now.' He was right, I bloody was. 'I can set it to trigger if you don't stay by my side. Or if you touch the windows or doors. So you'd best obey me.'

I tried to force out, 'Yes, *Master*'. But my tongue wouldn't work.

I watched for *Master's* hand to go to his buckle. When it didn't, I registered a pathetic gratitude, which clawed at the predator in me, who seemed, however, to have gone into hiding.

By the time *Master* shut off the tracker, I don't reckon I could even have told you my name.

Then there was a weird sensation, like I was flying.

Maybe I was back with you (or dreaming), because - *thud* – *thud* – *thud* – I could hear a heartbeat. Next was a blissful warmth. I closed my peepers, no longer caring about anything but the...

Hold on a tick.

As feeling came back to my locked limbs, I realised the warmth was water and someone with large, rough hands was vigorously rubbing my arms and legs back to life. Someone like...

Warily, I cracked open a peeper.

Bollocks.

'Don't fall asleep,' still gruff but not angry. I remained motionless, manipulated like a child by *Master*, in what I now knew was the claw-footed bath, which I'd seen earlier.

'Yes, *Master*.'

'Have you learned your lesson?'

'Yes, *Master*.'

'Can you stand?'

I nearly said, 'Yes, *Master*,' out of habit, which goes to show how easy it is to lose yourself in the mind-set. But then I remembered how insistent you'd been on honesty. 'I dunno, *Master*.'

'Good boy. Try.' When I hauled myself out of the bath, my legs were shaky. I managed to get back to all fours on the cream marble, however, which strangely no longer felt as awkward as it had. 'Now we just have your original punishment to deal with.'

Startled, I forgot my good intentions and stared up at *Master*. When I saw his hand shifting towards his belt, I hastily bowed my nut.

'Follow me to the training room,' *Master* ordered.

As slowly as I dared, I crawled after him, only to find *Master* waiting for me beside the St. Andrew's Cross. He'd laid out seven implements: an oiled prison strap, a rubber paddle with holes, a switch, a birch, a dragon cane (sodding hell), a heavy three-tailed leather tawse and a buffalo hide flogger. I paled.

'What did you think the *seven* stood for?' *Master* asked coolly, adjusting a restraint on the cross.

'I dunno...strokes or...minutes maybe, *Master*.'

'It will always mean implements. Face the cross.' I stood, allowing myself to be restrained at wrist and ankle. '30 strokes each. 210 in total. Count and thank me.' *The bloke was going to kill me. Master* ran his hard-skinned fingers down my arse and thighs. 'You'll mark up beautiful.'

Wanker.

Then *Master* stepped back, picking up the leather prison strap – *crack* – I jolted against the cross. A fiery sting burnt across both cheeks, making them twitch involuntarily on the holler.

'One, thank you, *Master*,' I managed through gritted teeth.

'One more thing: you think of escaping by passing out? Then we'll simply repeat the punishment tomorrow.'

When *Master* finally let me down off that cross, a blubbering, quivering mess, I was desperate to crawl to my cage and lick my wounds. I don't know how my cage had come to equate safety, but it was a pull. Almost like home.

Instead, however, *Master* pointed at the sharp log in the corner. 'Kneel'.

I stared up at *Master*: my mush tear-tracked and blotchy, my muscles still juddering from his abuse. And now he wanted me to kneel, like a naughty schoolboy with his scarlet behind on display, facing the corner on that painful wood? My mind baulked at the humiliation.

I edged back, until I saw *Master's* fingers tapping on his jeans impatiently. Then I was kneeling on that log, fresh tears falling, as it dug in needle sharp.

Master posed me for maximum discomfort: the log running just below my bare knee, with me in genuflecting position. Then he left the training room. I listened as the *clump*, *clump* died away.

When I was alone in the quiet, with nothing but my own agony and fear, I was disgusted with myself. Because all I wanted was for *Master* to come back. To not be alone.

I told you, I'd underestimated your dad.

Holding onto the game I was playing was as hard as holding onto myself.

As I clenched my hands behind my back, trying to absorb the building agony in my knees, I understood for the first time that simply surviving this month was the true caper: surviving as Light and not *Master's* boy.

That night, the clanging shut of the cage door didn't feel quite the degradation it had before.

I sighed in relief, settling down on the bars, as much on my stomach as I could. I yelped when my damaged knees came in contact with the metal.

'I am Light,' I whispered, mantra-like, desperate not to forget, 'I am Light, Light, Light...'

The next night, *Master* made sure I could no longer complain about not knowing the rules. He dropped *Rules for Blood Lifer Slaves* in a glossy corporate brochure, which was even stamped with the Cain Manx logo, on the floor in front of me.

I was kneeling beside *Master*, whilst he lounged on the leather sofa in the snug. 'Read it and memorise.'

'Yes, *Master*.'

'I'll test you. You'll earn punishment for each wrong answer.'

'Yes, *Master*.' I'd memorise it on the first read through, so intentionally earning punishment on my still tender backside..? *That deserved a medal.*

When I reached for the brochure, *Master* clutched my right wrist. 'First...' He snapped on a heavy stainless steel wrist cuff, which was magnetically locked. It had eyelets at the front, which *Master* was fastening to my left wrist. Then he was urging me to stick out my ankles; I watched dully, as *Master* bound them as well.

It was only when *Master* made me bow my nut for the metal collar that I recoiled, before I steeled myself. *It was just an act*; *I was still Light, and no one could take that away from me again.*

Then *Master* deliberately showed me the engraving on the metal – SHADOW: PROPERTY OF CAIN – before he placed the collar around my neck and screwed it shut.

I'd never felt so...owned. I blinked back tears.

'Now, what do you say when someone gives you a gift?' *Master* demanded sharply.

I jumped. 'Thank you, *Master*.'

Mollified, *Master* settled back with his newspaper, shaking the crisp pages. He glanced at me from under bushy brows. 'You see that, boy?' He jerked his nut towards a coat of arms, which hung over the fireplace. It was a triskelion of three legs, conjoined at the thigh; underneath it was the Latin motto: *Quocunque Jeceris Stabit*. I'd noticed the same words painted over every doorway in the circular hallway. *Master* leant towards me, his emperor's smile smug. 'Whichever way you throw, it will stand.' He turned a page, tracing down the column thoughtfully. 'Humans were made to be the leeches' masters. You have to be tamed. My family have always been slavers, of one sort or another. Now we're the saviours of our race.' He kicked the slave rulebook with his boot. 'Care you memorise your new bible, or I'll have you chiming tonight.'

When it came to it, I could only force myself to make two deliberate mistakes on the test, yet *Master* still had me chiming out when he opened those shallow drawers and used toys on me that... Some of the things I'll never tell anyone.

Afterwards, when I cowered at the bottom of the cage, I knew this was a battle of wills, even if *Master* didn't know the truth of it.

Yet now I wasn't so cocky I reckoned I'd win.

The next night, I didn't even think about protesting, when *Master* clicked a metal chain as a leash to the 'O' ring on the front of my collar and led me out of my cage, towards the pool room.

I managed to get a better butchers at the library, which was next door to the pool room. It was circular, with stacks of books ranked in spirals up to a high ceiling, arranged around an oak desk. There was a giant ash and elder triskelion mural on the floor. It must be *Master's* study as well – *jackpot*.

I forced my excited gaze down. I hadn't a clue if I'd be able to snatch a chance to rifle, especially now *Master* had added this choke chain. Yet for the first time since butting heads with *Master*, I reckoned maybe I wouldn't be the one with the antlers torn off bloody.

A tug on the leash – *and isn't that a sodding humiliating thing to write*? – and I crawled more rapidly after *Master* into the pool room, which was like a futuristic gentleman's club: the pool table was crimson velvet, shimmering silver chairs sprawled on each side below globular lights that were like space pods and a dome-shaped ceiling light bathed everything Midas-touched.

A summer storm was lashing the wide windows out in the dark; clouds veiled the stars.

Master tied one end of my chain to a leg of the pool table, like a bloke leaving his mutt outside the boozer, before setting himself up a game.

I still hadn't been fed or watered since arriving, although after my stint at Abona, the gnaw of starvation and claw of dehydration was at least familiar - reassuring even - like being tortured by an old nemesis, rather than a stranger.

I knelt there - shivering, starving and starkers - whilst *Master* casually leant for a shot. In every exposed inch of skin I felt I was just another one of this rich man's possessions.

'What do you think the wild leeches would say,' *Master* wasn't even looking down at me, as he lined up a shot, 'if they took a sight of you now, boy?'

Clatter – the ball hit the pocket.

I didn't look up. 'I dunno, *Master*.'

'Is that a lie?' *Master* bent low over the crimson table for another shot.

I stiffened. 'No, *Master*.'

'Would they accept you back as one of them? Respect you?'

I don't bloody care, you wanker - rebel here. 'No, *Master*.'

Clatter – another pocket.

I could hear *Master* taking a slow, appreciative drink. I licked my dry lips. 'Of course, they already can,' that same relaxed tone, the one *Master* had used with you about Fernando. 'Captain has a file on you. Photos. What do you reckon a Blood Lifer like him would've done with them, after your great fuss?' He ran the cue up and down between his fingers speculatively. I'd never felt so sick and...violated. '*This* is your life now: as my goog. You can't ever return to your old life again.'

Clatter – and another onion layer was lost.

Later, *Master* perched on one of the silver chairs in the pool room, balancing a tray of spuds and sweet Manx Queenies, which had been brought in by one of the short, sturdy servants, who I caught glimpses of moving between rooms with total indifference to me. It was like the imprisonment and torture of Blood Lifers was as humdrum, as if their employer was simply keeping a mistress. How many years had your dad been practising his skills for the local servants to be so blasé?

Hartford had said he'd been the first Blood Lifer bagged by *Master*. The thought of Hartford and the reason why I was suffering, steeled me.

Let my people go...

Sir had only ever been the slave driver: the true Pharaoh was seated on a silver throne, shovelling queen scallops into his bearded gob, whilst I knelt at his garlic stinking feet.

When my stomach growled, *Master* raised his eyebrow. 'Do you want some blood?'

Confused, I hesitated.

Rule 5A in *Rules for Blood Lifer Slaves* was... *A slave has no direct desires...* So could I *want* anything..? Rule 7B, however, was... *A slave will always be honest and tell the truth...* And I was bleeding hungry... Yet again, Rule 13A stated... *A slave will tell their Master all their needs, thoughts and secrets.*

'Your slave is hungry but it will only feed if you wish it, *Master*.'

Was that body, mind and Soul enough?

The stroke of *Master's* hand through my hair, told me it was. 'I knew I could learn you, boy.' Then he continued to munch his spuds, studiously slowly. When *Master* finally rang one of the stony-faced servants, and they delivered the blood, I sodding wished they hadn't. It was in an over-sized bottle with a rubber teat, like the ones you'd offered me. Then the wanker settled himself, holding it out between his knees, as if he was feeding a lamb. I scowled at the bottle and then up at *Master*. 'Don't be acting the gor. Drink.'

I shuffled closer, bending my lips to the teat. When I suckled, the blood oozed out, thick and freezing. I immediately gagged.

Human.

I fell back in shock, spitting out foaming globules onto the pristine white carpet, whilst *Master* swore and booted at me. But it was too late: I was swimming on the high. My peepers rolled back, my muscles juddering, as I giggled, at the same time as tears crept down my cheeks.

The bloody bastard.

At last I lay still, glaring up at *Master*.

Then *Master* was tapping his belt buckle, holding up - three fingers already?

I swallowed but I didn't stop glaring.

Didn't *Master* understand what *abstention* meant? The effect human had on a Blood Lifer, after a diet of animal alone?

Of course he did. *Master* had that file on me, courtesy of Captain, with all my *weaknesses*.

After five decades of blood abstention, the sadist intended to break it - break me - as if to prove I'd never been more than a parasite.

Starving and now overloaded, I shook, as I pulled myself back to my knees.

Master's peepers were crushed ice. 'Rule 2D states--'

'Yeah, yeah, a slave only eats what the sodding Master gives him and when he's told to. But *that's* human blood, and I'm not eating it.'

Tap, tap, tap - three more fingers – six.

Flushed with a creeping sense of mania, I wondered if *Master* would keep counting, once he'd passed his ten digits. Then I remembered, however, just how many implements *Master* had hanging from the training room's walls and sobered. 'It's human.'

'Aye, the Manxie donate it,' *Master* set the bottle down, before grabbing my leash and hauling me back to the snug, so fast I was dragged behind him along the wooden floor, bruising my jaw when I didn't react quickly enough to catch myself. 'The Cain family have been here on Ellan Vannin since before records began. Now we put money into schools, building works and jobs. Mann is our fiefdom.' *Master* unfastened the leash from my collar, slamming me into the cage. 'I'm an Independent MP in our Parliament: Tynwald. It's the oldest governing body in the world, boy. The Isle of Man Constabulary? Chief Constable Quayle's a keen member of our Blood Club. So the Manxie donate, and you'll never refuse food from me again.'

And I never did.

The next day, when *Master* held out the bottle, like it was feeding time at the farm, I latched onto the teat and sucked.

It was so freezing I nearly choked and pulled away. But *Master's* hand was suddenly twisted in my hair, holding me on. I had no choice but to keep drinking.

I took panicked breaths through my nose, as I forced down the manky blood, which still zinged through my bloodstream, awakening instincts I'd forgotten: a desperate wildness and howling power, which shifted me side to side.

I watched as *Master's* fingers moved to his brass belt buckle – one. 'Don't work yourself into a fidge. If you're a good boy, I'll take you out into the Estate, so you can have a pelt up and down in the woods. I need to cut some fresh switches anyway.'

I straightened. I needed to be outside now my cells were rushing with human blood and screaming for the chase of a hunt. I'd do almost anything for that.

When I caught *Master's* smile, I realised he'd engineered my response.

All evening, I was dead careful, trying to earn my reward. I couldn't sleep the day in the cage, restless with need.

That night, *Master* waited for me to open my gob obediently, like a baby bird, before he shoved in the teat.

When I suckled on it, I found the blood had been heated. I met *Master's* gaze over the bottle and felt this rush of...appreciation. It must've been reflected in my peepers because *Master* smiled warmly.

Master had never looked at me like that before: it felt bloody good. I hated myself. But at the same time? I was strengthened by *Master's* approval. No bloke had shown me that. Not since the day Nora, Polly and I had been playing out by the willow, and mama had stumbled towards us, her haunted peepers telling me the truth about papa, before she'd even begun to speak.

When I finished drinking, *Master* patted my nut. 'Good boy, let's take you for a run.'

I should've wanted to smash *Master's* patronising mug in.

Instead, I grinned.

When *Master* walked me on hands and knees out of a narrow back way, I sneaked a glimpse at the security code – 6 digits. Yet there'd also been four other codes between here and the private rooms.

I was beginning to grasp just how tough this caper would be. And I'd already been here... I didn't know how long. The days and nights melded into each other.

At least I'd survive as Light – *I am Light, Light, Light* – and return to you.

I risked a smile, remembering you hot against my back, as we tonned towards the coast on the Triton.

The carpet of wild garlic under the trees drove my newly blood heightened senses into thrashing overdrive; at last I understood the garlic scent on *Master's* boots.

When I darted and dove between the Manx oaks, ash, elders and wych elms, disturbing raptor-eyed pheasants amongst the brush, the heady scented mix of raw nature sang heavy metal *beat, beat, beat* to the resurrected Blood Lifer in me and called me to hunt in the warm of the summer night.

My partial fangs shot out. I laughed to the skies.

Christ in heaven this was glorious.

Master was somewhere in the black, with a 20-bore sidelock shotgun, held loosely over one arm; he used it to hunt the pheasants, which he bred on the Estate. He hadn't needed to say a word for me to know I must return when he called, like a hound.

But for now? This was my reward. And I was free.

I was running again at last – not crawling - an equal to First Lifers. I didn't know if I could ever be caged again. And I didn't mean in my new home behind the sofa in the snug.

Master had unleashed me.

Still high from the chase through the woods, which *Master* had boasted the Cains had planted themselves, since their Manxie forebears had sliced down almost every tree on the island, I dropped to *kneel*, as *Master* left me unchained in the hallway.

When the landline rang in the snug, *Master* shot me a warning glare, before clumping to take it, slamming the door on me.

This was it - my chance to spy on *Master's* study.

I peeked all around – no dour, sneaking servants. I had a gander through the library door at the circular oak desk.

Spurred on by the blood and the adrenaline kick of my night of freedom, I legged it into the library, over the mural of the three-legged man and launched myself at the Arthurian desk. I tore at the drawers. They were locked. I was too buzzed to do caution, ripping out the drawers, cracking the joints and then frantically searching the papers.

Nothing: just accounts. I began to panic.

The second drawer, however, held a list of names and locations, with slave names next to them. My stomach clenched. I quickly memorised them. Just in case.

Who am I? Patron saint of Blood Lifers?

I tore open the third drawer.

Reams of numbers - six digit codes - with a coloured key, which matched them to a layout of the Estate.

It was whilst I was absorbed in studying the codes, however, that I heard the polite cough.

Startling, I looked up.

Master was standing, with his hands clasped behind his back, examining me. To my alarm, he didn't look furious, more...disappointed.

Ashamed, I dropped the papers, folding to *kneel*. Vaguely, I wondered what was bleeding wrong with me. But it was buried beneath the wailing terror.

'You slink! I reward you, and in turn you be disobedient?' *Master* didn't raise his voice. Somehow that was worse. 'Why are you in here?'

I hesitated... *A slave will always be honest and tell the truth...* I struggled to shut out the oily, insistent voice in my mind. 'I dunno, *Master*.'

'Don't lie, you bad boy, or I'll have you scrooging and screwed-up for days.' I flinched, waiting for *Master's* fingers to move to his belt, but they didn't. 'What do you want with that?' He nudged the codes with his boot.

'Nothing, *Master*.'

'Were you trying to memorise them, so you could escape?'

'No, *Master*, a pathetic leech like me couldn't do that.'

Master relaxed then and laughed. 'That's true. You're such a stupid slowan you couldn't even remember your slave rules.'

At last my punishment for the deliberate mistakes in the test seemed worthwhile. '*Master*, may I?'

Master stroked his beard. 'Aye, boy.' Then unexpectedly he gripped me by the chin, his thumb digging into my jaw. I winced. 'I'll know if it's the truth.' He released me with a shove.

‘I’m sorry, *Master*.’ It wasn’t a lie: my skin pulsed with the need for punishment.

‘You will be.’

‘I was looking for a copy of my file,’ I forced myself to silence the nagging git slave voice inside my brain, ‘the one you gave to Captain. It made me dead upset what you said. I wanted to see what it--’

Master gripped my hair, wrenching my nut back. ‘*Wanted*? You’re not fit, boy. A slave has no desires. You exist only to serve. But I’ll learn you.’

I’d expected many things but not...

I was ordered to the low whipping bench in the training room, forced to lie on my stomach. My feet were raised on a strange wooden contraption, my big toes tied to it by a thick red string and ankles cuffed. I was restrained to the bench by my wrists, with a wide leather strap over my waist.

Master said nothing at all. He hadn’t tapped the buckle on his belt, held up a number of fingers, laid out implements or told me a number of strokes.

It was giving me the collywobbles.

Strapped face-down as I was, I might as well have been blindfolded. It was only when the first leather tawse whacked down bastinado-style on the vulnerable pink of the tender side of my right foot that I got what I was in for.

I yelped and struggled but I was tied down tight.

Master attacked both feet in turn with straps and rubber paddles, up and down from toe to heel, focusing on the arches. He turned my feet this way and that, as delicately as if he was examining them for injury, not thrashing the hell out of them.

I didn’t start bawling and begging, however, until *Master* broke out the canes.

At last, through the blurry fog of agony, I realized *Master* had stopped and was unfastening the restraints.

I was floating somewhere - not quite in my own body - but the tug of the leather being pulled around my middle dragged me back to a reality in which the punishment wasn't over.

Because that's when *Master* commanded, 'Stand.'

Quailing, I twigged that the psychological games were now beginning: on *Master's* order, I had to torture myself.

Cautiously, I swung myself round on the bench and then pushed myself up. My legs nearly buckled at the pain, which shot up from my bruised feet. Gasping, I tried to stand lightly on them, but *Master* placed his strong hands on my shoulders and pushed down.

I hollered.

'In the corner. Hands on head.'

I blushed. *Bugger it.*

I limped to the far corner, wincing on each step. When I finally heard *Master's* order to crawl and dropped to all fours, there were tears of gratitude in my bleeding peepers.

We Blood Lifers are all about the speed and skill of the hunt, and *Master* had given me a taste of that in the woods, only to steal from me the ability to even stand without pain.

After that, it felt as if there was nothing *Master* couldn't strip away from me.

Master led me back to the cage, locking me in without looking at me. I don't know why that hurt, after what the bastard had done to me.

Instead, *Master* left me alone in my cage, with nothing to do or see, except those white walls and the worn back of the leather sofa, for a long time.

I could hear him moving around the other rooms in the wing. He never came back into the snug, however, except once a night to feed me, through a panel in the bars of the cage.

The blood was freezing again and thick; I choked on it, as I struggled to get it down.

Master never spoke to me.

I asked permission to speak on the first night, although I'm not sure what I'd have said. *Master*, however, had simply shaken his nut.

As soon as *Master* had clumped out of the snug, I'd thrown myself side to side in the cage in frustration. My muscles were cramping, trapped in so small a space, yet buzzed on human blood.

I was blood addicted again: dependent on it and *Master's* feeds. I was restless and agitated when my blood sensed it was time, even though all this was artificial and against nature. Here I was, drinking human blood from a bottle, through the bars of a cage, instead of through the silk soft skin of a human neck.

I couldn't stop the blood dependency, or my dependency on *Master*. I was equally addicted to both.

I tensed in anticipation when I sensed *Master* was about to enter the snug, waiting in desperation for him to look at me. Speak to me. Even give me an order.

For him, I understood finally, to forgive me.

At last, one evening when *Master* was feeding me cold blood through the bars in stony silence, I couldn't take it anymore. '*Master*, may I?'

Master started to shake his nut but then seemed to change his mind. 'Aye, boy.'

Shocked I'd been given my shot, I collected my confused thoughts. I no longer knew what was acting and what was real, as if too many layers had been peeled back for the masks to remain. 'Your slave is sorry it let you down. It's learned its lesson.'

'You've learned it when I say so,' *Master's* tone was sharp but his expression had softened. 'You mustn't have secrets from me. Tell me what you wish.'

'Your slave wishes...to be allowed out of this cage again.'

'Why?'

This time the words came from somewhere deep inside me that I didn't know existed, ventriloquist-like. 'To serve you.'

That's when I tumbled down to a dark place, clutching my name like a rope.

Light, Light, Light...

Yet the more I repeated it, the less it felt like my name and the more it sounded like a nonsense word, with no connection to the slave crawling out of the cage and gratefully kneeling at its smiling *Master's* feet.

SEPTEMBER 3

If that'd been all the wankers had stripped away from me, then it wouldn't have taken so long to fight my way back to you.

But there's always more to lose.

One evening, before *Master* led me to the training room to be learnt my lessons, I knelt in silence at his knee, as he lounged in the high-backed armchair, perusing his newspaper and indulging in a cigar. Peepers downcast and holding myself perfectly still on the Victorian Oriental rug, I gazed at the reds and faded whites because they reminded me of the rug in my childhood drawing room.

The thought unsettled me with memories of kneeling at my papa's knee, as he puffed on his clay pipe and shook the billowing pages of the *Times*. I lost myself in the rug's threads; counting them, I was caught in the numbers.

Hours passed, as if I'd slept.

'Good boy,' when *Master* stroked my hair, I glowed, leaning into his touch.

It was as if I knew I should be screaming. Shouting. Swearing. But that I wouldn't.

Instead, I continued kneeling there, happy to be by the warmth of the glowing fire, free from the cage or pain. Content to have pleased *Master*.

And that's the first moment I let myself hide too deep in the dark. Only I didn't know it then.

When *Master* left to answer the harsh trill of the landline, I didn't even glance up. It was only when I heard my name – no, my slave name - that I was suddenly alert.

My true name - my Blood Lifer name - was one of the many things I'd let fade to black.

My name is... My name is....

'Slave shadow's a darling goog now, fair learnt. The auction'll attract high bids.' My nut shot up, but *Master's* back was turned. I tried to calm my panicked breathing. 'Aye, we'll put on a right party here on the Estate for the Blood Club. It's the best tack to boost confidence, after that unfortunate incident at Abona...'

Master continued to yak about business, as if he hadn't been nonchalantly planning to sell me.

No one's having you but me. No one's touching you but... I mouthed the words because I didn't have the bottle to holler them at *Master*. I no longer understood why I'd minded you saying them.

The metal collar around my neck (which I could feel every time I swallowed), read - SHADOW: PROPERTY OF CAIN. Your family already owned me.

A slave has no direct desires. But I did desire you, desired to be safe back with you, home in Primrose Hill. When I lay in my cage, it was all I dreamed about.

But an auction..? To be sold to the type of bastard, who got off on the specialised extras *Master* was offering..?

When I heard *Master* pace back to the armchair, I tried to still myself.

Master tipped up my chin, forcing me to meet his steady gaze, so tenderly the last thread of me unravelled. Then the tears fell. 'You must always tell me your thoughts and secrets,' *Master* murmured.

'Your slave is frightened of being sold, *Master*.'

'Why?'

'My Mistress owns me.'

'You're my property to sell.'

'*Master*, may I?'

'Aye, boy.'

'It would do anything to serve her again.'

I could see *Master's* apparent satisfaction, when he nodded. Yet his mush was grave. 'I don't know; you've been a bad slave for my daughter.'

I lowered my gaze. With every submissive atom of me, I tried to convince *Master* I could do better.

Master seemed to understand because he let go of my chin and petted my nut. 'Maybe if you continue to be obedient, I'll inform my daughter I've learnt you your lessons. Then she can come from across the water and decide. Will you try harder, if I arrange that?'

'Yes, *Master*, thank you.' I was panting, like an over-excited mutt.

'But remember, if you act the gor, you'll lose the reward. Then the auction goes ahead.'

From that moment on, I was lost.

Whether it was something in my file, or by watching the way we'd acted together at M.C.'s, *Master* had known to exploit my greatest weakness: *love*.

I was desperate not to be separated from you and flown, like another one of those glowing lights, somewhere around the globe to be a billionaire's plaything.

It wasn't a lie, what I'd told *Master*: I'd have done anything to get you back.

A month's undercover work now looked like the least of it; I'd be lucky if I ever saw you again. Terrified by that prospect – the stick - and thrilled about seeing you at last – the carrot – I jumped through every hoop and endured every humiliation. And the more times I did? The easier it became. As if my mind was being subtly reshaped.

Soon it was a struggle to even imagine I'd sworn at *Master*, fed from anything but a bottle or slept in a bed, rather than a cage.

One night, I was in the training room, placed in *nose* (a position I bloody hated): facing the wall on tiptoes, my wrists tied behind my back and my nose delicately holding an old Isle of Man penny with a triskelion motif - *whichever way you throw, it will stand* - to the wall. If I let the penny fall, I was in for a bleeding sore arse.

When I heard *Master* behind me, I tensed but he only removed the coin. 'When Grayse was little, and Marlane wasn't yet a woman,' *Master* unfastened my cuffs roughly, 'my wife loved riding in the evening by the coast.' To my surprise, *Master* was also clicking open the cuffs' clasps; they clattered to the floor. I jumped. Then I felt *Master* rubbing at my sore wrists. 'This yarn I'm spinning, it's a show but all true.' He fixed on new bondage cuffs. These were leather but softly lined with suede. If I hadn't been so tense, I'd have luxuriated in the comfort. *Master* shoved me hard onto my knees – *crack* – before working on my ankle cuffs too. 'She didn't come back, so at day-lift, I grabbed my shotgun and took a sight up the coast.' One ankle now had the leather cuff on, instead of metal; *Master* clutched the other, his fingers biting hard enough to bruise. 'I found her. Heart attack, they said. Still,' he pulled the last cuff on tight, before spinning me round and slamming me to all fours, 'no one could say why the horse was dead right next to her, its heart stopped just the same: until the Blood Life Council spun me a yarn, which was even more of a show.' He clicked on my leash. 'She's here.'

Master dragged me after him, without looking down.

I shivered at the thought of returning to *Master*, after what he'd just told me about his wife.

I'm sorry...but you should know the bloodied truth, even if you hate me, as much as your dad hates Blood Lifers. Even if you punish me for your mum's death.

At that moment, the wisp of hope I clung to was that *you'd arrived.* My heart hammered with joy and nervous anticipation.

Please let you decide to keep me.

How could I not be wary of your reaction to...whatever I was now? You'd always said you didn't want a broken *thing*...

Yet I'd survived, and you'd come for me: in the battle of wills, your dad might've chipped away at me. But he hadn't shattered me.

I was surprised when *Master* stopped at one of the bedrooms. When I'd had a gander in here before, it hadn't struck me as your style: a spherical bed slap bang in the middle, in satin scarlets and blacks, trapped by glass screens, which were printed with erotic photos of Blood Lifers.

Master unclipped my leash. 'She's waiting for you. Be a good boy and remember your lessons.' Then – *clump, clump, clump* – he retreated to the snug, firmly closing the door.

I was dead excited, yet something held me back. I was ashamed when I realised what you'd see: me, starkers, collared and in cuffs, crawling like an animal. I told myself you must know what to expect. But that didn't take away the bite.

Unable to raise my nut, I crawled slowly into the bedroom.

The first thing that was wrong was the smell. Not gorse and sunlight but leather and sweat.

Alarmed, I looked up.

The second thing that was wrong was the footwear. Not Fendis but black army surplus boots.

I scrabbled back against the wall.

'Dad told me he'd learnt you, liccle leech, but seems to me you be still a proper disrespectin' bitch.' M.C. stepped towards me, studded and spiked from head-to-toe; the only flesh showing was filmed through her black mesh top. I suddenly felt twice as starkers. 'Kneel.'

Conditioned now, even through my horror, I folded into position.

M.C. smirked. 'Good liccle bitch.' When she slunk towards me, I battled to stay still: to obey. M.C. stroked down my cheek with her black-nailed fingers. 'See? It just needed da right discipline to train you, innit?'

I kept my gob shut, even though my brain was whirring.

Why hadn't you come for me?

Christ I felt...abandoned.

M.C. prowled around me, trailing the back of her hand across my shoulders, as if assessing a purchase. 'Spoilt Boston brat never could share her toys.'

I stiffened. Sod it – M.C. wasn't *Master* and she wasn't my Mistress – she wasn't *you*. I shredded the wankering *Rules for Blood Lifer Slaves* and gave the bastard slave voice a slating. 'I'm Grayse's,' I whispered.

M.C.'s fingers transformed to claws, slicing into my right shoulder and anchoring me to *kneel*. 'You muggin' me off?'

'I'm hers - not yours - to touch.' Expecting a hiding, I licked my lips in a quick, anxious swipe.

M.C., however, only let go of me with a shove, before caressing my cheek again. 'You be no one's, you get me? An unwanted goog, sold to da highest bidder.'

'But Grayse--'

'Made her decision. She be gone back to dat neek Professor at Harvard. She don't want da Cain Company. And she don't want *you*, you feeling me?'

And yeah, *I felt her*, down deeper than anything *Master* had done to my body.

This was different because for the first time, I felt it deep in my mind.

You were what I'd been holding onto. My safe haven. Freedom. Love.

But if you didn't want me..? If you wanted Fernando instead..?

I'd opened your First Lifer peepers to the truth of the world, as I had for Kathy. Yet instead of embracing the darkness, you'd run from it. You'd chosen a life in the sun, which only Fernando could offer. I could've shared with you the wonders of a whole new reality, but it hadn't been enough: *I* hadn't been enough – and in the realisation of my worst fear, my mind began to break.

'*Liar*,' I hissed.

I could see the sudden alarm in M.C.'s peepers, as she reached for the tracker. Then she relaxed, as she sniffed. 'What, liccle leech? You reckoned she'd come running to save you? Da flower boy slave has a crush on its Mistress, innit?' Humiliated, I bit my cheek hard, tasting the tang of my own copper blood. When tears pricked my peepers, I fought for them not to fall. But I failed. M.C. leant down, wiping them away, before lifting them to her lips, as if savouring their saltiness. 'You ain't wallad enough to reckon my sis loves *you*? Grayse has never loved no one.'

I shook my nut, as if to deny M.C.'s words, but they stung.

‘Look, here’s da truth of it,’ M.C. slipped out her mobile, shoving the screen in front of me. All I could process was message after message between you...and Professor Zuniga Sanchez.

I didn’t know how M.C. had got hold of them. We should’ve known, however, that your family were monitoring us.

M.C was right. You hadn’t come back for me after the month. You’d let your sister have me instead: because of Fernando.

That’s when I stopped resisting. What was the point?

M.C. noticed the change in me. She prowled to the satin bed, which was between glass panels of male Blood Lifers. Then she patted the space next to her. ‘Lie down.’ Dazed, I crawled up and onto the bed. I lay on my back, with my legs spread and hands at my side. *You’d chosen Fernando... You’d left me here... You’d handed me over to your sister...* M.C. straddled me, the studs and spikes on her bondage trousers digging into my naked flesh. Her scarlet-tipped hair swiped my cheeks. ‘Maybe I’ll buy you. But you better show me how happy dat would make you, you get me?’ When M.C. clicked something to the side of the bed, the Sex Pistol’s “Submission” blasted. I wanted to howl. ‘Your file said you’d find dis tune heavy, yeah?’

M.C. gave a feral grin, as she licked her lips. Then she was snogging me, ferocious and fierce, biting my lips and fucking my mouth in fierce jabs.

You were gone... Back to your old life, whilst I was betrayed to slavery. This was no longer undercover: *it was real.* M.C. savaged my lip, sucking at the beaded blood.

Had you always known what this would mean? Always known my choice to return here would mean my abandonment?

I sank lower and lower, locking what was left of me tight and safe, where it couldn't be touched.

I stared up at the bright cloud light on the ceiling above the bed, as M.C. explored my body with experienced hands. I lost myself in the twists of white nylon tube wires and tiny lights, which had no edges, as if of infinite size. Soon I was flying in the unreality of the sky above, as down below a bint in leather violated my body.

And unlike you, she didn't stop.

She didn't bleeding. Stop.

That's when it started. When I broke.

Everything gets hazy after that, as if I was blanking out...breaking down...broken. Fragments left, only...successions of sensations and emotions...agony, fear, hunger, warmth, contentment and comfort...but each one in *Master's* power to give or take away. Only what he desired mattered. Ghosted, I didn't exist, except to serve *Master's* pleasure or take his pain.

My snatches of understanding were briefer still... *Good boy... Bad boy... Crawl... Lie Down... Corner... 300 strokes...* Limited to conditioned positions, orders, rewards or punishments.

Flayed truth? Once I'd stopped fighting, life became simpler – easier.

It flares me with shame but I'd retreated...somewhere else. And what was left? Knew how to submit. Obey. Accept punishment.

I was learnt: a good little doggy. Not a hero at all.

A true slave.

SEPTEMBER 4

I still forget you read this – not *Reader you*, the imaginary figment - but the real you.

This afternoon, when I was burrowed under my duvet, you came barrelling into my room, shaking this opened journal at me.

I tumbled out of bed into automatic *kneel*.

'Sodding hell...' Furious at myself, I made to stand, but you dragged me up with trembling hands, crushing me to you.

I stared down at the journal, which was crumpled between us.

Then I remembered: what I'd written about your mum's death. I didn't know for sure whether she'd copped it natural-like or at the fangs of a Blood Lifer. The Blood Life Council wouldn't have only exploited the weaknesses of Blood Lifers: there'd also be a fat file on you Cains as well.

'I'm sorry...' We both said at the same time.

Then you shook your nut. 'Naw, *I'm* sorry...that Marlane...that you were...for everything. I didn't abandon you, Light. I'd never abandon you.'

Too surprised to know how to react, I let you clutch me, as finally, I smiled.

At last it felt like I was back home.

You'd saved me, when I was lost.

When the pine crate was first delivered into your sitting room at the end of the month I'd spent on the Estate, I remember thinking, as the red nylon ropes were torn away and I was hauled out, that I hoped I'd please my new Mistress, as I had *Master*.

Master had stood over me on the last day, stern but patting my nut in the way I liked and ordered me to be a *good boy*.

There was bright light sharp in my peepers from a plastic chandelier of bottles and fishing lines, before I dropped to *kneel*. I shivered: it was colder here than it'd been in *Master's* snug. There was no rug, just a mahogany floor, which made me sad. I was careful, however, to keep my expression blank, like a good slave.

'You a bit *parky*?' My new Mistress laughed.

Confused, I hesitated. I didn't understand, so it was best to be honest and face the punishment. 'I dunno, Mistress.'

'Relax, it's just us now. Drop the act. I've been wicked frickin' worried, like, haven't slept or...' Pretty platform shoes clattered over the wooden floors towards me, and then soft fingers were caressing my cheek. I could smell gorse, like on my runs on the Estate: maybe Mistress lived near there too? That thought cheered me. When she tipped my chin, relieved at last I realised my new Mistress wanted the same from me, as my old one had – *pleasure* – I could serve her needs. I clasped my hands behind my back, opening my lips in preparation. Mistress, however, drew back, apparently dissatisfied. Anxious, I watched for her fingers to tap at her belt buckle but to my surprise, they didn't. It unsettled me. Whenever *Master* hadn't counted, it'd always meant he was planning a severe discipline session. How had I failed Mistress so quickly? When she raised her hand again to my cheek, I couldn't help the flinch. Mistress drew back. 'Let's go see if we can't get some clothes on you.' She sounded troubled.

Clothes. That I understood. Mistress was testing me. 'Mistress, may I?'

'May you what?'

Another test.

'May your slave have permission to speak?'

'What the frig is this?' Bewildered, I couldn't comprehend enough of Mistress' question to risk answering, even though I knew that meant automatic punishment. Still Mistress' fingers didn't go to her belt. My panic was building. At last, Mistress sighed. I'd disappointed her again. My stomach twisted. If only she'd give me permission to recite the rules, I could show her I knew how to pass her test. 'Yah, permission or whatever,' Mistress said quietly.

'Rule 9A: *A slave will not wear clothes.*'

There was a long silence. Then Mistress traced her thumb around the words on my collar - SHADOW: PROPERTY OF CAIN – and said brusquely, 'Go to bed. We'll talk tomorrow.'

I had a careful shufti around the sitting room: red sofa, two armchairs, a glass coffee table and a log bench with chair backs - but no bed for me. I could sense Mistress' rage, yet there'd been no order to move, and she hadn't clicked on my leash. 'Mistress, may I?'

'Just frickin' say it already.'

'Please could you tell your stupid slave where its cage is, Mistress?'

'Cage..?'

Then Mistress was clasping me around my neck and bawling.

Startled, I remained motionless, waiting for Mistress to calm.

At last, she hunkered down opposite me, gazing at me long and hard. 'I'll get you back, Light. I promise. Do you understand?'

'No, Mistress.'

Mistress spluttered something, which was half-way between a laugh and a sob. 'It doesn't matter. I will.' Then she straightened, as if composing herself. 'Follow me.' At last, a direct order. Proud to be able to obey, I crawled at Mistress' heel. She faltered, staring down at me. I wondered if I'd got it wrong again. 'It's a rule that Blood Lifers can't walk?'

'Yes, Mistress.'

When Mistress marched on again, I crawled after her, sensing the vibrations of fury thrumming through her.

I thought for definite she was leading me to the training room. I was sad I'd earned it on my first night but knew I deserved it.

It was unexpected, therefore, when the door Mistress pushed open, led into a simple room with a single bed, a cube bedside table and a blind over the window, which shone neon blue.

'This is your room,' Mistress was watching me closely. 'Do you remember it?'

As if a slave could possess furniture, let alone a room. 'No, Mistress.'

That sigh again. More disapproval. I shrivelled inside.

Mistress pointed at the bed. 'Lie down.' So it *was* pleasure Mistress required..? At least it was a clear position. Relieved, I climbed onto the bed on my back. 'Naw, I didn't...I mean...I don't...' Mistress sounded horrified, before she legged it, leaving me frozen in position for the rest of the night.

Over the next days and nights, I came to realise what a bad slave I truly was. Maybe I always had been. That's why *Master* had tried so hard to learn me. I was dead grateful to him now, regretting I hadn't tried harder: maybe then I'd have been able to serve my new Mistress like she wanted.

I was soon restless and agitated. Addicted to both *Master* and human blood, I suffered from the loss of both. I missed the wild chases through the garlic-scented forests, in the close black of the night.

Now I had no release. *Master*. Or blood.

When Mistress brought pigs' blood to me in a mug, I couldn't even drink it as she wished, assessing it from *kneel* on the mahogany floor of the sitting room, as if a puzzle.

Where was my bottle?

I hazarded a guess at tipping back my chin and opening my gob. Mistress slammed the mug down onto the coffee table, spilling the blood in a scarlet tidal wave.

Wrong again. Bad slave.

I thought maybe if I was a good slave and stayed in position, still and silent, as *Master* had taught – *no fidging* – then I'd please my new Mistress. Yet on the first day I tried it, Mistress ignored me entirely, skirting around me as if I didn't exist.

On the second day, Mistress started to scream strings of words, which I couldn't understand, or didn't make sense... *You can touch, move, talk... You're not a slave... Come back to me... Stop this, stop this, stop this...*

Mistress was shaking me. I wanted to stop doing whatever was enraging her. But I didn't know what *this* was.

Slap - Mistress clouted me, hard enough to knock me out of *kneel*. Then she clambered on top of me, pinning my wrists down. 'Naw, don't you frickin' dare get on your knees again.'

Tears welled up, I couldn't help it.

Master had never struck me: he laid out implements, showing them to me before he used them and warning me how many strokes. He never hit me in anger. But this was my Mistress now, and I was a bad slave.

From then on, I lived in continual fear of provoking Mistress because I was too stupid to understand how to serve and obey her. Her orders weren't direct, she didn't use the positions I'd been taught, punish me when I broke the rules or learn me my lessons. I never even saw the training room. There were also no rewards or approval. Mistress never once stroked my hair. I lay on my back on top of that bed every night, not understanding why Mistress never used me.

And I wished I was back with *Master*.

Yet the longer I was off human blood (and I guess, *Master* too), my mind began to slowly clear, like banks of a computer being turned back on. Flashes of another reality broke into my damaged brain. It hurt to even begin to imagine I could've been something else.

These sharp images flared jagged... A dark room, with floral wallpaper, me a savage predator with fangs latched into the throat of a First Lifer, a transcendent queen with a rose in her red hair savaging the human's neck on the other side, and I could feel the tug of her in the bond of our sharing... A scarlet flash of motorbike, and me tonning it, in this jacket with a worn gold ace of spades on the back... A bird with blue peepers, holding my hand under the moon on the moors, whispering her love to me...

They couldn't be real..? Memories? I couldn't be an actual person, who was powerful, loved and possessed a life – an identity.

Because if that was true...*what the bloody hell had I let happen to me*?

I burned with shame, until I didn't know whether it was worse to become the stranger, who was invading my brain. Or to stay safe as I was.

At least that way I wouldn't hate myself.

I was kneeling on the sitting room floor next to Mistress. The room was littered with pink Post-it notes.

Mistress had ordered me to follow her around the apartment yesterday, as she'd written the name of each object – STOOL, SOFA, GLASS VASE (for some reason that one had made her cry), until everywhere was a sea of pink. Then she'd calmly explained I could go on or touch anything, which had a Post-it attached. She'd even labelled the rooms, telling me that meant I could go into those without her permission.

I'd known it was a test but of course I'd simply replied, 'Yes, Mistress.'

I hadn't understood why she was so livid with me, when I'd continued to kneel at her side. I'd wished I was a better slave.

Mistress was working on her laptop. She often did – in silence - never reassuring me with a *good boy*, even though I kept as still as a statue. This evening though, she was distracted: her leg was jiggling up and down and she glanced at me every so often.

Finally, I thought, *this was it*: it was going to be one hell of a session. I clenched my hands and waited.

Mistress only, however, clicked something on the laptop. Then this music started up...

Mistress was examining me but I didn't know why. I knew better than to move out of position.

When Mistress hissed in frustration, grabbing my hair and twisting me, so I was gazing into her flint peepers, I jolted.

..."Lucy in the Sky with Diamonds"...

You - I was twirling you around this sitting room and you were laughing.

I scrambled back, as memories, like layers of an onion stripped away, reformed; image upon image recreated 150 years in an agonising rush.

I wrapped my arms over my nut, feeling like I'd bloody explode. I heard you scarper from the room, and I was alone.

Christ in heaven, I couldn't take it if...

Then you were there again, holding me. I could feel the wetness of your tears on my hair. You forced my hands away from my mush, pushing something into them.

Through the lightning crashes splitting my mind, I saw you'd stuck a Post-it note onto me, which was scrawled with one word: LIGHT.

When I met your intense gaze, you said, 'You're Light.'

I tried to rise out of the dark to you, to free my tongue from its shackles.

Light - I knew this word.

At last I recognised the man battling his way back into my head.

My name is Light.

'No one's born to be a slave,' you hugged me. 'I want you back. I need you back. And so do your family. We need you, Light.'

I blinked. I pulled away, before slowly raising my hand to touch your soft hair and the tears staining your cheek. 'You're real?'

You nodded.

'You didn't abandon me?'

You simply held me tighter.

And that was it. I couldn't fight it any longer: the shame of what I'd allowed myself to become or the knowledge of what I'd once been.

We need you...

I was that predator, with his fangs in the First Lifer throat. Powerful. Loved.

My family needed me.

I couldn't hide in the safety of the shadows any longer. I had to go back: to where I was loved. To where I belonged.

You're real.

SEPTEMBER 5

This is where it ends. Because of you.

When your dad and sister touched and broke me, they didn't have a scooby what they were unleashing: in me or *you*.

I doubt you even guessed at it yourself.

But I'd glimpsed the darkness in your flint peepers: I should've known you'd make a better Blood Lifer than your sister. *Sir* had buggered up my senses, however, so it took us nearly losing each other, for me to taste your Soul.

Yet when I did, I understood what'd been freed in you - and what Ashanti had meant about the preciousness of a life born from your own fangs.

'Oi...' You'd chucked a freshly laundered t-shirt at my nut, as soon as I'd sauntered shirtless into the kitchen.

'Get dressed, we're wicked busy tonight.'

'Alright, princess.' I dragged on the black t-shirt, before shrugging myself onto the shovel-shaped stool.

I watched amused, as you dynamo impressionist rushed about: *swiping* and *tapping*, waiting for the *ping* of the microwave, slamming a warmed mug of blood down in front of me and then slurping... *Buggering hell, was that black coffee..?* No wonder your detoxified, gluten and caffeine free body was bouncing off the bloody walls. Although you still looked blinding in the leather jacket, which

I'd nicked in Peckham. You'd taken to wearing it, as soon as you were *you* again, rather than Mistress.

I could tell you were planning something; I'd known for several days. Now, however, you turned to me over the lip of your coffee mug, with a wary anticipation. 'Fernando's calling any minute.'

Fernando – sodding perfect.

Away from the Estate and the psychological warfare, it was obvious you'd never have flown back to the Professor, leaving me to my fate.

We all have our hidden weaknesses, like the flaws in a diamond. *Master* and M.C. had merely exploited mine. I still couldn't hear Fernando's name, however, without wincing.

To be fair, you had been sending each other those messages...

I didn't say anything; I just gave you *that* look.

You rolled your peepers. 'I told you, he's not a bad guy.'

'And I agreed, decent bloke.'

We sat in silence; you with your black coffee and me with my blood. Then the *trill* of your mobile made you jump, before you raced to my side.

There was Alpha Geek on the screen, alone in the golden sunshine. An ivy-clad, red-brick building was fuzzy behind him.

Fernando wasn't speaking; he was gawking at me. He was leaning as close to the screen as he could without touching, like I was already laid out in his lab awaiting dissection.

Uncomfortable, I shifted.

You sensed the tension. 'You have news for us?' Still Fernando was stock-still, observing me. You glanced at me uneasily. 'We've been working on a way to... Fernando's been trying to crack the website on the Dark Web on account of we reckoned we'd upload the truth. And you finally did it. Right, Fernando?'

Fernando blinked. 'What..? I mean... How..? Or what..?'

'That's right technical jargon for a poor bloke like me to understand, Professor. But how about we save the evolutionary biology until after we save my species?'

At last, Alpha Geek snapped out of it. 'Aye, aye Captain.' He saluted smartly. 'So Gracie get you up to speed?'

'That'd be a no.'

'Let me put it this way then,' Fernando grinned, 'I control Cain Company's site.'

'That means we do,' you nudged me, '*you* do.'

It was strange. All these months powerless and now *I* had the control. Cain Company was hostage to my whim. Except it wasn't: it was testament to the deaths and suffering of my kind.

'What do you want me to programme? These magic fingers are at your service.'

'A memorial.' I stared straight at Fernando - Blood Lifer to First, night to day - and right then it didn't matter because we were united by the horror: that's what I was willing him to understand. 'I want every bastard who sees it to be so shocked they'll never forget. I want printed over those disgusting photos white crosses for the dead.' I tried to say *Ashanti* but I couldn't. 'I'll get Grayse to send you some names,' I mumbled instead. 'I want stamps for some, like...a crucifix.' I thought of Vesper. Her hopeful *kill me*, as her flayed fingers curled around mine. 'And the words *tortured...raped...starved* for others.'...The sensory deprivation hood, sucking blood in desperation from *Sir's* fingers, the white fire of the tracker, boiling water gargling down Hartford's throat, the *crack* of the bullwhip and every sodding thing that'd happened to me during my month on the Estate... 'I'll write some details and the like for underneath. No one'll be able to hide from the truth then.'

Fernando nodded. He was no longer puffed up with exultant pride. 'It's done. Later Miss Cain. And Light? We *will* have that chat about evolutionary biology.'

You dropped the mobile onto the counter. Then you were embracing me.

'Cheers,' I said softly, 'knew you were up to something.'

'The buck stops here.'

When I studied you, I noticed how pale you were. 'Hey now, what's this?'

'You were right. I took the money but not the responsibility.' You paused, before admitting in a rush, 'Mummy always hated Mann, I remember that. The Estate. She missed her real home. Her parents. She wasn't happy with... Never happy.'

'And me? Am I still a parasite? No right to walk the same streets as you?' I realised I was holding my breath.

'All I know,' you touched my cheek lightly with the back of your hand, 'is you're the man I love.' It was smashing to hear that from your lips, after feeling so fractured. The cracks were still there, however, and I couldn't help avoiding your gaze. Your peepers hardened. 'I've read everything you've written. You blame yourself for breaking. But you did it: we can bring the whole thing down - go for the jugular - because of you.'

I frowned. 'Sorry but I'm not following.'

'The *human camera*? The layouts and security codes you memorised? The fact dad needs a confidence boost for the company?'

I began to throb with roaring anticipation, my blood humming with a hunter's exhilaration. 'What's the caper?'

Your expression clouded. 'You'd have to act the slave again.'

'On the Estate?'

'One more night. Ever. Then you'd never have to fear again. No Blood Lifer would.'

I laughed. 'Don't think you really get us Blood Lifers but point taken.'

Then you were steering me towards the hallway, back to my room and tossing my motorcycle jacket at me, before thrusting a white sliver of an iPhone into my hand. 'Pack. Look, I'll call you with the... But first you need to sort your *business*.'

I was beginning to suss the plan. Yet even with the rage *Master* had freed in you, I wasn't sure you fully understood what this would mean.

I twisted you round to face me. 'If we do this, then we won't hold back.'

'Does that mean you'll introduce me to your family at last?'

I tried to smile. 'You won't miss them. But pissed off as you are right now, family is...family. And when we do this? Donovan and Hartford, they--'

'Are my family now. Like you.'

SEPTEMBER 9

Donovan is insisting I bear witness. He says I've already written so much in this *grotesque* journal I mustn't *split 'til the bloody end.*

Yeah, I know he's right.

I sodding hate that.

'It's a darling goog now; I learnt it myself,' when *Master* proudly patted my rump, I fought not to flinch.

Starkers, wearing only slave ring, leather ankle and wrist cuffs and collar - SHADOW: PROPERTY OF CAIN – I was kneeling in *kowtow.* My arms were outstretched, with the palms down and crossed and my forehead resting on my forearms.

I was the sculptural centrepiece on the vast ebony table, which ran the length of the Estate's neo-Palladian main reception. One hundred white and black candles (both the candles and their candleholders cast in wax), had been ranked with white on one side of my pale arched back and black on the other. Now it'd darkened outside, the dour-faced servants had lit the candles. They flamed and consumed themselves as they burned, like I was on a sacrificial pyre.

I heard the First Lifer's animated chatter increase around me, the *clink* of Champagne glasses and *hoot* of laughter, whilst the candles scorched me, as they melted en masse into dripping pools of opposing white and black: the spectacular theatre of destruction. I couldn't help remembering how Vesper's skin had melted too, just like I'd once been caught candle-like in the sun - before Kathy had saved me.

When I'd first crawled into the main reception at your heels, I'd had a sneaky butchers at the party preparations: servants bustling in penguin black-and-white tails, with Champagne flutes and miniature hors d'oeuvres on silver trays, whilst the crystal chandelier spiralled B – L – O – O – D - C – L – U – B.

Master had positioned me on the table, as Cain Company employees, corrupt Independents from Tynwald and Chief Constable Quayle (Mann truly was *Master's* fiefdom), as well as the Russian oligarchs, sons of Arab princes and brats of Silicon valley, arrived by chauffeured private car, yacht or helipad, or stayed as guests for the weekend on the Estate.

M.C.'s Crew, in leather, spikes, studs, tartan braces and tattoos prowled the edges as Security, coordinated by Red Mohawk and his mate Aviator.

Here was the Blood Club, gathered for the first time. Your dad was holding court, showing off his power, which had been diminished since the *hullabaloo* at Abona, with both his grownup daughters at his side.

And me - the sample product.

The fact not every member would've attended made me uneasy: all those glowing lights still existing around the world. I'd also scanned for Captain or any other representative of the Blood Life Council, but they either hadn't turned up - or hadn't been invited.

'It took strict discipline: leeches need to know who's in control,' *Master* was stroking my nut. It took all I had to remain motionless. There was a ring of Blood Clubbers huddled around *Master*, as if he was their guru. 'But there's not a leech I can't train. Our family have been slavers since Roman times. The Anglo-Saxons had no laws stopping us selling darling fair-haired boys and girls to Dublin. See, this isn't about race or species: it's business. That's why the Blood Club be in safe hands. My family know what works and we're not fearful to do it. We've traded with the brutal Norse traders and now with the Blood Life Council, leeches that they are. It's all merely business.'

'What a good boy the little chap is now,' a genial voice gave an oily chuckle, which oozed through my consciousness, with memories of lying strapped on a table at the mercy of this silver bearded man.

When *Master's* hand paused in its petting, I forced myself to relax.

Even though you were nearby, I wished I could see you. You'd promised you'd never leave me alone here again.

I tried to block out the sensation of *Master's* caresses and the thought of the Doctor, by imagining you were with me: you'd be bloody stunning in the strapless, crimson Alex Highbury-Lord number, which I'd picked out as your glamourous disguise for the night.

It was never going to be a piece of cake to pass myself off as the same mindless, broken slave *Master* had packed off in a crate to you.

No, not bloody *Master*, not anymore - Mr Finlo sodding Cain, slaver and all round tosser. But never my *Master*. No one's *Master*. Mr Cain was only a First Lifer playing at it, with the toys in his training room.

Well, soon he'd meet some true Masters and then *he'd* be the one *sodding learnt.*

Mr Cain's grip was now hard in the hair at the base of my nut: a warning not to *fidge*. I couldn't help the instant tension I'd hear the *tap* on his belt buckle. I held still, falling down into thoughts of deep submission.

Gradually, Mr Cain's grip loosened.

I could smell M.C.'s sweat and leather. And that's when M.C.'s fingers fondled my goolies. 'It be a good liccle slut now. I've taken it for test runs.'

'This Blood Lifer, slave shadow, I believe? He's quite the specimen. Is he up for auction?' A deep, male voice.

When I stiffened, M.C.'s hand squeezed my baubles, until my peepers watered.

'Naw, he's mine.' I heard you at last, somewhere in the throng.

'But you could offer the goog's services,' Mr Cain's gruff suggestion (and no way could you miss his underlying order), 'as a premium bonus for valued members - like our Chief Constable here - for a night or a weekend?'

'Na-ah, that's--'

'Grayse?' It was gentle but your dad's warning was as obvious as his hard grip in my hair.

'I guess important Blood Club members can play with him, you know, for goodwill.'

'Thank you,' Chief Constable Quayle was giddy with excitement; I bet he couldn't wait to get his flabby hands on me. 'A weekend with shadow would be much appreciated. And the extra services..?'

Mr Cain smiled slowly. 'Access to the training room is included, of course. Now Grayse, there are many of the bettermost men here, who I want you to meet,' Mr Cain patted your arm, 'MPs and aristocrats; you should think on marrying soon.'

M.C. snorted, as she gave my goolies a final twist, before letting go.

Even though I knew you wouldn't look at any of these wankers with anything but loathing, I still hated that your dad was husband hunting for you.

'First though,' Mr Cain turned to M. C., 'time for a demonstration. Marlane – lights.' Suddenly the main lights dimmed, until only the guttering of the melted candles and their holders, in puddles of black and white wax, like a chessboard with pieces ranked ready for war, remained flaming. And me - the sacrificial slave in their centre. 'Slave shadow will put on a show for us.' Mr Cain's announcement echoed through the vast hall.

I heard shuffling, as First Lifers entrapped me on either side.

Donovan, Hartford, Ashanti, Ashanti's girl, Vesper, marie antoinette, the Blood Lifers at Abona and every Blood Lifer, who'd ever been enslaved and then treated as entertainment by the Blood Club: I thought of them and I found the strength to endure.

I only understood then that a slave can't have a true conscience: you were right when you once threw at me in anger that I'd used you and maybe you'd have done the same but it didn't make it *right*.

If you're not free, your choices can never be truly your own. But you'd freed me, so now I was empowered to make my own choices and this was *my choice*: your choice, my choice and Donovan and Hartford's too. First and Blood Lifer united.

So I endured.

'*Kneel.*' I knelt up on the table. Mr Cain waited only a moment before he barked, '*Inspect.*' I stood fluidly, with my hands clasped behind my nut, as I balanced on tiptoe on the shiny surface of the table.

I hoped I didn't crash over onto those flaming pools of wax because that'd bleeding hurt.

I could hear the Blood Clubbers yakking about me. Although it does a bloke's ego good to know he's admired in *that* department, it's less reassuring to overhear the uses others intend to put you (and that part of your anatomy). Let alone the excited chatter about the nights with you, which they're already pencilling into their busy schedules and debates over whether blood and breath play are permissible – that's a *yes*, by the way.

Then Mr Cain began shooting positions at me so fast I almost stumbled. He *intended* me to because the first mistake I made would give fair reason to punish me. Except it wasn't *fair*, was it? I wondered how many other situations Mr Cain, when he'd been my *Master*, had engineered for me to fail, so he could condition me to feel I deserved discipline. Even ask for the punishment myself.

If Mr Cain wanted to punish me tonight, then I intended to make it sodding difficult for him. I moved to each position as fast as he said it.

I glimpsed Mr Cain's frustrated mug from underneath my lowered lashes.

'He is indeed a good boy.' I heard the Chief Constable congratulate, before patting Mr Cain on the shoulder, as if Mr Cain would be pleased I was keeping up with his gunshot rapid orders.

These naïve wankers didn't know the truth behind the Blood Club, with its Champagne and slaves.

But they would: *they bloody would.*

I couldn't help it. I looked up, straight at Mr Cain. And smiled.

Mr Cain's hand flew to his bastard belt, working at the buckle, which had filled so much of my narrowed world.

The dark wave of Blood Clubbers, however, took Mr Cain's sudden silence to mean the end of his circus show and they clapped: a polite ripple of applause.

That was when the screaming started.

My smile widened to a grin.

Mr Cain stood there - his black belt wrapped by its brass buckle around his fist - frozen in triumph, as if unable to believe he'd lost control on his own Estate. But then he saw the look in my peepers.

If you break a man, you know him better than he knows himself. And Mr Cain knew I was no longer his, nor was I a true slave - he understood just what he'd unleashed.

Like a herd of terrified wildebeest, snapped at by the jaws of submerged crocodiles, the Blood Clubbers crowded together, hoarsely calling to each other in their distress. The ones trying the doors or windows found them locked, which viral-bloomed their panic, as did the personal bodyguards, who hurled chairs at the reinforced glass windows: they didn't shatter. *I knew how that felt.*

The systems were on lockdown, except for one single back entrance, which we'd opened – or Fernando had. He'd hacked in, using the codes I'd memorised.

Turns out, the Professor *is* a decent guy.

The M.C. Crew snarled into walkie-talkies - pointlessly for the most part – because in our plan they were the first targets. There was nothing on the other end now but dead air.

M.C. stalked through the swarms, rallying the remaining punks.

Mr Cain was frantically scanning the hordes to work out who the invisible enemy was, whilst the Blood Clubbers - his acolytes only moments before

- were plucking on his sleeves, demanding information. Help. Freedom.

It sounded so bleeding familiar, I still couldn't wipe the grin from my mug.

Mr Cain wrenched himself away from the Chief Constable, who was wheezing in anxious gasps if *this was all part of the demonstration*? Then Mr Cain glared right at me. '*You*, boy. This is you.'

Belt tense between his hands, Mr Cain prowled towards me.

Let him come.

I swung my hands forward from behind my back, clenching them into fists.

Mr Cain hesitated, stumbling.

There was a sudden surge of First Lifers away from the atrium: they fell over white chairs, shoving each other over chaise longues and slipping on the black rugs.

Both Mr Cain and I glanced up into the shadows of the atrium's high entrance way.

And there they were: the fanged mugs of Donovan and Hartford, full Blood Lifer and no mistaking. They stalked from the shadows. They weren't starkers, collared or submissive. Even I shivered.

I waited for Mr Cain's attack on them - or me - to defend his Blood Club, Estate and daughters.

Christ in heaven, my every nerve sang *Halleluiah* because I was ready for it.

Stunned, I watched as instead Mr Cain scarpered. He hurled the oligarchs, Arabian princes and Silicon Valley brats out of his way, like playthings, as he struggled through the terrified throng.

The bloody coward.

All the agony and terror Mr Cain had forced me to face. And yet what was he? Give me Mr Cain, the training room and one day, and I knew now that the man, who'd been a god to me, would break. He'd shatter into smaller shards than I had.

I sprang off the table to start after Mr Cain. But then I caught Donovan's eye. Hartford nodded at me. We grinned. Mr Cain could wait. We had the jugular to rip out. Bloody.

After that? All was crimson and whirlwind death. We were Blood Lifers unchained at last. This was a Long-lived's revenge for over a decade's abuse. And it was *glorious*.

I trapped the sweating Chief Constable against the brocade wallpaper: strange thing was he didn't seem so keen to get up and personal with me now.

'Good boy,' Chief Constable Quayle tried to placate, licking his dry lips, 'good boy.'

'I'm not a boy and I definitely ain't good.' I seized the Chief Constable by his shirt front, before bashing the bleeder back against the wallpaper – *bash* – his nut smashed ripe – *bash* – crimson stained – *bash* – he slumped down in a heap of arms and legs.

Donovan (magnificent in indigo velvet and mauve eyeshadow), was letting Hartford take the pick of the Blood Club members. Hartford finished off the Blood Clubbers with such frightening relish the kills must've been personal. When I remembered the snaps of Hartford on the Dark Web, I hoped Hartford made the johns bloody feel it. When I saw a flash of silver, weaving the same way Mr Cain had fled, I wondered if Hartford had seen the Doctor too.

Donovan and I tag teamed what was left of M.C.'s Crew. My blood zinged, as I spun in circles, letting out every instinct, uncensored at last. I took down a punk in tartan trousers, jabbing and getting in an elbow strike. He staggered, before I swept out his legs from under him. Donovan dived on the punk then, fangs out.

I watched fascinated, as Donovan's newly grown fangs pierced the First Lifer's throat, pumping venom into his bloodstream. Paralysed, the punk jerked, as he fought it for the final few seconds. It'd been awhile since I'd seen the death of my true prey up close.

I wondered if I'd recovered enough of my fangs. It was fear...or shame...that I still wouldn't be whole, which had kept me from trying.

Suddenly, I was dragged backwards by a burly arm around my throat, which was crushing my windpipe and stopping the blood to my brain. White bursts of light danced in front of my peepers.

I clawed behind me at my attacker but reached only thin air. Desperate, I stamped down. Even with my bare foot, I caused a *grunt* and a weakening of the hold. I wrenched both arms off and twisted the joints back. The grunt increased to a shriek and – *pop* – the elbow joints went.

The bloke - Aviator goggles, red-faced and snarling – fell to his knees, spitting curses.

I booted Aviator over onto his back. Then I straddled him, wrapping my fingers around his neck: his limbs flailed, whilst his peepers were hidden fly-eyed. He scratched at me and kicked, but I didn't let up, not until he was as motionless as I'd been, whilst the centrepiece on the table.

It was at that moment I saw the black combat boots of red Mohawk standing over our bodies: one dead and one – *me* – having just strangled the life out of the other.

I slowly stood to face the bastard, who'd started all this: Head of the Retrieval Team in Bangkok, who'd hunted me on his monstrous black motorbike and trashed my Triton. He'd kidnapped me - not like a person - but like a wild bird, which'd been trapped and sold into captivity. A pet to be tamed and trained, presented in a gilded cage on some rich man's wall. From the moment Mohawk had shot me full of tranquillizers, I'd been a slave. My blood roared louder than those motorbikes. It wasn't terror I trembled with any longer: it was rage.

Mohawk's peepers were darkened, glancing from his broken friend to me.

We circled each other. How great a disadvantage I was at being starkers, however, was illustrated when Mohawk's first attack was a groin strike.

I doubled up, before I was caught to the kidneys. The tosser towered over me. Taught by M.C in the cage, this bloke fought dirty: he seized my goolies in a vice-like grip, crushing and twisting, until I reckoned he was going to rip them off.

Talk about irony: gaining my fangs but losing my balls.

I began to sweat...one more twist and... I bit Mohawk, with my ordinary, blunt teeth. I sank them deep into the wanker's chin. The zip of fresh human blood hit me kaleidoscopic.

Mohawk yelped, instinctively dropping my goolies and prising at my jaws, like you would a rabid dog. He hopped from foot to foot, as he tried to force me off.

I kept my gnashers clamped, however, working Mohawk back towards the central table. Then I let go of his chin.

Mohawk staggered, his hands flying to the crimson teeth marks. Like the Manx tattoo over his knuckles, they were a marking: for every Blood Lifer he and his Crew had bagged.

Before he could recover, I caught the bastard a roundhouse kick dead in his chest; he crashed backwards into the white puddled candles. Mohawk screamed, as the flames caught his mesh top on fire, and the wax stuck in pools to his skin. His scarlet Mohawk shot up, like a coloured birthday candle, as he shrieked, writhing with the agony of being burned alive.

Vesper, I thought, *an offering for you*.

It was then, however, that I saw you, crushed against the far wall, watching as my family tore and bit their way through the terrified First Lifers – your own species - who you'd betrayed, whilst I burnt a man alive.

Your mush was spectral. Death and killing weren't natural to you. Yet. They couldn't simply mean *justice*, without the guilt. The first time, of course, is always the hardest. I remember my own.

The reality - peepers wide open - is different to the theory. The real world is messy like that.

Hold onto my hand a little longer.

When I darted to you, I panicked when I noticed blood trickling down your neck. Without thinking, I pressed you harder to the wall, scenting the blood; *thank Christ it wasn't yours*.

Then, however, I could hear your heartbeat going like the clappers. I suddenly realised my mouth was stained crimson, as I scented your pulse point. My fangs itched.

I forced myself to draw back. 'I wasn't gonna...'

'I know.'

You, however, were still in shock. I stared around me.

For the first time, I saw the scene, as if a First Lifer. Hartford in particular had been busy: it was bloody carnage, where one side didn't even need weapons because they *were* the weapon.

Upturned trays of hors d'oeuvres were ground onto the black terracotta tiles, and shattered crystal Champagne flutes were like modern art, between displays of twitching bodies.

Donovan was dancing the Charleston, clutching a paralysed servant in black tie as his partner; I recognised the man as one of the minions, who'd delivered my bottled blood, whilst ignoring me, as if I'd been a piece of furniture.

I caught Donovan's sleeve as he passed. Then I jerked my nut at you. He seemed to understand, giving a nod.

I tried to smile. 'Come on, darlin'. Let's get you to the boat. Leave the clean up to me and my family, yeah?'

'Clean up?'

Right, well done wanker.

'You've done your part. Now you wait at the boat. That's what we agreed.'

I grabbed your hand, hauling you after me: that was the first time taking your hand didn't make me feel diminished to a boy.

You stumbled in your high-heels over congealing blood; you should've been prepared for it, considering you'd chosen *Heartbreak* for your bedroom.

When we reached the empty atrium, however, you yanked away from me. 'I'm not booking it outta here without you. *Clean up*? Who the frig are you going after?'

'Dat would be me, innit?' M.C. was sprawled in the baroque chair, which was crusted, as if by rough-cut crystals. She was trying to appear casual, like the party to promote the Blood Club was in full swing, rather than having wound down to a bloodbath. Yet I could see the rage simmering underneath.

I pushed you behind me, never mind your squeak of protest.

'Don't talk to him,' you were as furious as your sister. When M.C.'s dark peepers focused intently on you, it was clear you'd become her next target. 'Don't look at him or--'

'Touch it?' M.C. curled her tongue behind her teeth, as she sprang out of the chair, slinking towards you - anarchist tiger on the prowl. There was blood stained down her scarlet bondage trousers. It wasn't hers. You were shaking. Delayed shock or anger. Maybe both. 'Want to know how I made it scream? How I proper worked da bitch? Or taught it to be a good slu--'

'Shut your mouth,' you snarled. I caught your arm, holding you back.

M.C. laughed. 'All dis for some liccle leech? My crew? They be my family, you feel me?' M.C. widened her stance for the attack. I'd analysed M.C.'s cage fighting technique, but you were here and that complicated things. It put you at risk. And I wasn't about to kill your sister in front of you either. If I did, would you be able to look at me the same way? I remember every moment I've ever seen; I wish someone had saved me from witnessing the darkest. M.C.'s gaze flickered to me. 'You murdered my family for a toy.'

This was my opening. I hoped you'd understand. 'I'm not a toy.' I refused to do anything but meet M.C.'s killer's gaze dead on. 'I'm Light. And I'm a Blood Lifer again.' When my fangs shot out fully grown, it was like being reborn once more. 'Let's see you touch me now.'

When I sprang at her, M.C. stumbled backwards to the foot of the staircase, which swept up to the private rooms. 'Outside. Boat. Now,' I threw at you over my shoulder.

Then I dived up those stairs, like they led to my redemption and not the fight of my Blood Life.

I wove through the warren of corridors, until I reached the circular hallway with the motto above the doorways: *Quocunque Jeceris Stabit – whichever way you throw, it will stand.*

My guts clenched: *Master's wing.*

The door was open to the training room. I could see the black void, which had been the scene of my torture. Gags and bondage. Canes and straps. Pain and abuse. A tool kit for conditioning a slave. But I wasn't a defanged slave on a leash anymore; I was a fanged Blood Lifer. And I was free.

This was where it had to be.

If M.C. was so proud of what she'd done to me, let's see how she fared now she didn't have that bastard tracker in her hand. *And I had my fangs.*

'You want to be touched?' M.C. was standing in the doorway to her bedroom, like a threat.

I forced myself to grin. 'You find it that hard to get a date, do you?'

'Grayse don't. Not with humans. She don't need dutty leeches, when she has Fernando--'

'Give it a rest, you stupid bint. Fool me once, yeah? Grayse loves me.'

M.C. snorted.

'I didn't ask for your approval. I told you because I wanted you to know: First Lifers can love us Blood Lifers. They can love me. Have done twice now.'

M.C. seemed confused, as she frowned. 'And I told you dat Grayse don't love no one--'

'Just 'cos she doesn't love *you*, doesn't mean she can't love. It just means you're an unlovable bitch.'

M.C. exploded (as I'd hoped), in an uncoordinated flurry of knife-hands and palm-heel strikes, all of which were easy to block or let harmlessly slip past. Blinded by emotion, M.C. wasn't maintaining distance or strategy.

Who says I can't be master of the mind fuck too?

When M.C. growled in frustration, unbalanced by missing her punch, that was my in.

Suddenly I was swarming all over M.C., with an uppercut to her chin, which nearly took off her bloody nut.

Jab, jab, cross, jab, jab, cross, hook, hook, uppercut, jab, jab, cross...

Picasso-faced, M.C.'s mug was a shattered mess.

I'd driven M.C. staggering back to the doorway of her bedroom with a sidekick to her guts. She was struggling to breathe, as she spat out a bloody canine onto the floorboards between us. Like a hunted, man-eating tiger - wary but still dangerous - she swayed, glaring at me through swollen peepers.

I only twigged M.C.'s apparent weakness had been a trick, when I closed in for the kill: she swept both my feet out from under me, in a move so swift she could've been a Blood Lifer herself.

Then M.C. was bringing her heel stomping down onto me in an axe-kick, as I sprawled on my back.

Right onto my throat.

I choked, before rolling to the side, just as M.C. went to repeat the move. I tried to crawl out of M.C.'s reach, further into the bedroom, with its satin bed, which was enclosed by erotic Blood Lifer glass panels. Before I could escape, however, M.C. clutched me by the ankle, cranking on the small joints at the rear in an Achilles lock.

I howled.

I rode out the pain, allowing myself to fall limp, as if beaten by it. I could feel M.C. creeping closer.

When M.C. stroked down the back of my neck, I cringed. 'I be touching you, see?' Still I played dead. Then I heard her say, 'Guess what I found by the bedside? Only da tracker, innit?'

Then everything went white.

There was branching fire in the forests of my nerves. Nothing existed but my pain. I was flying.

M.C. was dragging me, like felled prey, across the wooden floor and then up onto her bed... *Lie down...* She was still inflicting punishment, my back arching off the sheets, as my hands convulsively opened and closed.

I was lost in the white. The cloud light was bright above; the twists of nylon and tiny lights were as if infinite.

M.C. must've eased down the tracker's level because my back hit the bed, although I still buzzed with electricity.

Please let you have gone to the boat.

Hartford had made Donovan promise - First Lifer and slaver's daughter as you were - that you'd be looked after like family. Hartford paid his debts. I trusted him. You were safer with those Blood Lifers, than anywhere else in this corrupt and brutal world.

If you'd gone to the boat.

'I'm gonna touch you. Den I'm gonna mess you up. I'm gonna learn you dat you be nothin' but a toy. Just like dad learnt dat bad leech cupid. Cupid fought - more than any other leech since - and we made it suffer for it. When we get cupid back... When dad...' M.C. hesitated, as if uncertain for the first time, 'retrieves both da two bitches.'

'Good luck with that. Last I looked, we'd eaten your Blood Club.'

M.C. increased the tracker's power. I gritted my teeth.

Then I shuddered, when M.C.'s long, wet tongue licked up my neck. 'And now you get to eat me, slut.'

I grinned, my fangs springing into place; my mouth was still stained crimson. 'Bloke with the red Mohawk? I just bit his chin. Do you really trust me near your soft and privates, luv?'

M.C. hissed, as she clouted me across the cheek.

With one final burst of effort, I rolled off the bed. As I thumped to the hardwood floor, I grabbed the base of the glass panel. And yanked.

M.C. only had time to turn in alarm, as the porn photos collapsed in on top of her – *smash*. They sliced her in bright slashes, scarlet on scarlet, whilst she bled out.

M.C. was submerged under the printed glass of fractured Blood Lifers, which trembled with her slight gasps.

I dragged myself closer to the bed. 'When you were raping me in here, you've no idea how much I sodding wanted to do that. So, cheers.'

I hauled myself over to the tracker, which M.C. had dropped over the side of the bed. Sighing with relief, I slipped it off, before I crushed it.

When I edged on weak legs back through the hallway and down the sweeping staircase, I didn't meet anyone. I glanced at the motto as I passed it – *yeah, M.C. wasn't doing much bloody standing anymore, was she*?

When I reached the atrium again, I found Hartford and Donovan had made good on their promise to *clean up*. Wisps of ash smoke curled between the Doric columns and fairy tale props, licking up the Goliath Manx cat.

You were gone.

I hoped you were safe on the speedboat, which was tied and waiting for us on the edge of the Estate.

When I poked my nut into the main reception, everything was silent, except for the crackling of the fires, which had been set. The air was thick with smoke and the pig-aroma of crisping human flesh, as antiques and modern furniture alike blazed side by side to the dying light of those one hundred pooling candles. Fernando had hacked into the mansion's fire system and turned it off remotely. The Blood Clubbers were melting down, wax-like. Because we were camouflaged predators, their deaths were still natural: if the heart attack didn't get them, then the smoke or fire would.

It wasn't as if we wanted our attack entirely masked: it was sending a message to the Blood Clubbers still out there, to the Blood Life Council and to anyone else, who intended to step into the Cain's shoes.

I guess that makes us terrorists.

Still, that's better than collaborators. Appeasers. *Or bloody cowards.* One thing I've come to know is you've got to live with yourself - no one else - every day. To face all you've done, failed or intend to do.

I prefer to think of us as rebels, anyway.

I left that white and black room, which was curling to grey, consumed by tongues of orange and red. I dived through the back passageways, whacking in the six digit security codes, which I'd memorised that time in Mr Cain's study: the price I'd paid had finally been worth it. I'd drilled the codes into all your nuts over the last few days and hadn't *that* been a delight with Donovan's grumbling.

When I reached the last code, I plugged it in and the cool, fresh air hit me, like life. I closed my peepers, resting back against the wall.

We'd bloody done it.

'Light, are you..?'

My peepers snapped open.

You weren't down at the coast: you were standing only feet away, assessing my many injuries. I sighed. 'I'm fine.'

'My sister?' I winced, looking away. But then your fingers entwined with mine. Surprised, I glanced up. 'So, I met your family,' you said carefully, 'I guess *my* family now. I like them.' I couldn't help but laugh. Your grin was too close to tears for comfort but full marks for trying. 'Hartford's wicked pissa. He was...kind. Not what I expected. They both weren't.'

'Yeah, we never are. So why didn't you go with them, like we planned?' I wanted to add – *like I told you to* – but I didn't quite dare.

'I wasn't booking it without you. Donovan had to stop Hartford from going back in, when I told him... When he knew Marlane... They both frickin' love you, don't they?' You gazed at me, as if you were surprised by this realisation. 'Hartford only stopped struggling, when Donovan told him sometimes there were things you had to do alone.'

'Wise words those.'

You nodded thoughtfully. 'I had to kick their asses to get them to go ahead on account of they wanted to stay and protect me. I told them there's no one left to protect me from.'

'Not quite true, sweetheart.'

You frowned. 'But Donovan said--'

'Your dad.'

You stared at me and then suddenly frightened, around at the black of the manicured gardens. The ragged clouds were streaming over the savage moon and the ancient stars. 'Right, let's go.'

'No arguments here.'

Your hand tightened around mine, as we sprinted across the lawns, your Fendis catching in the long folds of your ball gown. I guided you in the darkness: a First Lifer safe in my world.

It was when we were weaving through the Cain's personal wood, over the carpet of wild garlic, towards the coast that I first suspected we were being hunted.

Even amidst the firework-burst of raw nature, there was something else underneath, which my Blood Lifer senses - now fanged and free - were attuned enough to pick out. The *snap* of a twig, the *rustle* of clothing, the *thud* of a third heartbeat...and a gun *cocking*.

I glanced at you, stumbling alongside me in the dark. You didn't have a scooby.

'Sod it, this has gotta go.' I ripped up the hem of your dress to your creamy thighs, as you let out a gasp. Then I balled the desecrated satin, chucking it out onto the garlic.

Your dad was your hero and mentor. He was...your dad. I remembered my papa, his big hand in my small one on Regent Street... *You let go Light...*

Now your dad was hunting us through these woods, just like he'd allowed *me* to play at hunting here as a reward.

I couldn't fight Mr Cain, not like I had your sister. I couldn't kill your own dad in front of you. *And maybe the bloody wanker knew that.*

I pushed you ahead of me, resting my hand on your shoulder to guide you. If the bastard planned to shoot one of us in the back, then I was electing myself for the position.

The third heartbeat was getting closer. I remembered the night-time walks, which Mr Cain had taken; he knew this Estate in the dark, as well as he knew it under the sun. The bugger didn't get how close to being a Blood Lifer he'd grown over the past decade.

Suddenly, I heard the *startle* of pheasants, their ghostly *honks* and *beat* of wings, as they took to flight.

You cried out.

I pulled you against a Manx oak.

Bang.

I stared down at my right hand, which had been pressed against the trunk.

My hand was sprayed with pellets, which had ripped through the flesh, just as they'd shredded the oak's bark.

There was nothing but silence now in the black.

'*Bloody run*.' I clutched my wounded hand to my chest and snatched you to my waist by the other. I dragged you on, until I was half-carrying you damsel-like.

Then we were out of the wood and onto the open common, which was lilac with ling and luxuriant with gorse. *It smelt of you*. My right hand was a throbbing ball of pain; the thorny Burnet Rose bushes tore at my bare ankles. Something low and dark, with long hind legs, ran across our path: its tail was stumpy and its peepers were gold. Then it was gone.

My Manx cat, free at last.

Then I saw the cliffs, which led down to the cove and our speedboat, which was hidden amongst the damp boulders in the ravine.

We'd sodding done it.

'Grayse.'

No, don't. Please, don't...

At your dad's siren call, you were struggling out of my one-handed grip. Then you were turning round; just for a moment, you were looking back. But that's all it took.

'Daddy..?'

Bang.

The blast tore you away from me.

Then you were tumbling back, comic-slow in my horror, your chest scattered with pellet shot, which was worming deeper into your vulnerable insides and flooding them with blood. As you hit the heather tinted ground, you coughed scarlet. Our lips matched now.

I dropped to one knee next to you, overwhelmed by your false gorse scent, which was entwined with the real thing - your new bed. I grasped your limp fingers with my left hand, desperate to use my right one too. But it was useless. Blasted to pieces. Like you. I still tried: once, twice, three times... This sudden impotence - a broken doll - brought the first tears.

I'd saved Ashanti's girl, the other Blood Lifer slaves at Abona and brought down the whole slaving Empire. I'd kept my promise.

But if I lost you?

The price was too bloody high: it always was.

The *thud* of your heartbeat was slowing. Your lungs struggling. There was no magical A and E, to which we could airlift you in time.

There was, however, your attacker standing right behind me, the 20-bore shotgun, which he'd used on you, pressed to the back of my nut.

Tenderly, I placed your hand down on your chest, with a pat.

Your peepers were searching. Your stained lips were mouthing silent words. The desperation in your peepers for me to *understand* tore me in two.

I tried to smile at you reassuringly, before I gritted out, as the two barrels pressed harder, 'Come on then, you wanker, what are you waiting for? A slave's permission?'

I felt the barrel tremble with Mr Cain's rage - the tosser was bloody predictable.

I spun round, knocking the shotgun up, as Mr Cain fired, blasting the 20-bore into the night sky. I wrenched it from him. My strength, now I was unleashed, shrunk my old *Master* to a kid in breeches.

I walloped Mr Cain across the forehead with the walnut stock. When he collapsed to the heather with a *hmmpm*, I fell on him - all avenging angel - cocking his own shotgun at his temple.

Mr Cain was quivering like a baby rabbit.

Coldly, I scrutinized the little troll of a man, who'd once commanded me, kneeling at his booted feet. He was just a man – First or Blood – it didn't sodding matter. *Just a man.* 'The thing you didn't reckon on is no matter how you throw *me*, I'm the bloke who's always left standing.' Mr Cain cowered back. 'Dead big of you, shooting your own daughter. But you don't look so big now.'

'She's not my daughter.'

I met the bastard's gaze. At last I saw his defiance spark. I nodded. 'You're right: she's not.'

I hurled the shotgun as far as I could over the common, before wrenching the slave ring off my finger and pressing hard on Mr Cain's jaw. I forced his gob open, like he'd done to me so many times in the training room, before jamming the silver symbol of my slavery down his choking throat. *See how he liked being forced to gag on something.*

Then came the fangs.

Mr Cain tried to scramble back, but I pinned him down. His terror was delicious. He wanted to break me of my abstention?

All right then: *wish granted.*

I sank my fangs deep into Mr Cain's leathery neck. He struggled but then, limb by limb, was paralysed. It was the same as my punishments with the tracker, when a path of fire would take me over. I drew back, staring deeply into my ex-Master's peepers. I wanted Mr Cain to truly know what I was doing to him because he'd done it to me, Hartford and all those others. He was a poseable doll now in his own body...defenceless...like he'd trained us slaves to be.

When my fangs pierced Mr Cain's throat, I feasted as it was meant to be, under the face of the wreathed moon.

And it was transcendent.

I could feel my right hand knitting and mending, even as I fed, shuddering with the richness of the blood. And the beauty of the kill.

That's Blood Lifer justice.

When I tossed Mr Cain away, I saw Hartford and Donovan crowded around you. They must've heard the gunshot.

I stumbled to my new family, tears blurring them to ghosts.

Then we Blood Lifers held onto each other - a circle of three - as you died...

SEPTEMBER 10

You enslaved me. But in the end, you saved me. You saved us all.

There's no need to write anymore, however, because there's no First Lifer to read it.

Except, family's what you make it, right?

I came back tonight from my jaunt to the butchers to discover The Stones' "In Another Land", with its otherworldly harpsichord, blasting through the door and the boarded up windows of the squat.

I did a quick scan of the other 1930s council houses, which were huddled around our squat.

All quiet.

I shifted from one foot to the other. Responsibility: I'd never had it before and I hadn't appreciated how heavy a coat it was.

But then again - I do like a blinding coat.

Sighing, I was just pushing inside, when Hartford swung into the doorway. He dragged me in after him. 'Poor little bunny, why are you lurking alone outside?'

'How'd you..?'

Hartford grinned - it was smashing every time I saw him light up like that. 'For crying out loud, mac. Don't you reckon I can recognise your blood anywhere? We're family.'

I couldn't help the blush. It'd been a long time since any one had been proud to recognise me as *family*. In a smart wool tweed suit and with his golden hair Brylcreemed over the crown of his head, Hartford now truly was as dashing as any movie idol.

'The head of our little tribe returns,' Donovan strutted up from the sofa, 'don't bogart the blood, man.'

I passed the blood to Donovan, who dished it out into our array of tatty, mismatched mugs. I noted that in my absence, they'd tidied up, lighting the stubs of candles and shoving the sunken sofa to one side to make an impromptu dancefloor.

Cleaning up, dancefloor, lighted candles, my favourite record..?

Bewildered, I realised this was all for me.

Overwhelmed, I ducked my nut.

Suddenly, there were arms around my middle, which were dead strong, dragging me close.

'I'm gonna turn ya,' you murmured into my lobe, your lips soft and tempting, 'and scoop ya.'

'No arguments from me, darlin'.'

You spun me round. Bloody hell, you were going to be one powerful Blood Lifer: tall, steely and prodigiously intelligent, you scared the goolies back into me. And I was your Author.

I'd hoped you wouldn't be too changed by the transformation from First to Blood Life. Yet I hadn't been able to watch you bleed out on that common next to your dad.

I couldn't lose you.

In 150 years I'd never authored: no one's soul had ever called to mine before, except for Kathy's - *and she'd said no*. I'd watched Kathy die a natural death, after fifty years of love. It'd nearly destroyed me. I couldn't go through it again. Now you could evolve alongside me: a life born of my fangs.

When you'd been lying out on the heather, I'd whispered to your still body that I'd rebirth you into a glorious second life, hoping you'd understand. I don't know if you ever will. But I'll never bloody regret it.

'Hold on a tick,' I pressed my palm gently against your chest, 'I was thinking earlier about...when you were shot. You were trying to say something to me, but I couldn't make out the words. I just couldn't make them out.'

Your brows lifted. 'You want to do this now?'

I nodded.

'*I'm your Sun Girl.*' Your murmured words almost made me stop breathing. 'It's like, who knows what they'll think about, when they're about to die? But it was this mantra in my head, and I wanted you to understand. To know before...'

I flushed. Then I grinned, suffused with warmth, as if you truly were the sodding sun.

You smiled back, tracing my cheek with your finger. 'And for my Blood Lifer rechristening? My new name is Sun.'

This time when we kissed, for the first time it was as equals.

I was your Author - but rebel here - what did I care about outdated status? I set the rulebook alight, burnt to ash on the wind. You were mine and I was yours, bonded as close as it comes.

So we snogged each other and yeah - *it was bloody cracking*.

'Attaboy!' Hartford danced past me, spinning Donovan, who was resplendent in purple velvet. 'You're as goofy as me.'

'Leave it out, helmethead.'

Hartford twirled Donovan, who let out a startled yelp. *Never for a minute forget he's a Long-lived.* 'When do we get down to necking, like these guys?'

Donovan grinned, tossing his dark mop of hair out of his peepers. 'Right on.'

This was my family?

We needed a proper home, work, *life*... I don't reckon any of us even had a true identity. Not anymore. We were no longer the Blood Lifers we were before the Cain Company got hold of us: we were something new. We'd adapted yet again.

And you? You were just born, fresh to this dark world. Donovan and Hartford already loved you.

Yet I didn't have a scooby how to keep myself safe in this modern world, let alone my first ever misfit following.

Yeah, a family – this was my family.

You're one of us now. The Lost.

So many months of scribbling in these creamy pages, opening this burgundy journal and smelling the aroma of Italian calf leather. Now it's finished. You're not my First Lifer Mistress, so there's no need for a slave journal.

Light was never a slave. Shadow was the slave and he was never me. It was a fucked up First Lifer fantasy, which went up in flames.

I'm finally free.

Now comes the fun bit: when I spend the rest of our lives showing you that *you're* free as well.

It's going to be bloody blinding.

****

Blood Shackles over too soon? If you enjoyed *Rebel Vampires Volume 2*, you'll love the next book in the series, *Rebel Vampires Volume 3:Blood Renegades.*

Prepare yourself for the secret world of the Blood Renegades. Read on for an exclusive excerpt.

EXCERPT

REBEL VAMPIRES 3: BLOOD RENEGADES

*Don't forget me...*Sun entwined around me like a steel snake; her bite into my jugular was explosive rainbow end of days. I panted, squirming and gasping. Trapped in her embrace, I juddered. Then Sun was snogging me and I could taste my copper blood... *Don't forsake me...*

I could feel the vibrations of Hartford's anguished plea in his soulful song through every fevered atom. We curled around each other on the black cushions, which were piled on the lounge floor. Donovan was sprawled on the sofa, smoking wacky backy, serenaded by Hartford's new routine for the club. But it was meant for him because one thing I knew..?

Love.

...Live for me...

Hartford was singing to Donovan: the dead bloke he craved to resurrect.

I twisted Sun, splaying her over the cushions. She laughed in surprise. I'd forgotten how young she still was. 'My turn.'

I bit but gently. The moment when my fangs slid through her ivory skin was divine. Her blood was like coming home. Her body was quivering... *Don't forget me...* and we were snogging, both our bloods bonded as one... *Don't forsake me...* our hearts beating united... *Live for me...*

Crash.

Splintered door. Black balaclavas. First and Blood Lifers. *Shooters.*

'Bloody down.' I threw myself over Sun, shielding her. I couldn't hear anything over the *rat-rat-rat* of gunshots. The sofa's foam sprayed like snow.

Screams.

Christ in heaven, *Hartford.*

I peered up.

Dark shapes, like black ghosts, were thronging through our flat. A dozen at least.

Hartford was huddled by the wall: he was riddled with bullets. His breathing was laboured; crimson was seeping down his white shirt.

Donovan had dived from the sofa and was stroking Hartford's cheek, snarling at the bastard, who had his semiautomatic pressed to Hartford's forehead.

Enough was bleeding enough.

I stood up, straightening my shoulders. As if with a collective mind, the black balaclava bastards turned their shooters to point at me. Apart from the one who had his trained on Hartford. 'Reckon there's been a bit of a mix up, gents. So why don't you pack up and get your arses out of here. By the way, what type of Blood Lifer brings either a gun or a First Lifer to a barney?'

‘That’d be me.’

Bollocks.

****

Want to find out what happens next in *Rebel Vampires Volume 3: Blood Renegades*?

Order it today at Amazon or your local bookshop.

Then sit back and experience the secret world of the Blood Renegades...

DID YOU LIKE THIS BOOK?

Let everyone know by posting a review on Amazon and Goodreads.

Remember, please feed this author reviews – they’re better than chocolate (and Rosemary *loves* chocolate...)

Love Reading Gripping Fantasy?

If so, sign up to Rosemary A John’s VIP Email List to be notified of new promotions and never miss out on hot new releases.

Indulge yourself, grab a coffee and then dive into a Fantasy Rebel book – they’re fantasy for rebels.

Plus you’ll also receive Rosemary’s FREE and exclusive short story “All the Tin Soldiers”.

It’s our gift to you.

Visit Rosemary’s website to subscribe: rosemaryajohns.com

ABOUT THE AUTHOR

ROSEMARY A JOHNS is the bestselling author of the *Rebel Vampires* series. She wrote her first fantasy novel at the age of ten, when she discovered the weird worlds inside her head were more exciting than double swimming. Since then she's studied history at Oxford University, run a theatre company (her critically acclaimed plays have been described as 'uncomfortable, unsettling and uneasily true to life'), and worked with disability charities. She's a music fanatic and a paranormal anti-hero addict who creates spellbinding worlds, thrilling action, gripping suspense and passionate romances, all uniquely told. When Rosemary's not falling in love with the rebels fighting their way onto the page, she heads the Oxford writing group Dreaming Spires. She can also be found listening to Nirvana. At full volume. Or not found at all. When she's dived into her secret worlds again. WINNER OF THE SILVER AWARD in the Wishing Shelf Book Awards.

Hooked on *Rebel Vampires*?

Let the world know. Go to Amazon and Goodreads to leave a review today. Remember, reviews are better than chocolate - and Rosemary *loves* chocolate...

Reward yourself with another enthralling book by Rosemary A Johns. *Blood Dragons* and *Blood Renegades* are out now.

Discover Rosemary's dark scribblings online:

rosemaryajohns.com
www.facebook.com/RosemaryAnnJohns
www.twitter.com/RosemaryAJohns
https://uk.pinterest.com/rosemaryjohns1

Follow Rosemary's writing here:

https://www.amazon.com/Rosemary-A-Johns/e/B01JOJVTNE
https://www.goodreads.com/author/show/15571684.Rosemary_A_Johns

Go ahead and drop Rosemary a line at: rosemary.johns1@btinternet.com

Books by Rosemary A Johns

Rebel Vampires Series
Blood Dragons (Volume 1)
Blood Shackles (Volume 2)
Blood Renegades (Volume 3)

Member of a Book Club?

Share *Blood Shackles* with your group and delve into the free Reading Group Notes at rosemaryajohns.com

www.ingramcontent.com/pod-product-compliance
Lightning Source LLC
Chambersburg PA
CBHW051323250626
47155CB00007B/2425
* 9 7 8 0 9 9 5 5 5 7 9 2 5 *